ISBN: 978-1-62209-833-0
Manufactured in the United States of America
First Edition
Cover Design
Adina Mayo

THE GIFT
BY DYANNE DAVIS

Dyanne Davis TITLES:

An Imperfect Life
Hitting The Right Note
The Affair
The Critic
Another Man's Baby
Many Shades of Gray
Two Sides to Every Story
Forever And A Day
Let's Get It On
Misty Blue
The Wedding Gown
The Color of Trouble

Anthologies:
Continental Divide (Lotus Blossoms Chronicles 11) Anthology
On My Knees (Destination Romance) Anthology

Novellas
Santa Baby Flight 22
It's The Little Things
Taming The Bad Boy
Rebound Love
Just A Taste

Titles under F.D. Davis:

In The Beginning
In Blood We Trust
The Good Side of Evil (Carnivale Diabolique) Anthology
Lest Ye Be Judged

THE GIFT

Blaine MaDia sat on the jet, his eyes closed behind the dark glasses he wore so often now. It had taken him less than a week to survey the damage in his San Francisco apartment and start the rebuilding process. In the meantime he needed a place to live. So he was heading east to his spacious suburban home forty minutes west of Chicago

Funny when he'd flown to San Francisco he'd had thoughts of staying. Problem was, even with a psychic, life didn't always turn out as planned. For assurance he'd even drawn Tarot cards for himself. Too bad he hadn't asked if he would be burned out of his west coast apartment.

Lifting the glasses a tiny bit from his face to swipe at the sweat that had beaded between his brows, he allowed a deep breath of air to escape. He didn't want to take them off because for the past week he'd taken quite a bit of ribbing, some of it good-natured, some of it mean spirited. Mostly people questioned if he were a true psychic, why didn't he know his apartment was going to catch on fire?

In all honesty he'd answered, 'I'm not God.' Now he was tired of the questions, tired of all the answers. He just wanted to go home undisturbed. If he didn't wear the glasses, strangers would be pestering him with requests for readings. He accepted that as a price for his fame.

On most occasions he handled those requests with a modicum of dignity and humor offering his card to the person asking. He couldn't chance it now; he was in too weak of a state psychically. The fumes from the smoke had wreaked havoc in his body. He needed time to heal. Right now he could ill afford strangers pulling at his energy field. It was all that he could do to keep the barrier of energy surrounding his body, keeping out the thoughts of his fellow passengers.

Sleep was pulling at him when he sat up with a start. He rubbed at his temple feeling the beginning of what promised to be one doozy of a headache. Since the fire, dreams of his mother dogged him raggedly. There were so many questions he wanted to ask. If he could he'd eliminate the dreams, but for whatever reason they continued. *Not now* he thought not wanting to deal with the experience of the fire while sitting on a packed plane.

Trying to push the thoughts from him a searing pain warned what was happening wasn't about him or the fire but about someone entirely different. He closed his eyes in order to better focus his powers, to see who was having such an effect on him. Not since the first time he met Michelle Powers, his soul mother, had he felt such a dramatic reaction. Blaine wanted to know who it was who was having such a strong effect on him. And what was happening to his hard won self-control.

As he focused his energy the feeling became stronger until at last he was on his feet, standing, moving forward without wanting to, yet drawn to someone's pain. His hand moved unobtrusively through the air. Since finding his mother he was discovering new powers he'd never known he possessed.

He smiled to himself, the thought that he had only to put out his hand and connect with someone's energy surprising. After a lifetime of dealing with the unexplained, he was comfortable with his gift of clairaudience. He didn't have a name for this newest emerging gift.

The best way he could explain it was mining for energy. He used his hands much the same as he used his mind when speaking to those who had departed this life and were waiting. He focused.

Suddenly he stopped walking, his eyes landing on a woman of petite stature. Even from a sitting position he could tell she was short. He stood over the woman perusing her body in a quick perfunctory manner. She was slender also. His gaze fell on the woman's curly, dark brown hair and a lump formed in his throat.

Blaine stepped back as an irresistible urge to reach out and touch her clutched at his throat. It took all his psychic energy to resist the pull. A tightening began in his groin. Good Lord, not now. He panicked and moved backwards down the aisle. No woman had ever affected him so quickly.

"What is it that you want?"

Blaine stopped his backwards descent and looked down into the biggest pair of chocolate brown eyes he'd ever seen. For a moment he thought his heart would stop. Despite the woman's cold stare he felt drawn to her.

The sadness that had emanated from her to bring him to her now washed over him in waves. He clicked his tongue against his teeth trying to feel the woman's energy.

She'd placed a block to keep him out. Damn. That had never happened before.

"I'm sorry," he stammered. "My name's Blaine MaDia." He smiled at the woman while his skin began a slow crawl of awareness. It wasn't so much her looks as her aura. In looks she was ordinary with the exception of her eyes. It was the woman's aura that held an intense fascination for Blaine.

"I'm sorry, Mr. MaDia. Am I supposed to know you?"

Blaine tried again to probe gently at the woman's thoughts. When that didn't work he tried more aggressively, but still she held out against him, blocking any entrance. This stirred his curiosity making him wonder what it was the woman was hiding so possessively that she'd thrown up a shield against a stranger.

"Mr. MaDia, did you want something?"

Now he was standing there feeling like a fool, his own psyche open for probing, his defenses weakened. He knew better than to continue with his questions, yet he felt compelled to press on. Never in all the years since Blaine became a professional psychic had he ever used that gift to seek out females, or to impress. He was now embarrassed and could feel the flush of that embarrassment with the next words he uttered.

"I'm Blaine MaDia, the psychic on television." He gulped. The woman appeared unimpressed. "I was just walking, I didn't want anything." Blaine continued. Still nothing. The woman simply stared at him, her deep-set chocolate eyes turning to liquid cocoa. Now besides wanting to touch her, Blaine wanted to stand there and take a long drink from her eyes.

"I don't know you, Mr. MaDia and I don't mean to appear rude, but I'm very tired. I paid for two first class seats so I wouldn't be disturbed." She tilted her head slightly letting Blaine know she wanted him to leave.

"Sorry I bothered you," he murmured and turned to walk back to his seat. He paused and stuck out his hand toward the woman. "Nice to meet you Miss...Miss..."

He waited for an acknowledgment and a name, but the woman looked at him with mere curiosity, ignored his outstretched hand and cast her gaze back on the book in her hand.

Surely the woman had to be a psychic, Blaine thought. In the very least, she was familiar with psychic gifts because she was using them so effectively to keep him out. And he wanted in.

He set back in his seat amused and peeved. He was behaving like a hormonal teenager, trying to impress a girl into giving him her name. Still, knowing something and having emotional feelings about it were two different things.

The very thought of not knowing bugged him, when less than an hour ago all he had wanted was to be able to tune out the emotions and the thoughts of the people around him. Now, more than anything, he wanted to know what the woman four rows ahead of him was thinking. And why she'd thrown up a defense against him.

Blaine took his glasses from the perched position on the bridge of his nose and folded them into the clear plastic container that hung around his neck. He smiled to himself. He loved the three-inch case and the glasses that bent like spaghetti to fit into the case. He'd found them at a cheap boutique and thought they were cool.

He gazed around the cabin ignoring an inner command to rest. Sure he knew what he was doing. He knew that soon everyone in his section would recognize him and they would ask for readings. There would be a flurry of activity. Something in his experience no woman could let slide. Then, he thought, the woman with the chocolate eyes would drop her defenses.

He was fully aware his thoughts and actions were wrong. He had no right to violate another person's mind without their explicit invitation. And the code of conduct governing legitimate psychics prohibited such behavior. Still, he found himself smiling at no one in particular.

The need to know this woman was erasing his moral code. It only took a moment and a bit of gentle mental persuasion before the passenger across the aisle turned to him.

"Aren't you Blaine MaDia?"

"That's right I am."

"Wow. I can't believe it. I've been watching you on television for over a year and listening to you on the radio. I heard you wrote a book. Is it out yet?"

"No, it will be out in a month or so. Thanks for the support." Blaine smiled more deeply at the man, resisting the urge for further tampering. He could easily give the man a hypnotic suggestion to carry the fuss up an octave or two, but that wouldn't be necessary. Nor did he want to cross any more barriers than necessary.

Soon everyone in the first class section were clamoring, begging Blaine for a reading, telling him how much they admired him, watched him, believed him. Everyone that is with the exception of the lone woman occupying two seats.

Blaine tried again. She kept the invisible fence around her thoughts. In fact she'd fortified it and this time he knew it wasn't to keep out a stranger. This time it was personal. It had been structured to keep him out.

Taking out a small piece of paper from the notepad he always kept tucked in his shirt pocket he scribbled a few words on it and handed the note to the passing flight attendant who wrote on it and gave it back. Cassandra Boozer.

Smiling his thanks at the woman he handed her his card. "Call me. I owe you one." He didn't care that the woman thought it odd that he didn't just approach his fellow passenger, or as most people thought, his being a psychic he should automatically know the name of every person he met.

Sure that happened on occasion, but most of the times it didn't. Sometimes there was someone with such a strong personality that they would literally shout their name into his subconscious, much like the spirits he preferred to deal with.

There was only one other woman, one other person period, that had ever had a draining effect on him. And that woman was his mother from his only other lifetime. This feeling he had for this woman was extremely weak compared to the massive energized connection that had summoned him to his mother's side.

Still as weak as it was, Blaine was intrigued. He didn't feel she was someone from his past, either in this life or the one before it, but there was something about the woman and for some reason he knew he wanted to know her.

He stopped the thought as quickly as it had come wondering if it had anything to do with the cryptic message his mother's shadow self had delivered to him. He remembered Michelle's words clearly now. *"You'll find someone son."*

Could this Cassandra Boozer, the mysterious woman who feigned no interest in him or his reputation be the one he was looking for? He thought of her disinterested voice and cold stare. If she was the one, Blaine sure as hell hoped that her demeanor was just a psychic front. He had no wish to become involved with a woman with ice in her veins. No, with a woman like that he would only offer his professional services.

Again he felt the sudden tightening in his pants and lowered the paper he was reading to cover the bulge. Oh yeah, he thought, All I want to give her is professional services. With nothing left to do he decided to return to his seat and catch a quick nap.

Chapter Two

The air, hot and thick, rolled across Blaine's body as easily as it invaded his lungs. He fought to breathe, but it was no use. The cells of his body were quickly filling with the acrid smoke. The most he'd managed was a halfhearted cough, an attempt at clearing his lungs. Not now he thought as the smoke that filled his home descended upon him, robbing him of reason. Still he tried.

With his ebbing strength Blaine fought to live. But the battle was in vain. He was dying. He knew it as surely as he'd known the first vision he'd had was real. This too was indisputable.

His body went limp and his mind became a blank, clouded with the fumes. He couldn't think. But in a way it was peaceful, probably the only real peace he'd ever known. With nothing left to do his eyes closed of their own accord until at last he could feel his spirit letting go, giving in. He closed his eyes even tighter to enjoy the long awaited rest.

"Blaine, wake up! Wake up damnit! You will not die on me."

A smile tugged at his lips as he wondered about the voice. Was that really what death was like, hearing the voice of a loved one that was definitely too far away for it to be real. If anyone had asked him, he would have thought that was something for the dead to do, not the living. And as far as he knew his mother was living.

But he was a psychic, or had been, a medium who specialized in talking to the dead. He couldn't help but wonder how the conversation would go when he was on the other side.

"Blaine, wake up."

For the second time he heard the voice through the netherworld his mind had drifted into. It wasn't a dream. It was Michelle, his mother. But that was impossible. Michelle was in Hawaii on her second honeymoon. He was lying on a floor in San Francisco. Dying.

"Blaine did you hear me? I said wake up. I will not lose you again. I can't go through that pain. I refuse. Fight, Blaine, fight. If not for yourself fight for me. I love you and I need you. Fight, Blaine."

He could swear his head was clearing a tiny bit. He felt the touch of his mother's hand on his forehead. That was strange. She seemed to be testing to see if he had a fever. Hell, he was burning up. Of course he'd have a fever.

He wanted to tell her to go away, to leave him alone, but she was so damn insistent. What did she want with him anyway? She had a life. She'd patched things up with her husband Larry, and was well on the way to patching them up with her children from this life. What did she need with a reincarnated son?

"Michelle, let me go. This is what I want. I don't have anyone that gives a damn if I live or die. People only want me around to answer their questions about life on the other side, to tell them their future. They love me for that gift, but they fear me, the man. Go away, Michelle, leave me be. Even you, *my mother*, was afraid to touch me. What chance do you think I have that some woman will love me?"

WHACK.

Blaine couldn't believe Michelle had slapped him. The sting of tears followed another slap, then another until finally he caught her hands in his and her energy shot through his spleen replenishing him, giving him a renewed will to continue fighting.

"Why do you care?"

"Because I love you. You're a part of me, I'll never let you go again, I promise."

"But you promised my father, and you let him go."

"Only for a little while, Blaine, just a little while. Chance understands our lives are on different paths this time around."

"How can you be so sure? Maybe he feels the same, that you have no room for us in this life."

"Let's get you out of here first then you can ask your father. Chance will tell you the truth, you know that."

Blaine was on the precipice of indecision. For one moment he tottered there, a part of him wanting to give into the rest that awaited him, another wanting so badly to believe his mother's voice, to believe she wouldn't abandon him, as she'd done his father. He didn't begrudge her a happy life; he just wanted to be a part of it.

"Mother, I'm tired of being alone."

He felt the coolness of her hand as she once again touched it to his brow, and the smoothness of her cheek as she brushed her lips across his face. It was the first time he'd called her mother.

"You'll find someone, my son."

Her arms went around him and she cradled him as if he were a tiny baby, rocking and crooning to him, telling him over and over how much she loved him until at last he believed her. She would not leave him.

She smiled a beatific smile at him and passed her hand over his body. He saw the white light going through each organ and he visualized it recharging his cells. The fog was receding.

"You must wake up now, Blaine. I don't know how long I can sustain the connection. If you die, I die also and so will your father. Come, let me help you."

Blaine sighed softly as he looked at Michelle's face, contorted with pain. No, he didn't want her to die. The decision was made. He would live in order for his mother to live. He leaned heavily on his mother's shoulder, still confused as to how she was there, yet knowing she would give him no peace until he was safe.

He walked out of the heavy doors with her and fell into the soft grass burying his nose in the fresh mowed sweetness.

"You're going to be fine now," he heard her whispering to him as he began hacking the fumes from deep within his chest.

"I love you, Blaine."

"I love you too, Mother." Between coughs he reached to touch her cheek and she was gone, vanished into thin air.

It was in that moment that Blaine released all the tears he'd held inside of himself for thirty-two years. He saw his neighbors running toward him, heard the loud sound of the fire department and still he cried. He couldn't stop to explain to anyone that he would be fine.

He hadn't known in the beginning, but he knew now. There was an electrical short in his apartment. Somehow the fire must have started from that. That thought wasn't what brought about the undamming of his emotions. It was what happened while he lay there dying. Michelle, his mother had come to save him. Everything he'd ever wanted had come true. He finally had a mother in his life.

Accepting the oxygen the paramedics offered he didn't fight as they assisted him into the ambulance to be taken to the hospital to be checked out. He wondered if Michelle was aware of what happened. Did she know as she romped on the beach with Larry that her Astral spirit had traveled to him, to save him?

He closed his eyes. It didn't matter. He knew. And with that knowledge he moved from dream to dream.

Blaine awoke suddenly. He'd dreamt he was in a meadow filled with bright yellow flowers. All around him were birds of every exotic breed and color. He remembered looking around, reveling in the peace of the meadow when a small frightened cry broke his serenity. He moved toward the sound and found Cassandra huddled on the ground her chocolate eyes watery, her small face pensive and filled with pain.

"Help me," she pleaded with Blaine. "I'm in danger."

That was all he remembered before he blinked, waking fully to find himself still aboard the plane. He concentrated harder. Nothing. The woman was good. He could tell something wasn't right though. He looked at his skin that was now raised a quarter of an inch with hives. An increasing coldness settled over him.

Despite his better judgment Blaine walked toward Cassandra's seat before he could convince himself not to. Stopping a discreet foot from her he spoke.

"Excuse me, Cassandra. I was wondering if I could sit with you for just a moment."

"Why?" She stared at him and this time Blaine was sure the woman was made of pure ice, an ice that was burning like molten fire in his veins. He wondered for a second if this was what it was like for Chance and Michelle

No, he thought answering his own questions. The last thing those two had was ice. When they where within ten feet of each other everyone around them was consumed by the heat of their passion. If nothing else he'd love a opportunity at a passion like that.

So far his relationships had been limited in the past to a few weeks at a time. The most enduring had been six months and that lasted because they never saw each other.

No, after the first curious dates were over, the women feared him, feared that he was constantly reading their thoughts, evaluating them. At last they rejected him because as one date so eloquently put it, 'She didn't want to be with a man who could tell her when she was going to die.'

That time he'd half suspected that what she didn't want was a man who could tell she'd been screwing around. Lucky for both of them, things hadn't gotten messy with words like love.

But Blaine had hoped. He was glad he'd never shared those hopes with her. It was easier to watch her leave as so many others had done. He could merely smile and say "It's been nice."

A sudden surge of energy shot through him and Blaine stood still. An unexpected surprise, Cassandra Boozer was looking at him with extreme dislike. The woman's eyes were burning a hole through him and he wondered why the hell he was putting himself through this? She was up front from the start. She wasn't interested in him. What was he, a glutton for punishment?

"How do you know my name?"

Blaine swallowed wanting to lie, knowing she'd know and knowing if he did he wouldn't stand a chance.

"I asked the flight attendant."

"Why?"

"I was curious."

"Why?"

"I don't know." He attempted a smile, but the look on her face froze his smile at half-mast.

"Look, I don't usually do this. I just wanted to talk to you for a few minutes." He looked down deciding the only thing that might work on this woman was the sympathy angle. So he decided to go for it.

"You know wherever I go people know me, everyone's always wanting me to do readings. It's just so refreshing to have someone who doesn't know me and doesn't care what I do for a living."

"You're right Mr. MaDia. I don't know you. And, I don't care what you do for a living. But if I'm not mistaken, you announced that to me the first time. That strikes me as odd for a man who doesn't want to be recognized."

Blaine's mouth fell open slightly and he stared embarrassed into the chocolate veil her eyes had become. "I want to help," he said bluntly.

"I didn't ask for your help."

"Ah, so you do admit you need help?" Blaine tried smiling again to no avail. The woman was stone cold.

"Well, if you don't want my help, do you think it would be possible for you to help me?"

Just a slight movement, a turning of her head, a twitch around the corners of her lips. Blaine saw and was encouraged. At last something he'd said was having an effect.

"What kind of help do you need?"

"Well for one thing," Blaine leaned in closer. "I'm dying of embarrassment here. It would be a tremendous help if you could prevent this mishap from becoming fodder over everyone's morning coffee. Also," he plunged onward, "It would help my self esteem immensely if you would allow me to sit with you for a minute and maybe buy you a coke."

This time the smile on her face was genuine, as she moved her barricade from the adjoining seat making room for him to sit.

"The drinks are free, Mr. MaDia."

"Ah so they are. Sorry I forgot."

"That's a good one. What are you going to ask me next, my sign?"

Blaine tilted his head first to the left then to the right as he probed gently, so she wouldn't notice if she had the ability to do that as well as block him. Nope. No change. Her mental blockade was still in place.

"I wasn't going to ask you for your sign. And before you ask, no I'm not interested in reading for you."

"So how were you planning on helping me?"

She had him there. Blaine grinned. "Is it always so hard for a man who simply finds you attractive, to talk to you?"

"How do you know I'm not married?"

"Are you?" He asked.

"Don't you know?"

Blaine rubbed his chin vigorously before answering. She had too many damn defenses up for him to know anything. But then again, he would bet his months' salary that she knew that. He squinted before looking into her eyes. Yep, there it was in the depth of them, the sure knowledge that she was keeping him out.

"Are you psychic?"

"Why are you asking me?"

This time Cassandra was smiling and her smile melted some of the ice in her veins. Blaine liked her smile. Hell, he'd already decided he liked her, so her smile was an extra added bonus.

"Everyone's psychic to some degree, Mr. MaDia. We just all don't advertise it, or get rich from it."

Blaine studied her for a moment. "If I'm rich you're the one who can afford to pay for an extra seat on first class just so you're not bothered."

He waited for her snappy come back, but what he saw was pain etched into the soft lines of her face and for just a brief instant her wall failed and he once again sensed the sadness emanating from her.

"I'm sorry," he offered. "That was only meant as a joke. I didn't mean any harm in what I said." Cassandra looked away, but not before he'd seen the sparkle of tears in her brown eyes.

"I know you didn't mean any harm, Mr. MaDia."

"Please, can't you call me Blaine?"

His heart stopped as she eyed him from top to bottom, her lips trembled a slight bit and he observed as she appeared to have made a decision.

"Okay, Blaine, tell me the truth. What was it that brought you here to me?"Her voice dropped before she spoke more sharply. "I'll know if you're lying."

"Truth is I'm not sure why I came to you. I was just walking down the aisle and stopped by you."

In part that was the truth. But Blaine didn't want to scare her off, have her thinking he was reading her mind, knowing how hard she was working keeping her defenses in place.

He got the oddest feeling. She was scanning his mind. Slowly he slid the door open a tiny bit knowing what she would find, that he desired her. Her knowing that was preferable to having her think him a liar.

She smiled at Blaine then touched her palm to her head.

"I guess I could be paranoid."

"Cassandra, are you in trouble?"

"Believe me, Blaine, you can't help me. Stick to what you do best. Talk to the dead. You can't get hurt that way."

So she did know of him. He hadn't told her what his show was about. "I don't get it," Blaine smiled slightly. "Are you worried about me, or is it that you don't believe I can help?"

He waited patiently while she scanned his mind once more. He didn't like it and it took the patience of Job to pretend he didn't know what she was doing, to not slide his own mental blocks into place.

A different sensation hit Blaine and he began slowly to close his mind to Cassandra. He could swear he felt an evil male energy rummaging around in his mind. He didn't like the feeling one damn bit.

After what seemed like an eternity Blaine held his breath as he sensed a battle in Cassandra. When she spoke he realized she'd decided he could be trusted.

"I don't know why I'm telling you this, but I am. Yes, I'm in trouble. There is someone after me, correction, several some ones."

"What makes you think someone is after you?" He quirked one brow upward. "Are you a psychic?"

"Let's just say several members of my family are. As for me, I prefer not knowing. That's the way I live my life." She hesitated a moment. "You may as well know this up front, before you waste your time trying to woo me. As for being romantically involved with a psychic, that's about the last thing I want in this life."

It was too late for Blaine to stop the blink. She'd seen, as he'd known she would, but he never expected her to be so blunt about it. If he wasn't so amused he would be offended. He was highly sought after. True, no woman wanted him for long, but he'd never struck out without even making it to first base.

Cassandra Boozer presented a different twist. Women wanted initially to be with him because he was a psychic and this woman wanted nothing to do with him because he was a psychic. Damned if you do. Damned if you don't.

Blaine's eyes closed for the briefest of seconds. "Perhaps you were right. I shouldn't have bothered you." He stood to leave and felt the feathery light touch of her fingers on the back of his hand.

"I thought you wanted to talk?"

"I did. But I'm not a glutton for punishment. It's obvious to me that you were serious. You don't want to be bothered so I will respect your wishes and leave you alone."

"No, stay, Blaine." she interrupted him. "I've changed my mind."

"Why?"

"I don't know. Yes I do." She grinned. "I think if you're here talking to me I won't have to worry about you sitting in the back of me trying to probe my mind."

Blaine hesitated before smiling. "You knew?"

"A baby psychic would have known. You're pretty clumsy at this aren't you?"

He could feel the blush coming to his cheeks, something that was reserved for young girls, and something that he hadn't done since the first time a girl had popped her naked breasts in front of his face.

"It's not something I do a lot and I'm not proud of having tried it."
He watched while Cassandra appeared amused, melting more of the ice in her body.

"So why did you try?"

She caught his gaze refusing to release it. Damn she's good. "I don't know. "He stopped and looked up at her. "I really don't. I was trying to sleep. I felt this overwhelming sadness. I tried to ignore it, but it wouldn't go away so I tried to find the source. And here I am. "He looked into her eyes feeling a flush and prayed that he wouldn't get a hard on sitting next to her. He lowered his hand just in case, hoping to hide it if it happened.

"So you came because you sensed sadness in me?"

"Well," he hesitated. "It was a bit more than that. Anyway before I could stop myself here I was pestering you. Little did I know that you were a psychic."

He saw her raised brow and amended his words. "I didn't pick up on the fact that you hated psychics so vehemently."

She laughed and the sound washed over Blaine caressing him with warmth. There was no way on earth he could have anticipated the rush of emotions he felt on just hearing her laugh. He enjoyed it, glad for the knowledge that his hand was safely guarding the secret he didn't want to share with her. How the hell would he ever explain to a strange woman that he was as horny as any fifteen year old? He couldn't.

"I don't hate psychics per se." Cassandra laughed again. "I just hate the life and I don't want to ever be cast in that circle."

"But if you have gifts, it's a shame not to use them."

"Listen, Blaine, you may consider the things you do, hear or see as a gift. I don't. It's a curse and because of it my entire life has been cursed."

"Well, if that's true, why did you bother learning to block your thoughts?"

"Self preservation, something I picked up as a kid. That's the only good thing about this...this ability. It's also as far as I plan on taking this thing. But no one seems to believe me, and for that reason alone it seems someone is out to destroy my life."

"What are you doing to prevent it?"

"Running."

Blaine stopped short. That was it, what he'd sensed in the woman from his own seat four rows away. She was in a panic and she was running for her life. He wanted to help her. Surely her family had offered the same help. Hell, for that matter she could probably help herself if she wasn't so ashamed of having been blessed.

He started almost hesitantly. "There are things I could teach you that might help. You should at least protect yourself. This stuff is serious. If someone powerful is after you, they could destroy you if you're not prepared."

"Listen, Blaine, I'm not a fool. Like I told you, I come from generations of cursed people." She looked meaningfully at him. "Tell me your life has been a picnic." He cringed and she smiled. But this time it wasn't filled with warmth but bitterness.

"That's just what I thought. I have no idea why anyone would ever call having this a gift. I hate it." She glared at him. "I've prayed for many years for God to take it away, give it to any of the thousands of people that invaded my home as a child. Let them see the future for themselves, let them not be able to get a moment's rest because they can feel someone else's pain."

Blaine stopped her, feeling not just the mental blocks going into place, but her putting the oversized handbag between them erecting another physical barrier. He didn't want that to happen.

"I'm sorry for whatever happened to you, but it doesn't make this any less of a gift. Have you ever talked with anyone about this?"

Blaine couldn't help but think of his own childhood, not being wanted, shuffled from foster home to foster home until finally the state ran out of places that would take him.

He looked over at Cassandra, the anger making the corners of her mouth twitch. Yeah it could be pretty rough. He'd have to be a hypocrite not to acknowledge that fact. He imagined that she'd lived in a trailer park with a red neon sign blaring out to passerby's 'Psychic Readings.' Even now as an adult, seeing those signs embarrassed the hell out of him. There was nothing he could do about it. They had a right to make a living, yet there was something inside of him that still cringed to this day when people looked at him the way Cassandra was doing now. Something that made him feel lower than dirt, like he was doing something shady, bilking people out of their hard earned money.

It didn't help that every Tom, Dick and Harry wrote tales about psychics, not ever bothering to check, not doing even the most basic research. Then again why should they? The public would much rather see someone torn apart, made fun of, proof positive that everyone who claimed to have special gifts were frauds and fakes.

No, Blaine didn't blame Cassandra. He knew exactly how she felt. Only thing, he wasn't the enemy and he didn't like the way she was staring at him. This woman definitely had a way about her. She could make him get a hard-on in the nanosecond it took to breathe and just as fast she could dip that wonderful feeling into a bucket of ice making his body cold and the memories of his penis pressing hard and warm against his thigh vanish as though it never was.

Still Blaine wanted to remain in her presence. He'd never before wanted to plead with anyone to give him a chance. Never had the urge to tell people that there were many gifted psychics who only wanted to help others, despite the mental burden it placed on them. Defense of psychics had never weighed on him as heavily as it did now. Of all the people he could have convinced, it took a psychic to stir him up. He'd once wished people would at least investigate, or write to some of the professional organizations governing psychics. Hell, if people only knew there were professional mediums, clairvoyants, whatever they wanted to call them. There were thousands of gifted individuals trying even harder than the general public to clear up the misconceptions about them.

Ethical psychics would be the first to call the cops, to oust fakes, not out of jealousy but simply because they understood the basic principle of having a gift bestowed on them. Do No Harm.

"What are you doing analyzing me?"

"What are you talking about?" Blaine shook his head and blinked.

"You've been sitting there for five minutes staring at me."

"I was just thinking about what you said," Blaine answered softly. "I do understand how you feel."

"And now what? You're feeling sorry for me."

"No, I'm feeling sorry for me. If I can't convince you of what a marvelous gift we've been given…well." He hesitated not wanting to divulge too much, to tell her how he longed to meet the one woman who would understand him, and love him anyway. He would sound desperate and needy. What woman wanted that, or man for that matter? For a long moment neither of them spoke.

"Why would you even worry about convincing me?" Cassandra glanced backwards at the other passengers who were still talking animatedly, pointing at Blaine. "It seems you have a lot of adoring fans.

And as long as you pull in the big bucks what the hell do you care what people think?"

"Because I'm human," he answered her.

He watched her swallow, her slender neck hiding nothing. Her hands clutched at the oversized bag and she brought it to her chest.

"Blaine, I don't know how your parents raised you, but...," she looked down. "I hated my childhood, my parents and almost everyone else in my life. I hated my life, Blaine. If it had not been for two very special friends, I don't know how I would have survived. Thank God you had parents that didn't put you on display, that weren't always dragging you around to psychic fairs."

She shivered. "God it was awful."

"Did your parents love you?" He asked softly.

She blinked twice taken aback by the question. "Well they were parents, I supposed they did, but not enough to try and be normal."

Blaine was the one to give a bitter laugh. His eyes became hooded and he looked away.

"I sense your disapproval, Mr. MaDia."

"No, you sense my envy. I never got to have parents. I'm a product of the foster care system."

"You were better off."

"Yeah? I guess thinking I was a freak with no one to tell me I wasn't would be better than having parents tell me that I was special. That I'd been given special gifts and that I should embrace them and not be ashamed of those gifts, but use them for the good of mankind. I guess maybe you're right, Cassandra. Maybe I should sit here in my first class seat holding the world off, not bothering to accept any help from anyone."

"I'm sorry about your life, Blaine. But it was your life, not mine. Mine I hated. As for your haughty condescension, I didn't ask you to sit here. You came of your own free will. Remember that."

Blaine stared at Cassandra not needing his gifts to tell she was hurting, had been hurt a lot by her past. He should have been more sympathetic. She was right. He was the one who'd sought her out.

"Do you live in Chicago, Cassandra, or are you just visiting?"

He watched as the tension around her mouth begin to melt away leaving her skin with a dewy quality and leaving him once again with an extreme desire to touch her. There was no getting around it. He wanted her.

"What?"

"I just thought it would be safer for us to change the subject. I was thinking maybe for a night you could forget how much you hate psychics and look at me as a man. I'd love to buy you dinner."

"I'm not going to sleep with you."

"I'm only asking for dinner."

Blaine studied Cassandra as she studied him. He knew she was wrong. He would make love to her over and over again. He could almost taste her in his mouth as he looked at her. If he concentrated hard enough he would be able to caress her skin without moving so much as a muscle.

"It's been a long time since a man wanted me just for my body."

Blaine chuckled. "That's original. What is it that men want from you?"

"My powers, Mr. MaDia. I'm a twenty-first generation female psychic. There has been twenty generations of psychics in my family before me. Each generation getting stronger and stronger."

She stopped and looked at him. "You see, Mr. MaDia, my family only marry other psychics, that makes the bloodline that much stronger. If you've studied numerology at all you know that twenty-two is the magical number."

She grinned at him. "I'm supposed to be special, number twenty-one. I'm destined to give birth to the super psychic. Only I won't play along and lots of people are angry at me, including my entire family."

"Isn't there anyone else in your family who could fill this position?" He stopped and smiled at his unexpected pun. "I mean wouldn't a twenty-first generation cousin do as well?"

"You'd think that wouldn't you? Well, problem is I am the one with the direct line. Other branches of the family have no provable abilities. When I discovered what my family's plan for me was I rejected everything I'd ever known or learned."

"With one exception."

"Yes, you're right, with one exception. Like I said I only scan when I feel there's a danger to me. As for the blocks, same thing, otherwise I'm open all the time." She stopped and looked at him hard. "Someone in your line of work should really learn to be more adept at it. If you're going to do it, you don't want to get caught. I could show you how if you like."

"I thought you didn't like psychics."

"In general I don't." She smiled. "There's something about you." She looked down at his hand that didn't quite cover his obvious bulge.

"I'm not afraid of you. You just want to sleep with me. If you're going to go around crawling into a person's thoughts you may as well learn how to do it quietly so that you're not detected."

"I don't think it's something I'm going to be doing a lot of."

"Good."

She smiled at him and he couldn't help but notice the look of approval in her eyes.

***

From the last row of the first class section of seats, another passenger sat sipping on a glass of white wine, pretending not to notice the pair close to the front of the plane. He'd noticed all right. From the moment Blaine MaDia stepped on the plane he'd noticed. He recognized the man from all the television he'd done. There seemed nowhere a person could look now a-days without seeing his mug, smiling with the sincere, let-me-be-your- friend smile.

Yeah he was familiar with the man. He looked down his nose at most of the other people in his same field, thought he was better than them. What the hell did he know? He'd just gotten lucky that was all.

Well, it was okay the man thought to himself. Two for the price of one. It was only Cassandra he wanted, but no, she also thought she was too good for him. *Now look at her*, he thought, cozying up to Blaine MaDia as if he were God. He'd show her and he'd show him also.

He took another longer sip of his wine. He knew the man had a hard-on for Cassandra. He'd sensed it when Blaine opened up his mind and allowed the ice queen entrance.

Hell, it'd been easy. All he had to do was just waltz right in behind her. Blaine had never even known he was there, too busy trying not to touch himself. Oh yeah he'd seen that too, seen the way MaDia ran his hand down the ridge of his own penis, wanting to jack off right there in his pants.

No, he thought again. That wasn't what he wanted. Damn Blaine MaDia. He wanted Cassandra. It was Cassandra's hands the psychic had imagined was caressing him. Well they'd both burn in hell long before he ever had a chance to shove his penis into her. He'd see to that, the lying two-face cunt.

So she hated psychics. If that was true why the fuck was she laughing at that stupid show off Blaine? He tilted his glass to his lips and calmly polished off the wine.

Yeah, he'd show them both and he'd show the entire world who the real master psychic was. Fuck that shit about talking to the dead. Who the hell could ever prove any of that crap? He was going to talk to the living. And it would be loud enough to be heard around the world.

He laughed at his own joke. The prediction that could be heard around the world. Yeah that's it, and neither one of them would ever see him coming. He could mind fuck them anytime he chose. If Cassandra thought her puny blocks were really keeping him out she was stupid as well.

But mind fucking wasn't his ultimate goal for her. No, her he intended to fuck for real until she cried out his name and admitted that he was the one she needed, he'd make her beg for mercy. Then when he was done he would slit the cunt's throat. Then again maybe he'd save that pleasure until the whore gave him a son, then he'd kill her.

Blaine MaDia's appearance was just another interesting new facet of the game. He was going to cut off his balls and shove them down his throat. Let Mr. TV see that one coming.

Passenger number 12-A, sat back against his seat and smiled to himself over his plans. He didn't have to hurry. Let Cassandra think she was able to hide from him. He was enjoying the chase.

Chapter Three

Sighing contentedly not wanting to admit that Blaine MaDia was a wonderful lover she took a long stretch instead. *God I needed that*, she thought to herself, feeling some of the tension she'd carried for the past few months drain away.

"Hey, I thought you were buying me dinner?" Cassandra teased.

"And I thought you weren't going to bed with me," Blaine said and smiled.

She enjoyed the cocky smile he sported for just a moment longer before breaking his bubble. "I changed my mind."

"Why? Was it my charms or my good looks?"

"Neither. It was just knowing you'd never fit the qualifications. Blaine, where I come from you're a baby psychic. Sure you're good at what you do. But as far as I can tell... you're what?" She asked not mean spirited, "a first generation psychic?"

Blaine sat up not wanting to believe what she was saying. "Are you telling me you're in bed with me because I'm not good enough?"

"It's not that you're not good enough, you just could never complete the circle. I don't have to worry about being mother of a super baby. I didn't mean it as a put down."

"Did you mean it as a compliment?"

She didn't answer. He had known she wouldn't. Damn, damn, damn, he thought, damning himself for being so gullible. He had gotten carried away with wanting what Michelle had with Chance. For that matter he'd settle for what Michelle had with Larry.

Blaine refused to look at Cassandra as he climbed out the bed and stuck his legs in his jeans. He finished dressing in silence. When would he learn? Hell, he earned his living by telling others to stay away from painful situations, but when it came to his heart he always seemed to enter in blindly.

His gaze at last resting on Cassandra's face Blaine opened his wallet. Her eyes widened in dreadful disbelief. His own gaze followed hers to the wallet he held in his hand. He wanted to scream at her. Did she really think he was low enough to offer her money? With a snort of disgust he threw his card on the nightstand.

"My offer still stands. If you need me call." He walked to the door and paused turning back toward her. "But of course I'm sure there's nothing a first generation baby psychic can do to help you, is there?"

With that he left the room and walked toward the elevator. He blanked everything from his mind. He should never have trusted his lower extremities with making the choice. The rest of him was still too worn out from the smoke fumes. He should have waited. Now he'd totally expended all his reserve energy and he felt like hell.

***

Lying under the covers staring out into nothingness Cassandra sighed in annoyance. The couple of hours she'd spent in Blaine's arms had been wonderful. He was tender and considerate with just the right amount of machismo to make her feel she wasn't teaching him. She was glad of that. He knew what he was doing. She definitely wasn't teaching him. There was more to the man than met the eye.

When the hell had she lost control of the situation? She wondered and knew the answer immediately. On the plane. She should have never allowed him to sit with her, but she had. She'd enjoyed his smile, enjoyed talking to him and she wouldn't deny it. When she heard he was an orphan she'd used him.

It had been so long since she'd last had sexual release that she was bursting at the seams. She had to be careful whom she slept with. Someone was always trying to trick her into bed, pretending to be normal.

Blaine MaDia was that for her. He was normal. Sure he was a psychic, but there was no way he could possibly want her for siring a child. His bloodline didn't carry enough power.

She'd forgotten to tell him the other part of the plan her family had. She had to mate with a psychic of equal power. There weren't too may of those around, but enough that in the last several months she'd felt them coming to her at night, attempting to come into her body, trying vainly to make love to her. She'd grown up with several dozen psychics, all of them having received their training from the same master. Most of them she called friends, but it didn't mean they wouldn't be above trying to use her to fulfill the prophecy.

The one thing she hadn't lied to Blaine about was scanning and blocking for self-defense. As much as she hated the powers she was born with she used those two to protect herself.

It was wearing her down to keep a constant energy field around her for protection even in her sleep. It had felt good to just make love with a man for the pure pleasure of it. She glanced at his card.

He was right about one thing; there was nothing he could do to help her. The only thing she could think of that would stop the attacks would be to have a hysterectomy. And so far she hadn't found a doctor willing to perform unnecessary surgery on her.

One had looked at her strangely and told her maybe he could refer her to someone who could help. They both knew he meant a psychiatrist. He told her she watched too much television and movies that she sounded as if someone wanted her to have Rosemary's baby. Well to her that was how it felt. She would not be party to her family's plans. She'd decided long ago not to get involved with anyone from the psychic community. She would stay safe as long as she did that. Only now it seemed her time was running out. People were actively trying to force her to marry and produce an heir.

***

Blaine tossed an extra twenty to the taxi driver. The man had gotten him home quickly and had done as he asked, not bothered him with questions. He hated being rude, but that little scene at Cassandra's left him without the patience to handle mundane conversation. He needed to sort out his own emotions.

With a shrug he walked into his home, throwing his bag carelessly unto the sofa and making a dash for the windows. He'd been gone almost three weeks and his home smelled dusty, of stale air. Perhaps it was also because of the near miss in his San Francisco apartment, but he now craved fresh air.

As he opened the window his mind swiftly traveled to Michelle. She'd called him twice in California telling him she'd had a strange feeling that something was wrong with him.

He hadn't told her what had happened. Cassandra had called him a first generation psychic. That was a lie. It was obvious to him that his real mother had gifts as well. He'd not imagined what happened. She'd been there with him. She'd saved him and he'd called her mother.

The windows open at last Blaine smiled at his own foolishness. He should have guessed much sooner. His mother was also psychic. The business with Michelle appearing in his father's dreams, those weren't just accidents. By God she'd astral traveled to find Chance. Shivers skittered down Blaine's spine. He was excited. The love Michelle had for Chance spread to him. He knew this without a shadow of a doubt. He was alive because of her, because she'd appeared in his apartment and slapped him awake. He knew she was now able to Bi-locate.

Without a doubt he could prove it. She could be in two places at once. She'd been in Hawaii with Larry when another part of her had been dragging him from a burning building.

The thought of Larry caused momentary sadness. He touched the bracelet he always wore now on his left wrist. Blaine had found the family he always wanted only to lose them again.

Chance and Michelle had lived several lifetimes together, their last being as Jeremy and Dimitra. Somehow their love found them again in the twenty-first century and together they had found him. The son Dimitra had left behind when she died shortly after giving birth.

Only thing, they'd found each other too late. Michelle was married for over twenty-five years to Larry. It had looked for a time as if she might leave Larry and pursue her future with Chance. But in the end she'd decided her destiny lay with her husband of this lifetime.

Blaine rubbed his bracelet vigorously. It was a Mystic's idea of what would bring him, Chance and Michelle together again in the next life. He hoped it worked.

Chance had left Chicago and moved to San Francisco shortly after Michelle had gone back to Larry. That was one of the reasons Blaine got himself an apartment there. He couldn't bear to lose contact with father.

But it was Michelle to whom he felt the strongest connection. And it was Michelle whom he wanted to talk to now. He glanced at his watch. It was four A.M. Too late to bother anyone, even his mother with a phone call, but still he needed to hear the sound of her voice. He needed someone to erase away the hurt. He needed to feel love.

The phone was in his hand a second before he admitted that fact to himself. Damn, he hated feeling like that. It had never bothered him before she came into his life, but now, now that he knew what it was to have the love of someone who would always love you, he couldn't get enough of it.

The phone rang three times and Blaine almost gave up when Michelle's sleepy voice came on the other end of the line.

"Blaine, is that you?"

Tears filled his eyes. He wanted to hug her, cry in her arms like the child that she'd lost, the child he'd never had the chance to be with her.

"How did you know it was me?"

A moment of silence before she spoke. Blaine could picture her holding the phone, staring, wondering the same thing herself.

"I don't know. I just knew it was you, that's all. Are you okay?"

"Not really."

"What's wrong?"

He heard her mumble something, probably to Larry. He gripped the phone tighter. He should have waited until later.

"Give me a moment, Blaine. I'm going to take the phone in the den."

He waited while he heard her lift another phone. He could hear her footsteps as she padded back to hang up the phone beside her bed and walk back to where she'd taken the phone off in the den. He heard her settle in.

"Now tell me. What's wrong?"

"Nothing really. I was just feeling the need for a friend."

"At four in the morning? Come on, there's more to it than that."

"No really, I just needed to hear your voice."

"Blaine, something happened to you in San Francisco didn't it?"

He didn't answer.

"I knew it. I felt it. You were in danger. Tell me what happened."

"Michelle, do you mind that I think of you as my mother? I mean when we're alone... how would you feel...if...if I called you that?"

He'd had no intentions of ever blurting out his wishes to her. She had five children. She was trying hard to make her marriage to Larry stronger. The last thing she needed was him interfering. He could only be a reminder to her husband of Chance. He shouldn't have asked.

"Blaine, give me twenty minutes, I'm coming over."

"No, Michelle, there's no need, but just knowing you would do that means a lot to me."

"Blaine, you're my son, just as much as Derrick. You're not a bother in my life. Larry accepts that. He may not fully understand it, or believe it, but he accepts the fact that I believe you are my son."

"How did you know what I was thinking?"

"I'm your mother, I'm supposed to know."

"Thanks, Mom," he said teasing, testing the sound of it on his tongue not wanting to give away anymore than he already had. "Are you telling me that you're psychic also?"

"Just when it comes to you and maybe…"

She didn't continue, yet Blaine knew she was thinking of Chance. He rubbed his bracelet again hoping like hell it would work when the time came.

"Are you still wearing your necklace?"

"Yes. I'll never take it off."

"How about when you bathe?"

He heard her laughing on the other end of the phone. Everything about her had the power to change his mood. He loved having her in his life. She thought she was a lifetime too late, but she came just in time.

Michelle stopped laughing and turned serious once again. "Blaine, let me come. I need to see you as much as you need to see me."

"What about Larry?"

"Say the word and I'll come."

"I don't want to cause problems for you."

"Say the word."

"How about lunch?"

"How about now?"

"Lunch will be fine."

"How about breakfast?"

Blaine laughed. He truly loved having a mother. "I need to sleep, Mom. I just got in. Make it one pm. I'll meet you…"

"At the zoo?"

"Yeah," he answered loving the way she finished his thoughts. The zoo had become their special place.

* * *

Twenty minutes later Blaine was lying in his bed trying to console himself with the fact that he and Michelle had managed to achieve the impossible. They had been given a chance to complete a life they'd not been able to have a lifetime before.

Only it wasn't enough for him. He wanted children, a wife, someone to come home to at night, someone to rub his back, a woman whose feet he would massage at the end of the day. He could imagine helping her wash her hair, change the diapers and give the babies bottles. He wanted all of that. Despite the comfort he received from his relationship with Michelle he remained lonely. His mother wasn't enough to satisfy the craving of his soul.

He wanted a mate. Blaine tried not to think about a woman he only knew briefly, but more intimately than any of the women he'd had relationships with. Never before had he attempted to enter a woman's mind for his own selfish reasons. He'd only done that when invited through a reading. And never had he opened himself to be scanned by anyone.

He marveled at how easily he accepted Cassandra's explanation of being chased in order to produce a super baby. Then again he'd been doubted too much of his life to ever doubt anything. It seemed that more of what wasn't seen was truer than the things you could observe with your eyes.

He felt the flesh on his arms prickle with apprehension. That had been a mistake, her scanning him had left him open to someone else who wasn't interested in finding out if he was lying. Though the encounter was brief he'd felt a sinister intention.

His eyes became heavy. He no longer wanted to ponder what had or had not happened on the plane. He wanted to forget Cassandra, put her in the category of a one night stand and move on.

That was easier said than done, for as he gave into sleep his thoughts lingered on the smell and feel of Cassandra. His heart knew she was so much more than just a quick lay.

***

"I'm coming, I'm coming, stop the banging."

Blaine banged his toe into the dresser in his haste to make his way for the door. His attention fell on the clock. It was only a few minutes after ten. Michelle wasn't supposed to be here. She was to meet him at the zoo at one. Still he knew it was her banging on his door while ringing the bell simultaneously. Who else would dare to do such a thing?

"I knew it was you," he smiled at her.

"Of course you did." She pulled him into her arms for a hug then pushed him away slightly, observing him with a critical eye before embracing him once again.

"What's wrong with you?"

"I didn't tell you anything was wrong."

"You didn't have to, it was in your voice along with the fact that you called me at four to chat."

"I forgot the time."

"Liar."

Blaine smiled broadly at her. "We were going to meet at the zoo. Why are you here?"

"I couldn't wait."

"What about Larry, did he object?"

He watched closely looking for even the hint of deception. The last thing he wanted to do was cause problems for Michelle and her husband.

"Larry didn't object." She smiled, "he even told me to say hello to you."

At that comment Blaine arched his brow. Larry was not his biggest fan and he could not imagine the man sending him a warm greeting especially after waking him at such an ungodly hour.

"Okay, maybe that was pushing it a bit too far, but he didn't object. Now tell me what's going on. I didn't come here to talk about Larry. What happened to you in San Francisco?"

"You ask too many questions. How am I to figure out which one you want me to answer first?" He managed to duck out of the way as she swatted playfully at him.

"Okay, don't freak. I had a fire in my apartment in San Francisco, but…," he rushed on. "As you can see I'm fine."

"Blaine you may not believe me, but I knew something was wrong with you. Larry and I were at the beach and suddenly I felt as if I was choking and I saw your face. I rushed out of the water and called you, all the while praying that you were fine. I nearly went crazy when it took two days before I heard from you."

Now would be the time to tell her. He looked at her worried eyes and decided against it. What good would it serve? Besides her husband barely tolerated the idea of Michelle having a psychic in her life. He would freak if he found out his wife also had untapped powers.

"I'm sorry you were worrying about me. I didn't call sooner because I didn't want to worry you."

"That didn't work now, did it?"

"I suppose not." He reached out and took her hand in his feeling the warmth, reveling in her love, in the smile she was giving him. Yet, still it wasn't enough. For the first time in his life having a mother was not the most important thing to him. He wanted a woman to share his life.

"What's wrong, Blaine?" Michelle pried gently.

"Oh I guess I was feeling a little nostalgic for family. I met a woman on the plane trip home and it got me to thinking."

"About what?"

"How empty my life really is."

"How can you say that? You help so many people, you're admired by thousands, your phone never stops ringing and you have enough appointments to last a lifetime."

"That's business. I don't have anyone in my life."

"You have me."

Blaine smiled at his mother. "Not really." He saw her lips turn downward and her mouth opened to protest.

"Hear me out, Michelle. How many people do you think really believe our story, that you're my mother, besides you and Chance? I think everyone else thinks we're crazy. I'm not even sure if other mediums believe it."

"That doesn't make me love you any less. I believe it, that's all that necessary. And you believe it." She stopped short. "You do believe it don't you, Blaine?"

He detected a note of sadness in her voice. "I was there. I have to believe. And, I do not doubt your love. But I feel I'm taking something from your family every time we're together. I feel like a thief. I want someone to love and not have to feel guilty about it."

"This someone, is it the woman you met on the plane?"

Blaine jerked his head to where his mother sat observing him, analyzing his every word. Again he wondered how she could not have figured out she had psychic powers of her own. She was so in-tuned to him. Then again it had taken him a long time to put the pieces together and he'd accepted his gifts his entire life. Michelle evidently had run from it just the way Cassandra was doing now.

"Blaine." Michelle called to him softly.

He stared at her. He had almost forgotten she was talking to him. "I'm sorry." She was smiling at him now as though she knew a secret.

"What?"

"You're in love."

"What are you talking about? I simply told you I met a woman on the plane."

"It's not what you told me, it's what you didn't say. You're in love."

Blaine shook his head. "Women are the only ones who believe in love at first sight." He looked away knowing that was a lie. "Besides, the woman on the plane could be less interested in me."

"Why?"

"She doesn't like psychics."

"Oh."

Now Michelle's voice was annoyed, filled with a mother's righteous indignation. "Has she ever had an opportunity to get to know one?"

"She is a psychic. And from what she says an extremely powerful one. She says she's a twenty-first generation psychic." Blaine attempted to smile. "She told me that I'm a baby psychic, a first generation."

"Then to hell away with her. She's not worth your time. What's her name by the way?"

"Cassandra. Cassandra Boozer."

"Then to hell away with Cassandra Boozer, she doesn't know what she's missing. So what if you're a first generation psychic, you're good, too good for her, the snob."

While she fumed, Blaine laughed in amusement. "What if I could tell her I'm at least a second generation psychic, that my mother is also psychic?"

Michelle looked appalled Blaine noted. She rose from a sitting position and stood directly over him.

"That would be a lie and you don't need to lie to get a girl."

Michelle blinked and Blaine saw the shudder go through her body. He knew what she was thinking before she got the words out.

"Maybe your biological…"

He stopped her. "She's not my mother, you are."

"This time around she is, Blaine. Maybe she's gifted."

"She's not the one I was speaking of. Besides if I don't feel anything for her how can she be? I never believed she was my mother. I told you that."

"Yes, I know, but don't you ever wonder about her? What if she was gifted also? Wouldn't that help you?"

Blaine pulled Michelle down on the sofa to sit beside him. "You're my only mother. Maybe I'm putting too much pressure on you. It is asking a lot so if you'd rather I didn't think of you like that I could..."

Could what? Blaine knew his words were a blatant lie. No matter what Michelle's answer to him, she would always be his only mother. Instead of what he was expecting she surprised him.

"You know, Blaine, I was thinking about what your friend said, maybe it's not that you're a baby psychic, but a baby soul."

He stared at her dumfounded. What the hell was this? First he'd been insulted by the woman whose smell still lingered on him, who'd allowed him to make love to her, then allowed him to leave. Now Michelle was insulting him and she had the nerve to smile while she was doing it.

"Baby soul?"

"Don't go getting huffy. You pretend not to need anyone, even me. You offer to shut me out of your life and you and I both know how much you want me in it. I suspect it's the same with that Cassandra. You want her and you don't know how to make it happen, so you just pretend that you don't."

Staring at Michelle regretting his early morning call the frown was unpreventable. Maybe it hadn't been such a good idea after all. He wasn't in the mood to be analyzed this morning.

"Blaine, I only mentioned your mother..., sorry. Well, the other possibility because I'm not psychic and neither is...well neither of us have the gift."

Again he looked at her. Since the day she went back to Larry she'd not uttered Chance's name. If she thought about him she would have to think about what brought them together, and maybe just maybe she would have to admit that she did have powers of her own. She didn't want it. That was why she denied it. Granted, it wasn't an easy life. He felt his lips curving into a smile. He never could quarrel too long with Michelle. He'd waited too long for a mother to spend even a minute of it in dissension.

He reached for her hand and held it against his lips. "You're the mother my soul recognizes, the only one that matters, so lets get that straight okay. I don't need another."

"Good, we've lost so much time. I don't want to share you with anyone else, especially another mother."

"What about a wife and kids?" he teased.

"That I'll think about. Why? Who do you have in mind? And don't tell me that you're already picturing yourself with someone that hates you. That's not a very good match, Blaine, you're just asking for trouble."

Blaine chuckled, he'd asked for this, the mothering, the loving. He'd just have to learn to take the good with the bad.

"Listen, Michelle, would you mind starting the coffee while I take a shower? If you do," he grinned up at her "I'll take you out to eat before we go to the zoo."

He took her answer for granted as he turned and headed for the shower.

"We are not done talking. You can't change the subject so easily."

"Don't I know it?" He mumbled low as he closed the door and adjusted the spray. He had to admit Michelle was right about one thing. He should get his mind off Cassandra, but he couldn't.

He closed his eyes and immediately an image of her flooded his brain. She was pacing the room of her hotel. He saw her stop and pick up the card he'd left on her nightstand. He watched as she read it, then knew the second she became of aware of what he was doing. She turned around, a frown on her face and he felt a door slamming with force.

Wow, he thought to himself, this time he had not attempted to invade her mind, he'd only opened himself up to her vibrations, but she'd felt that also and from the frown on her face, she didn't like it.

Blaine opened the bathroom door to the smell of fresh coffee brewing and something else, delicious smells were emanating from his kitchen, but that was impossible. He didn't have any food and Michelle had not brought any with her.

With a smile he stepped into the kitchen. He eyed a plate piled high with food. "Where did this come from?" he asked.

"Oh a little of this and that and odds and ends."

"Eggs are not odds and ends. I didn't have any."

"I went to the store okay. You needed to eat and well I...what the heck? I needed to cook for you."

"I thought you were over that phase of taking care of other people needs."

"Taking care of your needs is taking care of mine. Listen, it's no big deal. It's breakfast and beside I have an ulterior motive. I want to know more about this woman you've fallen for. If she's going to be in your life I want to hear everything."

"Everything?" Blaine teased, "including all the personal stuff." He paused while Michelle blushed. He'd known that would stop her. "Just let me eat, then I'll tell you."

An hour later they were in the car driving toward the zoo. He'd eaten until he thought he would burst and then he'd kept his promise and filled Michelle in on the woman he'd met. He only kept one thing to himself: Cassandra was in danger. For sure this mother of his would want him to sever his ties.

While he was willing to concede that Michelle finding him had changed both their lives. It was difficult for her finding a full grown son. Sometimes she didn't know what to do. He was too old for her to diaper and give a bottle, but the look was always there in her eyes. She was right and he believed her. Michelle needed to mother him. He could only hope that the infant stage would end for her soon and that at least she would see him as an adolescent.

He pulled through the gates of Brookfield Zoo. Look who's talking, he thought. He wanted Michelle to not see him as a child and here he was every chance he got living out a childhood fantasy of having his mother take him to the zoo. He should feel ashamed. But he didn't.

Turning he gave a full-fledged grin. "Are you ready to go, Mom?" She seemed surprised for only an instant before she answered.

"Yes, Son, lets go."

She didn't wait for him to open the door, instead she got out on her on and came to his side where she immediately surveyed him, brushing back his hair, picking non-existent lint from his clothing, then looking at him with such love the intensity of her feelings for him startled him for just a moment. He loved her in that same undeniable incredible way. The feeling flooded through him surrounding him with such joy that his heart caught in his throat. She leaned into him and kissed his cheek.

"I love you, Blaine."

"I love you too," he answered her. No, this was one fantasy he would never let go of.

Chapter Four

Cassandra stared at the card in her hand then spun around. She'd felt Blaine MaDia's eyes on her, watching her and it was not her imagination.

She should have known better than to let her defenses down. To even sleep with someone she thought could do her no psychic harm was foolish. After all he was a psychic and apparently a more powerful one than she'd given him credit for.

An itching began in her hand and moved up her arm. A mild pain vibrated in tune with the beating of her heart right between her eyes. She could feel her third eye trying to open and she was damn if she would let that happen.

Cassandra hurriedly dumped the contents of her purse in search of the container that held her special potion and then she sprinkled a bit of bluish powder in the palm of her hand. She lapped the mixture up hungrily, squeezing her eyes shut, blanking her mind out, refusing to see anything other than the content of the hotel room. She no longer wanted to see things that weren't there.

She threw Blaine's card viciously on the floor. It was his fault. He'd made her laugh, he'd made love to her body and her soul and he'd invaded her world for a glimpse of her. She wanted to do the same to him and she hated him for it.

She rolled her tongue around in her mouth licking away the last residue of the powder. The vision was receding and with it her desire to spy on Blaine. She'd have to be more careful in the future. Seems like the baby psychic had a lot more power than she would have given him credit for.

Cassandra kneeled down and picked up his card tucking it away inside her purse. If she should ever meet the man again she would have to remember this moment. His innocent face and sexual attraction for her would not get in the way.

***

Excitement bubbled thorough his veins. He knew what it must feel like to be a child at Christmas. In a few short months his gifts had tripled, no they'd quadrupled in size and variations. For the first time being at the zoo with Michelle wasn't the balm his soul needed. If anything he'd felt restless remember how he'd been able to view Cassandra. He'd not tried, had not even known he had the gift of remote viewing and like a child he couldn't stop thinking about it wanting to try it out again to see if it would work. But he'd have to be careful, the lady in question wouldn't like the idea of him spying on her. Finally his inattentions had gotten to Michelle and she'd demanded he be taken home and that he get some rest and stop thinking about a woman who wasn't right for him. He'd agreed and she'd frown recognizing his promise as nothing more than a lie to placate her.

Now home he found himself pacing trying to figure out his next move. Seeing into the future, talking to the dead, those things were old news to Blaine, but these new gifts, the energy, just thinking about Cassandra and being able to see her, it was heady stuff.

He had to be careful, he had to investigate this, see if he could think of anyone else and get the same results, he wanted to be scientific in his approach.

Clicking his fingers on the edge of his desk, he thought for a moment. He needed a list. With his left hand he reached into the drawer to retrieve the needed paper and pen and was surprised to find his right hand had picked up the receiver for the phone.

Blaine smiled at his own actions dialing the number he'd not known that he knew. He waited until he was connected and then let out a breath doing his best not to bring her picture into his mind.

"My mother's very upset with you for your shabby treatment of me."

"I thought you were an orphan?"

"Well, I used to be."

"What are you talking about, used to be? Either you are or you aren't."

"Well, I was for thirty-one years, but I found my mother."

"What happened, did she put you up for adoption then decided to look for you after you made a name for yourself?"

"No, she died."

"Come again?"

"My mother died."

"Blaine, have you been drinking?"

The sound of Cassandra's voice was near making him giddy. "I don't drink or take drugs of any kind. They dull the senses."

He paused, knowing he'd hit on something. "Is that what you do, Cassandra?"

"This isn't about me, you made the call to tell me about your mother. The one who died."

Silence.

"I forgot," Cassandra purred. "You talk to them after. So your mother even in the spirit world, is displeased with my actions?"

"She's not in the spirit world. She's in the physical world."

"Blaine, I don't have time for games. What do you want?"

"I'm not playing games and as to what I want, well, I think that should be fairly obvious."

Again silence.

"How about that dinner I promised?" Blaine teased.

"I don't think that would be a very good idea. You shouldn't get too attached. I'm not into falling in love, Blaine."

He heard the catch in her voice. Hell, he would have had to be deaf not to notice it.

"Look how you reacted, after just one night. I don't think you can take it. All I want is someone I can sleep with occasionally, who won't ask too many questions, and who won't spy on me."

He found himself cringing inwardly at the unspoken reprimand. "I didn't mean for that to happen. It was an accident. I've never done it before and to be honest I didn't know I could. I was merely thinking of you and I saw you. I promise you I wasn't intentionally spying on you." He was going to say more when something very important occurred to him. If you're squashing all your gifts, Cassandra, how did you know?"

"I can only go so far in squashing them, besides it was late."

"It was early morning."

"It was late for me."

Blaine decided for once since meeting Cassandra to let the matter drop, he knew what she wasn't saying. She was taking something to tamp down her gifts, something that may eventually destroy those gifts completely. And without whatever it was, she'd seen him, or felt him watching her, he wasn't sure which.

"Okay, Cassandra, while I would love nothing more than to make love to you again, I would love to get to know you a little better."

"Are you going to play Sir Lancelot for me?"

"Doesn't every man dream of playing the heroic knight and saving his lady fair?"

"I'm not your lady anything, and I don't need you to save me."

"I know."

"Your feelings are hurt again, aren't they?"

"I was just wondering what my mother would say if she could hear this conversation. She'd probably tell me I'm nuts to want to bother with you."

"Seriously, Blaine, you've gotten me curious, this mother of yours, the one that died, that lives in the physical world, the one that doesn't like me, where did she come from?"

"Another lifetime." Blaine answered glibly. He laughed. "Have dinner with me and I'll tell you all about her. I'll even bring a picture if you like, to prove her existence.

"Why don't you bring her?"

"Because she doesn't like you."

"That's right. I forgot."

He heard the laughter in her voice a moment before his own spilled into the phone.

"Pick me up at seven."

"Thanks."

"Blaine?"

"Yes."

"This time I really do want dinner."

***

What had he done? He'd only meant to write down a list of people and research them, see if just thinking about them would bring a clear picture of what he was doing. Instead his hand had betrayed him. He remembered somewhere watching or reading something that said, if your right hand offended you, cut it off.

Blaine brought his right hand upward toward his face. He peered at it closely. Had it offended him? He smiled. He had a date with Cassandra Boozer. He'd say his hand did him a tremendous favor.

Cassandra hung up the phone and paced around the room scolding herself. Didn't she not five minutes before swear to stay away from Blaine MaDia. He was too damn nosy. All psychics were. They claimed to be naturally curious. She begged to differ with them.

She would bet anything that Blaine wasn't in her room spying on her because he was curious. No, he was nosy. If she hadn't caught him at it, she didn't know how long he would have continued.

Yeah, she needed to see him again, if for nothing else than to set some ground rules. Her body began a tingle and she admitted the sexual awareness, why not, the man was a babe and a damn good lover to boot, but to her he was a danger. She'd felt the tiny crack in her psyche, she couldn't allow him to penetrate any further.

Without warning the pain hit her with the force of an oil drilling rig. A wave of nausea overcame her and for a moment she thought she would faint.

Cassandra sank into the bed feeling violently ill. She was going to throw up, but if she did she would be weakened for the time it took to do it, so she took in one deep breath, allowing her lungs to expand, ordering the rush of clean air to go through her body to cleanse her.

Quickly she visualized a purple barricade around her body with the negative energy bouncing off her in waves and smashing to the ground into so much dust. Her intention had been to send it back to the person who'd sent it but then they'd know. They'd know that she did have powers she claimed not to have.

***

He knew it, he thought as he felt his lips curling into a smirk. He'd been following her for years now. He knew everything about her, her puny walls, her vain attempts to keep him out.

And he knew the smell of her, the feel of her body, but he knew these things as though he were a ghost. He'd only touched her astral body.

He wanted to touch her for real now, not in a dream, for even there she pushed him away.

He smiled. She had to be getting tired of this, he knew he was. Maybe tonight would be the night, maybe he'd actually make contact with her, go up to her and offer to buy her a cup of coffee.

It would be so easy to time his coming and goings when she was doing the same; he had the room right next door. For a hundred bucks the clerk had not bothered to ask questions when he said he wanted the room next door.

He had to laugh; the hotel boasted itself as giving the ultimate in luxury and safety for their guests. Well, he knew first hand that the guest's sense of well being could be sold for a measly hundred bucks.

He'd even heard her talking on the phone to that nothing show off. He'd wanted to rip his head off the previous night when he'd entered Cassandra's room with her. From everything he knew about her, she was supposed to toss him out on his ass.

Her routine so well known to him, that he'd even ordered up dinner laughing over how long it would take for the dimwitted psychic to see that he wasn't going to get into Cassandra's pants. But he was the one who'd been fooled.

It was all he could do to control himself when he heard the obvious sounds of lovemaking coming through the walls and Cassandra's screams of pleasures. If he'd owned a gun he would have shot through the walls and killed them both.

It had taken him hours to calm down. She soiled herself with the likes of that television psychic but wouldn't even acknowledge him.

Before it would have been merely an additional pleasure to rid the world of the man. Now it was a duty. He truly hoped the stupid bitch had made MaDia use a rubber. He would stand for no one's seed but his own to impregnate her, if she allowed that to happen through her foolishness, he would forget about all the things he wanted to accomplish, the son the two of them could produce. He would forget all that in a heart beat and just kill her for the sake of watching her die. Even now he could picture it.

He took a drink of his cold coffee, she'd better damn well hope Blaine MaDia hadn't dropped his seed in her womb, her life would be a hell of a lot shorter.

Chapter Five

The grin spread across Blaine's face. He was behaving like a school boy. One night with a woman he didn't know and he was feeling something he'd never felt before, maybe it had something to do with seeing Michelle. She always had a strange effect on him, making him want things he always thought he couldn't have, making him feel loved and yes, he'd say it, making him yearn for more.

He needed to get a grip, he was fast losing his focus. There had to be something else he could concentrate on, someone who needed his services.

There was a slight ping. He knew damn well what it meant. He had no business delving into anyone's psychic mess today. He wasn't fully charged from all he'd been through. He was in a weakened condition.

Blaine told himself all these things as he dialed his office. He needed something to take his mind off of Cassandra Boozer and he needed it fast.

"Hey."

"Hey boss, when are you coming home?"

"I'm back."

"In Chicago?"

"Yeah. That's home right?"

Blaine could feel his breathing slowing. It worked. Mundane conversation was enabling him to return to his own reality.

"So what are doing? Why aren't you in the office if you're back?"

That was Estelle. She ran his office with tight control and something in her little head told her she ran him as well. Today he was grateful for the woman's bossy demeanor. She was just what he needed.

"Listen Blaine," she interrupted his train of thought. "I could use your help on a small problem."

Blaine heard the hesitation in her voice and wondered what it was. She never, but never had an iota of tack, whatever she wanted must be something big to cause her to be embarrassed.

"Estelle, go on, you know if I can I'll help."

"I don't want to take advantage of you, but...I was wondering...that is if you don't mind."

"Estelle, spit it out, say what's on your mind, what is it you want me to do?"

"These news powers you have, I was just wondering if maybe you could help me find my earring."

"Excuse me?"

"My earring," Estelle rushed on and Blaine nearly laughed. If anyone was going to ask such things of him Estelle would be the one. And to think he thought it was a monumental issue.

"What's so important about your earring and since when do you use me as your lost and found?"

"It's not like that. It's just that my husband gave me the earrings and you know he doesn't give me many presents. I lost one and it means a lot to me."

He heard the sigh on the other end of the phone. He was teasing, but realized she was now wishing she had not asked for his help. That emotion was coming across loud and clear.

"Estelle, I'm sorry? I'll help if I can. I'll be there in an hour."

"Thanks, Blaine," she muttered.

Shaking his head in amusement he stared at the phone. He had what he wanted, an ordinary problem, something to take his mind off of the most incredible woman he'd ever met. He wouldn't think about the sex or he would never make it to his office to look for a lost earring.

An earring. He laughed out loud. The women in his life sure knew how to bring him back to earth with a bang. Did any of them treat him as the gifted psychic? No. They scolded him as if he were a child. And now they wanted him to be little more than a metal detector.

And he would have it no other way.

***

Every nerve ending in her entire body was on full alert. For just a moment Cassandra allowed the sensations to invade her body. She almost wished she could be as free as Blaine to enjoy the gifts she'd been given, but she wasn't. Maybe if it was only one gift. That she could handle.

But it wasn't just one gift. She was an empath. Feeling other people's pain was not the easiest thing in the world to deal with. To top it off she had others gifts as well. The gift of clairaudience and clairvoyance battled with her empathic gifts. Hearing, seeing and feeling what others thought was a burden she no longer wanted.

In the beginning she had known no other life, so she's voiced no complaint as night after night her parents paraded her before hundreds of people, each of them draining her as their pain became her own. She was maybe ten or eleven when she began to feel as if she was only born to fulfill some stupid prophecy. She was the vessel of the all knowing super psychic.

In time she came to know that her parents, her entire family were all a part of that plan, they trained her to take full advantage of her gifts.

It was on her own that she'd been led to a Mystic who taught her how to protect herself, to build different barriers to stop the public from draining her energy, to be able to help others without the damaging pain to her. Of course there was only so far she could go with that. It still hurt like hell when she touched someone who was suffering, but the pain no longer made her black out. It could bring her to her knees but she could stop it.

Cassandra wondered why her own parents never taught her that simple defense and became angered remembering the conversation she'd had with her mother.

"I don't want to go to the fair," she'd moaned.

"Why?"

"Because people always want to touch me and it hurts."

"Deal with it."

"What do you mean deal with it? It hurts and I don't want to go."

"Cassandra, stop whining you're going."

"Can't you help me, Mom? Tell me something to do so that I don't hurt so much?"

"There is nothing to do. The pain will only make you stronger. Now stop being so selfish and thinking only of yourself, those poor people need you."

Cassandra remembered how angry she'd been at her mother. That was the first time she'd really needed her mother only to have her lie to her. Of course it had taken her years to learn of her mother's lie. Not only was there something she could do she had learned it from a stranger, a Mystic who wanted nothing from her. That in itself was a first.

For many years it was only the old Mystic and her one true childhood friend Salvatore. He was the one who taught her to block out her thoughts and also how to enter into another person's mind.

She shivered at the memory of entering his mind. It was then she discovered he was in love with her. She wouldn't admit to knowing it, he was her friend, her best friend, she could never love him in that manner. Never.

Cassandra wondered what made her think of Salvatore. She'd not thought of how much he'd meant to her in a very long times. He'd left her to study and she'd resented it. When she thought of him it was always tinged with anger. But in his leaving her and the community to live in India he'd made it easier for her to break away. It was shortly after he left that she made the decision to disengage herself from the psychic community. On her own she'd experimented and finally hit on the right combination of herbs to stop the visions and the pain. Fear had stopped her from contacting her friend. Fear that he still loved her, fear that he'd be disappointed in her not using her gifts.

His knuckles rapped softly on the door. Blaine looked down at his hand and fanned his fingers outward. He wondered how thick the door was. He could feel this incredible build up of energy behind the door. No wonder he was drawn to the woman. She had to be ninety nine percent pure energy.

"Hello, Cassandra." He smiled when she opened the door. No other words would come they seemed to be stuck in his throat.

"Blaine we have to establish some ground rules. Okay?"

He was watching Cassandra's mouth yet he noticed that the beating of his heart had sped up a little. She was sputtering some nonsense about ground rules as though they were about to play a game.

"Blaine, are you listening to me?"

His smile was sheepish. "I'm sorry, I couldn't help letting my mind wander a bit." He saw the blush of color flooding her cheeks a second before she reached her arm out and pulled him into the room.

"You've got to stop ogling me. I'm not a pork chop and it's juvenile."

Damn, damn and double damn. That did it. Once again Cassandra had managed to take the steam away from what amounted to a pretty juicy fantasy he was having of her, of them, of the two of them doing-

"Blaine, stop it and come here, in this room or we won't be going out."

His eyes snapped to attention. "You sound like Michelle."

"Who's Michelle?"

"My mother, remember." He chided gently.

"Oh yeah, I forgot. The mother from another life."

Blaine could feel the recent desire draining away. He sat at the chair that was by the small writing table. He placed both hands on the desk making a cup for his chin. From that position he observed Cassandra. She was deliberately trying to anger him.

He laced his fingers together pressing on the nostrils of his nose. All this animosity because he wanted her. Why?

"Why did you agree to go out me?" he inquired.

"I don't know. I'm beginning to think it was a mistake."

Okay enough of this nonsense. To hell with this woman and her beautiful soulful eyes. To hell with the way his body had melted into hers and to hell with Michelle telling him to go after her.

"Listen, I don't have time for games. I have far too much to do and far too many people that I could be helping to put up with this."

Blaine walked toward the door to have Cassandra's words stop him.

"Did you find your secretary's earring?"

"What? What did you say?"

"I asked, did you find your secretary's earring."

"How did you know?" He watched as she cocked an eyebrow upward. "Oh yeah, I forgot you're the super psychic. No, I didn't find it."

"Tell her it's in the trunk of her car under a black bag she stows junk in."

"How do you?" he stopped himself. "I thought you didn't use your gifts?"

"Not ever using them would be like not breathing, I don't deliberately use them. Most of the time I'm flooded with unwanted information, this is just another example."

"And the rest of the time you what, drug yourself so you don't have to deal with life? And you call me the baby. At least I've learned to deal with what happens to me."

"Are you an empath, Blaine?"

"No." He looked at her in astonishment. "Are you an empath?" Now it made sense. He could understand why Cassandra chose to use something to block those feelings.

"What are you using?"

"Something I came up with. It's my own secret and I'm not sharing it. Listen, Blaine I don't want to be so bitchy, but we really need to clear this up."

Blaine looked at her, a knowing of her next words gnawing at his insides. If only he didn't feel such a connection to her he would tell her to go to hell. But he didn't, he stood like the obedient boy she apparently thought he was. It would be time enough later, after hearing whatever rhetoric she planned on spouting to show her that there was nothing in him that remained a boy.

An image of himself and Michelle strolling past the monkey cage flashed into his head. That's different, Blaine thought to himself and immediately pushed the unwanted thought away.

"Shoot," he said to Cassandra. "What is it we need to get straight?"

"Well for one, you have to promise you will not try and enter my mind ever again, no gentle probing, no nudging, nothing. And you have to keep your nose out of my affairs, no asking me about my childhood, no reprimands on what I do or don't do, no lectures on the wonders of psychic powers, none of that junk. And if the time comes when I find who's after me, no playing, Sir Galahad."

"I thought you called me Lancelot?"

Cassandra frowned and Blaine laughed. "I'm sorry, go ahead."

"Listen, Blaine, I'm serious. You could get hurt and you're no match for who ever is after me. Just leave it to me to handle, all right."

"But you're not handing things, you're running, you told me that."

"Blaine, I said no meddling. I don't even know why I'm trusting you. But I feel I can and I want to pretend to be normal for just a couple of weeks. I want to give into the lust I see in your eyes. And I don't want to worry about you trying to dig around in my psyche. Is that understood?"

Blaine watched the soft flesh of the woman's body change and conform until it appeared a rod of steel had been inserted into her back making her stand tin soldier straight in front of him, not giving an inch, not wavering in the least.

"Let me get this straight," he all but purred at her. "Are we friends or am I, pardon the pun," he laughed softly. "Am I to be just a layover?"

He stood there watching the blush cover her face. For all the steel in her composure he didn't think her skin could stretch far enough to include a blush.

"Blaine, I'm just being honest. There is no way I'm in a position to fall for you, and even if there was, I wouldn't allow it. Now," she said pulling her chin even straighter. "If you can live with that, that's what I have to offer."

"What, the use of your body while you're in town?" He wasn't going to let it go. Surely this was not the way true love began. It couldn't even be how 'like' started. This was simply an affair she was offering him, nothing more.

"I can't just turn on and off when you want me to." Blaine stared affronted that she would even ask such a thing of him. He followed Cassandra's gaze down the front of his pants and squirmed when they rested squarely on his crotch. He felt the familiar tightening making a liar of him.

"I do have some control," he muttered and turned away from her probing eyes, knowing he was hard pressed at the moment to prove it.

The sound of her soft laughter behind his back amused him. "Cassandra, I have a few conditions of my own." He remained with his back turned away from her as he commanded his body to obey him. He couldn't believe it, he'd never lacked such focus.

"You will not call me a baby psychic again," Blaine began.

"I didn't mean any harm," Cassandra attempted to interrupt.

"You will not order me about. As far as our sleeping together is concerned, it will happen only when I am in agreement. I will not be used to service you."

He watched as Cassandra's eyes dropped down again, a smile curving her lips. "That doesn't matter. I have enough self control not to follow through."

Blaine gritted his teeth together willing his blood to return from his southern regions. It was no use, neither his blood or his body obeyed him.

"I won't deny that I find you attractive and that you turn me on." He waited a moment as all of the blood in his body pooled into one area.

He smiled at her. "You'd know I was lying if I said I didn't want you. But I can resist the urging of my body, so let's get that straight between us. I would love to see you while you're in town, get to know you, become friends. If you can accept that, we can go to dinner."

Blaine walked toward the door before turning to notice that Cassandra wasn't following him. "What's wrong now?" he asked.

"You didn't agree to my conditions."

"And you didn't agree to mine."

They stood like stone statues each wanting the other to give in. Blaine stuck his hand out and watched as Cassandra tentatively took it.

"Shall we go to dinner?" Blaine murmured against the soft velvet skin of her cheek.

Cassandra took his hand feeling a fire of want and need curling in the pit of her belly, making her whole. It was a dangerous game she was playing with the baby psychic and she knew it. Sure she'd agreed not to call him that but she'd not agreed not to think it.

Chapter Six

Smiling at Cassandra he waited until she'd completed her order. "Steak, well done." Blaine ordered and snapped the menu closed. He waited until the waiter had left the table before he spoke. "Protein, just in case."

She blushed as he'd hoped she would. She didn't take the bait though; she merely took a sip from her wine glass and behaved as though he wasn't there.

This was going to be fun. He knew it without a shadow of a doubt. Without warning the positive feeling he had changed and he felt a sense of evil bearing down on him. His head swiveled behind to where the sensation was emanating and he saw a man fast approaching their table.

In an instant his head swung back to Cassandra, the man's gaze was riveted on her. In the same instant he saw recognition dart across her face and a huge smile appeared only a second before Cassandra rose from her chair with a war whoop.

"Salvatore, Salvatore, oh my God, how are you? What are you doing here?"

Blaine watched while the man she called Salvatore crushed Cassandra in his arms in a big bear hug and spun her around the room. It was as though he had suddenly become invisible.

Cassandra tears of joy fell on her cheeks and the man's fingers wiped them away gently as though Cassandra's skin was a priceless piece of art he didn't want to smudge.

Salvatore pressed his lips to Cassandra's as his hands caressed her cheeks. All the while she permitted this, ignoring Blaine. No, he thought to himself. Ignoring was too mild a word for what was transpiring. For those moments he didn't exist for her, only the man she'd called Salvatore.

It was becoming embarrassing, his date, her body pressed so close to another man that you couldn't get, well nothing between them, her kissing the guy and him fawning over her. He'd never claimed to be a saint, then again neither was he a fool.

"Would you like for me to leave?" Blaine offered as he stood to walk away.

Cassandra drug her eyes away from the man, but remained in his arms. It looked to Blaine as if she were trying to focus her eyes on him and having a hard time remembering who he was.

"I'm sorry," she murmured, "Blaine this is an old, old friend of mine." She looked again at the man. "He's my best friend in the whole wide world. Blaine, this is Salvatore Sharif."

With one arm still wrapped around Cassandra's waist the man turned and held out his hand to Blaine, his eyes dark and hooded, hiding secrets.

The tips of the man's fingers touched his and he cringed wanting to pull away, but Salvatore was faster pulling his arm into a viselike grip. He held on to Blaine and the only thing Blaine had time to do was throw up a mental block.

Ice flooded Blaine's veins and he found he was suddenly having a difficult time breathing. A never before sense of panic threatened to make him gag. He was in the presence of pure unadulterated evil.

Blaine fought harder to reinforce the blocks he had in place. He knew he was no match for the man squeezing his hand, draining his very energy from his body with just a touch. Hell he couldn't even make the man release his hand.

With a sudden smile Salvatore released Blaine's hand and turned again to press his lips to Cassandra. His gaze rested on her possessively and his hand roamed across her back before his eyes found Blaine.

His lips stretched into a smile that didn't touch his cold black eyes. He had issued a challenge.

Blaine remembered Cassandra's warning, don't play the hero. He sat down relieved to have received only a warning from her friend. Despite all his knowledge he was not in the same league as the man sitting across from him.

Blaine noted the way Salvatore strategically positioned himself between Cassandra and himself making Blaine the outsider.

"Salvatore, when did you get back?" Cassandra gushed.

"Oh not long ago."

Blaine noted the vagueness with which the man answered. Something wasn't right."

"How are you? Sal, I've missed you so much. You have no idea of what's been happening to me."

Cassandra hurled herself again into the man's arm and he felt like he himself wanted to hurl, straight into the nearest toilet. Blaine couldn't take anymore

"Sal, stay and have dinner with us. I'm sure Blaine doesn't mind."

"No, Blaine doesn't mind." Blaine stated sarcastically.

Sal turned cool calculating eyes on Blaine. "Are you sure?"

"Not only am I sure, consider it my treat." This time he was leaving. He peeled off several bills dropping them to the table. "Cassandra, we can do this another time. It appears you and your friend have some catching up to do. Go ahead. Salvatore, nice meeting you." He ignored the man's outstretched hand and moved past it.

Yeah right, he was going to shake the man's hand again. He didn't think so. Blaine walked away without a single complaint from Cassandra. In fact if anything he saw the relief in her face that he'd left them alone.

There was one thing he didn't have to wonder about anymore, would he be up to the task of helping Cassandra when and should the need arise? Hell no. He was not Sir Galahad, he had not acted in the least heroic.

Blaine dared a look over his shoulder. He stood beside a pillar watching the joy on Cassandra's face reaching out to caress him from across the room, but she wasn't looking at him, it was her happiness that furled about him, happiness he had not felt on any other occasion.

Blaine looked at the couple seated at the table. He didn't promise Cassandra anything about viewing her aura. His glance slid across to her dining companion Salvatore who was now devouring Blaine's steak as if he had every right to it, his glance resting on Cassandra as if he had a right to her also.

A dark cloud of angry energy rushed from Salvatore's body and sailed swiftly toward Blaine. Without thinking Blaine ducked behind the pillar. The man had done that deliberately, of that he was sure and all without taking his attention from Cassandra.

Blaine was angrier than he could ever remember being. He stepped from behind the pillar and attempted to walk back toward the table he'd so recently vacated. Two steps and he hit a wall.

What the hell. It appeared to be a powerful force field. He tried to sidestep it to no avail. No matter the direction he took he couldn't pass the invisible barrier. He stood for a moment fuming, observing the waitress and other patrons having no such problems moving around. No this barrier was meant for him alone.

He took one last look at Cassandra, she appeared to be not only safe but in good spirits having the time of her life. In that case he didn't mind leaving her. In fact he would feel like a fool if he didn't.

There was something about the man that spelled danger not only to him but to Cassandra. It wasn't just that he was jealous although Blaine wouldn't deny resenting the man's possessive manner toward what ten minutes ago had been his date.

No this Salvatore, this supposedly long lost friend of Cassandra possessed untold powers that he enjoyed displaying. In fact he'd gone to great lengths to make Blaine aware of those powers.

Blaine could not help but wonder about the matter of turning his body into a massive hunk of ice and all under the guise of an innocent handshake. Why had the man felt the need to show force?

And the deal with sending the dark energy and blocking him with an energy force field preventing him from confronting the man, although what that would have accomplished was anyone's guess. He should be thankful that he was not a smoldering pile of ashes on the restaurant floor.

If anything Blaine was not a fool. The man was dangerous. Blaine needed someone whose power rivaled those of Salvatore. There was only one person that he knew who could teach him. And with every instinct in him he knew he would need to know a lot more than he knew now. This time he would not call on his mother. There was nothing she could do. He needed an equalizer

Chapter Seven

"I can't believe you're not willing to teach me."

"You find it hard to believe I value your life? If what you tell me is true, you would be committing psychic suicide to go up against such an opponent. Combating evil is a complicated task at best. Psychic evil is not a game to be played by spoiled children."

"I find it hard to believe you're saying those words after what I told you. If you valued my life you'd teach me how to protect myself against this man."

"That one's easy, don't oppose him."

"I'm tired of this philosophical bullshit. I need some practical ways to handle this man."

"Why? Why do you have to confront this man? If it's your ego, you need to work on your spirit. Doing things for ego is not the way to go."

Blaine stared at the Mystic wondering why his old friend was being so difficult. Maybe he wasn't telling him in the right way. He racked his brain trying hard to determine if he'd left anything out. No, he was sure he'd told the Mystic everything that had happened.

"Listen," Blaine started, a new wave of fear welling up in his gut that his friend wouldn't help him. "My friend may well be in danger from this man."

"From what you told me before, I see no danger. You yourself said she was so overcome with joy to see this man that she cried. You said she barely noticed you leaving and did nothing to stop you."

Blaine paced back and forth. His friend was being deliberately obtuse. He should have known him better. Blaine had never once asked him a favor of such magnitude.

He found himself rubbing the bracelet he'd worn now for over six months. He stopped and stared down at it then at the old Mystic.

"You helped me to charge the bracelets, why won't you help me now?"

"I helped you with the bracelets to enable you to find your soul parents in the next life. They wanted this as well as you. There was no danger to you, or to them. What you ask me now could send you to the next life in the blink of an eye."

"You talk as if I had no powers of my own. I was able to block the man from entering my mind."

"Just barely, Blaine, just barely. You're weak. I can see the ripples in your energy field. You're in no condition to think of anything now except cleansing your spirit and resting. There's a darkness hovering around your aura, possibly put there when this man you want to go against touched you."

Blaine's hand reached out as though he could touch his aura and cleanse it. Coldness skittered down his back and lay claim to his entire body in a matter of moments.

He felt dirty, defiled, and now he felt dejected. "If you don't help me there is no one else who can."

"There are others who can help you Blaine."

"Who?" Blaine turned back to face his mentor watching his eyes carefully as they came to rest on his bracelet.

"You're not talking about--."

"Yes, Blaine, your soul parents. If the three of you were together and combined your energies, you would all be stronger."

"You know that's impossible. I could never place either of them in danger."

"You said you had no one else to turn to. I was just pointing out your options."

For the first time that he could ever remember, Blaine found himself getting angry with his teacher. "You know Michelle is rebuilding her life with her husband. I would never disrupt that, besides she doesn't even know she possesses any powers at all. And Chance, I don't think he has any."

Laughter rumpled from the old Mystic's throat and his eyes sparkled merrily. Blaine took a step back from the man, sure that somehow the evil that had touched him had rubbed off on the Mystic.

"Blaine, stop looking at me so strangely. I do laugh."

"I've never heard you."

"Because you've never heard me doesn't mean that I don't do it. If a tree falls…"

"Yeah, yeah I know, please no trying cliques. I need help."

"I need to finish my story."

First one eyebrow arched then the other. Blaine acquiesced. There was nothing to do but listen as the old man prattled on unmindful of the gravity of the situation.

"Blaine, I daresay you're becoming a bit arrogant lately with the increase of your powers."

"I'm not, I've never…" Sputtering was the best he could do and even then the old man's hand went up to stop his words of protest.

"For more than a year now you've been unfocused, since you first met your soul parents. Sometimes I wonder if it was a good thing that happened."

"What do you mean? Of course it was a good thing. I wanted this, and since finding them I've only…"

"Yeah, I know you've only gotten stronger." The Mystic interrupted him. "But you've become a wee bit cocky. You think you're unique, that you have a gift that only a few others have. Do you really think if the two of them, this Michelle and Chance were not gifted any of this would have been possible?"

"But they don't…"

"They don't what, have any powers? Or could it be they don't practice it, acknowledge it? Believe me, Blaine they both know. In their souls, where it counts, they know who and what they are. If you weren't so busy patting yourself on the back these days you would have figured it out for yourself."

"I did figure it out, that my mother has gifts." Blaine admitted a bit ashamed of the scolding he was receiving.

"And your father? Did you think his soul would have been able to receive the messages if he too were not gifted? They are old souls Blaine, linked through time and psychic gifts. This is only your second incarnation.

"True you have great powers, but you're just a baby psychic. You've spent too much time communing with the dead to develop your others gifts."

There was that word again. He hated it, baby psychic. Blaine didn't believe he'd become arrogant. Sure, he enjoyed playing with his new emerging gifts, but he never for a moment thought he was the only one that had been given such things.

"I never saw any evidence of anything in Chance," Blaine said trying once again to explain to his mentor. He didn't want the old man thinking he had become inflated by his own ego.

"And because you didn't see, it didn't exist?"

"What is it you want from me?" Blaine asked. "I didn't come here to talk to you about my parents or their gifts. I came to talk to you about helping me with a man that turned my arm into ice."

"You want to defeat this man?"

Blaine paused. "I want to protect myself from him."

"Then you need to begin at the beginning. You need to understand why and how you came into possession of the gifts you have. And to do that we have to examine your soul parents."

Blaine slapped his hand against his head. The last thing in the world he wanted to show his mentor and friend was disrespect, but the man was beginning to sound like a loon. With that thought he again heard laughter from the Mystic and knew immediately what happened.

"You read my thoughts didn't you? How? I felt nothing."

"Of course you didn't. Do I appear as a baby psychic to you? Do you think if I chose to do this, I would go stomping around in someone's psyche and leave evidence that I was there?"

"Why after all my years as a professional psychic is everyone suddenly calling me a baby psychic?"

"Blaine that phrase is not used as a slight. It is merely the truth. I didn't call you a charlatan or a liar. You are very gifted and you have it in you to be extremely powerful. I've tried to get you to expand your powers for years but you've resisted me, preferring to allow your body to be no more than a vessel for the spirit of the dead. You behave as though you were a television set, or western union. Spirits come, give you information, and then poof they're gone."

"I like doing it." Blaine was hurt. Never before had his friend said such harsh things to him. "Listen, I think I've taken up enough of your time I should leave now."

"I didn't say these things to hurt you, Blaine. I want you to listen to me. One day perhaps years from now you will be able to match powers against someone such as this man you described but you're not ready now. You are to me like a son. I want nothing more than to keep you safe."

The old man walked toward him and Blaine resisted the urge to move away. At the moment he didn't want to feel the touch of the old man's hand on his shoulder comforting him as though he were a child. Now he truly felt like the baby psychic.

"Blaine, what you do is beneficial to thousands. There are so many people who are afraid of death, who fear it for themselves. So they come to you not with their real questions of, what happens to me when I die? Where do I go? Is there a message from mom, dad, a friend?

"Sure these people are happy when they leave you, but it's not because someone came and gave them a message. It's because you gave them a message of hope. There is life after death. They don't have to be so afraid anymore. I'm not talking about what you do. I'm saying that you've been so lonely that you've been afraid to talk to anyone but spirits. It's time you moved beyond that. You have much work to do and I believe you're ready."

"So are you saying you'll help me?"

"As always I'm here for you, but you will have to be patient and do what I tell you. You will have to acknowledge that one day I will make another transition and you will have to be ready for that.

"You may one day have to call on these soul parents you found. If the need arise don't be heroic and try to go it alone. Is that a deal?" The Mystic stopped, looked down, held out his hands palms up, then smiled at Blaine.

"I can promise you I'll do all that you ask of me with the exception of causing my parents pain. That, I can't do."

"Not even to save your life?"

Blaine thought of Michelle's spirit coming to him in San Francisco to save him. "No, not even to save my own life."

"What about this woman you met, would you ask their help if she was in danger?"

"You're asking me if I would put my mother's life on the line for a woman I barely know."

"I'm asking if you would ask for your mother's help to save the woman you love."

"I don't love her, I don't even know her."

The Mystic smiled indulgently. "You love her or we would not be having this conversation."

"Even so," Blaine almost whispered. "I would not put Michelle's life on the line to save Cassandra."

"Cassandra?"

"Yes, that's the woman I've been telling you about." Blaine watched as lines of worry creased the old Mystic's face and he sank into a chair.

"Blaine, her last name, what is her last name?"

"Boozer."

"Oh my God. No, not my Cassie. The man, who is the man whom you fear?"

"I didn't say I feared him."

"Not now, Blaine, we'll deal with your pride later, who is he?"

"Salvatore."

"Salvatore Sharif?"

"Yes, I believe that is what Cassandra called him. Why, who is he?"

The Mystic stood and something fierce crossed his face. "I will help you."

"What is it what changed your mind?"

"My Cassie. As I love you like a son, I love her like a daughter."

"And this Salvatore, you know him also don't you?"

"Yes, I know Sal."

Blaine could feel the dryness in his mouth. "Who is he?"

"He is someone you do not want to go up against."

Blaine heard the fear in the older man's voice and that more than anything caused fear in him. "How well do you know him?"

"I taught him for years."

Blaine watched as the man's eyes became bright with unshed tears. "I was so proud of him. Never in my life have I witnessed someone as gifted as he. I taught him everything that I knew. He devoured it like a sponge."

Beneath the fear Blaine sensed pride, but the old man's fear quickly replaced that, wiping away any of the pride he may have felt.

"It was I who recommended that he go for further studies in India. He's studied all over the world, Europe, Egypt, India, China, you name it, he knows it. And he's mastered every teacher that ever taught him."

"Are you saying that no one…"

"He's strong." A shiver passed through the old man's body. "I had always prayed that my Cassie would one day fall in love with and marry Sal."

The man looked toward Blaine. A blank look of desperation filled his eyes.

"I was once vain also. I wanted like everyone in the psychic community to see the baby born of pure bred psychics dating back twenty one generations." He closed his eyes in silent contemplation.

"Can Cassandra handle herself with him?"

"No."

"You said that she's..."

"She has the ability. Salvatore has the training. Cassandra started hating her gifts, refusing to use them." He looked at Blaine. "She's an empath. It was hard on her."

"I know." Blaine nodded at the Mystic for him to continue.

"Cassandra hated the burden and people always filling their home at all hours of the day and night. Of course it didn't help that everyone wanted her to use her gifts to produce the super baby." He stopped and smiled.

"Is that what you wanted, for her to have a super baby?"

"Super baby is Cassie words, she's the one that felt that way. I wanted like everyone, to see if the legend was true, what would happen if two such gifted psychics got together and produced a child."

"What went wrong?"

"Cassandra didn't fall in love with any of the chosen ones. She rebelled and stopped using her gifts, stopped studying. Sal was the only psychic she would permit herself to be friends with. He's like a big brother to her."

"That's not what she is to him." Blaine muttered angrily. "He's in love with her."

"I don't know about that. Long ago he was madly in love with her, now he wants to possess her. He has all that he wants in terms of personal powers. He now wants an heir, Cassie's heir."

Blaine thought only a moment before revealing the final piece of information. If it would help him help her when the time came, he would suffer her wrath gladly. "Cassie told me someone is after her. She's been running for," Blaine stopped. He had no idea how long Cassandra had been running, she hadn't told him.

He swallowed, his head was pounding. Now he really did feel like a heel for leaving Cassandra with Salvatore.

"Stop with the guilt. It only causes self pity. You had no way of knowing about Salvatore."

"She told me she was in danger. I sensed an evil in the man. I should have known."

Blaine paced around the rooms, angry at himself for thinking he was becoming all he'd been meant to be. Cassandra was right. He was only a baby psychic. He couldn't even see what was happening in front of his face.

"Blaine."

The Mystic's angry voice snapped him out of it.

"You did the right thing. Salvatore will not harm Cassandra, not yet anyway. That will buy us some time. Like you he's arrogant. He wants to win her love. He will try that first."

He had to tell her. Blaine's mind raced to Cassandra. She thought she was entertaining a harmless old friend. She wouldn't be on the look out for danger. She should know. He should be the one to tell her. He ran his hands through his hair, distraught at the thought of something happening to her. "I…"

"No Blaine. You will not tell Cassandra your suspicions. She loves Salvatore, she will not believe you and we do not know that you are right. If you're wrong—"

Again Blaine saw a shiver run through the other man's body as he stopped talking in mid-sentence. Blaine focused all his energies on holding back the escalating panic. "If I tell her what do you think will happen?"

"Not only couldn't you help her, but Salvatore will destroy you and there is nothing I can do to help."

"What am I supposed to do, just sit here twiddling my thumbs?"

"Cassie is not your responsibility."

Blaine glared at the old man. She was his responsibility. He was the one who'd left her defenseless and alone. He'd known she was taking something to subdue her gifts and he'd felt the evil that emanated from Salvatore. He didn't care if the Mystic helped him or not. He would find a way to help Cassandra.

Blaine watched as the man's frail body puffed up. He knew then the old Mystic was planning on taking on Salvatore himself. The Mystic was powerful but he doubted he had the power needed now to take on Salvatore. He slid as many blocks into place as he could. Now was not the time for his friend to know his plans.

"Blaine, your blocks don't work on me."

If the situation was not so grave Blaine would have been amused. "That can become annoying you know. I don't like your doing it."

"No one likes it. Did Cassandra like it when you did it to her?"

"How did you...?" What a dumbass question. "No, she didn't like it. She made me promise never to attempt it again. But she knew I was doing it, you have me at a disadvantage. I can't tell. You're undetectable."

"Would you like to know who taught me?"

"Don't tell me, Salvatore."

Finally a genuine smile made the man's face shine with a new vitally.

"No. It was Cassie, but Sal taught her. He taught himself this particular blocking technique. It's about a hundred times more efficient than the method I taught you."

Again Blaine heard the pride in his friend's voice for Salvatore's powers. He was sure it wasn't petty jealousy he was feeling, but he did wonder how the Mystic would ever be able to put aside his pride in Salvatore in order to help him.

"Don't worry Blaine. I will not have any trouble teaching you."

"Are you sure you can? I don't mean to be rude, but since he is the one that developed it, how do you know it will work to keep him out.

"Sal taught Cassie how to keep him out of her mind when he was still very much in love with her and not so filled with his own greatness. She also taught me how to block him out. I will teach you."

"How did he develop a technique so powerful that you're afraid of him? I didn't think I would ever meet anyone with more psychic powers than you."

"That's because you limit the company that you keep."

The old man was changing right before his eyes. A spark of envy shot through Blaine. At the mention of Cassandra and Salvatore the man was suddenly ready to teach him, and he was filled with renewed energy, a zest for living, something Blaine had tried unsuccessfully to accomplish for months. Now just like that, it was done.

He tried to curtail his run-a-way feelings before anymore leaked out to his mentor that he was trying to keep hidden. "You're willing to teach me now?" Blaine asked.

"I believe that is what I said."

"Before any of this other nonsense about Chance and Michelle, about my learning about their supposed power? You're willing to forego snooping into their lives?"

"Yes that much you need to know, but believe me, if you attempt to go against Salvatore now you will lose and it will not be appreciated. Cassie will not believe anything bad about him. He will be the only one who she will believe. Only he can break her trust."

"But he won't show that side to her." Blaine said softly.

"That is my point. We don't know that he means her harm. He didn't exhibit that evil to Cassie or she would have felt it."

"They why did he show it to me? What was the point?"

"It was you," the Mystic smiled. "Perhaps he saw that you've become smitten with the woman he wants for himself. Maybe you should stay away from her, Blaine, until I can find a way to help you."

Blaine sat down alongside the old man. He ran his hand over the chair. He wanted nothing more than to use his powers to peep in on Cassandra, just to make sure she was alright. He decided against it. He would keep his promise to her for now.

"What if I'm wrong, what if Salvatore isn't the one after Cassandra? Are you telling me there are others out there with the same powers he has?"

"None has his powers, but yes there are at least a dozen men that I'm aware of and they all want my Cassie to be mother to their heir."

"What are we going to do?"

"Pray," the old Mystic answered Blaine and closed his eyes.

Chapter Eight

Cassandra sat across from Sal. They had long since finished dinner and went back to her room. She was glad to see her old friend for more than one reason. She'd begun to enjoy Blaine MaDia's company much too much.

The guy was cute, no doubt about it and he was a lot of fun. The way he looked at her didn't hurt either. What woman could resist having a man look at her with unbridled passion? For all her convictions on not falling in love, Blaine had her heading towards 'like' quickly. So Salvatore's interruption was a welcome one.

Now she sat, her legs tucked neatly beneath her smiling at him listening to the music in his voice. She could feel the gentle swaying of her body moving as though an island breeze was caressing her.

Sal did that for her, took her to all the exotic places he'd been, made her see and hear the same things he had. She could even smell the jasmine in the air from Egypt.

She looked at him startled by the look in his eyes. It resembled Blaine's except his was also filled with confidence.

"Sal, you look so different," she muttered breathless.

"You already told me that."

"Well it bears repeating.I love your hair long. I'd forgotten how black and curly it was." She smiled again at him. "You look like a gypsy."

He tugged on the gold hoop earring in his right ear. "I am a gypsy. Did you forget that?"

Cassandra cocked her head to the side, maybe she had. "I thought you were Egyptian." She looked at his dark coloring noticing for the first time two identical tattoos on Sal's cheek.

She moved to caress the markings and was stopped when he caught her hand.

"Why can't I touch them, what's wrong?" she asked.

"There's a price to pay for touching those."

"What is it?" She flirted right back.

"A kiss."

"Nothing more?"

"Not one of those chaste kisses you've been giving me. You've been thinking about that Blaine fellow from the moment he left the table. I want to make you forget him."

She glanced at Sal. There was something different about him, not just his smoldering good looks, or long dark hair. There was something intensely powerful about him and she found it exciting.

"I barely know the man."

"You know him better than I would want."

Cassandra started laughing. "Now I know you're teasing me. You would never be jealous of someone like Blaine. His powers are nowhere near yours."

"It's not his psychic powers I'm talking about."

"What then?"

"His powers of persuasions. He has to have something going for him to have charmed you when no one else could."

"Sal, have you forgotten? I plan to do without love. Don't worry, Blaine MaDia knows that love is not in our cards."

"And you my sweet, do you know that as well?"

"I know it," she whispered reaching her hand out to touch Sal's cheeks. "I could never love Blaine."

At her words Salvatore caught her hair in his hand and tugged causing her to wince in pain. Before she could protest further he was kissing her.

Conflicting emotions fluttered through her brain. Her limbs were on fire. She panicked as the fire made its way through her body. She wanted to push him away the fire was so painful. Then as suddenly as it began ice rushed over the fire putting out the flames cascading over and through her and she shivered in Sal's arms.

What was that? She finally managed to push him away, frightened at the intensity of emotions his kiss evoked, frightened at her total loss of control. She shivered even harder. She didn't know why, but she felt violated as though Salvatore had reached into her body and touched his fingers to her soul, branding her as his own.

"Sal, what did you do?"

"I kissed you."

"That was a hell of lot more than a kiss."

"Thank you."

"I didn't mean it as a compliment."

"You meant it as an insult?"

"I meant it as I asked it. What the hell did you do to me? I feel like you've put a spell on me or something."

She eyed him suspiciously. "Why are you back, Sal?"

"Don't I have a right to come home?"

"But you have considered this home in year. Why after all this time do I run into you in Chicago?"

"Coincidence," he answered.

"You and I both know there is no such thing as coincidence." She drew away from Sal and concentrated on using what he'd taught her years before. In all these years she'd never felt the need for such a strong block. Now she did. With that thought, she slammed her mind shut to her friend.

Sal sat calmly on her bed rubbing at his new tattoo. "I'm the one who taught you that."

"I know you are," she answered keeping the blocks in place. "Have you been following me, Sal?"

"You might say that I have."

Cassandra's face fell and the tears burned hotly behind her eyes. "Not you, Sal."

"It's not what you think. I came home only to protect you."

"Surely you didn't come to protect me from Blaine, you're the only one who's..., who..."

"Who's what, kissed you like that?"

"I didn't like the kiss."

"Why?"

"It made me feel like you were raping me."

The amusement in Sal's eyes turned swiftly to anger. He walked toward her and in that moment her knees turned to jelly. She feared if she would remain standing. With everything that was in her, Cassandra fought to remain in control of the blocks.

Damn, she thought to herself. For once she wished she had not used the mixture. For once she wished she was strong enough to block

Salvatore. She felt the blocks crumble one after the other and she whispered, "No."

"If I wanted to hurt you, Cass, I could. I said I came home to help you. I've been hearing things lately and knew you were in danger. I'm not about to leave you unprotected. First we need to clear up a few things. There will be no blocks between us. Do you understand?"

She was trembling. "Shouldn't this be my choice, Sal? If you want to help me, are you going to do it by force?"

She saw that her words were getting through to him. He backed away and dropped the last of the mental pressure he was exerting over her.

"Would you let me help you any other way?" he asked.

"Why don't you try?"

He smiled, a glint of amusement once again shining in his eyes. "How about another kiss?"

"I don't think so, Sal?"

"A kiss in good faith?"

Cassandra moved toward Salvatore, testing to see if his control was really gone. She placed her hands on the sides of his face and kissed him, ending it the moment she felt him wanting more.

"That wasn't nearly as much fun." Salvatore laughed.

"Maybe not," Cassandra answered, "but the other party should at least know what to expect and be willing." She pushed against his chest. "Now tell me, what have you heard?"

"I heard that the association is threatening to have every member of your family thrown out if you don't marry soon."

"They can't do that."

"I know it and so does everyone else, but the talk is just to make things uncomfortable for your family and friends. The most anyone can do is shun your family."

"This is crazy." Before she realized what she was doing Cassandra was up on her feet, her arms flailing about. "This sounds like something out of the dark ages."

"I agree." Sal smiled at her indulgently, lying back on the bed ignoring her histrionics. "This is all rumor and superstition, no one ever really believed it would happen but then it did, thirteen males and one female, all of them powerful, twenty one generations of carefully choosing mates to lead to this."

Cassandra shivered, the look in Salvatore's eyes telling so much more than his words ever could. He wanted what all the others wanted.

He wanted to mate with her, produce the long awaited child and she knew it had to happen soon.

"It's too bad for you that you're the only girl." Salvatore continued. "There are bound to be people doing everything they can to win your favor. And if that doesn't work, then they're still willing to try just about anything. And yes, I mean using their powers"

He laughed again and she didn't like it. "I hope you're not one of them, Sal. I would hate to think of you as my enemy. I love you. I always have. You're my best friend."

"Your enemy? Why would you ever think that? Tell me what it is about that Blaine MaDia that makes him appeal to you when you won't give anyone else the time of day? What does he have that none of the others have? What does he have that—?"

He let it drop. They both were aware he wanted to ask about himself. Cassandra was glad that he didn't. A feeling of dread began to slowly claim her and she fought against it, wanting to hang onto the moment she'd seen Salvatore's face in the restaurant. She was happy then. Now she was almost frightened of him. The worry she felt for Blaine she pushed to the deep recesses of her mind. She couldn't let Sal know that she cared at all about the man.

"Sal, think about it. Blaine MaDia is temporary entertainment."

She observed the thoughtful look on Salvatore's face knowing he was digesting her words, knowing he really wanted nothing more than to believe her.

"I thought you said you would never have a relationship with a psychic."

Cassandra laughed. "Number one, I'm not having a relationship with the guy and number two; I'm surprised that you acknowledge him as a psychic. My God's he's just beginning, he's just an infant compared to you."

Salvatore's face broke out in a huge smile and genuine joy made his eyes sparkle. Cassandra breathed easier as she sent a mental command to her lungs to take it slow. The flattery was working as she had hoped it would.

"You're right," Sal laughed again. "His powers are of no concern to me. But I saw the way he was looking at you."

His eyes darkened, but this time she was able to stop the leap of fear that had threatened her before.

"Come on, Sal." She hit him playfully, and then hugged him close to her. "Am I supposed to stop guys from looking at me like that? They always have. Remember all the guys you beat up for doing that?"

"Yeah, I remember," he answered her.

"So what are you going to do, start beating people up again? We're not kids any longer, Sal. You can't go around beating up guys for looking at me. Besides, I think you should first ask if I'm interested."

He eyed her thoughtfully and Cassandra moved slightly away from him. She knew he wanted to look into her eyes, if he didn't find the answer there he would scan her mind without the slightest hesitation.

Surprisingly after only a few seconds Sal broke the connection. His left hand came up and covered his face. She watched as he stroked the bridge of his nose then his eyes.

"I'm sorry, Cassie, I'm acting like a jealous lover."

"Or a big brother," she amended.

She didn't want to go down that road with Sal, didn't want to discuss what they both knew he wanted. If only he felt the same inclination to let it go she would have been happy.

"You will have to marry someone Cassie, and that someone might as well be a person who has loved you your entire life. One heir and you could get a divorce; you could even go after that skinny medium."

"I don't want him." She sighed. "Sal, I don't want to get married, ever. As for having a baby, do you really think I'd take a chance on passing on this curse to an innocent child?"

That did it. The calmness left Sal's face, his entire demeanor metamorphosed into any one of the other twelve men who sought her. He was offended.

It wasn't his words, but the stance and the glare in his eyes. She recognized the tremble beginning in her knees. Only Sal had ever been able to make her tremble in fear. She began backing away from him.

"Don't worry, Cassie," he purred. "I'm leaving now."

She eyed him. "You've always known how I felt."

"Yes, I suppose I have." He walked toward the door, paused then turned to look at her over his shoulder. His voice as soft as velvet when he spoke.

"Just some free advice, Cassie. You're rusty. You should have been able to resist me better. I know. I taught you. Right now I'd say Blaine MaDia is stronger than you are. Whatever you're taking to suppress your powers, I'd suggest you stop. I came home to protect you, but I can't be around you always. You'd better plan on protecting yourself."

"Is that an attempt to make me into something I don't want to be? No one can make me into this image the community has of me, not even you, Sal. You can report back that I'm not marrying anyone. And tell them Blaine MaDia is no threat, weak or not he's still a psychic."

Salvatore's eyes narrowed into slits and a smirk appeared on his face telling her of her mistake instantly. *Damn*, she thought to herself. *Why couldn't I leave well enough alone?*

"Me think thou doeth protest too much, dear, Cassie. You're trying awfully hard to protect a man you don't care for."

"Sal, leave him out of this," she pleaded. "We had one date and even then I left with you. I'm not asking you because I care about the man, but because he's innocent. He has no idea what's at stake and there's no possible way he could defend himself from any of you. But I ask you this as a friend, and because I love you."

She waited patiently the silence playing havoc with her body. She wanted to scream from the intensity of it. "I could never marry a man that was a bully."

She saw the lines of Sal's mouth turn upward until a small smile was framing his handsome face. In that moment she knew she'd bought Blaine some time.

"Then one thing."

"What?"

"Don't see him anymore."

"Done," she answered. "I wasn't planning on it anyway."

Her arms wrapped around Salvatore's neck, prolonging his stay at the door and she accepted his kiss, not chaste, but not sexual either.

She closed the door, her hands shaking, her insides humming with the need to feel the energy her body possessed.

She couldn't believe she's just given Sal encouragement. It was the only thing she could think of to buy Blaine some time. She thought of Blaine, his sweetness. She'd do damn near anything to keep him safe.

She raced to her purse and took out the empty film canister she kept the power in. She shook a little of the bluish dust into her open palm.

Salvatore was right, she was past rusty. She acknowledged the scalding tears cascading down her cheeks. She no longer wanted the responsibility of knowing what was going to happen, or feeling the pain of people she didn't even know hundreds of miles from her. The very idea was unbearable. Yet she knew she had to come into her own. She no longer had a choice.

Cassandra shook the powder back into the container. For two years she'd been running, only using enough of her abilities to keep her dreams safe, to prevent anyone from making love to her while she slept. Now that would no longer be enough. She needed her powers back full force. Pretending that she was inept had not worked anyway. She'd not fooled anyone. They all knew she was the chosen one. And they knew the power that ran through her veins.

Damn her for letting her guard down. Damn Blaine MaDia for making her laugh, for making her body respond to his touch. And damn him for not being strong enough to protect himself. Now she would be forced to do it.

Her fingers went to her lips. The memory of the kiss Salvatore gave her lingered still. He'd failed in his attempt to make her fall in love with him with that kiss. She closed her eyes and imagined Blaine's lips on hers, on her body and she smiled at the image of him smiling down at her.

He'd taken her completely off guard, making her care for him with just a smile. Now his smile would be the undoing for them both. Salvatore knew how she felt about Blaine. She would bet money on it. He'd boldly crawled into her mind. She'd done her best to hide those feelings, but she was never as good as him. For the last few years he'd been studying while she learned to concoct herbs to stop her visions, stop her knowing.

She needed to work and work fast to polish the cobwebs off her powers. She'd taken the first step. The powder lay safely tucked away inside her purse. She would keep it there until Blaine MaDia was safe. She had to talk to the Mystic. *God, please let him know how to help me.*

Cassandra crawled into bed, the tears still flowing knowing that soon she would not be able to look at another living soul without feeling their pain. Damn Blaine for making her care about him.

Chapter Nine

"What is it?" Blaine nearly barked into the phone. He was not his usual self. With only a couple of hours sleep he was a bit testy.

"Why are you yelling? If you didn't want to talk, you shouldn't have answered the phone."

Michelle. Thank God it was his mother. She would understand. "Sorry, I didn't get much sleep."

"And that's a reason for yelling?"

Blaine smiled, amused. Michelle was definitely making up for not being with him in their previous life.

"You're right, I shouldn't have yelled."

"That's better. What's wrong with you anyway?"

"I've got a problem."

"Can I help?"

"I doubt it."

"How do you know unless you ask?"

"Okay here goes. I need you to kick ass for me." He heard her laughter then joined in. It never failed, what ever the mood she could always brighten his day.

"So point me in the direction of the ass, and I'll kick it." Michelle answered him. "Is it that little snip you were telling me about, Cassandra...what's her last name again?"

"Boozer."

"Blaine, have you thought there might be something in a name? I mean Boozer, what kind of girl is she? Does she drink heavily? With a name like that you'd better inquire. Are you still running after her? Listen, I could set you up."

"Whoa, whoa." He had to put on the brakes. "Michelle, give me a little time to catch my breath. I haven't even had coffee...or...just slow down okay."

For a space of ten seconds neither of them spoke. Blaine counted on his fingers then waited. This mother of his could be stubborn. He would have to go first.

"Michelle."

"I thought you were going to call me Mom."

"Only on special occasions."

"What do you consider special?"

"Oh when you save my life, when I wake you at four am, things like that." He'd slipped in the part about her saving his life, hoping it would jog her memory.

"Are you angry with me?"

"Angry with you?" He was taken by surprise. "Why would you think that?"

"Well..."

"Michelle..." Blaine rolled his eyes and shook his head. "Is it the mom thing? I'll do it if it will make you happy."

"I don't want you to do anything that you don't want to do."

"Michelle."

Silence.

"Michelle, you're my mother right?"

"Right."

"We both know this, right?"

"Right."

"I'm thirty-two years old, correct?"

"Yes."

"You know that I love you, no matter what name I use, so don't let that become an issue with us. I'm an adult already. We can't go back and redo the last thirty-two years. And we definitely can't go back and fix a whole other life. Let it go okay?"

"But you're the one who asked me."

"I asked you if you would mind if I called you Mom when we're together," he interrupted her. He tapped on the base of the phone. "We're not together."

"You're a smart ass, Blaine."

He laughed out loud. "Mom, is there a reason for this call?"

"Call me Michelle," she retorted.

Again he laughed. "Lady, what do you want? You're giving me a headache."

"Good, then I've done my job."

"Your job was to give me a headache?"

"No, I had a dream about you last night. I sensed you worrying about something. I felt that you were in danger. I wanted to take your mind off your problem."

Blaine held the phone away from his ear and closed his eyes. He saw Michelle sitting at her home curled up in a chair her feet tucked beneath her, a green blanket partially covering her.

The Mystic was right, not only were his own powers getting stronger, but so was his connection to Michelle. Her powers were increasing also and she had no idea.

"Michelle, do you really want to help me?"

"Of course I do," she answered him without hesitation.

"Then go along with what I'm going to ask. Just humor me okay?"

"Okay."

Blaine heard the hesitation in her voice. "Don't be afraid," he rushed to assure her. "It's nothing that's going to hurt you."

Again there was silence and he could sense her growing apprehension on the other end of the phone. *Leave her alone.* The thought screamed out at him, but he didn't abide the wishes of his subconscious. He needed to know. He rushed forward with his request before she went into a full fledge panic.

"Michelle, I want you to close your eyes and breathe in slowly." He waited. "Are you doing that?"

"Yes."

"You have to tell me. I can't see you remember."

That was a lie. He could plainly see her shifting position in her chair, closing her eyes tightly. He smiled at that knowing she wanted to keep out anything she couldn't explain.

"Michelle, I want you to attempt to picture my face, tell me what I'm wearing and what I'm doing."

"You're crazy, I can't do that!"

"You can," he almost screamed at her regretting his tone the moment he'd spoken.

"Don't yell at me, Blaine."

"I'm sorry, I didn't mean to. This is just so important to me." He kept his own eyes closed attempting to slow the pounding of his heart. "Mom, please help me. I need you."

"The Mom's blackmail, isn't it?"

He heard the smile in her voice, saw it on her face. She wasn't offended that he was using his trump card. "Yeah, its blackmail, but I do need your help. Try please."

"Okay, you're standing up holding the phone to your ear."

"Don't strain, try again, relax your face, just picture me and tell me what I'm doing." This time his voice was gentle, cajoling, coaxing. "Tell me, what do you see?"

He went to the kitchen and placed his hand on the refrigerator. "Go ahead, Mom, tell me what you see."

"This is funny."

He heard the hesitant laughter in her voice. "What is?"

"I see you standing in your kitchen, your hand on the refrigerator door."

Blaine's head dropped to his chest and he cradled his face in his hand. It was true. He wanted to say something to her, tell her she'd done well, but he couldn't get the words to come.

"Blaine," he heard her calling his name, first softly, then with a bit of panic when he failed to answer.

"I'm here."

"Why were you holding your face, what happened?"

"You saw that?"

"I saw it. How?"

"How do you think it happened?"

"Well, I guess you're trying some experiment. I don't know. Maybe you're sending me your thoughts and I received them."

"Is that really what you think happened?"

"It must be. There is no other explanation for it. Tell me, when did you learn to do this? It's kinda cool."

Let it go for now, the voice shouted at him, *take it slow*. "I'm glad you think it's cool," Blaine answered her. "It's just something I'm fooling around with."

He stopped there; not telling her how knowing she too was gifted brightened his very soul. Not that he'd ever doubted, but this was the ultimate proof that she was indeed his mother. The Mystic was right all along. He should have never doubted him.

"Blaine, is that all you want me to do?"

Her voice drew him back. "Yes, that's all. Now what about you? Did you want something with me?"

"Like I said, I had this feeling you needed a bit of cheering up."

"Well, you've certainly done that."

"And you've certainly gotten me off the subject of Cassandra Boozer."

Blaine smiled, more in the mood to indulge his mother in her questioning of his private life. "Why do you think Cassandra has something to do with my mood?"

"I don't know. I just got this feeling. When her name came into my head, I saw a dagger. I don't know what it means, but I sensed this evil around her, and…"

"And what?" Blaine was curious now. "What else did you sense?"

"This is probably all my imagination, but I sensed that your being around her is dangerous for you."

"Do you think she's evil?"

For a moment he didn't think Michelle was going to answer him. He had to bite his lips to keep from demanding an answer. He'd almost yelled at her once, he wouldn't do it again. He'd just have to wait.

"No, I don't think she's evil. But there is something around her, some presence that is evil and if you remain in contact with her that evil will contaminate your life."

"How do you know all of this?" Blaine asked her softly. "Are you telling me that you're psychic, Mom?"

"Heavens no."

She laughed and Blaine's heart sank. He wanted to hear her say yes, ask him where the hell he thought his gift came from, but of course she didn't say any of those things.

"Blaine, you're the only psychic. I merely had a dream."

"That didn't sound like a dream, not all of it anyway. It sounds more like something you know, or at least feel." With his eyes still closed, he watched her, ignoring his resolution to stop spying on people.

She remained in her chair her eyes closed, her face peaceful, her breathing regular. Then he noticed the raised bumps on her arms. He saw as she pulled the blanket around her shoulders tighter, as if she'd suddenly gotten cold.

"Blaine, I'm probably crazy. It's just…well when I even think of her name—I get chills."

Blaine looked down at his own skin. He saw the identical bumps on his flesh and felt the chill cover him skittering up his feet encasing his legs and entire torso in ice. He thought of Salvatore and how with a mere handshake he'd frozen him.

"Michelle," he paused, the lump in his throat restricting his voice. "Mom, tell me something. Did you feel anything at all last night? I mean before you went to sleep?"

"I don't think so."

"Think hard. Are you sure nothing strange happened to you last night?"

"Hmm. There was one thing but…it couldn't have really happened now that I think about it."

"Why don't you tell me anyway," he coaxed.

"It was weird. I think it was more of my imagination or maybe just menopause."

Blaine was fighting to remain patient. He wanted to rush his mother's telling but knew from experience that would be impossible, especially given the fact that she was trying so hard to convince herself that it hadn't happened. He knew he had to be careful for now. Michelle didn't want to think any of the things she was seeing or feeling were real. If she thought they were, she would probably suppress them.

"Just humor me. What happened last night?" He asked softly.

"My right hand was frozen and the feeling went all the way up my arm. When it happened I got this picture of you shaking someone's hand and I sensed waves of evil emanating from the man."

"What did you do?"

"I told him to let you go, and then I poked him and took his hand off of you."

"How did you do this?"

"I was sewing at the time. I took my needle and jabbed him and he released you. See," she laughed embarrassed. "I told you it was pure nonsense. For a while I thought I was going crazy."

"Were you awake?"

"Yeah, I was sewing. Aren't you listening to me?"

Blaine smiled, now it was Michelle who sounded annoyed. "I mean are you sure this wasn't part of the dream you had?" He asked holding his breath, waiting for an answer.

"Of course not. Larry asked me what was wrong and I told him that my arm fell asleep. He laughed at me and asked; couldn't I find a less painful way of waking it up than sticking it with a pin?"

"Did you stick yourself?"

"No, but I guess from Larry's angle it must have looked like it. He came over and kissed my hand then… well…we went to bed. It was later; after I went to sleep that I had the dream about you."

Blaine wanted to stop himself from watching his mother. Damn he was going to have to at least teach her how to block her thoughts, and to know when she was being probed.

The idea of teaching her appealed to him probably more than it should have. She had sensed the danger same as he. He didn't want to involve her, but it was beginning to look as if he didn't have a choice. He needed to at least teach her to protect herself.

"Michelle," he began. "Would it freak you out if I told you that what you felt last night actually happened?"

"I don't freak that easily, Blaine, not after this past year anyway."

God how he wished that was true. *The three of you together would be stronger*. He had to get the Mystic's words out of his head. There was no way in hell he was bringing his mother into his mess.

He thought of Chance. His father would be more than willing to help him, of that he was positive, but he couldn't allow that either. Besides, all the power appeared to rest with Michelle despite what his friend said.

"Blaine, are you telling me that someone turned your hand and mine into ice last night?"

"Yes."

"That's impossible."

"I would have said that same thing if it had not happened."

"Who is he?"

"A friend of Cassandra."

"Harrumph."

Blaine sighed. "What's that supposed to mean? She had nothing to do with it."

"I don't think we can talk about this now. I hear the irritation in your voice. And if I want that I can get it elsewhere. I have to go."

"You woke me, now just like that you want to end the conversation?"

"I don't want to fight with you."

"Why not? Fighting will not make me love you less. You know that." His voice became soft and he whispered her name. "Please, Mom, don't hang up. I have something else to tell you."

"I know you do. That's another reason I have to go."

"You can't run from it forever." He heard the laughter coming through the wires, but he was still looking at her and saw the sad expression on her face. "Let me teach you." He pleaded.

"Blaine, I don't think Larry would be happy about any of this. I've asked him to accept a lot. We're happy."

"You know don't you?" He concentrated every molecule of energy in every cell, one distinct wish in mind. Instantaneously he was standing in the room with Michelle.

He kneeled in front of her. "How long have you known?"

"For awhile." Her hand reached out to touch his face, fat drops of tears ran unhindered down her cheeks.

"You saved my life. It did happen." Blaine whispered, wondering why he'd not picked up sooner that she hadn't answered him earlier when he joked about calling her Mom whenever she saved his life. "Thank you."

Michelle's arms came around him, pulling him closer, cradling him. Without words he knew he wasn't alone. He truly did have a family. He had a mother and a father and for sure his mother was gifted.

He crushed her to him, her tears wetting his checks. He lifted his hand to wipe them away and was instantly in his own apartment. He took a deep breath wanting to be back with her, but couldn't complete the journey. Glancing at the discarded phone he crossed the room to retrieve it. He lifted the phone to his ear. "Are you angry with me?"

"For what, Blaine? For thinking that if you were in trouble I wouldn't know it, and do everything in my power to save you?"

"No, for popping in on you like that. I've never done it before. I didn't know that I could."

Thoughts of Salvatore filled his mind and he sobered instantly. "Mom, we have no choice. He's going to come after me and I have to know you're protected. I don't want you doing what you did last night. This is a very dangerous man. I don't want him to find out about you."

"It's too late for that also."

"What do you mean?"

"I dreamt of him also last night. He's a very attractive man. He looks like a gypsy."

Blaine swallowed around the lump in his throat. He had what he wanted. Michelle had powers. She was acknowledging them. Damn, this wasn't what he wanted at all.

"I have to teach you how to protect yourself."

"Blaine I really do have to go now. That's your world, not mine. I don't need any protection. And I don't want any lessons."

With that she hung up leaving Blaine with a weight that pressed down on his chest with unbelievable force. He was consumed with guilt. Meeting him had thrown Michelle's life into chaos. Now she was in danger because of some genetic connection.

He thought of Cassandra, stubborn, skilled, but refusing to use her powers, and he thought of his mother, unskilled, but also refusing to even learn of her powers. How the hell was he going to help two such stubborn women who didn't want to be helped?

"God," he screamed out loud. "What am I going to do? Two women to protect, and I'm not strong enough to protect either of them.

Chapter Ten

Cassandra woke with a start. She shook her head to clear away the mental confusion. Her first thoughts were of Blaine MaDia.

She pictured his smile, his lean body with little more than peach fuzz covering his chest. She thought of his gentleness when they made love and the power in his embrace. She caught herself smiling. With the smile the image of Blaine became clearer until she found herself viewing his home.

Stop it, she screamed and retreated back into her own hotel room. This would never do. It was so much easier now without the powder in her system. She'd have to remember that.

Salvatore had taught her to bi-locate to others with a mere thought. They'd done it as a game, both finding the other in their bed, in the shower, anywhere the other was.

They were both so adept at it that they merely had to think the name and be in the presence of the other. If Salvatore knew she could visit Blaine that easily he would be angry. She knew that without a doubt. He considered their visitations something sacred between the two of them.

Even when they'd found out from the Mystic that it was called bi-location, he refused to accept it, making Cassandra promise she would never go to another living soul in that manner but him, and that she would never allow anyone to come to her but him. No, Sal must never know that she'd broken that bond. He wouldn't care if it was unintentional. He was extremely possessive about things he considered his. She knew his thoughts. She belonged to him.

That too was her doing, or rather her undoing it seemed now. She'd pledged herself to him when she'd been fifteen. He was her first love and her first lover.

As always when things became too tense for her to deal with at home Cassie found Sal. And as always he comforted her as he'd done for the past ten years. Only this time the comforting had taken a different turn. Lying on his bed, in his arms feelings of passion stirred between them.

It was Sal who'd pulled away protesting that they couldn't. And it had been her who'd begged him to make love to her, that she belonged to him, only to him. It was then she swore her undying love and devotion.

Her love and devotion for Sal never changed, but her passion did. She wanted Salvatore in her life forever, lovers could come and go. So she'd made a decision that she would go back to the way things were before they'd consummated their love. Sadly Sal never agreed with her decision.

Now he was back in her life, the one man who knew her better than she knew herself. He knew her strengths and her weaknesses. She could only pray that her love for him would not prove to be a fatal weakness.

He knew she'd been using something to suppress her powers. Now she had to allow him to think she was continuing to do so. That was the only edge she had on him and that alone was not enough to keep Blaine safe.

She felt him behind her and angrily slammed her mind shut before turning to face him.

"Salvatore, we're not children anymore. I don't want you bilocating to my bedroom."

"I thought you would enjoy it."

"You're a liar. You knew I would get angry. What are you doing, spying on me? What if I had a man in my bed? Would you care?"

"There shouldn't be a man in your bed should there?"

Cassandra refused to allow Sal to rile her anymore than he already had. She needed every once of energy she could muster to face him. She wouldn't play his game. Instead she fortified her blocks watching his face as his awareness of what she was doing became clear.

"I told you, you will not use blocks to keep me out."

"Sal, why did you come home? You said you came to help me, but up until now you've only bullied me. You're the one who taught me to block you. Now you get angry when I use it."

She saw him thinking over what she said. The years he'd spent away had served to make him not only stronger but harder and somewhat cold. A hard shudder ripped through her body making her aware of her feelings. She wasn't at all sure if she completely liked this new Sal.

"I'm sorry, Cassie. I guess I've been behaving like a show-off. It just angered me last night to see you with a psychic." His eyes narrowed, "especially when you've proclaimed that you would never date one."

"Don't be jealous, Sal. You and I have a history together. I love you. If I was going to be with anyone it would be with you, but I can't." She smiled again at him. "We're family, like brother and sister. We've seen each other naked."

"And I'd like to again," Sal quipped.

Cassandra blushed, knowing Sal was enjoying her discomfort. "Let's do this the right way. Leave and come to my door and knock." A moment before he vanished from her room, she made her voice stern. "Sal, don't do this again or the friendship is over."

His leaving gave her a moment to slip into a robe and concentrate on anything other than Blaine. Sal could probe her mind without even trying. She had a bone spur in her right heel. She concentrated on that, the pain, the difficulty walking when she first got up. If Sal was going to feel anything let it be her pain.

She was at the door before he had a chance to knock. "Good morning Salvatore. Nice to see you." She ignored the smirk on his face and kissed his cheek. Think of the pain she admonished herself.

It worked much better than she would have expected. She could feel the pointed end of the spur piercing her skin, making her stumble as she attempted to walk away from the door.

Sal caught her in his arms, a worried look on his handsome face making him once again her longtime friend, her brother.

"Cassie, what's wrong?"

"Nothing much, just a spur," she answered. Tears came surprising her and him. She never cried when she was in pain especially a pain she brought about with her thoughts. She leaned into Sal as he lifted her into his arms and carried her across the room to deposit her on the bed. His mind was on her and her pain and only that. He wasn't trying to read her thoughts. For that she was grateful. She was also grateful that she'd succeeded in diverting her thoughts. She mumbled a quick thank you to God that her powers had not left her. They'd only been tamped down temporarily by her use of the powder. She had a feeling she was going to need them.

"Why haven't you done anything about this?" Sal scolded her.

"I have."

"What did you do?"

"I went to the doctor a year ago. I got a shot of cortisone."

"Cortisone," he sneered, "You know what to do to stop this."

"I can't Sal. I was never much good at this anyway." He began massaging her foot and she sank against the pillows.

"Would you like me to take the pain away, Cassie? All you have to do is ask."

"What's the price, my soul, my body?" He smiled at her, but she refused to smile back. "I'm waiting for an answer, Sal. What is it you want?"

He put her foot back on the bed and peered at her. His dark good looks making her see him as a man, not just the kid she'd shared many a bath with.

"I'm glad you're back, Sal. I could really use a friend. But I can't have you ordering me around, breaking into my room, kissing me…the way you did the other day."

"What is it you want from me, Cassie? You know how I feel about you. I've never made it a secret."

"No, but you've never tried to force me either." She pulled her sore foot in close to her body wincing with the pain.

"Were you the one coming into my dreams, Sal? Have you been attempting to make love to me while I slept?"

Cassandra watched his face and body carefully for any signs that he was lying. There was no mistaking the anger in his jerky movements.

"What the hell are you talking about, Cassie?" He was suddenly holding her shoulders, shaking her, attempting a scan when she shook his hand off.

"That's what I mean, Sal. Don't do that. Don't scan me ever again."

"I was only trying to find who did such a thing to you. There would be traces of his energy left. I can find him."

"Not like that you won't." She stopped. "Are you saying that you weren't the one…that you haven't been trying…to…to?"

"To make love to you. No, Cassie, it wasn't me. I don't want you like that. I want you to want me as much as I want you. I would never take you by force." He laughed. "At least I don't think I would. But then again you might leave me with no choice."

"Don't joke about this, Salvatore, it's much too important," Cassandra chided him. "Someone has been trying this for two years."

"Why the hell didn't you contact me, tell me what was going on?"

"I didn't know where to find you."

"That's a lie, you can bilocate."

"Not all the way to India."

"How do you know? Did you try?"

"I don't recall you trying very hard to reach me either, Sal, and you knew where I was." She saw a smile creasing his face. He shook his head at her reminding her of the Mystic who'd taught them both. So now Sal thought she was a child.

"Cassie, how do you suppose I knew you were in trouble?"

"Have you been watching me?" She moved away from him and pulled a pillow in front of her body again feeling he was invading something very sacred.

"Of course I've been watching you. Did you think I could be gone this long and not give into the longing to see your face? You may not be in love with me, but I'm in love with you."

"Why didn't I know you were watching me?"

"Because of that damn powder you've been taking, that garbage you made."

"Why the hell couldn't you just pick up a phone, Sal? God!" She jumped from the bed wanting to be away from him. "Why do you always have to do things in such a grand way?"

"Well for one thing it was cheaper," he paused cocking his head to the side looking her over. "I wanted to see if you missed me. It didn't seem as if you did."

Cassandra closed her eyes. "If only you knew how much I missed you." She turned toward Sal wishing that she was in love with him. It would be so easy. No one would dare try and touch her if she were to announce she was going to marry Salvatore Sharif.

"You're right you know. I would kill any man who touched you."

Sighing she moved back across the room, feeling more than a little helpless. Cassandra sat between his legs her butt resting on the floor, her head resting on his strong muscular thighs. She drew tiny circles with the nail of her finger into the soft leather of his pants.

"Don't do that any more, Sal, no more crawling into my mind. I need to trust you."

"I'll try."

"You'll have to do more than try. Anything you want to know, I'll tell you." She watched while his eyes glittered in amusement.

"Then tell me about this man you're trying so hard to protect."

Cassandra stared at him, she'd not thought about Blaine once since Salvatore walked in the room. Her thoughts were on the pain in her foot. Now her thoughts flew to Blaine with the speed of light. She quickly pulled them away and continued staring at Sal.

"Cassie, I taught you remember?" He smiled. "You were doing a good job, but I'm not stupid. There's no inflammation on the bottom of your foot. The pain is something you induced. I love you, Cassie, but I'm not blind. I knew you were using that to cover your real thoughts."

"Are you going to hurt him?"

"I'm not going to let you marry him, and I'm not going to let you give yourself to him again."

If only she could have stopped the blush from happening. Damn. She couldn't. That as much as Salvatore reading her thoughts were a real give away.

"Cassie, you're too important to the entire community, not just the psychics here in the US, but across the entire world. Everyone wants to know what will happen. I can't allow you to be with him."

Her hand pulled back. She had every intention of slapping her friend. He had different plans. Sal caught her hand, bringing it to his chest kissing it.

"I'm sorry, Cassie. Like I said, I came home to protect you, and if I have to protect you from yourself then so be it."

She snatched her hand from his grip. "You didn't answer me. Are you intending to hurt him?"

"Not as long as you don't go near him and he doesn't come near you. You want to save the baby psychic, marry me, Cassie."

"Blaine isn't the danger to me, Sal. He's not the one who's been sneaking into my dreams. If you want to help me, you can start looking in a different direction."

"I have every intention of doing that. I will find him and he will be sorry. I promise."

His eyes turned dark and she was suddenly afraid of him. There was something that had never been present in Sal before. She closed her eyes, the vibrations getting stronger. No. She almost cried out loud, not Sal. She glanced over at him, the hard countenance of his face, the cold black of his eyes. There was no denying it, Sal radiated evil.

***

Salvatore Sharif, was unexpected. Damn, getting to the bitch was going to be much harder than he'd thought at first. He wasn't afraid. Hell, he welcomed a fight with his old nemesis.

Trouble was he hadn't known Salvatore was back in the states. No one had mentioned it. Lucky for him Sal had shown up before he had a chance to make his move.

Lucky for Blaine MaDia. He'd been one second from sending a mental barrage that would have killed him. He'd only stopped when Salvatore walked to the table.

He might not have to bother with that insect at all. He saw the way Salvatore looked at him, the hatred for the man emanating through his pores and caressing him like an ice cold breeze.

He laughed loudly. What a joke, make Sal chase MaDia, and the bitch chase Salvatore trying to keep MaDia safe. They would all be in a circle like rats chasing their tails. No one even suspected him. He could pounce on any of them any damn time he chose.

He laughed again. The game had just gotten more interesting. Salvatore Sharif was not the only one who'd been studying. He was also not the only one with an increase in powers.

Just think, three psychics for the price of one. The bitch would have no one to blame but herself. She should have known he was the only one to father her child. Stupid bitch. Stupid, stupid, bitch. He laughed and packed his bags. It was time to move to another hotel.

Chapter Eleven

Cassandra parked her car, her hand reaching into her purse to pull out her not so secret canister. She sprinkled an infinitesimal amount in the palm of her hand then pressed it to her mouth.

She closed her eyes for a moment before releasing her curled fingers to wipe all of the powder on the pocket inside of her slacks. Just in case Salvatore was watching her, she had to make it convincing.

She no longer held any stock in the promises he gave. Sure, he'd told her he would not enter her mind if she didn't attempt to keep him out. He'd only laughed when she answered that she would only attempt to keep him out if he tried to enter. They'd gotten nowhere.

If it were not for the fact that she was visiting the old Mystic she was sure he would be with her, plastered to her side as he'd been since he'd first made contact. For some reason Salvatore didn't want to see their old mentor. She'd take his weak excuse and be grateful for small favors.

She needed the Mystic to get a message to Blaine MaDia. She wanted him to tell Blaine to stay out of her life, that she wasn't interested, anything, as long as she didn't bring him into the mess her life had become.

Cassandra stepped over the threshold, immediately her senses were assailed by the memories of happier times, and happier places. Her and Sal running around the old man's legs, him teaching them everything he knew. What fun it had all been.

"Cassie, Cassie, I knew you would come."

She heard her teacher's voice from behind her and spun around eager to embrace him, but he wasn't there. True laughter bubbled up from deep within her. He remembered. Their own version of hide and go seek.

Eyes closed, she conjured up the man's face and saw him sitting outside amidst the trees waiting for her. "Long time," she whispered to the image in her mind before she walked out there.

"So, Cassie, you've finally come for a visit?"

For a long moment she didn't answer, feeling the old man's frailty beneath his robes as she touched him. She breathed in the scent of him, the spicy smell tickling her nose. "What is that you've got all over you?"

"Oh just something I've been working on, something I thought you, or someone else might need."

Cassie looked at the old man curiously. He knew about Sal, of that she was certain. Still it wasn't Sal of whom he was speaking.

"Hello, Cassandra."

She felt her heart lurch in her chest. A surge of joy shot through her veins. Salvatore hadn't harmed him. Before the joy left, she remembered Sal's warning.

"Blaine, what are you doing here, are you following me around?"

"I'm visiting my friend and my teacher."

She glanced curiously at the Mystic. "He taught you to talk to the dead?" Her tone of voice was almost insulting and she caught herself. "Why would you need anyone for that?"

"Talking to the dead, as you put it, is my choice. There is value in my work whether you approve of it or not."

They stood glaring at each other for a moment before the Mystic placed an arm around each of their shoulders. "There are no enemies in this room."

"What are you talking about?" Cassandra stopped herself, glancing once in Blaine's direction then back at the Mystic.

"Blaine, would you mind giving us a few minutes? There is something very important I need to talk about with Cassie."

She felt a small nudge and immediately thrust her finger upward toward Blaine. "Don't you dare. I've had more than enough of men invading my mind."

"I wasn't going to…" Blaine attempted to protest.

"Save it," Cassandra answered glaring at him. "Now would you mind leaving?"

"Actually I would. I was here first. How's your friend Salvatore?" he asked ignoring the Mystic's look of reprimand and the surprised look on Cassandra's face

"I'm sorry about last night, Blaine, but Sal's an old friend. I hadn't seen him in years." She looked toward the Mystic then back at Blaine. "I was only repeating the request. I wasn't the one that asked you to leave."

"Not with words, but you did want me to go."

Cassandra turned her face into granite. "Are you determined to have this conversation here, in front of an audience?"

"Why not?" Blaine answered. "We had an audience last night."

"Well fine, but I warn you, you're not going to like what I have to say. I told you on the plane, I wasn't interested in you. I've repeated it at least a dozen times. So I don't get this hurt or betrayed act you're putting on. We had one date, Blaine. One date does not a relationship make."

Blaine walked toward Cassandra. She was right. He didn't like what she'd had to say. He stood as close as was decent to stand with the old man there watching the two of them like a hawk.

"We didn't have the one date. I think you owe me that." He surprised himself and he could tell by the audible gasp from her that he'd surprised her also. But he'd thought of Michelle, of what she'd told him. He did keep himself closed off not wanting to get hurt. Now he was putting his feelings on the line. He did want to see Cassandra again. He wanted to make love to her over and over. He wanted a relationship.

"I can't see you, Blaine."

"Can't see me, why? You're not married or engaged? Neither am I. I could understand your not wanting to see me, but what's with the, can't?"

"Damn it, Blaine, if that's what it will take, I don't want to see you again. There, now are you satisfied?"

"Not quite." His hand snaked out and pulled her in closer. With the pads of his fingers he gently caressed her cheeks.

"Blaine, maybe you shouldn't."

He heard the Mystic's voice. There was no turning back, he felt Cassandra tremble beneath his touch, her gaze boring into his own and he lowered his lips to cover hers.

Together they were swirling toward a beacon with a zillion twinkling lights. It was as if they were caught in a rainstorm of fairy dust. He'd come home, regardless of what she said, he felt her tightening her embrace, her hands pulling him closer. There was no denying she felt what he felt.

His senses were completely taken over by the emotions he was having on touching Cassandra. He never wanted to let her go.

Slowly and with great reluctance he ended the kiss, his lips but a fraction away, he could still feel her heat, see the moisture from his tongue beaded on her flesh. Her eyes glazed, her fingers still clinging to him.

"It was just a kiss, Blaine."

"Like hell," he laughed at her and walked away. He had to. He was hotter than he could ever remember being and the evidence wasn't something he wanted his teacher to see.

He walked toward the front of the small house. "You've got your privacy," he muttered.

Cassandra watched Blaine leave before turning toward the Mystic. "I can't see him."

"Why?"

"Salvatore is back."

"You're not in love with Sal. Why should his return prevent you from seeing Blaine, if that's what you want to do?"

Cassandra sat in the only comfortable chair in the room. "Why are you being difficult? You've always known that I had no plans for love, marriage or babies. Why are you surprised now?"

"Because, Cassie, you can't plan love. It just happens."

"I don't know Blaine. I've just met him. I just want to stop it before it goes too far… before…"

"Before what, before you find out I'm right that your heart has betrayed you? And will wonders never cease, you've fallen in love with a psychic?"

Cassandra shook her head. "The guy is funny, okay. I'll give him that, and he is a good kisser, but that's all." She brought her attention back to what was important, keeping Blaine safe. "Look I don't know how you know him, but you can make anyone listen to common sense. Just help me convince him that we can't see each other again. It's for his own good."

She'd said too much. She could tell from the heightened awareness that came into the Mystic's hazel eyes. They suddenly appeared to burn with some inner fire.

"Cassie, you keep saying you can't see Blaine. I think there's something more going on here. Has someone told you not to see him, Sal perhaps?"

At that moment she wanted nothing more than to lie. "Salvatore came home to make sure I…I…" she stopped and stared at the Mystic. "I don't really know why he came home. He said to protect me, but he's only been making demands."

"Did he threaten Blaine?"

"Not really, he just told me nothing would happen to him if I don't see him."

"Is that why you don't want to see Blaine, you're afraid something will happen to him?"

Cassandra glanced toward the kitchen. "Nothing serious would have happened between us anyway, but…well, I don't want him hurt because he has a crush on me."

"Since when do you let Sal boss you around?"

"I'm not worried about Sal hurting me." She looked down before allowing herself to meet her mentor's eyes. "Sal's different. I can't begin to describe the power I feel he has." She hesitated, a fraction of a second, not wanting to betray Sal, but needing to say the words to someone who'd once loved Sal as much as she had. "There's something wrong. He's into… I don't know. I think he could be using his powers for, well, you know… evil purposes."

"How do you know this?"

"I don't, but he kissed me, and I…Well it's hard to describe, but he made me feel strange. I just don't want him to take it out on Blaine because I won't marry him"

"Did he ask you to marry him?"

"Yeah."

The Mystic laughed. "Cassie, he's asked you to marry him since you were twelve. What's so different about this time?"

Cassandra looked again toward the kitchen. "With all the pressure for producing this super baby, I think Salvatore will do everything in his power to make sure that baby is his and that includes harming Blaine."

She covered her face with her hand. "I feel so disloyal talking about him like this, but I can't help it. He made me feel a little afraid of him."

"And you plan on protecting me, by not seeing me again is that it?"

Her head swung around toward Blaine. "Did you?"

"No, I eavesdropped," he answered smiling at her. "You never told me not to do that. You merely said for me not to enter your thoughts."

"Blaine, this isn't funny."

"Sure it is, think about it. This whole thing sounds like some SCI-Fi drama. You've got this powerful sorcerer, who wants to steal the princess and take her to his castle. This is the twenty-first century. Cassandra, he has no power over us. We're adults."

He looked first at Cassandra then the Mystic for confirmation. "The only problem I can see is if you're in love with the guy. Are you?"

He waited his heart pounding, wondering how he was going to gracefully pull it off if she said yes. He crossed his fingers and stuck his hand behind his back.

"No," she answered finally. "I'm not in love with Sal. But I'm not in love with you either."

"Maybe not right now, but I think you must be in 'like' with me, you cared enough to try and protect me."

"I would do the same for anyone who couldn't protect themselves."

"Well, don't worry about me."

"Children, children," the Mystic scolded them as though they were five years old. "As I said before there are no enemies in this house, here we're all friends. As for you, Blaine, I think you'd better take Cassandra's warning seriously."

Blaine stood, running his hand through his hair. It was getting a bit longer than he liked it, but lately he hadn't had a chance to cut it.

"Cassandra, I want to see you."

"No."

"I'll keep calling you, coming to your hotel until I wear you down. Now the only way I can think of for you to know if your friend Sal has not turned me into a Shish kabob, would be for you to be with me."

"Blaine, if word gets out that I'm dating you, Sal will not be the only psychic that you will have to contend with. And I guarantee you that the others haven't spent their time talking to spirits. They've learned how to control people."

She peered at him. "You have heard of psychic attacks haven't you?"

"Of course," he answered sounding just a bit offended. "I'm not as dull-witted as you seem to think. I know it's real, but I can protect myself, I promise you."

"Not against Sal."

Blaine didn't answer. She was right and all three of them knew of it.

A light shone from Cassandra's eyes. "That's why you're here isn't it? You're trying to learn how to combat him."

Blaine laughed in spite of himself. "You too?"

"Yes."

Something in the tilt of her head, Blaine had expected this moment to come at some time. He remembered the Mystic's warning that in spite of everything Cassandra loved Salvatore. He wasn't surprised to hear her next question.

"Why did you feel you needed protection from Salvatore? He did nothing but shake your hand."

"It was just a feeling I got." He hadn't lied, it was a feeling, an ice cold feeling that ran through the length of his arm, a coldness that overwhelmed him to the point that his mother became aware of the danger. Yeah, he'd say it was a feeling.

"So I see the baby psychic is learning."

"I thought you weren't going to call me that anymore."

"Lighten up, Blaine, I was only kidding. Tell me more about this feeling you got. What brought you here and how long have the two of you known each other?" She paused glanced over at her teacher, *our teacher*, she amended her thoughts.

"You didn't mention that you two knew each other."

"Remember we haven't had much of a chance to talk. Besides, I didn't know you knew the teacher."

"So what happened, you got tired of talking to your spirit friends?"

She was teasing him and he found himself liking it. In fact he more than liked it. Cassandra laughed softly and Blaine fell in love with her in that moment. The sound of her voice, even teasing him was what he wanted to have for the rest of his life. It was quick, but then again he'd prepared a lifetime getting ready for the right woman. Cassandra was that woman.

Not attempting to mask his feelings from her Blaine looked directly into her eyes. He wanted her to know. "I was thinking about you, I thought you might need my help."

"Against Salvatore?"

This time her laughter wasn't so charming, but he loved her none the less, even though at this particular moment he was beginning to find her quite annoying.

"Yes, I decided I needed to know more just in case you should need me."

"Blaine, you could never compete against Sal."

"In no way?" He watched the blush cover her face.

"Get your mind back on the matter at hand. I'm talking of his powers. You're not even close to being in his league." She hated scolding him, but this was serious business. "Beside that, I have nothing to be afraid of from Sal. He would never hurt me."

"I heard you from the kitchen saying you were afraid of him."

"You're awfully nosy aren't you? Well, you didn't get it straight. I was scared for a second or two, but not for myself, only because he's changed, and I don't think it's all for the best. I think he likes his powers maybe a little too much, but afraid of Sal." She laughed. "Sal would never hurt me. He loves me, always has. It was you I was concerned about," she said pointedly.

"Don't waste your concern. I can take care of myself." She was starting to piss him off. If it was only concern he could take that. But the woman thought he couldn't take care of himself and that in itself irritated the hell out of him.

Chapter Twelve

As the tension mounted the Mystic shook his head then laughed. He was overjoyed to still be alive to witness one of the most unexplained miracles of life and love. But his enjoyment was short lived. Now was the time for making peace. Once again the old Mystic stepped between them determined to stop their petty squabble.

"Blaine, I'm sure Cassie meant no harm. Cassie, it's been a long time. Your being here, your concern for Blaine tells me that I should be concerned also. Tell me what happened."

He speared a look in Blaine's direction. "This time there will be no interruptions, is that clear?" He glared at Blaine before tapping his finger to his lips indicating that he wanted Blaine to remain quiet.

Blaine swallowed. He'd been properly chastened, but of course he would do as the old man asked, he had too much respect for him not to obey. He cringed burning with embarrassment as he flopped down on the floor, his arms resting on the purple velour cushions that were scattered about the room. He turned first toward Cassandra then the teacher.

"Go ahead," he smiled half heartedly. "I'm all ears."

Cassandra glanced first at Blaine not wanting to talk with him there. But the teacher had vouched for him. Besides she was in the teacher's home she thought as she turned toward the Mystic. "Sal came to my room this morning." She saw the smile cross the old man's face.

"Don't. I didn't find it amusing. We're no longer children I don't want him popping in and out of my bedroom. Besides, I didn't get the feeling he did it for old times sake, but more to spy on me."

"How long was he there before you knew?" The teacher asked.

"Only a few seconds." Her voiced was subdued. She was ashamed that it had taken her even that long to know Sal was in the room.

"Then last night you didn't take it?"

The Mystic stopped speaking as Blaine looked toward him questioningly. Now they were both annoying Blaine. "I know she's taking something to suppress her powers. I'm not a fool." He stopped when the Mystic glared at him. Once again he was firmly put in his place.

"Why didn't you take it?" The old man's attention had returned to Cassandra.

A visible shiver ran through Cassandra's body. "I don't know. I just got the feeling last night that I needed more protection. I need...I just didn't take it."

"Do you think Sal knows about your taking something?"

"Oh he knows alright," Cassandra laughed. "I want him to think I'm still taking it. That may give me the only edge I have over him."

"That's not true," the Mystic interrupted, "your powers are just as great as Sal's. It's just that he's more fully developed and he relishes the things his mind can do. You on the other hand hate it. That's the only difference."

"Are you saying I have a chance to help Blaine? I mean keep him safe?" She saw Blaine bristle at her question and shook her head.

"How strong are Blaine's powers? Can he manage without me?"

The Mystic looked Blaine over. "He may surprise you, Cassie. He's extremely strong, but like you, he hasn't developed his powers to the fullest. He accidentally learned of other talents less than a year ago, and like you he's refused further teaching."

The Mystic laughed then, loud and boisterous startling both Cassandra and Blaine before he continued talking. "He thought it was so easy to talk to spirits, that it would keep him safe from dealing with the living. Well, Blaine, my boy," the old man walked over to him. "It looks like the living has found you." He chuckled. "Go on, Cassie, what else happened with Sal that brought you here?"

"Sir, it wasn't just Sal." Cassie apologized to the old man. "I came here specifically to see you, to ask for your help. The attacks are getting stronger."

"You came for training?"

"Not originally. I wanted you to talk to the community. You're well respected. I wanted you to convince them that this super baby they're waiting for is just legend. I wanted to be free to live my life."

"And now?"

"Now I know that's impossible. I know no one's going to let me go."

"Did Sal tell you that?"

"Not in so many words, but he said, I have no choice, that he would make sure I didn't marry or fall in love with someone who's not suited for me."

Cassandra heard the old man chuckle again and turned to glare in his direction. He was holding Blaine by the shoulder one hand clamped over his mouth.

She squinted at the two of them. "What are you two doing?"

"What's necessary." The old man laughed louder. "I had to physically restrain this errant son of mine. He would crush Salvatore with his bare hands, wouldn't you Blaine?"

Blaine rolled his eyes, but didn't speak.

"Good." The Mystic smiled. "Good."

"You're waiting for me to tell you that I spoke of you to Sal, aren't you Blaine?" Cassandra asked looking directly at Blaine.

"Well I did, but I didn't want to. He doesn't like you. That's what scared me; there was so much hostility when he spoke of you. He said if I want to keep you safe that I wasn't to see you."

Blaine removed his teacher's hand from his mouth. Do you want to see me, Cassandra?"

"Maybe. I don't know." She shook her head. "Blaine, it's hard to give you an answer. Maybe I would have if this didn't happen. But now it's not worth it. I couldn't stand it if you got hurt especially, when I'll never fall in love with you."

"Never say never." The teacher interjected.

"Why don't we both just concentrate on learning more to protect ourselves?" Cassie replied, ignoring the Mystic as he looked from one to the other of them.

"Will you still go out with me?" Blaine persisted.

"No."

"Please."

"No."

"Cassie," the Mystic interrupted. "Blaine's not as helpless as you might think and he's not a first generation psychic. His mother also has powers."

"Don't." Blaine turned to the teacher his eyes pleading. 'I don't want her in danger."

"From what you told me, Blaine, she might already be."

"I don't think it's a good idea to speak of her. The less Salvatore knows of her the better."

Blaine watched as Cassandra turned and began walking in his direction stopping inches from his face, the scowl on her face fierce.

"Are you telling me that you think Sal would do something to hurt your mother?" She bellowed, before turning toward the Mystic. "Are you buying this nonsense that this guy found his parents from a past incarnation and they managed to hook up in this lifetime? I don't believe it. And frankly I don't know how the two of you could either."

She placed her hands on her hips. "For God's sake, Blaine, you're famous. You don't think someone would want to use you for your fame, just make it up and come to you with claims like that? You don't think people know you're an orphan? Listen, you weren't just hatched this time around. What about your biological parents?" She closed her eyes.

"It's not bad enough that I have to deal with someone wanting to impregnate me, now I have to worry about protecting a man who believes this crap. And I come to a teacher for help in increasing my powers and finds he's in cahoots with a nut. God," she screamed loudly, "why don't I just get it over with and do us all a favor and marry Salvatore? There is no way in hell we can prevent it. We're all wacko."

Blaine glared right back at Cassandra. Okay maybe he had fallen for her too quickly. Because it sure as hell wasn't love that he was feeling for her now. He was angry that she thought he was a nut, but to think Michelle would try and trick him, hell who did she think she was? Let the teacher help her, he was through with her, let her marry Salvatore. Who the hell cared?

Without a word he walked from the room. He cared. He cared a hell of a lot and he didn't want to. He would continue his training. He wanted to, beside that, if the mess did spill over to his mother, she was the one woman in his life that he'd never walk away from.

Damn Cassandra Boozer and damn her for having such kissable lips, and soft dewy skin and eyes that he got lost in. *Hell Blaine*, he fussed to himself. Why don't you just damn the world while you're at it?

***

Her powers were back full force. It served her right for the way she'd treated Blaine. Cassandra looked away from the Mystic, unable to bear the disappointment in his eyes. She was ashamed of her actions. She watched Blaine leave the house, continued watching until he got in his car and drove away. She sensed his hurt, it was palpable.

"Cassie, I've never seen you behave so rudely. I'm ashamed of you."

"I'm sorry, Sir. I just don't get the deal with this reincarnated mother of his."

"Do you believe in reincarnation?"

"Yes."

"Why?"

"It just makes sense."

"Then why don't you believe Blaine?"

"Because it doesn't make sense."

The Mystic smiled. "You can believe in a concept without having proof because it makes sense. But a man that claims to have proof in the concept you believe in, you call him wacko and say it doesn't make sense."

"It's just that I've never met anyone who actually thought they knew someone from another incarnation, it just doesn't seem possible." She cringed under her teacher's close scrutiny.

"Do you believe I've become so old and frail that I would fall for anything, just because it's some new age fad? I'm not that bored with my life that I have to invent new things to keep the juices going. No, Cassie, I believe him. I've known Blaine since he was a very young boy, maybe five or six. He's always stated that he has lived before."

"At that age?"

"Even younger. Blaine was brought up in a series of foster homes and orphanages."

"I thought those didn't exist any more."

"There's not a lot of them around today, but for the most part when he was growing up, they had no choice. No one wanted him around. He was a little kid with a big knowledge, everyone was afraid of him."

"How did you learn of him?"

"We have our ways. We always hear of promising talents, so I traveled to see him. No, I didn't connect with the spirits that he did, but everything he told me was accurate."

The old man smiled at Cassie. "He could recite entire conversations. I could ask questions. He didn't just give general things, like, 'your mother is at peace.' That's not what he does on his show either.

You really shouldn't judge him unless you know what you're talking about."

"Are you telling me that he actually has two way conversations with the dead?"

"Yes, I'm telling you that. But he's so much more than that. He just does what he does for a living, because he found he was more easily accepted by the dead than by the living. I doubt if any of them have ever called him a wacko, or me either, for that matter. I take great offense at that, as I'm sure Blaine does."

"Then tell me about this mother of his, how did he find her, and why so late in life?"

The old man smiled. "I think I've caused enough damage for one day. Anymore about his mother and he'll have to tell you. He doesn't want her name mentioned and I have to respect that."

She'd been properly chastened she thought as she stood staring at the old man finally curious, knowing he would divulge no more, still she had to ask. "What about his birth mother, his biological mother from this time?"

"That's a good question. And I don't think it would be breaking a confidence. Blaine is not an old soul yet he feels and think like one. I think so much parental love went into his last lifetime that his soul recorded it and he couldn't accept anyone else as his parents."

"You don't consider the woman who gave birth to him this time around to be his mother?"

"I can't, if he can't," he smiled, "but I call the couple he believes are his parents, his soul parents, and I believe that's every bit as important as genes. Matter of facts it's their genes that are imprinted on his soul."

Cassandra stared thoughtfully at her mentor for a moment. "I didn't intentionally offend him. I'm worried about him and I'm worried about myself." She glanced away, something else on her mind. It had been eating at her from the moment she'd told Sal she was coming to see the Mystic. "What's going on with you and Sal? He refused to come with me to see you."

"Sal doesn't want me to see the change."

"You know about it, don't you?"

"Yes, of course. I've seen him several times since he left. He's bi-located each time. He's too cheap to pay for a plane and he likes the power." In spite of himself the old man laughed.

"Did he tell you he'd popped in on me?"

"He didn't have to. He was always disappointed that you didn't try and reach him. He said he never even sensed you thinking about him. That was all he'd ever say."

"That's not true. I've thought about him a lot." She watched the old man's face sadden. "I'm sorry, Sir. I know it's a lie. I didn't want to think of either of you. I'm sorry. I just wanted to have a normal life."

"No one can blame you, Cassie, not me, not Sal."

"I should have written him. He wrote me you know, he even called and he emailed me. I never answered him. Do you think when he came and found me with Blaine, that he thought Blaine was the reason I hadn't called. Could he blame him for that? Maybe he believes I've known him longer than I'm admitting to."

"I think he knows the exact moment Blaine entered your life and when things changed for you."

"Nothing's changed."

"Yes, Cassie, things have changed. Something happened with you and Blaine. You're not the same girl who's been on the run. Before, you ran, but it was different, now you're terrified. I sense it in your soul. And like you said you're not afraid of Sal, so it's not for yourself that I sense this fear. It's for Blaine. He's changed you somehow, made you care."

Cassandra felt the burning tears that happened to her only on rare occasions. "It's not just Blaine I'm worried about. Sal's not the one who's after me. He told me that he wasn't the one who'd been chasing me."

She stopped and stared straight into her mentor's fiery gaze. "You have no idea how badly I wanted it to be Sal. I would have been able to reason with him." She shivered and turned away. "Sal came home because of the danger to me. I now have to take this whole damn business more seriously. Sal's being here tells me that. As for Blaine MaDia, I'm terrified. I should never have let my defenses down and talked to him. I thought he was no threat, he could do no harm, what the heck. So I let him sit down with me."

"And you let him touch your soul."

"It's been so long since I could just relax my guard, he made me laugh." A sigh escaped her and she smiled. "I've never had a man look at me in that way. He made me feel so beautiful, so wanted."

"There are lots of men that want you, Cassie. You're beautiful."

"I'm not," she protested. "We both know that. But Blaine made me feel that I was. In that short period of time I was special to him. All the other men in my life, who've wanted me, wanted me only for my uterus. They wanted me in order to fulfill 'THE' prophesy."

"Not Sal." The Mystic offered.

"No, not Sal. Well, not the old Sal. This new Sal also wants my uterus." She would have laughed but it wasn't funny.

"But you don't feel for Sal after all these years what you feel for Blaine after one night." The Mystic said without hesitation.

"Am I that easy to read?"

"I've known you your entire life. To me you're an open book. Blaine may think you have no feelings for him. I know better."

"Don't tell him okay. If you care about him, let him just disappear back out of my life."

"What are you going to do, Cassie?"

She heard the concern in her teacher's voice. "I'm going to get Salvatore to help me find out who's after me. Together we'll defeat him."

"What if the man you're after turns out to be Sal?"

"It isn't."

"How do you know?"

"I trust him."

"Cassie, that's a contradiction. You're here because your instincts tell you that you can no longer trust Salvatore. You're hiding the fact that you've stopped taking that vile concoction you created. You said you sense something evil in him. Is that true? Do you sense evil in Sal?"

"Yes, but he loves me. That's still there. I would trust Salvatore with my life."

"Be careful, Cassie, it might just not be your life on the line. Do you trust Salvatore with my life, or Blaine's, or the life of Blaine's mother?"

To that Cassandra had no answer, instead she said, "Then, we'd better get to work in case I'm wrong."

***

He laughed at how it easy it was to follow people, to observe their every move and not have them know it. There was a great deal of fun in that.

The man laughed to himself. This game of cat and mouse was becoming more interesting by the hour. His little mouse had just brought in another player.

The old Mystic had never been one of his favorite people. From the time he was a boy the man had looked at him with suspicion, refusing to teach him. Now that he thought about it, it made perfect sense. All of them in one fell swoop.

This would take a bit more time than he'd planned. But he'd waited this long, a little longer wasn't going to kill him. He laughed to himself. No, it would only kill them.

Of course he'd have to get rid of Salvatore first, he was the strongest, and then the old Mystic would come next. MaDia was barely a thought. What was MaDia going to do to him, send the spirit of the dead after him? He laughed again.

How he wished he could save Salvatore for last, let him see what he was going to do to his precious Cassie. The bitch. But thinking like that was far too dangerous. He needed to remain focused. And to do that he had to take out his old foe first, regardless how much he would relish him knowing he had the woman he couldn't get.

For the time being he'd suspended using his powers to keep tabs on them. Good old American technology had come through. He laughed again as he brought his binoculars up to his eyes. This was almost too easy.

Chapter Thirteen

The sky was a beautiful shade of purple with just a hint of orange peeping over the top of the ever increasing clouds. Cassandra stretched, feeling tired and famished. She'd worked for six hours straight with her teacher, stopping only once to go to the bathroom.

Now she rolled her head around on her shoulders wishing for just one drop of water. The old man had forbidden any form of nourishment for either of them, stating it would make their mental clarity sharper. In a way she believed it worked. She was more focused, sharper than she'd been in years. Though pleased with the progress she was still hungry and tired.

She turned pleading eyes on the teacher and gave him what she hoped was a sad smile. "Come on, aren't you tired, just a little?" she teased.

"No, Cassie I'm not. But if you're so weak that you would let the need for food and drink disrupt our studies, then by all means you're welcome to stop practicing and go find something in my kitchen to eat."

With the insult ringing in her ears she sprang from the chair and was rifling the refrigerator in a matter of moments. As hungry as she was, she did have the common decency to pour the juice into a glass when all she wanted was to open the carton and let the liquid flow down her parched throat.

After two glasses of juice, a hunk of cheese and a handful of grapes she returned to the room to find the Mystic smiling at her.

"You're smiling at me. I thought you would be angry, disappointed that I couldn't continue."

"No, Cassie, I'm very pleased."

"Why?"

"Two reasons. You went two hours longer than I expected and you did not let me distract you from what you wanted with my taunts."

She felt herself coloring. She didn't feel proud of stuffing her face, just the opposite. "I don't understand what you're saying. I didn't do anything brave, I was just hungry. I ate."

"And that was your act of bravery. I don't feel it's boasting to say you hold me in somewhat high esteem. Yet you defied me and my wishes for you. You ignored my demands on you and did what you felt was right for you and your body.

"Cassie, doing that showed great fortitude and determination. It shows a will that can not easily be broken, which you're going to need to fight not only Salvatore, but who ever is after you. I'm not as worried about your safety as I was when you first came to me today."

"You didn't think I could learn?"

"I had my doubts. It's been a long time since you studied. And I had no way of knowing what effect those herbs would have on you. I'm pleased."

"So, are we done?"

"For the night. Why don't you remain here? You'll be safer and I won't have to worry."

"Salvatore's going to be very upset." As she thought more about it she smiled. "I believe I'll take you up on your offer. Do you think he'll come?"

"Who, Salvatore or Blaine?"

Damn she wished she didn't blush so easily. Actually she didn't remember blushing this much until a few days before, when she'd met Blaine. The teacher was right; she was spending a great deal of time denying she was attracted to the man. Just remember, she scolded herself, attraction does not equal love.

"Salvatore will not come tonight, not in the physical, nor will he send his spirit." The Mystic answered her at last.

"How do you know?"

"I know Salvatore."

"Do you think Blaine will come?" She ignored the old man's knowing smile.

"Only if he's invited."

"Is that always the way he is, invitation only?"

"No, but he knows you will be here and he will not come unless you want him. You will have to do the asking."

A gasp passed Cassandra's lips. "You expect me to call him, why?"

"Because you're the one who insulted him."

Cassandra stared at the old man, stunned when he opened his hand and held out a piece of paper. She knew without looking that it was Blaine's phone number. But how? The man had not moved from his seat. Of course, the Mystic still had many tricks he'd not taught her.

She palmed the number into her own hand. "Okay, but I'm only calling to apologize for my rudeness. I'm not asking him to come over."

"That's fine, whatever you want." He laughed and walked into the kitchen.

Her palms were slick with sweat. She wiped them against the cotton shirt she wore, feeling nervous. "I'm only checking to make sure he's okay, that's all."

She dialed the number and waited nervously for someone to answer. The feminine voice threw her off. She shook her head slightly; of course it was his office. The man did have a job.

"Yes, may I speak to Mr. MaDia please?"

"Who's calling?"

The woman's voice had a hint of possessiveness about it, and for some reason it annoyed her. "Tell him Cassandra Boozer would like to speak to him."

Her fingers had just begun to strum against the back of the chair she was sitting in with a bit more force. She glanced once at her watch. Over three minutes he'd kept her waiting.

"Hello, Cassandra. Is there something I can do for you?"

She almost laughed aloud at the cold formality. After working from mid-morning she was fast losing her patience. He was sulking like a child. "Jez, Blaine, I'm sorry okay. Get over it. Listen, you can come back and finish your training, if you don't mind me being here."

Now it was his shot, she'd apologized and she'd even gone out of her way to invite him over. He should be grateful. She heard him sigh.

"I didn't know you had the authority to say who can and who can't come to the teacher's home."

"Suit yourself. Come or don't. It's your choice."

"You're right, it is."

With that the phone went dead. Of all the nerve. She spun around at the cackling sound behind her. The Mystic was laughing at her.

"Is he coming?" he asked.

"I wouldn't know. He said it's his choice."

The sounds emanating from the Mystic grew louder and more annoying. She'd never heard him laugh this much her entire life.

***

What an annoying woman. Blaine glanced at the phone for the first time since coming to his office. Yet he couldn't deny feeling a lightness that had evaded him.

His appointments were back to back, and for the first time since he began making a living from his gift he'd not felt rewarded. Instead he heard the Mystic's voice in his head, calling him little more than a television.

All day long that was how he'd felt as he relayed messages back and forth through the rift between life and death he had managed to penetrate. Talking to the spirits was different today, it drained him. His smiles to his clients were forced, his words of comfort halfhearted.

Now this half-ass apology from Cassandra and it was as though the sun had decided to shine again. "Estelle," Blaine called to his secretary. "Are we about done? I need to leave."

"We're done." she yelled back.

"Good, he answered her, "I have just one call to make then I'm outta here."

Blaine dialed his mother's number trying hard to think of an excuse that would not be a lie. He didn't need to hear her telling him that being around Cassandra was dangerous, but he didn't want to lie either.

"So you're canceling our date?" Michelle answered the phone, no hello, no waiting to see who was on the other end, no explanation. Blaine smiled. How could she not accept that she was gifted? It was who she was.

"How did you know it was me?" He teased her.

"Nothing special, Blaine, I just knew. I've had the feeling all day that you were going to call and cancel. Am I right?"

"I'm afraid so, there's something I have to do."

"Yeah right."

"Michelle."

"Don't start on me."

Blaine could not help but laugh, she was continuously proving his point. "Michelle, you always know what I'm going to say before I have a chance to say it. And since you know I'm going to ask you to get some training, let's suspend your objections. Let me teach you, even the basic, just how to block your thoughts, okay?"

"Blaine, why don't you go meet Cassandra and leave me alone?"

"Aren't you going to warn me about her?"

"I already have and you didn't listen. Now it's too late."

"What do you mean it's too late?"

"You're already in love with her."

"Why do you think that? I've only known her a few days."

"Are you denying it?" Michelle laughed.

"I'm not confirming it. I just want to know why you think that I do."

"It's in your voice and your energy. I feel it, your happiness, your love."

"Do you approve?"

"Does she love you?"

"She's worried about me."

Blaine waited, while Michelle held the phone, silent. He trusted her, this mother of his that he'd known a little more than a year. She had good instincts; they were proving to be better than his in personal matters. If she said that Cassandra didn't, or wouldn't care about him he would not pursue it. He waited with bated breath wanting to scream at her to hurry.

"She cares for you, Blaine."

At last an answer. "Are you sure?"

"I'm sure." She laughed, "If I wasn't, would it have prevented you from seeing her?"

"No, but I would have made myself control my emotions around her. Are you sure she cares, really and truly? You're not just telling me something you know I want to hear?"

"I would never lie to you," Michelle scolded him. "You're not mistaken in your feelings, she's the one."

"You know what this means don't you? I mean your being able to tune into me and to pick up vibes from Cassandra?"

"Of course I do," Michelle quipped. "Now I'll never be free of your clamoring for me to expand my gift."

"Will you listen to me?"

"One thing at a time, Blaine. Your love life is the issue here, not my gift. I don't plan on making a living at this. And I also don't want another year of chaos in my marriage."

"Michelle?"

"Blaine, go meet Cassandra, she's waiting for you."

He heard the click of the phone. He smiled for a moment at his mother's stubbornness. Then the realization of their situation hit him. He would have to teach her to protect herself whether she wanted to learn or not. But right now she was right. He wanted to see Cassandra.

Chapter Fourteen

In less than an hour Blaine was walking through the front door of the Mystic's home. He didn't bother to knock. The man's home was always open to anyone that cared to enter. That thought had never bothered him in the past. He never worried about his mentor being able to take care of himself. Now he wanted to have him lock his doors.

"So you decided to come?"

With a weary sigh he turned in Cassandra's direction. "Yes." He proceeded past her to the corner where the old man was waiting, smiling at him as one would a favorite child.

"Did you bring dinner?" the old man inquired pointing to the bag and pizza boxes in his arms.

"Well, I know how you are when you become involved in psychic research. I know you don't eat or allow others around you to eat."

For the first time since coming in the room he smiled at Cassandra. He could almost hear the rumbling of her stomach. He could sense her mouth watering from the spicy aroma given off by the pizza.

"Here, help yourself," he shoved the boxes toward her having decided to longer torture her. "I know you're starving."

In less than a second Cassandra had opened one of the boxes and was wolfing down a piece of pepperoni and sausage pizza.

"I bought a vegetable pizza also. I thought you'd want that."

"Not on your life," she mumbled between bites. "This suits me just fine."

Blaine smiled at his teacher holding out the paper bag he carried to the old man.

"I brought you fruit, yogurt and cheeses. I even found some of that wild honey that you're so crazy about."

As the old man rummaged through the bag, Blaine made himself comfortable on the floor next to Cassandra. She was now working on her third slice.

"Mind if I join you?" He watched while she looked up from her eating.

"I'm sorry."

"Don't be. I did owe you a dinner."

"It's just," she gave a sidelong glance at the Mystic. "It's been a long hard day."

"Tell me about it. I know the drill, no eating, no drinking, make yourself strong for the battle."

"What battles did you ever fight?"

"Do you think what I do is easy? Every time I give a lecture there is always a ton of negative energy coming at me. So many people not only don't believe what I do, they want to see me fall on my face, to expose me if you will. And not all the spirits that come through are nice. I face a battle each time I do a reading for people."

"But surely you don't come here, to the teacher before each work day begins."

"No, but he has taught me how to take better care of myself." He nibbled on the pizza. "I wouldn't dare eat junk like this while I'm working." He took another bite and chewed thoughtfully. "I think we'd both better enjoy this pizza. I think it's going to be the last junk food we have for awhile." He glanced at the Mystic, "hopefully we get to celebrate our victory with another pizza."

"We're not fighting together, Blaine. I'm going to get Salvatore to help."

"But…"

"No buts." She stopped eating, full for the moment. "I'm sorry for being such a witch earlier, but that doesn't change my mind. You're not really involved with this. I don't want you to be."

"I am involved, your boyfriend threatened me."

"My friend."

"Whatever. He threatened me and I don't plan to just fade into the background. I want to date you, that is, if you want to date me." He had the grace to add.

"But—"

"You think Salvatore is powerful and dangerous, I get that. Like I said, I'm not going away. But I'm also not a fool. I'm not taking any chances. I plan on doing whatever I have to. This guy will not control my life."

"Blaine."

Blaine glanced toward the Mystic. He'd almost forgotten the old man was still in the room.

"Blaine," the Mystic spoke again, "perhaps you should tell Cassandra of your experience with Salvatore last night."

"I thought you said…"

"Never mind, tell her."

Cassandra was staring at him, a not too friendly look on her face making him feel awkward.

"Yes, tell me what did Sal do to you last night? Remember, I was there. I saw nothing."

"Are you calling me a liar?"

"How can I? You haven't told me anything yet."

Blaine closed his eyes. The woman was really getting on his nerve. Too bad she didn't say that before she was full. He may have been tempted to withhold the pizza until she was nicer. In spite of her annoying smugness, he grinned at her. It was nice to think of all the mean things you would never actually do. It kept one humble.

"You may not have seen him," Blaine said sternly, "but I felt it. He shook my hand and my entire arm turned to ice."

Cassandra couldn't help it. She laughed at Blaine. She had never heard of such nonsense. Sure she sensed power in Sal, but nothing of that magnitude.

"I think Sal took a little trip through your mind. Perhaps he planted the idea there and you thought it was happening. He's good. I have to say that for him?"

"You sound as if you're proud of him," Blaine fumed. "Am I missing something here? Didn't you say this morning that he appeared in your room to spy on you and you were uncomfortable? Are you sure he was there? Are you certain he didn't just put a thought in your mind that he was?"

"I'm not prone to flights of fancy, I'm more—"

"More what, more in tuned, more evolved? Well, Ms. Boozer, you weren't evolved enough last night to see what was going on in front of your face. It was not my imagination, and beside that it wasn't the only thing he did."

"What else?" she smirked knowing her smirk irritated Blaine.

"Cassie," the Mystic reprimanded. "You're being rude again."

"Sorry," she muttered. "Go ahead, Blaine, tell me what Sal did to you in a room filled with people yet no one noticed anything out of place."

"He sent this dark energy cloud toward me."

"Why? If Sal wanted to hurt you he wouldn't have to lay a hand on you."

"I don't know why."

"You know, Blaine, you're making Sal out to be some—I don't know, some psychic vampire."

"They do exist you know."

"Yeah, I know, but Sal's not one of them."

"How do you know? You keep yourself so doped up I'm surprised you even know your own name."

Cassandra was on him in a flash, pummeling him with her fists. Blaine let out a groan of surprise when one punch landed in his jaw. "Damn, stop that."

"Cassie," the Mystic pulled her off Blaine. "Cassie, calm yourself. Blaine, you stop it this instant. Cassie does not take dope."

"I don't care what you call it, she's taking something. It might as well be dope; it turns her into a zombie."

Cassandra stood for a long moment consumed by anger. She gripped Blaine's hand and closed her eyes tightly concentrating on the old man in the room with them.

As abruptly as she had taken his hand, she released it. "Now, you know why I don't want to feel."

Sinking down to the floor Blaine held his head in his hand until finally he was able to look at Cassie and the old man who'd taught him so much. "How long have you known you had cancer?"

"For some time now."

"Why didn't you ever tell me?"

"There was no need for you to know."

"But you're in great pain. I could have helped."

"Do I look like I need help? The two of you have been viewing me all day, thinking that I'm weak and frail. Yes, yes, I've read your thoughts, both of you. Well, I'm old but that's all. I can still handle myself and I can still teach the two of you what you need to know. Now I suggest you makeup and play nice. I need to put this fruit away." He slapped at Blaine's hand as he attempted to do the chore for him. "I can do it."

For several seconds Blaine stood wetting his lips unable to form the words. No wonder he didn't have any luck in relationships, he was too damn blunt.

"I'm sorry," he turned in Cassandra's direction. "I knew of course you were an empath, but to feel what you actually go through. I can understand why you'd want to subdue the feeling."

He didn't know what he expected, but it sure as hell wasn't her laughter or the snarl in her voice when she spoke.

"Do you really think you now know how I feel? My God, Blaine, that was controlled, that was a few moments of feeling someone's pain. Do you know that if I hadn't discovered the herbs, this would be constant? This is not something I can turn on and off. I walk in an elevator and I'm bombarded with the emotions, pains, thoughts and feeling of every single person on there. In a crowd of thousands I become paralyzed with fear and pain. And you say you're sorry for calling me a doper, that you know how I feel." She wiped the back of her hand across her nose feeling her resentment build.

"It's all that I can say." He stared at her, at the tears streaming down her face and the pain she must endure always made his heart ache for her.

"Don't touch me," she warned as he approached, his intentions clear to her.

"Shh," he said as he folded her in his arms. "I'm sorry." He kissed her cheeks, her hair, her earlobes. "I'm sorry," he repeated. He held her tighter as she clung to him, the tears unabated letting go of some of the pain, some of the anger.

"You're right," he whispered into her ear, "compared to you, I am a baby psychic." Her surprised hazel gaze met his own when she turned her tear streaked face to his, her lips slightly parted.

He sure as hell hoped she was inviting him to kiss her because there was no way he could prevent himself from doing so.

Their lips met timidly at first before his hunger for her changed the kiss of comfort into one of passion. There was so much heat in her mouth and Blaine sought her warmth.

He pulled gently on her tongue urging her to participate in an ancient ritual and dance of passion. Their tongues intertwined moving backwards and forwards. Feeling for the bumpy texture sent other sensual changes flooding through his body.

He kissed Cassandra with his eyes open wanting to watch her emotions play across her face. She smiled gently at him then closed her eyes and accepted him fully allowing him another glimpse of what she was capable of feeling. He felt her reaction to his kiss, felt the heat beading between the vee of her thighs. Through her eyes he saw the drops of moisture gathering at the base of her femininity and he felt her stomach muscles clench with awareness and desire.

Never in his life had he ever experienced so intense an emotion. He sensed her drawing back and instantly knew why. She was revealing more than she'd intended. With the pads of his fingers, he traced the nerve endings of her spine and felt the ripple of pleasure. He wanted to know her deepest feelings for him.

She trembled in his arms. "They're my own feelings, Blaine. You have no right to them if I don't want to share them."

He pulled back disappointed, but respecting her wishes. "Does that mean I have to stop kissing you?"

"In the manner you're kissing me, you do."

"Is it always like this for you?" He really wanted to know, he prayed that he was the only man with whom she'd shared such a kiss.

"I've never let anyone feel that part of me, never."

"Not even Salvatore?"

"Not even Sal."

"But you said he kissed you."

"Yes, but I said it made me feel strange. I didn't say I enjoyed it."

"Did you?"

"Blaine, that's none of your business. You have two choices: you can either kiss me again, or you can wait until the teacher comes back and puts a stop to it."

He wasn't dumb, he wanted nothing more than to taste her lips, suck on the nectar that was her. "Easy choice." Blaine whispered.

Once again he was pulled into a fantasy world of desire so intense he could feel it in every cell of his body. Her breath went into his mouth and revitalized him. He was pressed against her, his erection straining for release and he wanted her with every fiber of his being.

"Damn," he muttered hoarsely, "I don't want to do any studying tonight."

"Neither do I."

"I want you," Blaine whispered pressing himself even closer to her if that was at all possible. "Come home with me."

"I told the teacher I would stay here. He's worried about my safety."

"Tell him you're going with me. I'll protect you." He caught a glimpse of the smile she was fighting. "Okay, so I won't protect you, but I will make love to you and make you forget."

"There's a problem there, Blaine."

He halted at the sound of her voice, it was no longer joking or teasing, but tense and he sensed the honesty within those few words.

"What's the problem?"

"I want to be with you, for now anyway. I want to make love to you and I want to do as you said. I want to forget everything, I want to let go completely."

"I don't see a problem with that, I want you to let go also," he leered at her

"But you have to promise me, that you will not take advantage of me."

"I don't understand."

"Shhh, let me finish."

"I want to give to you what I've never given to anyone, my complete self, and if I do that I would be vulnerable to your invading my thoughts. I don't want you doing that, ever. Especially not when we're making love. I have to know I have a safe haven in your arms."

Blaine rubbed his hands back and forth across Cassandra's back willing to give any promise if it would mean he could make love to her, if he could feel what he was actually doing to her body. The thought intrigued him making his already hard flesh jerk forward.

"Are you planning on doing the things you've done to me already?" Again he felt his penis jerk in anticipation. "I mean are you going to share your body responses with me?"

"I don't know, I might, but I just want to make sure if I do you'll only go where I take you, not take advantage of the moment, not try and find out things I don't want you to know."

"I promise."

"Then let's go."

"Does that means you're no longer worried about Salvatore?"

"Let's just say the power of lust is stronger right now than Sal's threats. I hope we don't live to regret our decision though," she ended. "You still game?"

"If this is the way I have to die, then lead me to my death." He tapped Cassandra knowing that like him she'd been so caught up in their discussion that they had not noticed the old teacher was back in the room and was observing them.

"What are you talking about, Blaine? You two are doing so much whispering, I've been straining to make out the words."

Both Blaine and Cassandra laughed at the Mystic knowing that if he wanted he could easily find out the topic of discussion. They respected the fact that he didn't choose to do so.

Cassandra stretched, "I'm sorry, I've really done enough studying for the day. I can't work any longer. How about tomorrow?"

"Actually I'm bushed also," Blaine said, not looking in her direction. "I think we should wait until tomorrow, you know get an early start."

"Don't you have appointments tomorrow?" the old man asked.

Blaine noticed the twinkle in the Mystic's eye. "I do, but I'll get here as soon as I can."

"Then by all means the two of you should get a good night's sleep." He straightened his body into his full height. "Just remember this is not a game and I want the two of you to be extremely careful."

Blaine eyed the Mystic. "You're not going to do any psychic spying are you? I mean..."

"I know very well what you're thinking. I wouldn't dream of peeking. I'm not a voyeur. My only concern is for your safety. You do know that Sal is going to find out. His link with Cassie is strong, you will not be able to keep it from him. Think hard, is this really what you want to do and is it worth it?"

There was a tightening in his groin as well as the one in his throat. The Mystic was right. This wasn't a game. Being with Cassandra for him was worth it, but he wouldn't be the one to answer the question. Blaine's eyes turned toward Cassandra

"I'm through running." Cassandra looked first at Blaine then the Mystic. "I'm going to reclaim my life and that means doing what I want. Yes, Sal will know, but neither my body nor my heart belongs to Sal. It's mine to give to whom I choose. It's worth it."

"Blaine?"

"Blaine," the Mystic called again.

He was stunned, she may not have realized what words she'd spoken, but he'd listened to her. She was not just offering him her body, but her heart as well. "It's worth it," he said softly not wanting to break the spell that was weaving his heart with Cassandra.

Chapter Fifteen

"You're giving me your heart?"

She smiled at him, the words had tumbled out of her mouth without thinking and she'd not had a chance to pull them back in. Saying them felt so natural, so right. What the hell had Blaine MaDia done to her? She felt bewitched, under a spell.

"Don't make more out of my words than they mean."

"I heard you."

"I think you heard what you wanted to hear."

"Maybe. Can you blame me for wanting you to experience the same things I am?"

"Blaine, we're not kids. Love at first sight is a myth, it doesn't happen. We had great sex, that I will admit, and I'll also admit I want to have it again. But it doesn't go any deeper so stop searching."

She watched as he pulled the key from his pocket and opened the door. Without asking he'd known that she didn't want to make love to him at her hotel with Sal in the next room. Chances were they wouldn't live to complete the act.

She entered blinking as he switched on the light, bathing the room in brightness. "I like your home." Cassandra said as she walked around peeking here and there, touching his personal mementoes, feeling his energy in the room.

"Thank you."

Suddenly it all felt awkward, just what the hell were they supposed to do, rip each other's clothes off and race for the bedroom? She was slightly embarrassed. She was behaving like a bitch in heat.

She smiled suddenly, maybe that's why all the eligible psychics had begun turning up at her doorstep, maybe she was sending off some psychic pheromones that were letting them know, psychic in heat, perfect time for creating super baby.

"What are you thinking about?"

Blaine's voice startled her. She'd forgotten for a moment that he was in the room with her waiting to finish what she'd so unashamedly allowed to progress at the Mystic's home. Now that they were alone, she didn't know what to do.

"Cassandra, if you've changed your mind, we don't have to, we can just sit here and talk."

She glanced at Blaine, saw the firmness of his flesh pressed against his pants, the bulge making her want to laugh. Sure talking would be fine with him, still she appreciated the fact that he was willing to say the words.

"Blaine, why don't we sit for a couple of minutes maybe have something to drink?"

"Are you talking about wine, or juice? I don't have any alcohol in the house."

She caught the look in his eyes, he was embarrassed. Do you have a problem with alcohol?"

"No," he answered. "I just like keeping my head clear…not that you don't. I'm just saying…"

"Blaine, it's okay. I know tons of psychics who don't believe in polluting their body. I was just thinking, well don't worry, a glass of water would do."

"Are you sure? I can go out."

"No, Blaine, it just feels as if my throat is suddenly dry." She held her hands in front of her body. "Look at this. I'm shaking like a leaf."

Her gaze caught his and the look he gave started trembling in the tips of her toes. Oh God, she moaned in her head. This man is doing something to me. She watched as he walked toward her. He'd better hurry and get the water or she would explode.

"Cassandra."

"You can call me Cassie," her voice was quivering, "Every one else does."

"Then I won't. I don't want to call you what everyone else does. I want what I call you to be special."

He was standing so close, so very close. God, she was burning up. His fingers touched her check, so gentle, so strong, she was tingling. He began rubbing her face, just that one finger and she felt the heat generated by the friction.

She breathed in pulling lightly on his essence, it was good, his energy bright. "Stop," she warned, she knew what was happening. They were heading for a spiritual mating. Before it had only been physical. There would be no way she would be able to retrieve her emotions if they continued in this vein.

"Blaine, can you feel it?"

"Can I feel the energy surrounding you? Yes, I feel it. I can see your aura glowing?" he smiled at her.

She'd never had anyone tell her that her aura glowed. She wished she could see it. She gazed into Blaine's half closed eyes, the desire stark and raw. He wanted her and the knowledge caused a ripple that went to her soul. She wanted to see what he saw in her.

"You can, you know," he whispered against her lips.

"Can what?" she asked half afraid of the answer.

"You can see what I see in you. Close your eyes and touch me."

"Where?"

"Anywhere."

She thought for a second of what he'd said, she's not felt him enter her mind. Then how did he know what she was thinking. "Blaine, are you reading my thoughts?"

"No, I'm reading your eyes, your body, your face, your emotions are all there. You're so much like my mother." He stopped and smiled.

"I'm sorry," she said for perhaps the tenth time. "Maybe one day you'll introduce me to her."

"Maybe, just not right now. Believe me, my mother is the last person on my mind at the moment."

Cassandra smiled as Blaine's finger dipped into her blouse. Suddenly she was pressed against the wall while volts of electrical currents shot through her. Damn! What was happening? It wasn't like this the first time, or even close.

"Close your eyes, Cassandra, and let go."

She did as she was instructed and with her third eye she saw the pure golden glow surrounding Blaine. She relaxed and saw another energy form entwine with his. It was her own essence, her energy.

She barely noticed that Blaine had removed her blouse. The tiny breeze that ripped through the room cooled her skin, but not nearly enough to put out the heat that he'd started.

He nibbled at her ear, his hands moving downward fanning the flames of her desire. She watched in amazement as together their combined energies blended together and became one. The feelings were indescribable.

"I'm falling in love with you, Cassandra."

She heard his words a moment before he lifted her in his arms and his lips claimed her, swallowing the no, she wanted to say. She remained in his arms feeling his steps, one by one, knowing they were moving toward his bedroom.

She opened her eyes surprised to witness the glassy look in Blaine. "It's too soon for you to know," she managed at last.

"I've waited a lifetime to know."

She watched as their combined energies grew even brighter. She was no longer viewing this through the third eye but through her physical eyes.

"Blaine, stop talking," she moaned. "Just keep touching me." The mattress beneath her was as soft as a cloud. She imagined it becoming a part of her body also. She wanted to feel Blaine inside her, but he was moving too damn slowly.

His lips were moving from her mouth to take her nipple, "Oh God," she screamed out loud, her pelvic muscles tightening. He moved away and smiled knowing what he was doing to her.

"Blaine."

"Hush," he commanded, "just lay back and enjoy."

He didn't have to ask her twice. She clung to him greedily, enjoying the texture of his tongue on her breasts, the slight chill as he blew on the area he'd kissed. She shivered when his tongue tracing liquid fire swept across her belly and dipped into her belly button.

She knew his intentions. She wanted him so badly she could not keep anything from him. For a moment she thought how unprotected she was and it didn't matter. She didn't want a block stopping her from enjoying the deliciousness of the moment.

She spread her legs giving him easy access to his destination. He smiled again at her, his tongue never losing contact with her skin. It was a wonder that he could do what he was doing and undress her at the same time. But he'd not only managed that feat, but excelled at it. When he peeled away her only indulgence, silk panties he looked at her with reverence and bent to place a kiss right above, yes. Oh. God.

He was there, her hips jerked spasmodically as he dove into the center of her body. She wanted to hold on, fought to with every thing she had in her, but from somewhere deep inside the urge to let go became too great.

Their energies had now become one and somewhere in the center of the whiteness was a vivid blue mixed with patches of red. Why not? She thought. She was on fire.

"Blaine," she whispered "I hope you're feeling this. I don't want to make the journey alone, come into me now."

Her body jerked again. There was no way in hell she was going to be able to wait for him.

"Please, Blaine," she begged. "Let's do this together."

He rose from her wiping his mouth with the back of his hand, his face contorted by lust, his energy field so much a part of her she could not tell where she ended and he began.

"Blaine," she was moaning now like a common whore, she didn't care, she wanted him to put out the fire he'd started in her. "Blaine," she writhed on the bed, "hurry."

"Your wish is my command," he said as he lifted her hips from the mattress. He pulled her body forward onto him. His shaft found her center, then the whole of him delved in, plunging deeper and deeper taking her very breath away. He was so hard. She'd never known such firmness. He plunged in and out, each time making her scream when it seemed he would lose contact, and then when he almost had her begging he would be inside her again.

Cassandra wrapped her legs tightly around Blaine's middle. She was determined to hold on. She couldn't bear for him to leave her body, not for even an inch. His sweat was dripping into her face; she licked it away with her tongue.

"Cassandra, I love you," he said once again then lunged himself forward quickening his pace, pounding away harder and harder, her legs cramping from trying to hold on.

She screamed out loud convulsing with the strength of her orgasm and with it went the last of her control. Blaine was inside her physically, spiritually and psychically. They had become one. Her soul touched his and she wept for the sheer joy of the contact.

Bound together, she floated with him into a realm she'd never been before, somewhere she didn't even know existed. She reached out for Blaine, fearful of the intensity of the pleasure rippling through her.

"I'm here," she heard his voice calling to her softly. "I'm here." She had arrived at last to the spot she'd been searching for all her life. He was home or she was, she didn't know which. She only knew their souls had mated, they were joined together for now, for always throughout all eternity.

"Cassandra?"

"Yes."

"Are we still alive?"

"I don't know," she answered, "but if this is death, all I can say is, WOW!!"

Blaine chuckled, at last getting some reality base indications that he was pressing his body into Cassandra, that she still laid beneath him. He felt the quiver of her muscles trying to un-kink.

His arms slid beneath her hips and he flipped her over so that she was now positioned on top. "I'm sorry. I didn't think about how heavy I must be."

"Blaine, the first time we had sex in my hotel, it was wonderful, but it was nothing like this. What the hell happened?"

He laughed at her. "Simple, we fell in love." He brought her head down, kissing her lips, biting her tender flesh. "We didn't have sex, Cassandra, we made love because we are in love."

"But I'm not—"

"Not what? Not in love with me?" He laughed again. "It's too late, I don't believe you. Our spirits joined together, you touched my soul and I touched yours."

"What the hell," Cassandra groaned. "Okay already, I'll admit I feel something for you that I've never felt for anyone else, but I won't go as far as to call it love. I've never been in love, Blaine. So how am I supposed to know that this is?"

"Trust your mind and your heart. Trust me," he whispered before capturing her lips with his teeth. "There is nothing to fear."

Damn. He wished he hadn't said that. He saw the moment the awareness dawned in Cassandra. She rolled off him and curled up at his side.

"What we just experienced may very well have signed both our death warrants."

Tears were in her eyes. That surprised him. "What can Salvatore, or anyone do to us for that matter?"

He watched her, loving her more than ever as she rose up on one elbow a frown creasing her brow, an annoyed look crossing her face.

"I'm not trying to be insulting, Blaine, but the world I live in, was raised in, is far different from yours. Don't you realize that people can be killed literally by the power of the mind? Do you think all the junk on television or in the movies is made up? Hell no. The movie about that kid setting her enemies on fire, Blaine, that happens. In the real world it happens. I know many psychics with the abilities to get inside your head and make it boil until it explodes.

Cassandra exhaled and gave Blaine a sharp look. "When you say they can do nothing to us, make damn sure you're ready to pay the price. What we just had, I wouldn't trade for anything, but make no mistake, I was in no condition to protect you or myself. I was totally and completely open to any and all psychic attacks. I had no defense, Blaine, neither did you. While our souls left our bodies and mated, anyone could have taken control of us. We can't let this happen again."

Blaine's face fell. "You're finally admitting that you love me and you say we can never make love again?"

"First I didn't say that I love you. I said, I don't know what I feel. Second, I have to figure out who's after me. I have to take care of that first. In the meantime I've got to figure out a way to convince Sal you still mean nothing to me."

"Forget it."

"What do you mean? He'll kill you."

"I mean forget it. I'm not hiding and I'm not going to allow Salvatore to control our lives, not now, not ever." He growled playfully at her. "Don't worry I'm a quick study. I'll learn everything the Mystic has to teach me and I'll be the one doing the protecting."

He saw her smile, before she turned her face into the flesh of his belly and began laughing. He tickled her for a few seconds then gathered her in his arms. "Cassandra Boozer, I love you. And I will protect you."

Chapter Sixteen

The spirits were having a devil of a time coming through. Blaine could barely concentrate enough to allow it. His mind remained on Cassandra throughout his appointments.

Her taste tickled his senses and once or twice he'd even made a sexual reference to a client. Both times he'd covered it up and blamed it on the disembodied phantoms. He gave all his clients a free reading, they were thrilled and surprised, but he didn't feel right taking their money, he'd not done his best for them.

Besides Cassandra, he now had the dead scolding him about the dangers he was about to expose himself to. What was the deal? Didn't anyone think he could take care of himself?

Estelle was surprised that all during the day he'd buzzed her and said no charge. Finally she'd poked her head in and asked, "Are you going to be able to pay me this week? I mean, we do have to make money."

"Don't worry," Blaine laughed at her. "Listen, just for today, no fees, okay. I just feel too good to take money for this today."

Estelle had frowned at him. "Are you sure you're all right? Maybe I should call a doctor or something, maybe I should call Michelle."

His mother? He laughed at his secretary and shooed her out of the office. There was one thing the woman had said that made sense though, he should call his mother, tell her that he was in love officially. Tell her that Cassandra loved him in return. After all she'd predicted it. She'd told him he'd find someone.

There were a thousand questions he wanted to ask, mainly if it had been like that with her and Chance. Was it like that for her with Larry?

But she was his mother for heaven's sake. He couldn't ask her about her love life. Could he?

***

The deep masculine voice on the phone startled Blaine. It was a weekday; he'd not expected Larry to be home."

"Hello, Larry, how are you? This is Blaine."

A few moments of silence before Larry answered him, his voice pleasant, but wary.

"I hope I'm not disturbing you or interrupting anything, how are things?"

"Oh fine."

With a bit of amusement Blaine noticed the dip in Larry's voice as the weariness increased. The man was still unsure of him and his motives toward Michelle. Only time would solve that. For now all he could do was make inane conversation. "Good, good, I was wondering if you and Michelle would like to have dinner with me this evening. I have a friend I would like for you to meet."

Again there was hesitation. Blaine didn't know why he'd issued the invitation. Larry was still uncomfortable around him, and he understood. Usually he only invited Michelle out when Larry was at work, or had an evening meeting.

"I think that can be arranged. Let me get Michelle for you."

Blaine was taken aback. He didn't believe Larry had accepted the invitation, surely he could sense that it was a quick excuse that he'd thought of.

As he waited for Michelle to come on the line he attempted to find a way to gracefully get out of the hasty invitation.

"So Blaine, Larry tells me you want us to meet your friend."

"Yeah, I guess so." He didn't try to mask his dismay, and as he'd known she would do, Michelle started laughing.

"Blaine, that's so sweet of you," she cooed. "Larry and I would be happy to meet you for dinner."

"Yeah right," he answered in return. "I know why you're so anxious, you're just plain nosy. You want to get a good look at Cassandra and grill her. But why does Larry want to come? He's not very fond of me, we both know that."

"Well, it's improving. Maybe this will help."

"We'll see."

"Listen, Blaine you've got to have faith and a bit more self control," she chuckled. "Next time don't invite people anywhere if you don't want them to accept. What time and where do you want us to meet you?"

Blaine thought for a moment. Since it appeared he had no choice in the matter, his mother was going to meet the woman he loved, he may as well bring her fully into his life. Let her meet the Mystic also. That should be a real hoot. He could just picture Larry in his expensive suit seated next to a man that wore robes and beads. Oh yeah this should be fun.

"Tell you what, Michelle, let me call you back later with the details." He hesitated not wanting to ask, but not wanting to have to talk to Larry again before the evening.

"Would it be possible for you to call me back here at the office?" Blaine finally said waiting for her to laugh again. It didn't matter he decided as he pushed on. "Call me in, let's say an hour?"

"Sure," Michelle's voice lowered. "You haven't asked her yet have you?"

"No, I haven't, Ms. Smarty. Now would you give me a chance to do that?" He smiled at the sound of his mother's voice teasing him. God how he loved her.

"Call me back." Blaine repeated. He hung up the phone making himself relax. There were times when he talked to Michelle when he was sure the cellular memories were surfacing just from hearing her, and he wouldn't want to let go of her, didn't want to ever sever the contact.

But now he had to call Cassandra and arrange for the two women in his life to meet. He only hoped Cassandra would not spoil the way he was feeling with anymore smart ass comments. Before he could make the call he turned in surprise at the sound of the Mystic's voice strumming though his mind.

"Blaine, are you tuning into our vibrations?"

It was definitely the Mystic's voice. He heard it clear as a bell. Before all that had happened in the last few months he would have doubted his own sanity, now he took everything as truth until it proved otherwise.

"Blaine, listen up. This is practice for Cassandra, she needs it. If you have someone in your office, get rid of them. You have thirty seconds."

Blaine sat in his chair and waited. He didn't need thirty seconds. He was alone. He tried hard to send a message back to his mentor, to let him know he'd received his message, but could tell instantly his thoughts lacked the necessary power.

He felt a slight breeze that carried Cassandra's scent. What the hell? He looked up in awe into her smiling face. "Cassandra, are you really here? I didn't know you had this gift also."

"It's one I've gotten a bit rusty at. Didn't I mention that Sal and I did this all through our childhood? I'm practicing, you don't mind do you?"

"Of course not, he walked toward her, this spirit Cassandra felt just as real as the physical one. She smelled the same, he dipped his mouth toward hers. He wanted to see if she tasted the same. Hmmm. She did.

"Blaine, stop." She pushed at his chest, "this is very serious, I'm working. Hard." She smiled, "now I must return." She looked around the room, "give me something so the teacher will now I was successful."

"I gave you a kiss."

"I mean something tangible." Her eyes looked over the top of his head and his gaze followed.

"A bottle of juice? It's my calling card."

"Good," she answered walking toward the small refrigerator. "I like your office by the way."

"He hadn't realized that she'd never been there. They knew practically nothing about the other, except they had the ability to touch the other's soul and according to Cassandra there wasn't going to be any more soul touching. Blaine cringed. Cassandra was right he would help her study and study as well himself. The sooner they foiled Sal and whoever the hell else, the sooner he could experience her in his arms again.

She was walking toward him a mischievous smile on her face. "I have to go now, just one quick kiss."

He held onto her hand. "I want to ask you something first, would you have dinner with me tonight?"

"Yes," she smiled, "I will."

"Do you mind if my mother joins us?"

Cassandra blinked. "I don't think we're ready to make announcements."

"It's just a dinner, please." He hated adding the please, but to tell his mother Cassandra didn't want to meet her wasn't an option. No way in hell was he prepared to do that. She would doubt all over again that he was making a wise choice in dating her.

"Sure, I'd love to meet her."

"Thanks. One more thing," he ignored her raised brow. "Do you mind if her husband joins us?"

"Your father?"

"No, remember, I told you this." It was obvious she hadn't listened, or in the least that she hadn't taken him seriously.

"My father lives in San Francisco. They're not together because when they found each other in this lifetime, Michelle was married to Larry. They had no choice but to wait for another reincarnation to be together."

"Does her husband, Larry believe this stuff?"

"No."

"What does he think of your relationship with his wife? Does he know you call her your mother?"

"He can't stop the relationship, Michelle wouldn't let him. I'm not sure if he knows that I call her Mom." He bit his lips. "I don't do it all the time anyway, just sometimes it pops out. Most of the time I call her Michelle. But yes, he knows I believe her to be my one true mother."

"He's okay with this?"

"No, but there's nothing he can do. Believe me, I try to stay away from him most of the time."

"Then why the family dinner tonight?"

"I opened my mouth and invited him and he accepted."

She laughed, reminding him of Michelle. She'd laughed also. "Cassandra, I think it might be fun."

"For whom?"

"Well for us. We can laugh about Larry's disbelief later in bed." He reached for her drawing her into his arms.

"Or Larry and I can laugh about you and Michelle. Remember I'm not so sure about this either. The jury is out on this one."

"It's funny that you chose that particular cliché."

"Why?"

"Because Larry's an attorney." Cassandra laughed again and just like that she was gone.

Within seconds the phone rang and Blaine snatched it up. He'd known the Mystic would call. "Will you come?" Blaine asked the old man.

"Why now? I've asked you several times to meet these soul parents of yours and always before you said no, the time wasn't right. I told you your mother's gifted, that she should start training. Again you said no. And now, you want Cassie to meet her and you say yes."

Blaine smiled. "Sir, she has to meet the woman I'm going to marry."

The Mystic didn't answer, making Blaine wonder if he'd heard what he said. "Did you hear me?" he spoke louder making sure the old man would hear.

"Don't shout at me, Blaine. I heard you. But don't count on that. There are too many obstacles in your way. This isn't a game. The entire community will be up in arms over your relationship. Everyone has been waiting for the prophecy to be fulfilled."

"You sound disappointed."

The Mystic's voice brought a chill to Blaine's heart. If he didn't see a future for him and Cassandra... *no*, he amended, that wouldn't matter. It would bother him if the old man would rather she was with Sal but it wouldn't stop him from pursing a relationship with her.

"Do you have someone else in mind?" Blaine inquired keeping his voice low and respectful.

"Don't take offense, Blaine. Cassie loves you, this I know. Allow an old man just a little while to grieve one of his dreams."

Blaine was silent waiting for the man to finish his thoughts.

"When one dream dies another is reborn, cheer up, Blaine. You can't blame me for wondering what powers a baby created by Cassie's genes and someone of equal powers would produce. You're a psychic, tell me, aren't you even a little curious?"

"Not curious enough to give her up." He heard the old man chuckle, yet underneath Blaine still sensed the grief the man felt.

"Blaine, if I were you I still wouldn't count on marrying Cassie, not just yet anyway. She has mentioned no such plans, in fact." The teacher's voice lowered an octave or two. "She's planning on leaving as soon as this is over."

Now it was Blaine's turn to be silent. "Will you come to dinner with us?"

"Cassie told me that you invited Larry as well."

Another chuckle. So far Michelle, Cassandra and the Mystic had laughed at him. He wondered if Larry had laughed at him also.

"Yes, I invited him."

"This should prove to be most interesting," the old man quipped. "I wouldn't miss it for anything, just tell me when and where and I'll be there with bells on."

"I hope you don't mean that literally." Another laugh from the old man.

"Are you saying you disapprove of my wardrobe? Would you like me to look more conventional to meet your mother, a suit perhaps?"

Blaine knew the Mystic was reprimanding him. The chances of the old man even owning a suit were slim at best.

"I'm not asking you to change, just don't go overboard with adding things trying to teach a lesson on tolerance tonight."

"If I did that, then I would be the one who needed the lesson on tolerance. Haven't you been paying attention to anything that I tell you? Aren't you worried about how Cassie might dress?"

Blaine licked his lips, he could care less if Cassandra wore nothing at all, in fact he'd prefer that she didn't.

"Blaine, get your mind out of the gutter."

Blaine laughed, "Cassandra will be just fine."

"Apparently she will be because she isn't going back to her hotel to get any clothes. Sal is there and she doesn't want to run into him, so her attire might surprise you."

"I'm sure it will," Blaine murmured, "I'll be by to pick the two of you up around seven. Will that work for you?"

"It will be fine, just don't put more into this than there is. Blaine... I don't want you hurt."

"You mean by Sal?"

"No, I mean by your heart, be careful."

With that the Mystic hung up the phone and Blaine waited for his next appointment. When his mother called, he would give her the information. They had plenty of time to worry about the bad guys. Tonight he wanted to introduce the woman he was going to marry to his mother. He didn't care what Cassandra or the Mystic said. And he sure as hell didn't care about Sal and the psychic community's input. He would marry Cassandra, and it would happen in this life.

Chapter Seventeen

A smile lit up Blaine's face. Cassandra was dressed in a white silk shirt he thought. He couldn't really be sure because he'd never seen a shirt that came below the knees before. On her head she sported a strange white wrap. He cocked his head to the side and studied her.

"Do you like what you see, or do you disapprove?" Cassie asked in a soft flirty voice.

"Oh I like it," Blaine laughed, "I just don't know what the hell it is. But I like it." He turned his head a slight bit to study her more.

"The teacher said you had no clothes, where did you get this?" His smile broadened. "Don't tell me this belongs to the teacher?" he pointed at her head.

"Let's just say we're mixing a little psychic energy with a little old fashioned voodoo."

"Ahh, I thought what you were wearing looked familiar. Why did you choose that combination?"

"I didn't, but don't worry Blaine—"

"Cassandra, you really believe what you said about me don't you?" Blaine's smile had dropped. He didn't want to feel hurt, not tonight. He forced a smile back on his face and asked again.

"You really believe that I'm a baby psychic?" he sighed. "I could live with that maybe, but now it seems you think I'm ignorant as well." He shook his head and wagged his finger at her in reproach.

"Do you really believe I think voodoo is some evil spell casting ritual?" Blaine asked. "Give me enough credit for having at least studied other religions. I know the origin and the intent."

"Sorry, Blaine."

"You should be." He didn't want to smile at her, but the translucent fabric she was covered in would have drawn a smile of appreciation from him regardless of her words.

"This wasn't necessarily directed at you. But you have to admit there are a lot of psychics who don't know the first thing about voodoo and what it means. I'm pleased that you know they observe a lot of the same principles that other religions believe in."

"And suspended belief for most of the world." Blaine countered. "To believe in psychics, energy, reincarnation, astral travel, bi-location and the casting of spells require suspending belief in the things you were taught."

He looked away for a moment reflecting on his own past. "I've been called a fraud enough times in my life to not hand that label out so easily."

"But everyone says you look down on the psychic community." Cassandra looked away from him preventing her from looking into her eyes.

Blaine smiled in earnest. "I thought you'd never heard of me?" He stood watching the blush cover her face wishing he had time to make love to her to check out the blush over her entire body.

"Well, you were too damn cocky when we met. You behaved as if I was supposed to be impressed that you have a television show, and radio broadcast, that your talking to the dead set you apart somehow from the rest of us, made you better."

"I never intended that to be the impression I gave." Blaine frowned in thoughtful contemplation. "I guess I have been guilty of unfair judging. It was never the people themselves; it's just all the advertising, the blaring neon signs made it so hard for me to be taken seriously." He grinned at Cassandra. "Listen, let's call a truce for tonight and start all over. Cassandra, you look beautiful."

"Thank you, Blaine."

Oh yes, he'd fallen heads over heels in love with her. He stood for a long moment grinning like an idiot, loving the way she said his name. She was now grinning at him. "I love the scarf on your head. I hear it's very effective in covering your crown charka."

The Mystic poked his head around the corner. "Is it safe to come out now? Have the two of you finished fighting?"

Cassandra and Blaine laughed together, reaching their hands out to each other. "We're done," they said in unison. "We've called a truce."

"Good," the old man nodded at them, "I'm surprised you ever managed to fall in love, you're always so busy griping at each other." The man spun around. Done with his pronouncement he tilted his head to the side and issued a dare to Blaine. "Am I conventional enough to meet this mother of your?"

With an arm around the old man's shoulder Blaine shook his head in amusement. "You look great. Conventional, no." He took in the man's sandals, his long flowing robe of purple and gold. He too wore a covering on his head.

He held the door open for his passengers, his curiosity getting the better of him. "Okay, tell me you two, why are you covering your heads? I know what the covers mean, and I'm not objecting to it, it's just," he stopped and looked at the Mystic. "I've never known you to wear one before. Why tonight?"

He almost missed the looks that went between Cassandra and the Mystic. "Trouble right? Sal?" he asked.

"Let's just go enjoy dinner." Cassandra pleaded with him.

This wasn't something he could just let go of. "What happened?"

"Sal did make his presence known briefly. I felt him around the fringes of my consciousness."

"As did I," the Mystic interjected. "Though for what purpose I'm not sure. Salvatore could have easily barged in or just bi-located, he can do that as easily as breathing. He needs no practice."

"Here's an idea, why not something even more conventional like picking up a telephone and dialing the number, or just coming over. I don't like this guy," Blaine fumed.

"You never did."

He sighed again. The Mystic never minced words, just short, sweet and to the point. "Lets forget it for now; at least he didn't stop us from going out."

***

For the most part their drive to the restaurant was uneventful. The Mystic and Cassandra did the bulk of the talking while Blaine alternated between fuming over Sal's interference in their lives and worrying about Michelle's reaction to the both of them. Why the hell hadn't he gotten to know Cassandra better before having a meet the parents' moment? He groaned in exasperation and once again when The Mystic and Cassandra laughed at him without asking what was wrong. Being in the constant presence of psychics could be annoying. This was the first time he could remember hoping for things to go well for him. Generally he rolled with the punches, but this was important. This wasn't something he could just let go of.

He was on edge as he pulled the car into a slot at the restaurant, more nerves jangled as he helped first the Mystic then Cassandra from the car. She smiled and kissed him on the cheek, a sure sign she knew how he was feeling. Then he heard the laughter from the Mystic at the same instant he felt the loving pat on his shoulder

"Blaine, if this mother of yours is all that you believe her to be then I don't think you have a need to worry. Let's go. I'm anxious to meet her. With a couple of deep breaths and a sigh Blaine gave his teacher a timid smile and led the way.

His gaze locked with Michelle's the moment they entered, *LaTanya's House of Soul*. Show-time, he said to himself and clasped Cassandra's hand expecting Michelle to make a beeline toward them. Instead she was looking puzzled at the Mystic.

Bad idea, he thought to himself, hoping his mother would be able to make a quick recovery. Her reaction somewhat surprised him. From Larry he would have expected blatant curiosity, not from Michelle.

It was the opposite, Larry was warm and friendly his glance barely lighting on the old man before going to Cassandra and staying on Blaine.

"It's very nice to see you, Blaine. Cassandra, it's a pleasure meeting you. And, Sir, I didn't catch your name," Larry said smiling at each of them in turn.

"He doesn't use one," Blaine started to explain. "We simply call him the Mystic, or Teacher." He waited for a sign of disapproval from Larry. Nothing. Larry smiled, he actually smiled and said, "Well then, Teacher, it's nice to meet you."

Michelle was still staring at the Mystic with an awed expression on her face. She appeared to have no interest whatsoever in Cassandra. Blaine looked his mentor over, his attire was different, but in LaTanya's, he was not out of place.

Since Michelle's attention was still on the Mystic Blaine looked around the cozy room. The place was a virtual melting pot. The booming business made him smile. His friend LaTanya had earned a Ph.D. in business and now was in the process of making a pile of money. It seemed every endeavor she touched turned to gold.

No, the Mystic was definitely not out of place here. Even Larry accepted the man and was way past cordial, to friendly, seeming to be fascinated with whatever story the man was telling him.

Blaine sidled up to Michelle. He hugged her close in order to whisper. "Stop staring at him like that." He saw his mother blink as though she wasn't aware of her own actions.

"I'm sorry," she murmured, her gaze still fixed determinedly on the old man. At last the Mystic turned in her direction and his face lit up. A smile broke out and he too stared back at Michelle in wonder.

Blaine watched the pair, something strange was going on. It wasn't just general curiosity or rudeness that had kept Michelle's attention, it was something more. *Oh my God,* he thought, don't let this be another soul from her past, Larry will freak.

In that moment Michelle recovered and walked toward the man, taking both his hands in her own. She smiled warmly at him then embraced him as though they were old friends and the old man did likewise. Neither of them said a word but it was obvious the two of them were not strangers.

It was a relief when they were finally seated. Michelle remained unusually quiet, smiling gently in the Mystic's direction most of the evening. None of the grilling of Cassandra was done. In fact the entire evening turned out to be much better than Blaine could have hoped. It was a complete success.

"Hello, Cassie, I've been looking for you."

Blaine turned toward the sound of the voice, not having to see the face to know who the words came from. Damn, damn and double damn. A few more minutes and this would have been a normal family dinner, now it would end as something more.

"Am I interrupting something?" Salvatore looked at everyone at the table holding each of their gazes for a second or two. When his eyes landed on Michelle he tilted his head to the side, and rubbed the palm of his hand while looking at her.

Blaine glanced toward his mother. She was angry, she was glaring at Salvatore. Blaine's own glance went quickly from his mother to Salvatore.

Hell no, he thought and stood up. There was no way he was going to allow Salvatore to hurt Michelle. It was obvious he knew she'd stuck him with a sewing needle.

"Actually the party's over, Sal. Everyone was just leaving."

"Surely Cassie and the teacher can spare a few moments for me," Salvatore grinned. "You might want to see your guests out and join us, Blaine. It might prove interesting."

Salvatore's eyes never left Michelle's face. That more than anything was the reason Blaine gave in to Salvatore's request. Who was he kidding? Blaine mused silently. The man had demanded, not requested.

"Larry, Michelle, it was nice of you to join us. I'll talk to you soon." Blaine said as he moved toward them. He tried to usher the pair out of the room. Halfway to the door Michelle stopped and put her hand against his chest.

"Would you stop pushing me? I can walk." She snapped angrily.

"I'm sorry," Blaine muttered looking down wanting her to run as far and as fast as she could.

"I know who he is, Blaine."

Blaine glanced in Larry's direction. "If you do then you know you need to leave now. Don't worry about me. I'm with the teacher. I'll be alright."

Michelle was frowning. For a moment he didn't think she was going to leave, then Larry tugged her arm and she tilted her face toward him.

"Blaine," Michelle held her arms out as though for a kiss, when he leaned in she whispered in his ear, "I'm ready to learn now." With that she turned and left the restaurant with Larry.

Blaine stood for a full minute looking out the door watching Michelle and Larry make it safely to their car. Putting his mother's life in danger was not the way he'd planned to get her to advance her powers.

His heart stopped as he waited for Larry to start the engine. When it turned over without incident Blaine breathed easier.

"I absolutely positively hate him," he repeated to himself as he walked back to the table to confront Salvatore.

"You seem to have a habit of showing up at dinner as an uninvited guest."

Salvatore smiled in his direction and rubbed his palms, a hidden look in the depth of his eyes. Blaine almost rose to the bait. He wanted to slam his fist into Sal's face, to tell him he'd better stay away from his mother. When the clear realization hit him that Sal didn't know who Michelle really was he calmed himself. Sal was baiting him and he'd almost fell for it.

"Why are you here, Salvatore?"

"Good, MaDia, skip the amenities and the pleasantries. I like that. I'm here to take back something that belongs to me. I came for Cassie."

"You have no right," Blaine growled, "Cassie—"

"Cassie is an adult. She can make up her own mind." Cassandra interrupted Blaine. "I do need to talk with Sal, he'll take me back to the hotel."

"No. You came with me. I'm taking you home." Blaine felt hands on his shoulders. The Mystic was pressing his bony hand into his flesh.

"Sal, why haven't you been to see me?" The Mystic asked the question calmly as he refocused the conversation. Blaine knew it was to give him time to cool off. If he hadn't known it, the teacher's fingers digging into his flesh would have told him. Blaine held his temper determined to get control of his emotions and listened at the conversation that floated around him.

"I've been busy." Salvatore answered the Mystic.

"Too busy to see your old teacher?"

Blaine wanted to shove the old man's hand away. The presence of a calm other than his own entered his body and he found himself relaxing. He was feeling downright giddy. Damn it, the Mystic, Blaine laughed, he didn't care. This feeling was wonderful. Sal and Cassandra both cast glances in his direction. He didn't care.

"Yes, Sal, why have you been such a stranger?" Blaine muttered sarcastically. Blaine felt the old man's grip tighten considerably making him shake his head to clear it. If he didn't know better he'd say someone slipped him a Mickey, he felt higher than a kite. He eyed his glass suspiciously remembering he'd had nothing to eat or drink since Sal's unwanted appearance. His first impression was correct, the teacher had done something to him, was still doing it, he realized as the man's knuckles settled into a sensitive spot.

Ouch, Blaine whispered inside his head, but kept the words silent. He would not allow Salvatore to sense weakness in him.

"Cassie, I've narrowed down the list to three men who could be after you. I think we need to combine our powers and work together before any innocent bystanders get hurt."

Salvatore barely glanced at Blaine, then the Mystic. "No offense, sir, but I think together Cassie and I can handle this."

"As you wish, Salvatore. Should you need my assistance I will be here." The Mystic directed his words to Sal, but his eyes pierced

Cassandra letting all at the table know it was her to whom it was truly offering his assistance.

"Blaine, I'll see you later. Take the teacher home, it's getting late."

He didn't believe her. Cassandra was dismissing him. This was the second time Salvatore had come and she'd chosen him. He watched mutely as she rose from her seat to stand besides Salvatore. *Unfreaking believable.* Blaine's tongue was stuck to the roof of his mouth. He wanted to shout at her to go to hell, but he could barely move and talking was out of the question. What the hell did the Mystic do to him?

It was only after Salvatore and Cassie had left the premises, did Blaine feel the ability of speech return to him. "I don't believe you. What did you do?"

"Save your life and the life of your mother."

The Teacher had the audacity to smile at him.

"Would you like to thank me now?"

Of all the nerve. Thank him? Hell no, he didn't want to thank him. He only wanted to take him home. For a moment Blaine wondered if the teacher had pulled similar tricks on Salvatore, perhaps that was the cause of the tension between the men. Whatever it was, it didn't matter. None of it, not the Mystic, not Salvatore and not Cassandra. At this moment he was so angry that he didn't want to question the Mystic on just how he'd saved his life. More than likely it had something to do with keeping him from putting his foot in his mouth. Damn his temper.

Realization dawned on him. He was lying. His heart plunged the depth of despair. The Mystic mattered a hell of a lot to him. As for Cassandra, he loved her, that wasn't so easily shoved away. He needed psychic training ASAP. He would not lose those he loved to the psychic community, nor would he lose them to whomever was chasing Cassandra. And definitely he wouldn't lose them to the arrogant jerk who claimed to love her. Perhaps he did, but Cassandra wasn't in love with Sal. She loved him. Their souls had mated. No matter what he tried, Salvatore could not break that kind of bond. And Blaine would fight to protect their bond until the last breath left his body.

An evil laugh rang in his ears and gave him chills. It was past time for thinking about studying. Action was required and required immediately.

Chapter Eighteen

Cassandra drove away with Sal, doing her best to keep her mind open, knowing that Sal was gently probing her despite his promise not to. She hated it, hated the feeling that she was a willing accomplice in his violation of her thoughts.

Nevertheless, she sat in his rented car and took it, for Blaine, the Mystic, and for Blaine's mother. She'd seen the way Sal had looked at the woman. If her sitting here with Sal meant he would not harm the people she cared about, she would do it.

Besides, she really did need Sal's help. One villain at a time. First she would do as he'd asked, combine forces until the man who was chasing her had been psychically neutralized, and was no longer a threat. Then she would tend to Salvatore.

"You're thinking of him, Cassie. I can tell."

"Of course you can, Sal. You're probing my mind, and you promised not to."

Laughing Salvatore turned his head in her direction. "I did, didn't I? But you went against our agreement."

"The agreement was, not to keep you out."

"It also included something about your not seeing MaDia."

"No, that was your order, Sal. I decided you can't tell me whom to see."

For a long moment there was laughter, deep, throaty, rich baritone laughter, and despite herself Cassie found her body shivering with the melodic tones.

"No kidding. Sal, you can't tell me who to date."

"I wasn't kidding. You're not to sleep with him again. Am I making myself clear?"

She heard the warning behind the words and her heart went cold. "What the hell happened to you, Salvatore? Why are you behaving like this? I know it's been a long time, but you can't just march back into my life and take it over. You said you came to help me. Damn it, prove it, tell me what to do to end this."

"Do you think it bothers me that you're calling me Salvatore?"

"I don't know you anymore. What's wrong with you?"

"I said I came home to protect you …and other things. Marry me and you'll never have to worry about your safety."

"No, Sal. There has to be another way."

"You're worried about MaDia, that I might do something to him. I wouldn't have ever believed it. Cassie, are you afraid of me?"

Cassandra shifted uncomfortably in the seat not wanting to let him know that somewhere in her heart she feared him.

"Have you become something that I won't like, Sal? Are you now working your gifts to the detriment of others?"

"Ohhh, that sounds so scary," Sal mimicked her, making fun of her fears. "What, do you see, horns coming out of my head? Do you think I'm an evil monster? Maybe I'm working for the forces of darkness."

He laughed. This time she didn't hear the music, just the sinister intent. For just the briefest of seconds she sensed something else about Sal, almost as if someone was inside him, sharing his body.

For the rest of the ride Cassandra remained quiet. She stood meekly alongside Sal as they rode the elevator to her floor.

"I'm staying the night," he said.

"Excuse me." She turned in his direction. "You weren't invited."

"I'm staying the night. I'm going to link with you. When you fall asleep I will be there to protect you, let the bastard try and come in your dreams. I will see him."

"I don't know if I like what you're proposing, you're asking me to willingly turn over my mind to you, to be used as your playground."

"Now you offend me, Cassie. I love you, but be careful. What I suggest is a way to capture this man who would take what's mine. Believe me, when I make love to you, you will be awake and you will beg me for more."

For a fleeting second she thought of Blaine and the connection their souls had made. She could not imagine begging Salvatore. She looked up and Sal was smiling at her.

"Let's try something," he began, "you try and not bring Blaine in your thoughts when we're together and I'll do my best not to probe his mind to find out his biggest fears and use them against him."

He smiled coolly again. "By the way, the woman at the table, the one that glared at me. Who is she?"

"She's a friend of Blaine's."

"Not a relative?"

"No. Blaine is an orphan. Stop it damn you." She slammed her blocks into place and reinforced them with the newest method the Mystic had taught her. "Don't scan me, I'm telling you the truth."

"I know, besides that, I checked MaDia out. But there is more to his relationship with the woman. I felt the connection, and when he jumped up to put himself between me and her, it confirmed it. Maybe he's screwing her also," Sal threw out. "Ever think of that Cassie? Maybe you're not the only one."

"Sal, I wish I knew what happened to you, you're so crude. You were never like this before." Anger propelled her from the elevator and to her room. She attempted to close the door in his face but he merely laughed and walked into her room. She was trying hard not to tremble, not to scream out for help, not to think of anyone else besides Sal.

She stood waiting for an apology. None came, but she caught a glimpse of the boy she'd loved her entire life. In a flash he was gone and this stranger in her friend's body stood looking at her, a smirk on his face.

She watched him as he sauntered toward him, his dark looks brooding, his eyes lit by some inner fire. Her eyes skimmed him and she gasped out loud. She couldn't believe it, the bastard was aroused. Her anger was what he wanted.

As he came closer she could feel something happening in her body, the flushing of her skin, the tingle of excitement. *This is sick*, she thought to herself. *I don't want Sal.*

He stood by her whispering words she didn't understand. They sounded slightly Egyptian, but she wasn't sure. All she wanted at that point was to fall into his arms. His smile was all knowing as if that had been his intention all along.

His hand reached out and with his long slender fingers he caressed the bare flesh of her arms. Her entire body was tingling and she tried hard to stop her body from responding. She attempted to think of Blaine, but couldn't remember what his face looked like.

As the pads of Sal's fingers tantalized her flesh she was aware of the harsh sensation that began at the tips of her toes and was now traveling the entire length of her body.

"Sal, don't," Cassandra whispered weakly into the air, knowing that he was going to kiss her, knowing that she didn't want him to yet her body was leaning into him and her arms wound around his neck.

She kissed him savagely, tears of frustration running down her cheeks. She was burning up with a fearsome desire. "Sal, stop this," she pleaded with him, "it's not right."

"Tell me right now that you don't want me to make love to you and I'll stop," he breathed huskily, his flesh pressed hard against her.

Cassandra closed her eyes and poured everything she had into concentrating. Every block she threw up came crashing down as the moisture from his tongue lapping the underside of her ear steamed her vital organs. She couldn't resist him and God how she wanted to.

She stood under his gaze unable to stop him from unbuttoning her blouse. Within moments he'd popped her breasts out and was licking one after the other furiously. Her limbs were trembling in ecstasy. Her hands clutched his long raven hair. "Sal, Sal," she moaned, "don't."

He stopped and looked into her eyes, with one finger he wiped away a tear, and then he shoved her away from him in disgust. "You're weak."

She buried her face in her hands and sobbed loudly. She felt dirty, her body burned even now from the touch of Salvatore's hands and with almost everything in her she wanted him back, wanted to feel his hardened flesh between her thighs. Despair filled her soul as she continued to weep.

She looked up through the tears to see Salvatore looking at her with disgust. That should have been enough to stop the burning lust she was feeling, but it wasn't. She wanted nothing more than to have him put out the massive fire he'd started in her belly. But somewhere some inner awareness whispered to her, *he'll never be able to quench the fire in your soul. Only one man can do that.*

Once again Sal's arms slipped around her cradling her from the back. Once again she felt his hardness jutting into the flesh of her behind. She knew why he was holding her now, he'd sensed her thinking again of Blaine and he wanted to squash it. For the first time Cassandra believed Salvatore would have no problem getting her into bed. He was right. For a short time he would be able to make her forget Blaine, he would probably also be right about having her shout out his name and beg for more, she was on the verge of doing that. She gritted her teeth cursing herself for having tampered with her powers wishing she were mentally stronger. She gave one last try and felt something Salvatore's hold break enough so she could at least think.

"Take the spell off, Sal, try it without your magic." He withdrew and laughed. After several moments she found the courage to turn toward Sal, her tears now dry.

"Did you think I was going to take you?" His eyes darkened and he looked away over her head.

"That's exactly what you were going to do. And that makes you a liar and a coward." She was betting on his arrogance to make him break his hold completely. The one thing he'd never liked was for anyone, mainly her, to think him a coward. "You said you wanted me to come to you freely." Cassandra countered.

"You're saying you didn't."

"Cut the crap, Sal. You and I both know you put me under some subtle hypnotic spell."

"Cassie, even if that were true no one can be hypnotized to go against their nature. So if you were under my spell you could have broken it any time. Beside, I only did that to show you how much you need me here. I'm so disappointed in you." This time Sal was the one who turned away. "That shit you've been taking has fried your brain. If you can't stand up to me when you're awake, Cassie, how the hell do you ever expect to fight a psychic vampire in your sleep?"

Cassandra sniffled turning her head to the side. "Are you saying you were only testing me?" She knew he was lying but she'd play along. She needed time.

"Yes."

"But I felt your arousal."

"That," Sal laughed at her indulgently as though she were an ignorant child. "I can get my body to cooperate at will. You need to learn to do the same. It may be your only defense."

Cassandra's cheeks were burning. "You're saying you didn't really want me then, that this was all just some learning experience?" She was embarrassed as hell that he'd breeched her defenses so easily. She uttered a prayer that she'd not lost her gifts.

"Exactly, Cassandra." Salvatore turned away from her and walked toward the bathroom. "You need more work than I thought."

Staring at Sal's retreating back for a long moment Cassie was angered at the laughter she heard in the bathroom. Was she a joke to him, just a horny joke?

Damn, Cassandra thought to herself. She'd never wanted to be in love. Before Blaine, she hadn't made love to a man in months. Now it seemed she had an over supply of males, only right now they were both angry and disappointed in her. However one was extremely dangerous and the other she had to protect. She happened to need the help of the dangerous one in order to protect the helpless one.

She pulled her night gown out of the drawer and slowly began to undress, this was Sal after all, and like he said, he didn't want her, not now anyway. Sal was correct. It had been much too easy for whomever it was to come into her dreams. She could still feel the slimy hands on her body if she concentrated enough. She would work with Sal, she would give him access to her mind, let him be her guard. Hell, what did she have to lose? He'd probed almost every thought she'd had already.

There was a tiny stabbing pain over her heart. Something about the whole setup didn't feel right, yet Cassandra wasn't sure what it was. Until she knew, she had no choice but to combine her powers with Sal's.

"Are you ready to begin working?"

Sal was out of the bathroom. She hadn't heard him return, he was stripped down to his boxers, deep purple silk. Once again she felt a tingle of excitement, only this time was worse. She knew he didn't have her under a spell at the moment. But his earlier touching of her before had rekindled the memories of her giving herself to him freely. That was the one bond that she'd been unable to break. They'd been each others first.

Sorry, Blaine, she managed to whisper as she looked away from Sal. I wish you could have been my first in everyway.

***

This wasn't as easy as he'd anticipated. The move from the hotel had become necessary after Salvatore's arrival on the scene.

He'd already lost an entire day trailing Salvatore. Once, he'd almost been caught. If only he'd been able to enter Sal's mind to probe a little, see if he'd slept with Cassie.

He'd figured it out. Everything had to be timed just so, the baby had to be born on October thirty-first. There were only a couple of months left to impregnate Cassie if the baby was to be born this year. And he'd be damned if he waited another year to make this happen.

He had to make a move and make it soon. He'd seen others in town. He'd known automatically they were after Cassie. But they were fools, they hoped to win her affections with flowers and candy and talk of love and the combining of powers for the greater good.

He had no such illusions. Cassandra Boozer would never fall in love with him. That he was aware of. She'd always treated him as some invisible entity, the only smiles he'd ever received from her had been ones of pity when they were children and Salvatore had punched him in the nose drawing blood.

That was the only time she'd ever looked at him. And her pity he didn't need. Besides she'd walked away with Salvatore in the end anyway. He'd heard her gently scolding Salvatore, but still she remained with Sal, always loyal to him, never looking at anyone else.

Well now he had a debt to pay to both of them. He was no longer a loner on the fringes, trying desperately to make friends, to make Cassie fall in love with him. No, he was no longer a boy. He was every bit as powerful as Sal.

She thought she knew Salvatore so well, she thought the rest of them were dangerous, little did she know she'd just delivered her soul willingly into the hands of the devil. Sal wanted to fulfill the prophecy. He wanted the same power the rest of them sought.

He rubbed his hand across the bridge of his nose as though he could still feel the sting from Sal's fist twenty years later. Sal would stop at nothing to be the father of the child of the twenty-second generation of the most powerful psychics and neither would he.

Chapter Nineteen

Pacing had been the first order of business. Then anger at himself for not having better control of his emotions surfaced. That vied with the guilt for having placed his mother in a position where she could now be harmed. If only he'd listened to her warnings. But now as she'd said, he was in love with Cassandra Boozer, the woman who'd helped him to bring the danger into his mother's life. As much as it pained him to admit it, he was woefully unprepared to protect her. And protect her he must. His determination to study with the Mystic was now his primary concern.

Breathing in a cleansing breath he focused his energy to take on the battle. His resolve firmly in place Blaine called Estelle and left a message for her to go into the office the next morning and cancel all his appointment for the next two weeks. He had no time to make contact with the spirit world. Luckily he could shut that part of his brain off when he chose. For now, he had to do what he should have done years before. He had to train and embrace every gift he'd been given. His mother's life depended on it as well as his own.

He wished desperately he could push thoughts of Cassandra from his mind. He knew as long as she was with Sal, she was safe, at least physically.

His job for now was as the Mystic pointed out, to train so when the time came he would be ready. Within seconds of completing his call he heard the Mystic's snort of disgust,

"Blaine, are you done with your call? We've wasted enough time."

The old man's voice blasted him out of his reverie. "Yeah I'm done. Let's get started."

For a long moment Blaine felt the old man was angry with him. He stood watching him, not speaking, his face stern with hard lines, something that Blaine never remembered seeing before.

"What's wrong?" Blaine asked.

"You're too scattered," the old man replied. "If you're going to be able to tune into other's vibrations you must be focused."

That sounded to Blaine like an out and out insult. Didn't anyone think what he did, his work, took focus? He was becoming increasingly annoyed with being treated as a novelty.

"You're too sensitive," the Mystic barked, then sighed.

Blaine could feel his cheeks coloring. "I never felt you entering my mind. How are you able to do that without detection?" he asked.

"Easy, Blaine. You should be able to do that also, secondly you should never be that easy to read."

"But you just said…"

"I know what I said, it's not a contradiction. You should be able to scan anyone's mind without them knowing, but you should never leave your own mind open to such a scan."

Blaine was puzzled. "Are you saying I should be able to scan even Sal without his knowing it?"

"Yes, exactly."

"And are you also saying that Sal would be strong enough to not allow such a thing to occur?"

"Precisely," the Mystic beamed in Blaine direction. "Now you're catching on."

"But you're contradicting yourself."

"Ahh, it may seem so, but there is a method, a window of opportunity when even the most vigilant is susceptible."

"How the hell am I to know when anyone is open? How am I to spot Sal's weakness or whoever the hell's after Cassie? They're all stronger…" he hesitated, not wanting to admit it out loud. "They've had more practice in this area."

Again the Mystic beamed. Blaine didn't get it. How could the old man smile at a time like this? Maybe he really was becoming senile.

"No, not yet," the Teacher replied to Blaine's thought. He chucked before continuing. "I will let you in on a little secret. Your innocence will work in your favor. No one, and I mean no one will suspect that you can do this. They've written you off as not a threat. They will not be looking for this from you."

"Okay, I can get on board with that. But tell me, what good will it do me to learn to scan without detection? I don't have a laser beam in my eye. I can't blast people with the power of thought."

"Oh but you can my innocent son."

Blaine looked at the old man. "Are we talking about killing someone, I mean literally taking someone's life?"

The Mystic walked away from Blaine, he appeared to be deep in thought before he turned back.

"Do you know at this very moment four psychics are contemplating ending your life?"

"How do you know that?"

"I tuned into the energy of the higher consciousness, their thoughts are a part of that consciousness, so I heard."

"You're just saying that."

The man smiled, his face looked sad. Blaine watched while the old man walked back toward him stopping inches from his face.

"Blaine, you must be prepared to do whatever is necessary."

"I have no plans on…you know. I think this is getting out of hand. Maybe we should just go to the police."

"And tell them what? 'Someone is thinking bad thoughts about me. They might even wish that I were dead." He laughed. "What do you think they can do? You must listen to me and be prepared to defend yourself even if it means taking another's life to save your own."

"I won't go that far." Blaine answered.

"If you refuse you leave me with no choice."

Blaine glared at the teacher. "And that choice would be?" He already knew the answer, he just wanted to hear the Mystic say it.

"Blaine, you have a secret weapon at your disposal. Use it. Use her. She wants to help."

"You're talking about my mother. I'm not bringing her into this mess."

"Blaine, she's extremely gifted."

"She's had no training. Besides, I seem to be the only one she's connected with. Her gifts are in evidence when it comes to me." Blaine remembered the strange way Michelle had reacted to the Mystic and he to her.

"You know my mother, don't you? What is this, some past life reunion? Who is she to you and how the hell do you know so much about her?"

"Trust me, Blaine, it's not always wise for one to reveal all they know. As for your mother, not only does she have untapped powers, she has powers of the ages with her. And she's remembering. She will be a mighty force to be reckoned with."

"How do you know all of this?"

"Trust me. I know."

"Who are you? I mean really, who are you? How do you know my mother?"

"Who am I? You've known me for over most of your life. I'm your teacher, your mentor. As for your mother," he hunched his shoulders. "I scanned her mind."

"I don't believe you. There's more to the story."

"Perhaps, but now is not the time to tell it. Suffice it to say that with a little training, her powers, along with her full memories of how to use them will be restored and she will be a great ally."

"I don't want to use her. I don't want her hurt." Blaine glared at the old man. "I won't let anyone use her in this war, not even you. My primary goal right now is to protect her."

"What about, Cassandra?"

"She has Salvatore."

"She's going to need you also. And me. And your mother."

"Me, she has. My mother stays out of this."

"What if she decides on her own that she wants in? What can you do to stop her?"

"I'll go to her husband. Larry won't like it and she's not going to jeopardize her marriage for a few moments of playing parlor tricks."

"Blaine," the Mystic voice thundered loud, he was quacking with anger.

"This is not a game. Look at what I did to you in the restaurant, you felt drunk, helpless, and that I did out of love, just imagine if the reverse were true."

That did the trick. Blaine stopped in his tracks ashamed of his earlier reactions to whatever it was the old man had done to him. "Why did you do that anyway?"

"Because Salvatore was looking for a chance to hurt you. He wouldn't have tried anything in front of Cassie, or in my presence but he was observing you. He even scanned your mind, Blaine, and you weren't aware."

"How do you know? I didn't feel anything."

"Because I was there. I shoved him out and I placed an impenetrable barrier there."

"It's not there now."

"Of course not you fool. Even I can sustain something like that for just so long. If Salvatore had not left when he did we both would have been open to him. It takes a lot of concentration to protect the minds of two people at once. Especially from someone as strong as Sal. Now are you ready to begin working, or do you want to keep playing around?"

Blaine knew he should not ask the question, not after the scolding. But he wouldn't be able to work anyway, not with this on his mind, not until someone helped him to make some sense out of it.

"Why did she leave with him? I thought she was beginning to feel something for me. I know she doesn't want to but," he swallowed, his eyes closing against the painful lump in his throat.

"She does love you, Blaine. Don't you understand? She knew as well as I, that she had to get you away from Sal. She didn't want you to blurt anything out about Michelle, nothing to alert him to the fact that she's your soul mother."

"Do I look that stupid?"

"Not stupid, just emotional. And when you use your emotions in battle you will not win. You have to use your mind. You're gifted, extremely so. I didn't know until tonight just how gifted you really are."

"What are you talking about?" Icy tremors ran through his body, all of this had to do with Michelle, his mother but how, how had meeting her alerted the Mystic that Blaine was capable of more?

Blaine looked into the old man's eyes trying hard to fathom the depth, find out his secret. All he got was a deep scowl and a, 'tsk tsk.

"You will find out nothing I don't want you to know. You should know better. In due time all your questions will be answered. For now, let's say you are blessed."

"Blessed?" Blaine cocked his head to the side. "How do you mean that?"

"Blessed to have me for a teacher and to have Michelle for a mother. Furthermore you're blessed to have someone as wonderful as Cassie fall in love with you. Now no more questions, lets begin with something basic. Even you should muster up enough concentration to handle it."

In the twenty-five plus years he'd known the Mystic the old man had never called him stupid. Now in the space of a few days he'd called him every conceivable kind of idiot in the book. If anyone asked his opinion on the teacher's method, he'd have to say he didn't believe that was the way to motivate someone to work.

"But I didn't ask you did I? Now let's begin."

Of course, Blaine thought. The teacher always get the last word.

"That is correct, now hush and concentrate. Close your eyes and envision a bright blue light surrounding your entire body. Let the blue extend about nine inches out in all directions.

"Good, good. Now I see it. Okay, place a white sphere above your head, relax, Blaine, breath deeply. Keep the blue surrounding your body." The teacher was as excited as a little kid. Then the displeasure.

"Don't let the ball touch your head." The old man screamed and nearly broke Blaine's concentration."

"Blaine this is basic kid stuff. Keep the ball above your head. Hmm."

Blaine heard the old man's deep sigh and ignored it. Anyone watching would think this was the first time he'd ever done this particular exercise.

Crack.

What the hell was going on? Blaine's eyes popped wide open. The old man had swatted him with a ten inch thick ruler. Blaine wanted to laugh in spite of the damage done to his pride. "Why did you do that?"

"Because you're losing focus. Your mind was not on your work. Now begin again, go back to the visualization."

The teacher smiled to himself as he observed Blaine's aura. He was intentionally pushing him hard, not praising him, going so far as to insult him. The things he was doing were to make sure when the dust settled Blaine came out of this alive. He was a part of his heart and he'd loved him from the day he'd laid eyes on him. Perhaps he was being a bit too harsh. Maybe he should try a bit of praise.

"Good, good, now let sprinkles of silver fall across your body but be sure to retain the blue barrier." Very good, very good, keep that position for a few moments then breathe deeply and bring your body back slowly, retain the field around you, keep it real."

"How was that?" Blaine asked.

"It wasn't bad."

"Not bad?" Blaine smiled, "I think I did great."

"Don't get too pleased with yourself, you had too much trouble achieving the desired aura and you lacked focus."

"But I did it and I kept it for…" he stopped to look at his watch, "at least ten minutes."

"There still isn't time to pat yourself on the back. That's basic psychic self defense and you had better learn to sustain it for more than ten minutes at a time."

"Will this work against Salvatore?"

"Of course it will, but you need to keep practicing three to four times a day and holding it longer each time."

"So, what's next?"

"We're going to work on your keeping me out."

"Then are you going to check on Cassandra, make sure she's…" Blaine hesitated almost embarrassed to continue. Surely the old man knew he wanted to know if Cassandra was falling for Salvatore's charms. Even if his teacher knew, he'd never say it out loud.

"I mean are you going to check on her just to make sure that nothing's happened to her with Salvatore."

"Blaine, we're not working for the goal to be when you're done you get to barge in on Cassie. I'm not going to be your spy. I'm not going to bilocate to where she's at. And I'm not going to probe her mind."

"I could do it myself."

"Then why don't you?"

"She made me promise not to." Blaine smiled. "She didn't make you promise."

"She didn't have to. She knows I would never invade her privacy without contacting her telepathically and asking for permission."

Blaine should have been chagrinned but he wasn't. It was hard to focus on psychic lessons of mental alertness when all he could think of was Cassandra in Salvatore's arms, maybe even in his bed. He was being childish, he admitted to that, but still the feelings remained with him.

The teacher was watching him, growing disappointment mounting on his face. He smiled sadly and for the first time since they'd begun to study, Blaine felt ashamed. He truly must be a baby physic, or he wouldn't be having so much trouble focusing.

"Blaine, you're not a baby physic, far from it. You just aren't aware yet of your own powers. You've forgotten and now I know that all that is needed is to teach you what you've forgotten. Besides, you're still having some difficulty believing all of this is real and you're too concerned about what Cassie is doing with Sal."

"Would you please stop reading my mind?" Blaine mumbled.

"I wasn't reading your mind but your face. You're feeling down on yourself and you shouldn't be."

The old man sighed. "Salvatore isn't the biggest danger to Cassie, Blaine. He never was."

"Then why?"

"Because at some time you'll have to confront him. But for now he's on our side."

"How can you be so sure?"

"Because while he was scanning your mind, I scanned his for a moment."

"I thought he was too strong to ever allow that to happen."

"He was scattered, his energies partially diverted by his emotions. His jealousy over your relationship with Cassie caused a moment of weakness. Believe me he won't make that mistake again."

The man chuckled and Blaine glared at him. This time he was sure the Mystic was proud of Salvatore.

"You like that he's so strong don't you?"

"A teacher is always pleased when a student excels and passes him."

"But you said he's now evil, so did Cassie. And my mother sensed it as well. How can you still be proud of him?"

"For his accomplishments," the Mystic chuckled low. "Blaine, a parent does not abandon a child when they do something wrong, you feel sorry for that child and responsible for him, especially if you taught him the skills he uses to intimidate others."

"Is that it? You're feeling guilty for having taught Salvatore. If that is true, why are you trying to teach me techniques that can destroy?" He watched in silent contemplation while the old man sat and looked forlorn before answering him.

"Blaine, I love Sal as I love Cassie. I hope none of my children will ever have to face each other in anger, but I'm no fool. There is a real possibility of that and I know it. I also know that Sal is much stronger than you, not by birthright, but by learning, and I don't want you hurt."

Blaine stood back to stare at the teacher wondering how deep his pride in Salvatore went. He hesitated to ask but in the end couldn't resist. "If it comes down to a choice and you can only help one of us, which will it be?"

"You're blood, Blaine."

"What did you say?"

"I said you're like blood to me, a grandson."

"That's not what you said, you didn't use the word like, you said I am. What the hell are you talking about?"

A cold chill swept over him. He was afraid he knew. Somewhere inside of him he'd always known. From the moment he met the Mystic he felt a connection to him that went much deeper than that of friend or teacher. He felt they were blood, now the old man admitted it.

"Blaine, let it go for now, don't even bring the thought into your subconscious. Just know that I love you."

"Because?" Blaine persisted.

"Because you're one of my best students, just like Sal and Cassie. I love them also. Now if you're done with your interrogation of me maybe we can get back to work. Keep me out of your thoughts."

Blaine looked at the old man. A mixture of anger and fear filled him and for the first time in a week he turned his energies inward and concentrated only on the spirits that were desperately trying to come through. The Mystic disappeared as did thoughts of Cassandra and Salvatore. He listened only to the voices that had comforted him for as long as he lived.

As he listened he hardened his heart against the Mystic. The man had always known the amount of pain he carried not feeling wanted, not having any family and he'd never said one word, not one blessed word.

A surge of energy entered him and he fortified his mind. His teacher would never enter again unnoticed. He would make damn sure of that.

***

Four hours later it was the Mystic who called a halt to their studies. He was tired. A few hours before, Blaine would have insisted the old man retire and get some rest, now he taunted him.

"What's the matter old man? Is it getting to be a little rough for you?"

The Mystic stopped in his tracks, his shoulders slightly bent and turned toward Blaine. "Why the hostilities?"

"All this time you knew and you never said a word."

"I didn't know until last night, until I...until... I met your mother."

"You had to have suspected."

"I didn't know. Are you going to blame me for not knowing? What could I have done differently? I could not have loved you more than I already did. Blood made no difference. Have you ever felt there was a time I didn't love you?"

"I could have had a family."

"Blaine, I didn't know for certain." Tears sprang to the old man's eyes as he amended his words. "I was never sure. How was I going to tell you what I suspected?"

"That's why you wanted to meet my mother."

"That was one of the reasons. I suspected it, but you never wanted me to meet her, and I respected your wishes."

Tears were falling down Blaine's cheeks unchecked. "Just say the words. Tell me that my mother is your daughter."

"You already know that, Blaine."

"I want to hear you say it."

"Fine, the woman you know as Michelle, your soul mother is my daughter. Only in our lifetimes together she was not Michelle, nor was she this, Dimitra that she was when she gave birth to you. She was called Dharma. I named her."

"You named her Dharma?"

"Yes, it means dedication and reason to live. She was my reason for living, she was my pride and joy for many lifetimes. It also means, meaning of life and she gave my life meaning."

"Is she the one you kept trying to find each lifetime?"

"Yes, but after she no longer wanted it, I never could. I don't know what happened. I always retained my memories and for many lifetimes so did she. Several times she was reborn as my daughter. And always in each new life, I named her Dharma."

The old man smiled and Blaine could see that he was getting lost in his memories. He didn't want that, not now. He wanted to know more. He threw a pillow against the couch and gestured toward the teacher to sit. "Please," he added. "I want to know how you managed to lose touch."

"I don't know," the Mystic replied sadly. "The last life we shared there were great debates and ill feelings against psychic, seers. We were called evil, wicked and people became afraid of us and shunned us. My daughter wanted to live a normal life. She was so powerful. She was wonderful. How I envied her, her control and her accuracy. Lots of what I know today I learned from her several lifetimes ago."

"Then tell me why you retained your memories and she didn't."

"That one's easy. I wanted to. I was never ashamed of having been given a gift. I never believed that I had to conform. I always knew that we were all a part of the total consciousness of God and that life never dies but continue. I did extensive soul travel to imprint it on my soul, who and what I was. By the age of three I always regained everything and it was that way with your mother for many lifetimes. The last time we were together she had no idea who I was and thought I was nuts. I believe she would have turned me in as a heretic had I not escaped. Since then I've always hoped and prayed to find her again and that she would want to remember."

Blaine looked in the old man's direction. "So that's what was going on in the restaurant. Michelle remembers you."

"Yes."

"Why now?"

"I think it has something to do with you. I think she wanted so badly to find you that her soul opened up and she's now ready to reconnect with her powers and hopefully with her true father."

"Wow." Blaine sat back in amazement. "I don't know what to say. Didn't she ever have any other children?"

"Not in the lifetimes we were together. Her husband who I suspect is the same man she found again, this soul father of yours—I have a hunch that the two of them were so much in love they had no room in their lives for a child until you."

"And then I killed her."

"What are you talking about?" The Mystic looked puzzled for a moment. "You mean her dying shortly after giving birth."

"Yeah, if they had continued their habit of not having children she would have finished that lifetime as Dimitra. She would have lived to be old with Jeremy."

"That's nonsense. Both of them must have really wanted you or they would not have had you, simple as that. Anyway it's her love for you that's brought her back to her soul's path. She loves you fiercely."

"That's why you said I wasn't a baby psychic?"

"That I've always known. Of course then I didn't know your true parentage." He rubbed his lips his look turning serious. "You know what this means. I hope you can keep this to yourself. You may have the lineage, but you lack the discipline. If word of this gets out before we're ready we're all going to be in trouble."

Blaine frowned.

"Blaine, don't you understand?" the old man explained patiently. "You could very well be able to produce the twenty-second generation baby with Cassie."

"But how?"

"For at least seventeen lifetimes your mother has been a powerful psychic, now in this one I sense it. So she could very well have lived through several more lifetimes without being aware of her gift. When she bequeathed you with her gifts...," He thought a moment. "You could very well have the gifts in this lifetime of the twenty-first generation psychic we've all been waiting for.

"I thought this prophecy thing had to be different generations, not the same person reincarnated."

"So did I, but think about it for a moment. What if it's one person living each lifetime themselves and at the right moment passing the banner so to speak to a new generation that will herald in the long awaited prophecy?"

"You're saying I could be a twenty-first generation psychic?"

"Precisely and your child could be the one that was talked about."

Blaine laughed out loud. "I don't believe this." He thought of Cassandra's condescending tone when they first met and of Salvatore. "You're saying I'm in the same league with Cassandra and Salvatore, right?"

"I'm saying you have the ability to exceed them. But Sal has spent his entire life studying. I don't know if we have time for you to cram."

Blaine laughed. "In your face, Salvatore."

The old man paused frowning in Blaine's direction. "Blaine, don't get so cocky. I would love to become reacquainted with my daughter before you blow her cover."

"I would never do that."

"Not intentionally but just then I saw the pride in your eyes. The same way Salvatore let down his defenses and allowed me to enter his mind because of his jealousy over you, you could allow pride to do the same. Now good night. I'm going to bed, try and put this out of your mind for now."

"One more question, please."

"One more only."

"Is that why you helped me with the amulets for Michelle and Chance? You wanted to see them find each other again?"

"No. Remember, Blaine, at the time, I didn't know. Even if she had not been my Dharma, I would have helped you. It's extremely rare for souls to find each other and know it. I wanted to give them every opportunity."

Blaine rubbed at the bracelet he wore on his arm looking the old man in the eye. "What did you do to these, to ensure we'd find each other?"

The Mystic smiled. "An ancient ritual that I won't tell you about now. I will tell you that I imprinted my soul on each item."

"Why?"

"Because I hoped that they were who I thought, and by imprinting my soul it would contain blueprints of theirs from all the lifetimes we spent together. And of yours," he smiled at Blaine. "We're blood."

"What if you had been wrong?"

"Their own souls were imprinted also, so if I was wrong they would still find each other."

Blaine stood reaching out a hand to help the old man from his cramped sitting position. "Do you think that's why my mother recognized you in the restaurant? She's been wearing that necklace with your soul blueprint for months."

"Perhaps." The Mystic smiled.

"So...you...?"

"Enough for one night, Blaine. I'm going to bed."

And so he did.

Chapter Twenty

Something was amiss. Cassie's eyes opened as she mentally shook herself trying to free herself from what appeared to be a tangle of strong vines.

With her eyes now opened she realized the strong vines were Salvatore's arms and legs thrown over her. For one long moment she lay still watching him sleep, separating her thoughts from his with the feeling they'd shared more than she intended.

He smelled good, even after sleeping he reeked of an exotic scent that could not be duplicated. It was not bottled but strictly Sal. She observed his strong features, his thick, dark hair, and the waves fighting with the natural curls for dominance. He was one beautiful man.

Her heart quickened. It would be easy to imagine herself in his arms night after night making love to him, having his babies. She loved him and he loved her, why not give him the baby everyone was clamoring for?

Baby. That's it. She grabbed a handful of Sal's beautiful dark hair and yanked with all her might. "Get the hell out of my mind, Sal."

He smiled sleepily turning toward her. She was right, he'd planted that damn thought.

"Good morning."

"Don't you good morning me. What the hell did you think you were doing?"

"Come on, Cassie," Sal unfurled his long body and pulled Cassandra into his arms. "You act as if this is the first time we've ever slept together."

He practically purred. She couldn't believe it "Don't say it like that. We've never…never done anything but sleep. Not since…not since. That was a long time ago. Now let me go or you're not going to have to worry about ever having kids."

She felt his lips brush the back of her neck and his hands push their way under her nightgown. For one long moment his fingers caressed her body before moving downward and making a home between her legs. She was trembling. Even she didn't know if it was from fear or desire.

"No, Sal."

He kissed the back of her neck again and moved his hand away. "You're not my prisoner."

Cassandra shook her head slightly to toss the hair out of her face. True Sal was no longer holding her, but he'd used the wrong word. She was his prisoner, something had happened to them during the night to make her that. With great reluctance she moved away from him. Her body was craving his touch and her mind was quickly following suit.

"What did you do to me, Sal?"

"What are you talking about?"

So that's the way he wanted to play it. He wanted to make her say it. Then when she did he would pretend it never happened.

"I feel like I've been drugged."

Sal laughed and rolled on his side to peer out at her from beneath his long silky lashes. He tried for a look of innocence but Cassie wasn't fooled. Alright, two could play that game. She would pretend as well, she'd ask only about the night's experiment.

"Did the bridge work, did anyone try anything?" She asked softly, keeping her tone flat.

"Not last night, but I did pick up some interesting tidbits. You made love with MaDia again. I warned you not to."

"Warned me, you warned me? Who the hell do you think you are?" Cassie was angry now, no longer afraid of what Sal would do to Blaine. She'd deal with that later. She threw the covers back with a flourish.

"Sal, you don't own my body."

A chuckle greeted her. Sal was now on his back smiling at her, an amused look on his handsome face. "What did you do to me, Sal?"

"I think the question should be, what did you do to yourself? I think those herbs or whatever the hell you concocted has made you delusional."

Cassandra could feel her face coloring. She'd never felt the need to defend having made the potion. The Mystic had understood. Even if he hadn't, well so be it. She looked at Sal and now she almost felt ashamed of having tried to protect her psyche.

"I didn't have a choice."

"There's always a choice, you just weren't interested in finding it. You took the easy way out. You drugged yourself until you lost the ability to think. Now you want to blame me that you feel something for me, that Blaine MaDia just might not be the right man for you. So it's easier to say I planted that thought there."

"I don't doubt that you would, you put the bridge there. You weren't supposed to go into my memories, only be there to guard my dreams."

"I didn't go into your memories. You dreamt of him."

Cassie stopped, she didn't remember doing that. She was becoming confused, not knowing what was real or what wasn't.

"Do you think I'll get my full powers back?" She asked suddenly frightened and missing the comfort of having her powers at her disposal. She didn't like the feeling of having her senses scrambled. Even with the herbs she'd never felt this disarmed.

"Not in time." Sal got out of the bed and walked to stand beside her. "I've seen several men in town who could possibly be after you." He smiled. "I believe I dissuaded a couple."

"What did you do?"

"Don't worry. It was nothing permanent. They knew the risks they were taking. They knew I would be here to protect you, that I would never let them near you."

She frowned. "If you're here to protect me from them, Sal, tell me who's going to protect me from you?"

***

Waking with a start he rubbed his eyes and attempted to focus. "Something's wrong." Blaine sat on the lumpy sofa and repeated his thoughts to himself. The old man hadn't bothered to answer.

His eyes closed involuntary and he used his fingers to pry them open. He would not bi-locate to Cassandra's room. "Damn," he muttered aloud.

"You're doing better, Blaine."

Blaine turned to look at the teacher. "I thought you were sleeping."

"No. I've been observing you, waiting for you to sense something, waiting to see if you made the right choice."

"Did I?"

"You're still sitting here; you didn't invade Cassie's privacy. I'd say you made the honorable decision."

"Then tell me," Blaine glared at the old man. "Why do I feel so damn lousy?"

"Because you're jealous, Blaine, but you're learning more control over your emotions. That's going to be important. Now I'll put your mind at ease. I'll contact Cassie."

"You're going to bi-locate?" Blaine asked in surprise.

"No, I'm going to use the telephone." The teacher laughed as he made his way to the phone.

Within a matter of minutes the Mystic returned and smiled at Blaine. "Cassie's fine. She's coming over."

"Good," Blaine answered and stretched his legs out in front of him. He could relax at last.

"Sal's coming also." He heard the Mystic's words as his body tensed and the long sought peace evaporated. He needed a shower and he needed a caffeine fix to be able to abide being in the room with Salvatore. As soon as he'd showered he made a dash for the nearest restaurant and had several cups of coffee before returning to the Mystic and his admonitions for him to behave.

***

"They're here."

"And you want me to do what exactly?" Blaine's response to the Mystic was less than respectful. The old man had told him earlier to get out of his snit and he'd tried. But it was difficult to ignore that the woman he'd fallen in love with had spent the night with another man, that she trusted someone other than him to protect her. Maybe he should tell her that he possessed the blood line as well as Sal.

"Blaine," the Mystic put his hands on his shoulder to stop his pacing.

"Please put all thoughts of the things we talked about out of your mind. You're not ready and neither is Michelle. Don't allow Sal to find out about her."

"I don't know if I can stop him."

"Don't be afraid," the teacher answered him. "You're much better than you think. Just remember while Sal is here you must remain on guard. The moment you feel him begin to probe, throw up a block."

"What if it's too late?"

"Then I will help you. Don't worry, I'll keep my eyes on Sal." With that he went to open the door that was never locked.

While fighting for dominance over his emotions he continued to pace. Hearing Cassandra's voice as she greeted the Mystic annoyed him and took him from his course. Patience had never been his strong suit. Her scent hit his nostril and a blinding rage overtook him. "Did you get much work done?" Blaine spoke to Cassandra unable to keep the accusation out of his voice.

"Some," she answered him, but he noticed she wouldn't look at him. He was right. Something was wrong.

"Well, MaDia, good morning, didn't know you'd be here." Salvatore smiled at him and Blaine wanted to knock his perfect teeth out and not with psychic energies. He felt a small tingle and threw his blocks into place glaring in Salvatore's direction.

The man laughed at him and walked by Cassandra allowing his hand to casually caress her body. Two fingers lingered on her hips and she didn't bother to remove them.

Blaine was fuming. He wanted nothing more than to remove Salvatore's hand personally. He took a step in his direction and stumbled slightly. It felt as if a hot poker was stabbing him in the foot. He glanced at Salvatore who was smirking at him then over at the Mystic. The Mystic's face carried a warning and Blaine knew it had been his mentor's way of telling him to stop.

"Cassandra, we need to talk."

"Not now, Blaine, maybe later."

Her eyes wouldn't meet his. He wanted to leave all of them alone, together. The teacher who thought he was too impulsive, the master psychic who viewed him as a joke, and the woman he loved who viewed him as, what? He didn't know.

Salvatore was smiling at him his hand still touching Cassandra. Blaine fought down the demons that battled within his body. He would not concede so early in the game. With all his energies directed on the task, he regained a little self control. "Nice to see you again, Salvatore."

"I'll bet it is." Sal laughed and walked toward Blaine his hand held out in greeting.

Blaine's head dipped to the side and he eyed Salvatore warily. The man was testing him, but he didn't give a damn he was not about to shake hands with him again.

"If the two of you are finished with your pissing contest, maybe we can put our heads together and come up with a plan not only to find out who's after Cassie, but how we can combine our powers to protect her."

The Mystic glared first at Sal then Blaine. "For now this is a team effort. The two of you can behave as dogs fighting over a bone when this nasty business is over."

Blaine bristled. He didn't like being reprimanded, and especially in front of that obnoxious jerk who kept looking at Cassandra with open lust.

"I'll put my feelings aside if everyone else will," Blaine offered, wanting for once not to appear to be the immature one in Cassandra's eyes.

Sal grinned at him. Blaine could easily see why Cassandra or any other woman for that matter would be seduced. The man looked like some Egyptian god come to life. The glances he bestowed on Cassandra were adoring and filled with a promise. A promise Blaine hoped he'd never get to keep.

"There is no animosity in my heart, Teacher." Sal drawled before looking toward Cassie. "I want to keep Cassie safe, and her new little playmate as well. I am curious as to how he can help us though. Is he going to call on the spirit of the dead to combat the living?"

That did it. "Why you arrogant, pretentious, egotistical son of a…"

"Blaine, stop it."

The agony of betrayal washed over him as he looked down at Cassandra, at her chocolate eyes and he moaned inwardly. She'd all but ignored him and now she chose to scold him. Blaine pushed her hand from his arms, disappointment mounting in his heart.

When he dared to look toward Salvatore the man was lounging against a pillow, Blaine's remark not seeming to have made the tinniest dent. He glared in Salvatore's general direction until he looked up and caught Blaine's gaze and hunched his shoulders.

"Blaine, I didn't know you would take offense to that remark. Sal said feigning innocence. "That is what you do for a living isn't it? I've seen you on television and I've heard about you from others. Are you ashamed of what you do, Mr. MaDia?"

Who did he think he was fooling with this act? Blaine glanced toward the Mystic and found his mentor's face furrowed in disappointment. Cassandra's, well her expression was hard to read. Okay, so maybe he'd fallen a little too quickly. He'd been warned of the relationship between the two, and now when the chips were down he saw who she wanted. He would stay and help. But to hell with his feelings for her. To hell with loving her. To hell with Cassandra Boozer.

Chapter Twenty-One

Hour after hour Blaine sat listening as Salvatore took the role of teacher, training them of things even the Mystic was not aware of. Every few minutes he endured Salvatore's cutting remarks framed as genuine concern. I'm not going too fast for you am I, Blaine? MaDia, do you understand this concept? Blaine, would you like to try building a golden bridge? That's good, MaDia, you're learning."

Blaine didn't know which he hated more, the man's condescending tone or his patronizing manner. If he didn't have his own reasons for staying, he may have left the three of them to find the villain on their on. None of them seemed to need him in the least anyway.

The Mystic was obviously impressed with the knowledge Salvatore had managed to pick up. Could he be that easily swayed by psychic powers that he no longer sensed the man's evil intent? A better question was did either of them really believe Salvatore was imparting all the information he knew.

"Blaine, have you ever heard of the phrase, bi-location?"

Salvatore's drawling voice was pulling him, making him aware of the painful situation he'd found himself in. He couldn't help but think back on the past couple of weeks when he'd woke to find his home on fire. Being there was preferable at the moment to being in the room with Salvatore Sharif. Did he really look that big a fool that the man would dare to ask him such a simple question? Even a novice knew the meaning. Before Blaine could answer, Salvatore smiled at him and began explaining.

"Bi-location is the ability to be in two places at once. There are even novices who are able to manage this and are unaware that their spirit or astral body has left their physical body and done some traveling.

"Of course I don't imagine that you would have had much use for this gift. I mean no offense, but again, you do deal primarily with the dead." Salvatore laughed.

Blaine decided to play along, be the buffoon in Sal's little side show. "What's the good of being in two places at once?" he asked.

"Well, say someone wanted to commit a murder, they could very easily have an airtight alibi and send their astral body to do the deed."

Blaine wasn't blind or deaf; the man had issued a threat, or a warning. What the hell was he doing and why were Cassandra and the teacher sitting as though he'd said nothing? Okay, he'd still play. "Is that the only thing it's good for?" Salvatore laughed. The sound of his voice grated on Blaine's nerve.

"There are many reasons why a person would do it. Cassie and I did it a million times as children, just to be close to each other, to feel each other's warmth."

Blaine watched as Salvatore's hand slid over to Cassandra. He continued talking without missing a beat. And Blaine wanted nothing more than to wipe the smugness off of the man's handsome face. Well there was something else he wanted but he couldn't have it. He wanted to wipe away Cassandra's memories of Salvatore, to have the two of them never to have shared a past. He wanted to replace himself in all the images she had of Salvatore.

"We did it to comfort each other when we were in pain." Salvatore continued. "We shared our baths, our food and our beds. We shared our hearts."

Salvatore stopped talking and the air hummed with energy. Virulent male sexual energy. Our bond can never be broken he said softly gazing at Cassandra with obvious love.

A private look passed between Cassandra and Salvatore and it strengthened Blaine's resolve. Oh yeah, when this thing was over he would put Cassandra the hell out of his life.

A fragile feminine energy tugged on the fringes of his consciousness and he heard her whispered words. "Let it go."

He didn't want to hear any more of her thoughts. Her eyes were fastened on Salvatore while her mind whispered sweetly to him. What kind of woman was she?

Blaine tore his eyes from her. How much of this was he supposed to endure? It was taking the good sport thing to a new level, one he could no longer maintain.

"Listen, like you said, Salvatore," Blaine bit the words off. "You're all a little more familiar with psychic self defense and psychic battle than I am. I think I might be making your lessons go slower, so maybe I should call it a day, see you all tomorrow."

"Blaine, we need you here, four of us working together will be stronger."

Blaine turned toward the Mystic, not this time. The old man would not shame him into staying. He'd not spoken up before, not one word in Blaine's defense.

"I'm sorry sir, but as Salvatore has kindly pointed out I make my living talking to the dead. And if I don't tend to my clients, then I'm out of a job."

"You took two weeks off, Blaine. I know that."

Sal was smirking at him. Why was the Mystic embarrassing him like this? Why couldn't he just let it go? He needed to talk to Michelle, to his mother. She was his only constant.

"I enjoyed meeting Michelle last night. Who is she?"

Blaine glared at Salvatore. The bastard had invaded his mind, read his thoughts. He then glared at the Mystic, he was supposed to help. He saw the Mystic returning his glare and heard his words. "You were warned to keep up your defenses."

Enough with the games. "It's none of your damn business who she is." Blaine retorted.

"Temper, temper," Salvatore laughed. "I was just asking a polite question."

"Nothing about you is polite and I'm sick of sitting here playing these games. I know you're holding back on us. You probably already know who's after Cassandra if it's not you. And I'm not so convinced that it isn't. You'll stay the fuck out of my mind, or so help me, I'll—"

"You'll what? You're no match for me either physically or psychically. What do you plan to do, get a few ghosts to scare me? Ohhh, I'm so scared."

Salvatore rose from his lotus position, his height impressive, his dark brooding looks intimidating. Before Blaine had a moment to think, he felt Sal's hands around his throat squeezing the life out of him. He could feel it coming, he was about to black out yet Salvatore was standing several feet from him, his arms at his side.

He thought of Michelle. *Mom, I'm sorry I didn't listen*, Blaine whispered to his soul and instantly felt Sal's fingers being pried from his throat. Blaine coughed several times, rubbing his neck with his hand knowing very well that now Sal knew. He'd led him to her. He shouldn't have thought of her either before or when he felt Sal's fingers squeezing him.

Now Salvatore was standing there, a Cheshire cat look on his face. "So we have another psychic in the mix." Sal laughed loudly. "This just keeps getting better."

Blaine turned toward Cassandra who looked at him with tear filled eyes before glancing toward the Mystic who glared at him with the first true anger Blaine could remember. And it made him tremble. What had he done? Oh God, what had he done?

***

She answered the door before he could ring the bell. "Mom, I'm sorry, he knows who you are."

"Don't be," Michelle answered. "He would have found out sooner or later anyway."

Blaine was angry, his anger turned inward on himself. "He baited me for hours. Like a fool I caved. I gave in and I led him straight to you?"

"Blaine, its okay, don't worry about it." His mother tilted his chin toward her. "I'm only glad I could help. But I don't think he intended to actually hurt you. He wanted to prove to himself that I was the one who interfered before. I was unable to let it play out. He was hurting you and I couldn't just sit back and allow it. We both reacted the way he knew that we would."

Blaine touched the pads of his fingers to his neck. "Yeah I got the same feeling. He laughed at me."

"And probably at me," Michelle admitted.

Blaine allowed the anger to fester, to fill his veins with its energy. "I didn't want to involve you. I wanted to protect you, make sure he never knew of your true connection." Now he looked downward. "Maybe it would have been better if I had never gotten involved."

"You knew didn't you?" Blaine brought his eyes upward remembering, you can see into the future. That's why you warned me not to become involved with Cassandra. You knew what was going to happen. Why didn't you tell me?"

"Blaine, I thought for a time I was going crazy. I hated having visions. I hated even more having them come true. I had convinced myself they were only dreams until that day I found you. After finding you I had no choice but to admit to myself what was happening. I just didn't want anyone else to know."

"Why not me?" Blaine almost moaned. "I told you how my life had been, how lonely I'd been as a child, how people thought I was crazy. Why didn't you ever tell me then you had went through the same thing?"

"I told you that I couldn't go through what you did, and I didn't. I knew what would happen. I chose not to allow it in my life."

"But you accepted me, you believed I was your son, you believed Chance was my father, your husband, why couldn't you accept that you had a gift?"

"Because I didn't want it."

"Why?"

"I had my life to live, this life. I have a husband who doesn't believe in reincarnation, I have five," she stopped and looked at him. "I have six children, the five from this lifetime don't believe in anything they can't prove. Only one believes enough in me that he doesn't think I'm crazy."

Blaine smiled. "I like your son Derrick."

"Thanks, he likes you too." She hesitated. "I wanted to protect them, Blaine. I didn't want them and most of all I didn't want Derrick to lose faith in me. I wouldn't be able to handle it if he thought I was crazy."

"Does he think I'm crazy?"

"No, just a little strange. But I'm his mother. I don't know if he could take me being…, I don't even know how to say it."

"Then let me say it for you. You're a psychic, Michelle. You were born a psychic, you've lived many times as a psychic and now you're remembering those gifts once again."

He watched while his mother closed her eyes. He could sense her fighting her tears; feel the agony as she was torn between loving him, a reincarnated son, and her husband and children of this life.

"I've put them through so much this past year. Larry has truly forgiven me for having an affair with Chance. He's accepted you. How much more could I ask him to accept?"

"Does he accept that it wasn't just an affair you had, that Chance is your husband of many lifetimes, does he accept that Chance is my father? Does he accept me as your son?" Blaine didn't know why that was important to him, but it was.

"He accepts that I know who you are. He trusts me enough to believe me after all that we've been through. He just doesn't know how to deal with this. He's an attorney. He's used to dealing with facts."

Blaine closed his eyes. "I'm sorry, perhaps I should go."

"I'm not going to abandon you, Blaine. Maybe you misunderstood me. I said I didn't want to put my family through any more craziness. I didn't say I was willing to sacrifice any part of my family for the comfort of the others. You're my family too, as much as they are if not more. Whatever is happening I'm going to be there with you."

"How much do you remember?"

"Enough to know that I don't know enough. I'm rusty," she smiled, "at least a couple of lifetimes of rusty, but I'm not closing my eyes any longer. No one's going to take you from me, and Salvatore will not harm you, not as long as I can prevent it."

"He's strong," Blaine sighed, "very strong."

"I know, but I'm not afraid."

"What are you going to tell Larry?"

"As little as possible."

"What's your plan?"

"I have to relearn everything I've forgotten."

"When?"

"There's no time like the present."

"You're talking about going to see the Mystic. Sal's still there."

"I'm not hiding from him, Blaine, and neither are you?"

"This is not your fight, Michelle."

"It is now. You've made it yours and for some reason Sal has taken a personal dislike for you. You're my son. When he tried to hurt you, he made it my fight. Now let's go. It has been too many lifetimes since I've seen my father."

Blaine looked at this mother of his and he was overcome with the desire to weep. Why had he not listened to her? None of this would have ever happened, none of it. It was all his fault.

"It's not your fault, Blaine. It was destined to happen."

Blaine stared at her in surprise. "Mom, you can," he gasped aloud. "You can read my thoughts." He smiled in spite of himself.

"Too easily, Blaine. We don't need to let Salvatore know everything. If we can keep the fact from him that the Mystic is my father that will make everything easier, until we figure out his true motive. Now before we go over there suppose you tell me everything from the beginning and leave nothing out.

***

"That's incredible," Michelle murmured when Blaine had finished his tale. "A super baby, a child born on the solstice. This is extraordinarily unbelievable."

"Tell me about it, but after finding you I find nothing impossible," Blaine admitted.

"Considering what you do for a living, I wouldn't have thought you would disbelieve anything." Michelle joked.

Out of the blue something clicked. Blaine saw the glow in his mother's eyes, felt the surge of energy go from her body to his, much as it had the first time they'd met. He didn't know if he would ever get used to such a supreme connection. He avoided thinking of the connection his soul had made with Cassandra. Probably a freak occurrence, it could never happen again. Even if it could, he would never find out. He would have nothing else to do with her.

"You know, Blaine, I think I know why Sal hates you so. I think somehow he knows the truth. He knows it's not any of the other psychics that the prophecy speaks of. Somehow he's figured it out. It's so hard to believe but that has to be it."

"Then why is he working to help us keep Cassandra safe?"

"For two reasons: to eliminate the competition and to make her believe in him and trust him, maybe even agree to marry him." She glanced in Blaine's direction. "How would you feel about that?"

"I don't care," Blaine snarled. "She can marry who she pleases."

"You're no longer in love with her?"

"No."

"Then why are we both risking our lives to help her?" Michelle stood still facing him, waiting for him to admit the lie to her and to himself. He did neither.

"I'm not in love with her. I resigned myself a long time ago to a life without a woman. I'm helping only because the Mystic asked for my help. As for Cassandra, when this is all over she can go to hell. Or better yet, she can go to Sal."

"Blaine, make no mistake about this, Salvatore is the real danger, not the ones after Cassandra. They are not nearly the threat that he poses."

"The Mystic and Cassandra both think Sal is not the one." Blaine looked around Michelle's home, wanting for a moment to focus on something else. He wanted Sal to be the bad guy. He wanted to be the one to help Cassandra.

"Blaine, you're not listening to me. Where are you?"

He blinked. "Don't worry, I'm back. Are you sure about this? Do you really think Sal is the enemy? He said he returned home to protect her."

Blaine could feel his cheeks burning. He didn't want his mother to think he was naive enough to believe that lie. "Listen, I know he's in love with her, but Cassandra trusts him, she doesn't think he will ever do anything to harm her." Blaine continued looking away not wanting to see disappointment or fear for him in his mother's eyes.

"When this is all over you will have to confront Salvatore. You're his enemy, Blaine, not Cassandra. He came home because of you, not because of her."

"He didn't even know I existed. How could he possibly know that I would meet and fall..., I mean how could he know I would meet her?"

"I knew Blaine and I'm so, so rusty. Sal's not rusty. I want you to be ready when the time comes. You have to learn all that you can and focus. Don't ever allow him to use your anger against you again." She looked away, "Or your fear."

"What are you talking about?"

"Don't fear death, Blaine, for in trying to hold too tightly to your life you will lose it. It is only in letting go that you will realize that your essence is eternal and nothing will destroy that. If nothing else the very fact that we found each other again in this life should convince you of that."

"Are you saying that I'm afraid of Salvatore, afraid of dying?"

"It was your fear that I sensed. Don't be ashamed of that. I'm just telling you because I want you to be prepared. Whatever happens, however this turns out it's not the end of us."

What the hell was she talking about? She sounded as though she was trying to prepare him for her death. Now he was scared. He was terrified, not for himself but for the people he loved, for his mother who he'd pulled into this mess while trying to keep her out of it. He didn't want her to die. It had taken too damn long for him to have a mother. He wasn't ready to lose her.

"I know life's eternal, I remember my other life."

"Then why are you afraid?"

"It's not for me, it's... I don't want to lose you."

"You'll never lose me son, never. I'll love you until the end of time and beyond. Remember like the soul, love never dies."

Michelle came toward him and he opened his arms to envelope her, his tears mixing with her own. "Mom, I love you. I promise I'll protect you."

"That's not your job, Blaine. You're not forcing me into anything. You're helping me to be who I was always meant to be. Thank you. Thank you for making me remember and appreciate my gift."

Blaine held onto his mother for dear life. He may not have understood what powers were truly available in the psychic ream, but now he no longer doubted.

Chapter Twenty-Two

Ahh, a group effort. So the big bad Salvatore Sharif needed help. The word was he'd always boasted he could take on a hundred psychic warriors and never break a sweat. He wondered what happened. He only had eleven to worry about.

It was good that he'd enlisted the aide of the Mystic. It would make it easier to get all of them at once. The Mystic he understood. But why Sal would chose to work with someone as lame as MaDia he couldn't fathom a guess. Probably wanted to keep in eye on the man, keep him out of Cassie's pants. Yeah, Sal wanted all of that for himself. But he wouldn't have a chance to sample it. He'd underestimated MaDia, and the slut had slept with him. But he would not underestimate Sal.

How Salvatore had managed to talk the bitch into letting him take over her mind he didn't know. The moment he tried to enter last night he felt the strong male energy and hurriedly left before Sal was even aware of his presence.

He'd allow Sal to help take out the others, not even knowing where the true danger lay. Then the true battle would begin. This was going to be so much fun. Enough hiding out, enough staying in the shadows. Twelve of them, each powerful in his own right. Salvatore had dispensed with two of them. And he'd gotten rid of another three himself.

He smiled to himself. The men had never known what hit them, a mysterious virus the doctors had called it causing instantaneous and irreversible paralysis.

He knew Sal had not used all his powers, he'd merely rendered the men useless by draining their powers. They would be lucky if they remembered their own names after this. He laughed, a horrible cackle he had to admit. Sal could have those juvenile games. But he was playing for keeps and that meant playing hard.

There were five more to go then the battle would fall between him and Sal. They would be the last of the psychics alive with the capability to fulfill the prophecy. Blaine MaDia didn't concern him. He would kill him merely for sport, for fucking Cassandra, a woman that belonged to him. He deserved to die for that alone and for thinking he was always better than the other people in the community. He wondered what he would think when he lay drained of any psychic powers, not even enough to call a ghost or two to save him.

The man laughed again. If Blaine were lucky maybe there would be a ghost waiting to greet him at the pearly gates.

***

Blaine walked in front of Michelle, his stance protective. Something about the whole think niggled at him. It didn't feel right, but his mother insisted on coming and there was nothing he could do to stop her. She was determined to regain all she had lost. She would have come to the Mystic with or without him. In that case he had no choice but to shield her with every once of energy in his body. It hurt that even she thought he wasn't up to the task. She, a woman who until a little over a year ago, ran from him, afraid to touch him. Now look at her, he thought and glanced back. She was embracing being different, it appeared that her acceptance of being gifted had come rather quickly and with it that same subtle knowing, that called Blaine a baby psychic. He was damn sick and tired of it.

"Why are you smiling at me?" Blaine inquired of his mother.

"Oh I don't know. Maybe I like knowing you approve of me, yet there is still this thought that you want desperately to protect me. And there is no need." She smiled. I'm ready for this. I guess I'm enjoying being who I am." Her lips thinned and her eyes sobered as she touched her hand to Blaine's shoulder. "Blaine, don't."

"Not you too, Michelle." Blaine licked his lips pushing the pain away. He'd been doing this his entire life. His mother had just gotten started, yet she was doing as all the others, treating him as if he were no more than a novice. "Please don't insult me," Michelle. "I have my thoughts under control. You'd better just hope it's not the old man himself who gives it away."

As if on cue the always unlocked door was opened by the Mystic. He stood for a moment scowling at Blaine. "I'm disappointed in you."

"As I am in you," Blaine answered. "He was choking the life out of me, you didn't lift a finger."

"Neither did you."

"There was nothing I could do."

With a snort of disgust the old man shook his head. "You're hopeless." His glance turned to Michelle as though he'd just noticed her. "I see you brought your mother. Welcome to my home, Michelle."

"Thank you sir," Michelle answered and glanced over the old man's shoulder. "Do you mind if I include myself in this?"

"No, you're more than welcome."

Michelle released the death grip Blaine had on her shoulder and moved into the room. She glanced once at Cassandra, her look apparent that she held her responsible for the trouble. Her gaze landed on Salvatore the same instant as Blaine's.

Salvatore smiled coolly at Michelle before coming up to her. He dismissed Blaine by not acknowledging his presence. "It's nice to see you again." Salvatore said to Michelle.

"Sorry I can't say the same," Michelle answered him, her back straight as she moved an inch or two from Blaine's protective grasp.

"It surprised me that you were able to remove my hands. I didn't pick up anything from you last night."

"That's strange, I thought you did." Michelle answered. "I thought it strange that you would play such parlor tricks. Surely a man who thinks he's as powerful as you can find something better to do with his time than sneak attacks. Blaine was not ready for you. He had no idea that you were going to become physical."

She laughed right into his face. "That was a very cowardly act."

For a moment Salvatore bristled, and then he smiled. "You're right. Next time I will announce my intentions. This time I only did it to confirm what I suspected. I wanted to meet Blaine's helper."

"I'm not Blaine's helper. If you insist on there being a next time, Blaine can and will take care of himself. You're a bully, and I only interfered because of the manner you acted in."

"Ouch." Sal laughed this time. "I get the point."

"Silence!"

The one word roared like thunder while all in the room turned in the direction of the Mystic.

"We have a lot to do and if we're not all committed we may as well forget it."

"I'm willing to work on this if they are." Sal grinned first in Michelle's, direction then Blaine's.

***

Things were definitely becoming more complicated by the moment. Salvatore appeared to be enjoying the verbal sparring with this soul mother of Blaine who she had to admit had thrown him for a loop. It wasn't that she didn't know souls reincarnated into different hues, different races if you will. Michelle's skin was the same toffee brown as her own. She'd just not been prepared for it. No one had thought to mention it. But apparently she was the only one who'd given it a thought. Sal wasn't concerned neither was Blaine of the Mystic. She finally had a window of opportunity to tell someone what she'd discovered. She'd prefer it be the Mystic but his shields were up and his energies focused on protecting Michelle who wasn't behaving at all as thought she need protecting. She had one choice left to her and moved in his direction. "Blaine, I need to tell you something."

He refused to acknowledge her. She tried to enter his mind but found it blocked to her. She almost laughed. The baby psychic was learning. She was impressed. But right now she had to tell someone about Salvatore.

"Blaine, please, we don't have much time. You have to listen to me." Cassandra was whispering to Blaine as loudly as she dared while Salvatore's attention was focused on Michelle.

Blaine's eyes raked her over and he forced his body to remain rigid. She would not win him over again with sweet words and mournful looks.

"That is not Sal." She whispered urgently.

"What the hell are you talking about?"

"I'll explain later, just trust me. That is not Salvatore. Something is wrong."

"You know what, Cassandra? I don't give a damn who he is. I'm here to help you get through this mess. After it's over you can sort out who he is. Alone. Like you said in the beginning, it's been fun."

Blaine turned on his heels and walked away from Cassandra going up to his mother and pulling her toward a comfortable grouping of pillows. He was tired of her sparing with Salvatore and he was tired of trying to hold in his pain. He wished he'd listened. He wished he'd never met Cassandra Boozer.

Quick tears came to Cassandra's eyes causing her to wrap her arms around her body to stave off the coldness of her tears. She had to get hold of herself before Sal noticed. So far she'd managed to keep her true feelings for Blaine tightly under wraps.

Blaine thought she and the Mystic would have allowed Sal to kill him that they weren't aware of what was going on. It had taken all the strength she possessed not to rush Sal. All she'd wanted to do was bombard Sal with her own energy, make him turn Blaine loose. But she'd remained rooted to the spot she stood in, knowing without a shadow of a doubt that Sal would not kill him.

It was in those moments she'd glimpsed Sal's pain. Something wasn't right. She sensed a struggle was going on inside of Sal's spirit for dominance. Someone other than Sal occupied his body.

She would have smiled in relief that it was not her best friend, her protector, her brother, who had the veil of evil wound tightly around his body, but there was no time for celebration. No time to even pray that Blaine would free himself.

When Blaine had finally begun coughing, taking in gulps of air in relief, she thought he'd been able to combat Sal. Then Sal's words "So there's another psychic in the midst." And she'd known. Blaine had not freed himself, someone else had.

Cassandra glanced over in Michelle's direction to find the woman looking back at her, her eyes so cold that she shivered. It was obvious Blaine's mother held her responsible for the trouble they were in.

Didn't anyone understand that she'd never asked for this, never wanted it? Who the hell in their right mind would want such an awesome responsibility, to be the mother of the world's most powerful psychic? The very idea of it was a bit intimating. She was not up for the task, had never wanted it. Blaine had only become involved because they were both lonely and horny.

Damn, she should have stuck to her original plans, never screw a psychic, even if he was a baby psychic. No good could come of it. She glanced once more in Blaine's direction.

Oh yeah, he'd frozen her out. He thought she'd betrayed him. That much was obvious without reading his thoughts. Without her concoction all of her powers were coming back full force. His heart was breaking and it was tearing her apart that she couldn't comfort him, couldn't tell him how she really felt. For within the pain she sensed his hatred. Oh this was bound to be a ton of fun.

Barely an hour passed before Salvatore stood and stretched with his cat like grace. He glanced down at Cassie and smiled. For a moment she sensed the presence of her old friend.

"I think it's me," Salvatore said lazily, "but this all appears to be a monumental waste of my time."

Cassie stared up at him missing the quick glance she'd gotten of her lifelong friend. "What are you talking about?"

"Well, no one here really wants me around," he paused. "With maybe the exception of you sweet, Cassie, and even of your loyalty I'm not sure."

"Salvatore," the Mystic scolded. "We all agreed we're in this together. If we combine our gifts and learn to work for the greater good we can protect Cassie."

"That would be wonderful, but somehow I've been thrust into the role of teacher with some mighty disagreeable pupils." He looked toward Blaine and Michelle.

"Admit it old man, with me gone you can teach them what they need to know. As for the combining of our powers, I don't see how any of you will be able to enhance mine."

Cassie cringed. She couldn't believe Sal would talk to the Mystic in that manner. "Salvatore, you don't have to be rude," she said rising to her feet. He turned to face her a darkness permeating his spirit.

"Are you now wanting to challenge me, Cassie? I warned you not to push me. My love for you will only allow me to tolerate so much." He grinned. "Especially when I'm so conflicted about your divided loyalties."

Cassandra tamped her temper down. Her body became flooded with cries for help. She blinked, looking at Sal, knowing she was right. Somehow someone had gotten at least partial control of Sal, but how? She didn't have time to wonder about that now. She had to answer him.

"Sal, I don't want to fight with you, but there is no need to be disrespectful to the Mystic."

He smiled at her, his lips full and lush, his eyes laughing at her. He walked toward her and a chill crept around her heart. She watched Blaine looking at her and Sal with disinterest.

"I will never hurt you, Cassie."

She looked into his eyes, the eyes of her friend and she clutched his hands to her heart. "Sal," she moaned. "Fight it," she whispered.

His lips brushed her lightly and she wound her arms around his neck holding him close to her before he gently pushed her away enough to search the truth in her eyes, to cup her chin and once again kiss her lightly. Then suddenly his touch and his kiss changed.

From a kiss filled with love and friendship it quickly changed to one of total dominance. Cassandra felt the strangeness of the kiss and glanced over Sal's head at Blaine. She tried to plead with him that she didn't want Salvatore, but it was no use.

She was not in control. She knew the moment her legs turned to jelly and her lips returned the crushing torrent of emotions. She tried to keep her eyes open, to maintain a link with Blaine, but she couldn't. They closed to the lust Sal was generating in her body and she held him fiercely, not sure herself of what was happening.

It seemed that it had been forever before Sal released her and smiled a victorious grin in Blaine's direction. Then in front of all he ran his hands over her body, tweaking her breasts. Her nipples puckered and hardened, amazingly evident through the sheer blouse. With the pads of his fingers he ran his hand down her body, along every curve, resting at last on the vee between her legs.

Salvatore smiled at her as she trembled in shame and in need. She wanted him, yet she didn't. Blaine's pain was rushing at her in waves almost dropping her where she stood. She looked over at him and saw his face. A storm cloud hovered around his aura. She saw Michelle's hands on him holding him firmly in place. She was relieved when Sal released her and laughingly left the house. He'd branded her his whore and left.

When the door closed Cassandra sank to the floor and cried in her hands. It was back. The torrent of emotions she'd fought against for the past several years were back and they were coming at her in such a rush that she couldn't discern where they were coming from. Never had she ever felt such a barrage of emotions, anger, hatred, pain and confusion and she sensed somewhere in the midst of all that, victory.

Focusing her energies Cassie ordered her mind to assemble the emotions. The victory was easy to categorize it was Sal's. He felt he'd won. She sent a beam of white light straight to the heart of those feelings and it dissipated. The confusion was pulling at her. She looked up, the tears in her eyes making it difficult to focus clearly. Yes, the teacher owned the confusion. He didn't know what had happened. *Well join the club*, she thought. Neither did she. She pulled in a deep cleansing breath before making the emotion vanish from her. The anger and pain were intermingled, coming from both Michelle and Blaine.

Blaine. Oh God, Blaine. What did she look like to him now, a harlot who spread her legs for any man? To allow Sal or whoever the hell was in his body, to fondle her so unabashedly in front of Blaine and his mother was unforgivable. She didn't blame either of them for the waves of anger. Still she had to try and explain.

"Blaine, I couldn't stop him. I couldn't stop myself."

"You didn't try."

"That wasn't Sal."

"I heard you call him by name and if I'm not mistaken that is the same man you introduced to me as Salvatore."

Blaine was being cold. He had to be. Michelle and the Mystic were both watching him for signs that he would crack. Even now Michelle held on tightly as though she thought he might snap. None of them knew what he was capable of. Not even he knew he could sit still while a knife was plunged through his heart and repeatedly twisted.

"Wait, Blaine. Let's hear Cassie out."

Blaine wasted barely a glance for Cassandra as he watched the Teacher put a warning finger on his thin lips. *Of course the teacher would believe her*, Blaine thought. He wanted to. He'd said he loved her like a daughter.

Blaine was hurting and he didn't want to hurt. He was feeling betrayed by the people he loved most in the world. He glared in the direction of the Mystic. It was just as he'd thought, once again the old man's, actions proved greater than his words. What happened to the blood bond when Sal was choking the life out of him? He'd not lifted a finger to help him. And now, just a few tears from Cassandra and the Mystic was trying to find a reason for her behavior.

"Quickly everyone, sit on the floor. Closer, closer." The old man shouted and sat down to join them.

Blaine was startled by the Mystic's spunk. He seemed so different, not so frail, he was gingerly stretching his limbs. It looked as if he'd taken an anti-aging potion. The Teacher had peeled twenty years off in a matter of seconds.

"Close your eyes and meditate."

Even Blaine followed instructions without questions. What else was there to do? He moved like a robot, doing what was asked only.

"Okay now you may open your eyes."

Blaine was startled. They were completely encased in an energy bubble of iridescent colors. White and purple danced about them. *I must be losing my mind*, he thought as he looked first not wanting to, toward Cassandra and then to his mother. Michelle's face wore a huge smile as she looked on in pride at the Mystic.

"I can only hold this for ten or fifteen minutes," the Mystic explained. "We'd better talk fast. No one can hear us or scan us now."

"We can do twenty if I help." Michelle offered.

This was a day for surprises. Blaine was again startled at the words that came out of his mother's mouth. Even he didn't know how to construct an energy barrier that would protect the four of them. He noticed Cassandra's look of awe at Michelle's offer, but didn't offer herself. Was there finally something that someone else could do that she couldn't?

The Mystic gazed at Michelle while Blaine looked on. "Are you sure you're ready to try this?" The Mystic asked her.

"As ready as I'll ever be," she answered.

Before anyone had a chance to breathe, the colors of the energy force field shifted and changed, the colors dancing around in glee it seemed.

"Now," the Mystic ordered, pointing to Cassandra. "What was that all about?"

"It's Sal. I think someone has possession of him."

"Are you sure? I didn't sense anything."

"I'm positive. Things have been different from the moment he returned; only I didn't know what. But there's something about him kissing me." She blushed and looked toward Blaine before turning away. "I can't help yielding to him. I don't want him," she murmured quietly.

She chose to ignore the derisive snicker from Blaine's direction. "I could feel Sal inside, calling out to me to help him."

"How in the world could someone have taken control of Sal? He's too smart for that, too strong," the Mystic asked shaking his head in wonder.

"How about too arrogant?" Blaine piped in.

"That's it." Michelle leaned in closer. "I don't know him, but I felt something myself, like two parts of one warring with itself. There was a moment that I sensed his admiration for me. But in a flash it was gone and all I could feel was his contempt."

"Now that I think on it, I too sensed a difference, not just the arrogant disrespect, but something vile and totally evil. For long stretches it would not be there, and then it would resurface." The Mystic closed his eyes in anguish, embarrassed he'd not known. "How could I have believed that was my Salvatore?"

Blaine couldn't help but notice the spark of hope that darted across the Mystic's features. The man was clutching at straws wanting to believe that his student had not turned evil.

"With all due respect, sir," Blaine interrupted, "I think you should examine your reasons, both of you." He spared no more than a glance in Cassandra's direction. "You both want him to be as you remember, so couldn't it be that you're inventing a reason for his behavior? I didn't feel anything lurking beneath. What I witnessed was definitely evil through and through. If what you say is true, it's too late anyway. He's evil." Blaine looked around the bubble. "He's evil," he repeated.

"What if he isn't?" Cassandra spoke softly.

He glared at her in return. "What difference does it make? We've made him our ally, brought him in. He knows as much as we do about all of our gifts, and what's more, he knows about my mother." This time he glanced at Michelle. "What more do you suggest? We have no more secrets."

Michelle touched his arm. "Yes, Blaine, we have one more that he doesn't know."

"I don't care," Blaine fumed and turned away. "Salvatore, or possessed Salvatore, I still don't like him."

"But if he is possessed, if Sal's inside we have to help him." Cassandra turned pleading eyes on Blaine. "He's my friend. He would do the same for me."

"Well, he's not my friend and the guy has made my life miserable from the moment I met him." He attempted to hold Cassandra's gaze until he saw the first crystal drops of tears forming. He turned away. "Don't manipulate me with tears," he ordered and turned silent.

"I'm sorry I ever called you a baby psychic, Blaine." She spoke softly as the first fat drops rolled down her cheeks. "That's not what you are. You're a baby in everything, including love. How can you say you love me and not love the people I love?"

Blaine remained silent, but turned an indignant glare up a notch or two. He wasn't going to let her get to him.

"Teacher, how do you think this happened and is it possible that we can help? Cassie's eyes were hopeful turned toward the face of the Mystic.

"It had to be voluntary." The Mystic answered her. "That's the only way. Sal must have for whatever reason allowed another entity into his body."

"Why the hell would a psychic do a dumb thing like that?"

Blaine waited while Cassandra, the teacher, and his mother eyed him with awed curiosity.

"I thought you wanted out of this conversation?" The Mystic grinned in his direction before answering Cassandra.

"Well simple, psychics are human, lets not forget, and sometimes a little too curious for their own good. I think Salvatore learned almost everything there is to know about every gift there is. He probably became bored and turned to magick."

"Magic?" Blaine mumbled and wished he hadn't spoken. Again the trio was eyeing him as if he'd somehow wandered in by accident.

"No, not magic. Magic is only an illusion, the tricks of magicians. Magick is real and can be deadly." The Mystic looked directly at him this time. "Lots of psychics delve into that realm and there is nothing wrong with it unless you turn to the practice of dark magick. That always hurt the practitioner."

"Despite the fact that it's apparent you all believe I'm limited in my knowledge of the paranormal, I assure you I'm not. I'm well aware of the difference between magic and magick. I only asked in order to be sure which you meant. And if as you say Salvatore is using magick then if he brought this on himself, why are you all worrying about him?"

"Because I love him, Blaine. Because he's a good person and deserves help."

"If he's so powerful, why can't he help himself?"

Michelle touched his arm, her eyes asking him to be gentle. He looked away. He didn't want to be gentle with Cassandra, didn't she hear, Cassandra had just said she loved Sal. Did his mother really want him to offer to help? A pang went through him and he closed his eyes tightly against the emotions flooding his bones, making him weak. He didn't like it, he had enjoyed having a mother, having her love and support. Now he'd just had the first inkling of how he'd feel if it were denied him. It would kill him.

As if she sensed his fears, Michelle reached for his fingers and squeezed tightly, her eyes probing his. "I will never stop loving you, Blaine," she whispered into his mind. He held her glance for only a moment before looking away. The knowledge that she could read him so easily left him feeling bare, and needy. He didn't like it.

"I don't really know if we can help Sal," the Mystic admitted. "He will have to help us defeat what ever entity is in him."

"What if you're wrong? What if the entity is truly the real essence of Sal?"

"We have to try," the Mystic answered him. "If it were you, I would try."

"But I wouldn't be stupid enough to allow an entity to take possession of my body."

"No? Isn't that what you do when you talk to your spirit friends? When their voices come from your mouth what the hell do you call that?" Cassandra's voice was angry and her angered energy caused a ripple in the barrier.

"Careful," he heard both Michelle and the teacher caution her. She glanced at the barrier, her words stopped, but her glare remained lethal.

"They don't take possession of me." Blaine defended. "That only happens when I allow it for some special reason for a minute or two."

"Then what's the difference? Maybe Sal only meant it to last a minute. How do you know?"

"I don't care what his intentions were," Blaine firmly reaffirmed. "I'm not risking my life or my mothers' to help him."

He watched while Cassandra's anger melted and her look changed to pity. He glanced away quickly and was greeted by disappointment on the Mystic's face. Not allowing his gaze to linger, he turned to his mother.

Her eyes mirrored the same disappointment as the Mystic. Not her too. From Cassandra and the Mystic he could take it, just barely. From Michelle, the look pierced his heart.

In the blink of an eye, it was as though a giant sword had moved down under the energy shield and severed him from the other three occupants. He felt more alone than he'd ever felt in his entire life. The intense hurting burned him through to his soul. If he'd never tasted real love, he glanced at his mother then, toward Cassandra. If he'd never made love with a woman who claimed his very soul, maybe he could go back to the way things were. Now, there was no way. He couldn't, he didn't want to ever feel alone again.

"I'll help," he offered grudgingly not wanting to, but unable to bear the loneliness.

"You don't have to." Michelle ran her fingers over his hands. "I'll help."

"Not without me, Mom. Don't even think it. You won't be battling anyone without me at your side." He held her to him his eyes searching out Cassandra.

"This entity, why is he here?" Blaine asked looking directly at Cassandra for the first time since she'd arrived at the Mystic's home.

"Because like everyone else he has plans to impregnate me. Even I'm not sure which one of them came up with that idea, Sal or the person inside him. But I still have to help him."

"And then after this is all over and we are successful in saving Sal, what then?"

"We'll deal with that when we save him," Cassandra answered.

Oh yeah, this day was going about the way Blaine figured. His entire psyche was aflame with puncture wounds. Inflicted by the three people he loved most in the world.

Damn, was there any wonder he chose to speak primarily with the dead? All these years not once had psychic vampires attacked him. Not once had he ever had to try and save an evil psychic possessed by a more evil entity. Not once had he risked the life of his soul mother for any of this unbelievable nonsense.

Until now.

Damn right, give him the dead. Any day.

***

He sat in his car several blocks away and tapped on his parabolic microphones. What the hell happened? The thing was working fine, but for the last twenty minutes he hadn't been able to hear a word from the Mystic's home, not since Sal left abruptly.

He'd laughed at that bit of news, finding it ironic that the Mystic's prized pupil had called him little more than a bumbling old man. He licked his lips. Those hadn't been Sal's exact words, but it meant the same. Sal had dismissed the Mystic's help. Now the game was really getting interesting.

He'd even learned the name of the woman who'd been at the restaurant the night before. Somehow she was connected to MaDea. Sal didn't like the woman, that was obvious. It seemed she must have been a psychic, but very rusty. He'd only gathered that because of Sal's remarks about teaching her.

Well with the microphone on the blink he'd better go. Besides, two people had already come up to him and asked if he were in some type of trouble. He knew if they came out again they would call the cops. How paranoid people were. They behaved as if every one was reading their thoughts. God, how he wished he could dare tune into the thoughts of his prey. But he couldn't, not now, it was getting too dangerous. Besides he wanted no chance of their reading him and knowing who he was.

He tossed the microphone onto the back-seat and laughed out loud. He didn't need his psychic gifts to spy on his prey. No, all it took was plenty of money and a good solider of fortune magazine. Hell you could buy whatever you wanted nowadays.

He pulled quickly out of the parking space just as he spied the shop owner peeping at him from the closed blinds of his shop. He was getting hungry anyway, time to grab a bite to eat.

Several blocks away he pulled over, the various fast food signs beckoning him. With his newspaper in hand he opted for one that would allow more than a quick drive through. He wanted to sit. His adrenaline was going so fast he needed some protein to slow himself down. He always got like this when he was so close to Cassandra that he could smell her scent. And she never had a clue. The bitch had better get a clue soon. Time was running out, there were only five more psychic to take care of.

The thought flittered across his brain that the legend spoke of thirteen male psychics. Well, that part was wrong. There were only twelve. For a mere nanosecond he thought of Blaine MaDia, but dismissed the thought. Since he'd entered the picture he'd checked him out, dug into his background probably even more thoroughly than MaDia had done when he'd tried to find his family.

He'd hired the best private investigator to look up the skeletons in MaDia's closets. All that turned up was a stupid teen who'd given him up at birth. A deeper search into several generations of her life revealed that the people were nothing more than poor dirt farmers, ignorant at best, insane at the worst.

Psychic gifts, that was a laugh and a waste of his time. Still, even though he didn't prove a threat, he was going to kill MaDia. He should never have fucked around with him, and he definitely should have never fucked Cassandra. Ah, it would be good to eat and relax for a few minutes he thought as he opened the heavy glass doors and started to enter the restaurant.

"Norman, Norman Bates, how the hell are you?"

Norman turned slowly. He eyed the psychic facing him, knowing that in a moment the number would be cut down to four. He was a bit annoyed at himself for being seen by any of the others, but he'd have to get over that. He was smarter than the rest of them; he'd just been careless that's all.

"Yates, you know it's Yates," Norman said turning to face his prey.

"Don't go getting testy, Norman. You know we called you Bates throughout our childhood. Norman Bates, good old Norman."

Norman eyed the psychic icily and repeated, "My name is Norman Yates."

"What the hell difference does it make? Bates, Yates, you're still Norman and you're still a bit strange."

Norman stood stark still and watched the man laughing in his face, knowing he didn't have a clue what would happen to him.

"So, Norman, why are you in town? Surely you don't expect Cassie to choose you? My God, that's ridiculous," the man laughed at his own joke.

Norman opened the door of the restaurant once again and held it open, allowing the other man to enter first. They placed their orders, moved down the line and picked up their trays, before Norman spotted a table near the back, opposite an exit door. "Perfect," he whispered aloud.

"Oh, what was that, Bates? What are you mumbling about?"

"I just found a perfect table where we can talk in peace." Norman led the way to the table, noting it appeared to be an area that was avoided by others. To ensure this he sent out a line of energy. Only a fool would attempt to cross an invisible barrier that pushed them away.

"Now, Norman, you never said why you are in town."

"The same reason you are."

"You're kidding?"

Norman sat patiently while his dining companion perused his appearance. He knew he didn't look much different than he had in childhood, hair too long and shaggy, thick and dark brown, his clothes acquired from "Nerds Are Us" and his ten inch thick coke bottle glasses. Yeah, he was aware of what he looked like.

Only now the look was deliberate. He had contacts that did the trick and a hair stylist that flirted with him like crazy whenever he walked into her salon. Even his clothes had changed. But for what he was doing, he preferred to not garner a second look, to remain indescribable. Why not, he was indestructible he may as well be invincible.

"I'm sorry, Norman, but there is no way in hell Cassie will marry you. I don't mean any offense," he waved his hand expansively. "But look at you. You couldn't get lucky in a monkey whore house and you had a bag of bananas."

Norman glared at the man seated across from him with full knowledge that his glare like any other look was disguised behind the incredibly thick lenses. The joke was lame. David Spade had used it a dozen times.

"And you think Cassie would choose you?" Norman asked. "Why? What makes you so special?"

"Well for one thing we're friends. We were in the same crowds, hung out at the same places. You must admit, Norman, you never did. You were always sort of an odd duck."

As if he'd actually thought about what effect his words might have had, Norman watched as the psychic pursed his lips.

"Norman, none of this should come as a shock to you, you've never fit in. But besides all that, you never showed any inclination toward any real psychic powers. Sure there are many generations of psychics in your family, but it looks like when it came to you, it skipped a generation."

The man laughed heartily and Norman felt his own lips curl up, into a smile perhaps. In the blink of an eye, Norman reached his hands into the pocket of his pants, and with deft fingers separated an object from among the others he carried. He rubbed the smoothness for a moment, caressing it, savoring the power. He stared at the smiling face of the psychic, another of his childhood tormentors and his decision was made.

With the object firmly clutched between the pads of his fingers, Norman brought his hand up from his pocket and opened his palm.

It took a moment for the psychic to stop laughing to dry his tears of amusement, allowing his vision to clear and focus on the object Norman held.

The moment he did, Norman's smile became genuine, stretching until it seemed his lips touched the tips of his ears.

He held the red crystal heart in the palm of his hand, and closed his finger tightly around the object. He laughed softly. Now it was his turn.

He watched in amusement as the man's face turned an ashen white, his fingers clutching at his throat, his words feeble and muttered between ragged breaths.

"Bates, Bates, stop. What the hell do you think you're doing? Bates"

Norman picked up his soft drink and pulled on the straw, allowing the icy liquid to quench his thirst, as his hand closed even tighter, closing off any sound. The pasty white face turned an ashy shade of gray.

Norman took in the last bite of his sandwich and polished off the few remaining fries before finishing the few sips left of his drink.

His smile was broad now, as he leaned closer to the dead man. With the forefinger of his left hand he held it under the nose of the corpse. Nothing. Good.

He wanted to make sure. Norman was nothing if not precise. He didn't like loose ends, no leaving the man to be found and revived later. With a calm of a job well done he carefully picked up his trash and deposited it in the can, and then he returned to the table for one last look.

"By the way, I don't like the name Bates. My name is Yates, Norman Yates. He looked at the corpse one last time before leaving from the exit door a few steps away.

Well Sal, he thought, if you want in on this game you'd better get busy. You're two behind.

Chapter Twenty-Three

Blaine stood off to the side observing his mother talking with the Mystic. He felt like what he'd been all his life. An outsider.

"I like her. Your mother's very protective of you." Cassandra smiled at him slightly, but he didn't return it.

He inclined his head slightly toward Cassandra. His brow lifted, but he didn't speak.

"You have every right to be angry."

She was trying and he acknowledged that much, but it was a case of too little too late. When Sal was around it was as though Blaine turned invisible. He didn't like it.

"Don't you think I had a reason for what I did, for treating you so cold?" Cassandra asked.

"Sure I believe you had a reason. I'm just not very interested in hearing it at the moment." He glanced again across the room in amazement. Michelle Powers, Psychic Extraordinaire. Unbelievable.

"You're afraid for her, aren't you?"

Cassandra's words cut through him like a hot knife forcing him to turn fully toward her. He had every intention of telling her that when this mess was over, when she was safe he wanted her out of his life, wanted nothing to ever do with her again.

"Blaine," she whispered her breath falling on his cheek. He was lost. He crushed her in his arms while his body trembled with fear.

He ran his hands over her back down the small dip stopping at her buttocks and holding on there. He had yet to kiss her. Holding her was binding him tighter than ever. To kiss her would be giving her control of his soul. He didn't want to, he couldn't.

As he lifted his head, her eyes were open, her lips trembling. "I'm so sorry I hurt you," she murmured. The rest of her words he swallowed with a kiss.

"Shush, it doesn't matter."

"I never wanted to involve you in this. I had no idea of the magnitude of the situation. Blaine, I understand why you hate me."

"Hate you?" He placed her hand over his heart. "You're an empath. You tell me. Do I hate you?"

He felt her energy waning and her body softening, curving into the hard ridges of his own, it was like butter melting. She closed her eyes and gave a little sigh, falling a nanosecond before he caught her in his arms.

"Cassandra," he crooned rubbing her face, her hands, "Cassandra." The Mystic rushed over as did Michelle.

"What happened to her?" Michelle asked Blaine, one hand on his shoulder the other touching Cassandra's brow.

"She'll be fine," the Mystic assured Blaine. "Remember she's an empath, she feels emotions perhaps a hundred times stronger than mere mortals. What happened, what were you talking about?"

"My feelings for her," Blaine muttered, not wanting to divulge more.

"You hate her that much?" the old man asked.

Blaine's eyes grew wide. He shook his head glancing from Michelle to the old man. Didn't they see Cassandra in his arms? How could they think he truly hated her?

"He doesn't hate me," Cassandra said in a slightly weakened voice. "He loves me."

"Cassie, I thought you had that under control. You should not give into the emotions of others so easily," the Mystic scolded.

"I'm sorry sir, but it's been such a long time and since I..., well you know once I learned how to turn off the feelings, I just haven't had a chance to get a good grip on them."

Cassandra was feeling better. She looked into Blaine's eyes. "I've never felt such honest love, not for me anyway. It just took me so by surprise. I thought you were just... you know..."

"Using a line." Blaine filled in for her. "How could you think that after what happened?"

Cassandra smiled shyly remembering how their souls had mated the second time they made love. "I didn't stop to think about it."

Neither Blaine nor Cassandra missed the looks that passed between Michelle and the Teacher.

"Blaine, you did use something, right?"

Blaine stared at his mother for a moment not understanding what she was asking. This was going just a bit too far in his opinion. Mothers had there place in the lives of their children, his bed was not one of them.

"We're not children, if that's any of your business," he replied testily trying his damnedest to remember. He knew for sure they had the first time.

His eyes slid over to Cassandra. How he wanted to ask a silent question, but he'd made a promise. He would never for any reason enter her mind. He had only one option left to him, he'd have to do it the old fashioned way.

"Are you on anything?" he whispered knowing the Mystic and his mother were listening.

"No, there's never been a need."

Now Cassandra was eyeing him strangely, her eyes becoming frightened, as she closed her hands protectively around her abdomen.

"Surely you don't think?"

Blaine smiled weakly. "I'm sure I used something, I just can't remember that part too clearly, can you?"

"No." she answered truthfully. "Wouldn't that be a hoot?" She laughed, "Wouldn't that just take the air out of everyone's sail if the blessed vessel became pregnant by the baby-psychic? Sorry, Blaine. I find the entire thing ironic."

"Blaine's not the baby you think him to be, Cassie." The Mystic walked over to her placing his hand on her shoulder, he looked toward Michelle.

"What are you talking about, what's going on? If you're talking about her being his soul mother, that still doesn't make any difference. Okay, she had some latent powers in a previous incarnation, and some residual now. Surely that's a long way from the prophecy."

"Cassie this is Michelle's twenty-second incarnation and Blaine's second. In Blaine's last life he was the first child born to two great psychics. Both husband and wife were powerful and lived many lives together, perfecting their gifts, finding no need nor wanting children until they decided to have Blaine. Michelle died shortly after giving birth to Blaine, but before she did she passed her gifts to her infant son. When she did, he became in a matter of speaking a twenty-first generation psychic."

Cassie was trembling. "That's not the way the prophecy reads. This can't be right." She glanced at Blaine in horror, feeling betrayed, yet seeing his love, surrounding herself in it. She pushed away the feeling of betrayal, for surely this would be too incredible.

"Okay, go over this from the beginning. You say that the whole thing is topsy turvey and Blaine is descended from a woman with many incarnations. What about the part that said powerful? I'm sorry," she smiled at them, "but Michelle isn't powerful."

"Not now," the Mystic admitted. "But she's forgotten a lot more than you'll ever learn and we're going to bring it all back. Believe me, she is powerful. And remember this, she passed her powers on to her son, her gift to him. The gift of a dying mother."

The room was spinning. "How do you know all of this?" she asked, her knees going weak again as she reached her hand out for Blaine. "You just met her last night."

For a long moment no one spoke. Cassie knew within the very marrow of her bones. She knew. Oh God, how had she gotten herself in this situation? She'd been running for years from the prophecy, from the community's powerful psychics, to run head long into the arms of the baby psychic, to find he wasn't a baby after all.

She shuddered. She still didn't want to be used to fulfill some stupid prophecy. She would be the heralded mother of a super baby. She sent up a prayer to whoever might be listening. *Please don't let me be pregnant and I'll make sure there's not another chance of it happening.*

She pulled away from Blaine, feeling the texture of his skin as she did so. Damn. She'd given the man her soul. She was bare. She had nothing left to give. The thought of not being able to be with him tore at her, but she couldn't, that was not her destiny.

Blaine eyed her, knowing without reading her mind what she was thinking. He'd felt the very moment she'd withdrawn from him. He'd also felt the moment when she acknowledged her love, there in his arms. There were no longer any doubts. Whatever was between her and Sal had no bearing on how she felt about him.

And this thing wouldn't either. Neither of them would allow a thousand year old, stupid legend to dictate their lives.

"Let's take this one step at a time okay? First we have evil villains to fight. We have to what, perform an exorcism on Sal? And then fight off the other psychic vampires?" Blaine laughed to lighten the moment. But he laughed alone.

He saw the corners of Cassandra's mouth pulling slightly until she was smiling at him.

"I don't think I ever mentioned the word exorcism."

"Well don't forget we're talking about Salvatore. It would take nothing less."

She laughed, and once again Blaine pulled her into his arms. Of course his having a relationship wouldn't be easy. He was crazy if he'd ever imagined that it would. Like every aspect of his life, he would have to work damn hard to make it into what he wanted.

He kissed her deeply, inhaling the essence that was hers alone. At last he moved away slightly, remembering that the teacher and his mother were both watching him. It didn't take Cassandra touching him for him to feel the tightening throughout his body. But this close to her, it was damn near impossible not to. He smiled at her, and moved several inches from her, making sure to stay turned from the others.

A bolt of pure unadulterated lust shot through him, softened only by love. "Give me a moment," he whispered, "then I'll be ready to play Sir Lancelot for you."

***

Sal put the phone down. Someone else was helping him with his job. His sources had confirmed that fact. The news of a psychic dying of a heart attack in a restaurant was unbelievable. Sal knew all of them. They'd all played together, studied with the Mystic.

"You won't get away with this."

"Oh but I will. I already have," answered the voice that spoke from within. "I am Salvatore Sharif. I look like him, I act like him, and all who see me, think that I'm him."

"But you're not, you tricked me. You can't keep my body. I'll find a way out."

"Well, my friend, until you do, I know how to silence you." He poured three fingers of the scotch into a glass and drank greedily, laughing as he did so, laughing as the voice of the soul he inhabited was drowned away. Alcohol always seemed to have that effect on psychics. That was one of the reasons a lot of them never drank he supposed. But he had no such problem. This body didn't belong to him. When he tired of it he would find another.

With the pesky voice stilled, the new and improved Salvatore as he liked to think of himself went to the bar. He was meeting with two of the psychics he'd spotted in the hotel.

The only thing he'd not been able to get complete control of was his host's ability to kill with psychic energy. He'd tried twice, but the most damage as far as he could tell was to give the men headaches and memory loss. He wished he could do more. He would have enjoyed the challenge.

He wanted to see if either of the psychics he was meeting had taken off the moral brakes. Someone had made the kill and he wanted to know who. Maybe he'd learn something from them, some means to defeat Sal and keep him in the shadows for the rest of this lifetime.

He held his hands out toward his face smiling at the reflection he saw in the mirror. It was a good body, no doubt about it, lean and trim, and good looking. He would be happy to remain in the vessel if the ornery psychic would just behave.

"Sal, you wanted to see us?"

Sal turned toward the two men, smiling broadly at them, taking in their fear. "Yes, I did. It's come to my attention that someone is eliminating psychics, taking them out of the running."

"We heard the same thing." the shorter of the two answered him. "Matter of fact, he laughed nervously, "we thought it might be you."

Sal laughed.

"Well is it?" the same man asked. This time neither of the men moved a muscle, waiting undoubtedly for an answer from Sal.

"Why don't we get a table?" Sal suggested.

He followed the men toward a table and began a gentle push, he felt their barriers firmly in place. They were no fools, they didn't trust him. They were protecting themselves against him.

"Okay, Sal, we know you have something to do with what's happening. None of us came here looking for trouble. We came in the spirit of healthy competition. "All we wanted was a chance to ask Cassie to marry us. We're her friends also, but since we got here one after the other psychic have been dropping like flies. So now we've decided to stay together."

"We heard about Todd." This came from the taller of the two.

"Todd?"

Both men looked at Sal, their eyes closing against some knowledge Sal didn't possess.

"Are you saying you don't know Todd?" Again it was the smaller of the two who chose to speak. "He was killed a couple of hours ago."

"I heard he died of a heart attack."

"We thought you didn't know him."

"Well no, but I did hear of a psychic being found dead in a restaurant. Apparent cause, heart attack."

"At thirty four, highly unlikely. He was supposed to meet us. When he left us earlier in the day he was fine." It appeared the shorter psychic had made himself spokesman for the two.

"Are you accusing me?" The smooth cultured voice of Sal slammed into both men striking a cord of fear deep within their souls. Sal knew and was pleased.

"Are you saying you had nothing to do with it?"

"I am." Sal smiled big and bright. "It must be someone else." He ignored the looks the men gave each other.

"How many are left?" The taller man asked.

"Six have been eliminated." Sal replied. "There are twelve of us in all, that leaves six, the three of us and three others. I can only name two more, Carl Conroy and Daniel Weathers."

"Don't forget Norman Bates."

"Norman Bates," Sal's eyes widened. "Who the hell is he?"

Again the men looked at him, neither saying a word.

"Well if he wanted to be in this he could, but Norman never showed any inclination toward having any seeable gifts. So I guess we're down to five, beside us that leaves two more." This time it was the shorter of the two, the spokesman.

Sal smiled, waved his finger in the air, ordered a drink, then proceeded to tap a cigarette from a nearly empty pack and lit it. He inhaled deeply, ignoring the fact that the men were staring openly at him.

"I told you you won't get away with this. They know I would never smoke or drink. They know I treat my body as a temple. They know you're not the real Salvatore."

The entity occupying Sal's body spoke to Sal's soul. "Then you should have been more careful who you invited into your temple?"

He picked up the glass of his just delivered drink, and drank, laughing at the shocked looks on the faces of the men.

"I'll save you boys a bit of trouble, you all remember how close Cassie and I have always been. Well last night when we…, well after we finished, I proposed to her and she accepted."

"Are you telling us that you...?" Again it was the voice of the shorter psychic.

"That I made love to Cassandra Boozer? That's exactly what I'm telling you. At this very moment she could be carrying my son." Sal chortled.

"So where is she?"

Again from the runt. Sal was getting awfully tired of the man. For someone so small in stature he certainly had a big mouth.

"She's with the Mystic." Sal offered impatiently. Until I find the nut that's harming our fellow psychics, I wanted to keep her safe."

The men looked for a long moment at Sal, before the taller one this time decided to speak.

"If that's true, Sal, I think we'll head home. No need for us to stick around."

"I didn't think there was any reason either. Now if you two run into Carl or Daniel, why don't you tell them for me." He laughed again. "Once the last psychics leave town, Cassie and I should be able to begin our lives. We'll invite you for the christening." With that Salvatore rose and strode off, ignoring the fact that he had not paid his tab. Let them get it, he thought. After all he'd just saved their lives.

***

"What the hell was that all about?"

"I don't know, but I meant it when I said we're leaving. That isn't Sal."

"What are you talking about?"

"Didn't you notice the way he acted? The drinking, the smoking, he was down right vulgar and telling us about sleeping with Cassie. He was bragging. Sal would never talk about Cassie in that manner and would kill any guy who did."

"Do you think Cassie is in any trouble? Maybe we should stick around and help her."

"No. If she's with the Mystic, she's fine. Besides, you forgot how powerful Cassie can be when she chooses to. We'll just give Carl and Daniel a call and get the hell out of here."

"Do you think we should try and find out if Norman is in town? Maybe we should warn him to stay away from Sal and Cassie?"

"Naw." It was the shorter psychic again. "Norman would never have thought to come here. I doubt if he ever heard of the prophecy, or the equinox or anything. Let's just call the others, get our things and hop on a plane. Something's wrong here and I don't like it."

With that, the men paid Sal's tab and left.

Chapter Twenty-Four

"That's Todd." Cassandra turned from the television screen and gazed sadly at Blaine. "They said he died of a heart attack. I don't believe it."

All eyes were riveted on the screen until a long sigh filled the space. A sad mournful sound of wailing, the grief of many caused them all to turn in the direction of the Mystic.

"I didn't want to tell any of you, but strange things have been happening for the past week or so. Todd is the sixth psychic to fall prey to whatever's happening."

The Mystic's voice held more than a note of sadness. It held fear. "Todd was the first to die. There are two others in the hospital as we speak, and another two who I think with intense aura cleansing will be healed, but impaired. Their gifts are gone. Stolen."

"Is it Sal?"

Blaine watched the differing emotions play across the faces of the people he loved. He rolled his eyes to the top of his head in disgust before spearing them all with a glare and concentrating on the teacher, refusing to look away. They thought he was afraid.

"Look I'm only asking," Blaine said.

"I don't think Sal could have done them. Well he could have, but I don't think he did." The Mystic answered, his eyes fastened on Cassandra. "He was with us when Todd died and he spent last night with you, when someone attacked Eric."

"Eric, Eric Swenson?" The color drained from Cassie's face at the knowledge. All these men were friends of hers. They'd grown up together, played together, studied and learned at the hand of the Mystic. Why would anyone?

She felt a sudden pang of guilt. Her. They all wanted her and this damn baby they thought she could produce. But to hurt all of her friends. She shuddered, her mind going blank, eagerly accepting the arms Blaine wrapped her in.

"Who's next?" she whispered. "I never wanted any of this to happen. Maybe Sal was right. Perhaps I should just agree to marry him. Then this would end. No one else would have to suffer."

"But you said Sal wasn't himself." Blaine's arms tightened around her possessively. "Besides you're not in love with him." He smiled at her and she smiled back.

"No, I'm not," she answered. "But I don't want any more of my friends hurt." She trailed one long finger down his cheek. "I don't want you hurt. Ever."

Her glance slid easily to include Michelle. "I'd never forgive myself and I'd never be forgiven."

The Mystic was somber. "We'd better turn this off, forget what's happened, we can't change that. Let's concentrate on our lessons, on increasing our own powers." He gazed lovingly at Michelle. "You've gotten a lot back quickly. I wish we could call—"

"No." Blaine stopped the old man before the words could come out. "Hopefully this will be over soon. My mother has a life to return to, a husband. Did you forget about Larry? He's not into any of this." He glanced at his watch then back at Michelle. "How are you able to stay out so late?"

"Larry knows I'm with you. He trusts me, and he trusts you to look after me."

"Yeah right. If only he knew that it's always you who's doing the rescuing."

"Well, the four of us have to make sure and come up with something, so he never has to find out. And, Blaine, thanks. I couldn't ask Chance to come back. It was too hard for him to leave."

Blaine glanced toward the Mystic, watched as he sighed then heaved in a breath of resignation before he spoke.

"I know daughter, it's just that I also know the strength we would have if the three of you were united together in battle. There is no doubt in my mind that we would win. We would all be safe if the power the three of you have was combined.

For a moment no one spoke. The Mystic held Michelle's gaze. He was more aware than any of them of the bond forged through time between Michelle and Chance. He'd lived with them through time after time and witnessed their devotion.

It didn't surprise him in the least that once again their souls had found each other. The only surprising thing was that they hadn't waited for each other as they'd always done. He prayed that somehow they would be able to accomplish all they had to do without Chance's aid. If they had the luxury of a year or even a few months it would be no problem. But now, with the fifth element gone they would be severely weakened, like any star that lost a part of itself.

They were mortally wounded. They could no longer count on Sal. If Cassie were correct, if Sal were possessed; to continue to train in his presence was signing their death warrants. It would be total suicide. They really could use Chance's energy, the Mystic thought. But like Blaine, he too didn't want to disrupt Michelle's life, nor that of her husband Larry. Only thing, without Chance it was possible that none of them would get to live out this lifetime.

Together the four of them studied, their senses on the alert for any sound, any word. They could all feel it, an unspoken knowledge that they were working crippled. Whoever heard of a four pronged star or pentagram? If only they could have used Sal until they'd completed their work.

"The phone rang, startling them out of their somberness.

"Sal, is that you?"

Cassandra turned worried eyes to the group, flashing for them to throw up mental barriers.

"Cassie, I'm in trouble, help me."

She felt a sudden stab of pain, and clutched the phone to her ear screaming out his name. "Sal, where are you? I'm coming."

"Sal's in trouble," she shouted over the pounding in her heart, thinking of Todd, wanting to get to him before it was too late.

"Stupid bitch." Norman almost screamed into the phone. He'd not had a chance to tell her to come alone before she rambled on.

"Sal, hold on."

"Cassie, come alone. I don't want everyone gawking at me." Norman smiled to himself at how much like Salvatore he sounded. He'd fooled Cassie completely.

"What's going on?"

Norman recognized MaDia's voice in the background. What the hell was he doing there still?

"It's Sal," he heard Cassie explaining. "He's in trouble; he wants me to come alone."

"No way," MaDia screamed. "No damn way are you going alone. If he wants you, I'm coming too."

"So am I."

That voice must have belonged to the woman. Norman still didn't know who she was, but it didn't matter. He didn't want a freaking circus. He only wanted Cassie.

"Sal, Blaine and Michelle are coming with me."

"All right, just hurry, Cassie." Norman made his voice weak. "Cassie, I'm sorry," he whispered and hung up the phone.

Norman slammed his fist into the wall. Damn stupid, stupid bitch. This could have ended if she wasn't so fucking stupid. All she had to do was come alone, that's all. How much more simple could it have been? He'd planned to fuck her all night long if necessary until he felt his sperm go into her and he didn't doubt that he would be able to tell when that happened. Now he had to readjust his plans.

Well, it might be better anyway. While they were all preparing to save Sal, he would pay the old Mystic a visit. This should make up for his spoiled plans.

***

It had to be said. Someone had to voice it. He sure as hell wished it wasn't him, but as he looked round the room he knew none of the others would voice his concerns. "Cassie, What if that wasn't really Salvatore? Did the thought ever occur to you that this could be a set up?"

Blaine was frowning slightly, trying his best to be the voice of reason. He judged by the doubting looks in the faces staring back at him that they believed his motives were simply altruistic.

"Blaine, I know Sal's voice. Something's happened to him. Maybe he even tried to rid himself of the entity. I don't know what happened, but I don't have time to argue with you now. I'm going."

"I never said I wasn't going." Blaine sucked in air through his mouth and blew it back out making as much noise as possible.

"We're all going," the teacher stretched. "We're stronger if we stay together."

"No."

"No?" The old man turned in amazement to face Michelle. "No. Who are you suggesting is not going?"

"I don't think you should go," she answered. "If this is a setup, Cassie may still need your help and all of us together would prove too easy a target."

The old man was silent for a moment, and something happened in that time. Blaine had a vision of the old man lying dead. It was so real he shivered.

"I think Blaine should remain here to keep the home fires burning, I'll be of more help." The Mystic outlined his plan as though Michelle hadn't voiced her objections. "No offense, Blaine, but you can't give the assistance that I can. I'm better." he said quietly.

Blaine thought of his vision. No way was he going to allow his mentor to be put in immediate danger. "That's right, you are, Sir. But you're also our last line of defense. Who better than you to make sure this place remains safe? If Michelle, Cassandra and I need to retreat, you will be the one we run to."

Flimsy yes, but it was the best he could do at the time. The smile spread across the face of the Mystic. "At least your thoughts of me being feeble have disappeared." The old man touched Blaine's shoulder. "You can't prevent my death, Blaine. If your vision is true, it will happen "

"But..."

"No buts, you can't hide anything from me."

"Then why...?"

"Why am I agreeing to stay? Because you're right. Someone should remain here to ensure that things are not defiled. As much as I want to accompany you, I think I would worry more about leaving you alone here without anyone to watch over you."

Blaine frowned at the old man.

"I'm sorry," the Mystic amended. "Cassie and Michelle have you to look out for them. They're very lucky. I'll stay and guard the castle."

He turned and walked away as a smile broke across his craggy face. Blaine couldn't help but smile also. Yeah they all knew the order of things. He was going with the women so they could keep an eye on him. He was damn tired of this baby psychic routine. As soon as this was over, he made a solemn vow to himself to study night and day. His powers had increased tenfold. The only thing he could admit that he needed was more focus. He looked toward Cassandra. That was no good. She was the cause of his distraction. He felt himself start to harden. Even in the midst of danger he wanted her.

He glanced across the room to where Michelle huddled in quiet conversation with the Mystic. She saw him touch her necklace, the one he'd given her. And again a wave of remorse hit him. What had he gotten his mother into? If they made it out of this in one piece he wouldn't be able to blame Larry if he forbade him to never see her again.

He walked toward her, noticing that they stopped talking as he approached. They both had worried looks. He frowned for a second before laughing, here he was worried about her and she was worried about him.

"Stick close to me," he ordered his mother, "I'll help you with your blocks." He noticed the old man's left brow quirked in amusement.

"I found that I can build a bridge, a link for you." This time the pair was openly smiling at him. "Just stick close to me, I'll protect you."

"I know you will," Michelle answered, and kissed his cheek swatting his shoulder affectionately. He watched while she said goodbye to the Mystic, a strange gleam in her eyes, a kind of sorrow, a knowing. But just as quickly as it came, it disappeared, and she assured him they would return soon.

"Call if you need us." Blaine said to the Mystic as he followed Cassandra out the door wondering why they didn't all just bi-locate to where Sal was. "Teacher humor me and lock the door behind us, please."

"You know I have an open door policy."

"I know." Blaine smiled. "But we do have several evil entities about. Can't you please, just lock the door?"

"A lock will not keep out anyone determined to gain entrance and most assuredly it will not keep out a psychic who has the power of magick."

"Will you just humor me this once?" Worry for the Mystic was making him lose focus. Perhaps none of them should be going. But Cassandra would go alone and his stubborn mother would follow. He had no choice to go with the women regardless if they thought he could protect them or not.

"Grandfather?"

"Emotional blackmail huh, Blaine?" The Mystic laughed. "I'll lock the door."

Chapter Twenty-Five

This was a bit redundant. They'd gone to Cassandra's hotel and checked her room and Sal's. No Salvatore. They'd gone to the bar and had been told Sal had been there earlier, that he'd had a drink with two men and left. Calling him had been an exercise in utter uselessness. Until this moment Blaine had been holding back on speaking. He couldn't any longer, his feelings about the Mystic were intensifying. He was worried about the old man. It surprised him when Michelle was the one to voice her thoughts.

"We've been driving forty minutes, Cassandra. Can't you get anything?"

Michelle's voice was a bit impatient and Blaine couldn't blame her. They had not spoken a word since leaving the hotel with the exception of Cassandra ordering Blaine to drive north. He was still driving north.

"Isn't there anything?"

"Nothing."

Blaine heard the slight sniffle in her voice and knew she was worried if they were too late.

"Why don't we go to him? Just bi-locate."

"He wouldn't like it."

"What are you talking about? If you're trying to save his life—"

"Sal's proud. He'd rather die than for me to break my promise to him."

"Why would you be breaking a promise? I don't understand." And this time Blaine was truly puzzled.

"I couldn't take you with me."

"You don't need to. We can do that on our own." His voice sounded annoyed, it was because he was.

"No, I don't mean that." Her eyes flew down. "I promised Sal this would always be something special for the two of us."

"Thousands of people can do this. What are you talking about?"

"I know they can, but still I made a promise to Sal. I can't allow you to go with me, not in that manner, we have to keep trying to reach him."

"If we don't do something soon, it may very well be too late," Blaine warned.

Cassandra sat back, her head against the cushions. She opened the window for a little air, and tuned into Sal calling him. Nothing. Then suddenly and without warning. a slow awareness crept into her big toe and continued until it tingled along her spine. With sudden force, pain began rumbling throughout her body making her weak

Her fingers reached out to claw the back of the seat and she managed to moan. "Turn around, it's the Mystic, it wasn't Sal. We have to help the Mystic."

A quick glance told Blaine that Michelle had left her body. She was gone to be with her father. A cold knot of fear claimed his soul. Cassandra's eyes were glazed over and she appeared to be in some type of trance. He couldn't very well leave her to pull the car over and bi-locate after his mother.

The three of you are much stronger together. Will you put your mother's life at risk to save the woman you love? He remembered the Mystic's words to him. With everything that was in him Blaine had been certain when he answered, "No," to the Mystic's question. He'd been certain that he would never endanger his mother, but he had.

He looked backward toward the sound of the moaning. No, he couldn't save his mother, to do so would mean leaving Cassandra to whatever was happening. The only think he could do was to get to the Mystic's home in record time.

Blaine prayed harder than he ever had in his entire life. He prayed for God to take care of his mother. He prayed that whatever the hell Cassandra was going through she would be done with it quickly. He prayed for the life of the Mystic and he prayed for the safety of his father. When he thought he was done praying he prayed for the soul of Salvatore. For Cassandra's sake he prayed they could save him.

***

"So old man we meet again."

The Mystic turned toward the voice, instantly erecting an energy force field. He almost laughed remembering he'd told Blaine a locked door could not keep out evil. And he had locked it. Blaine had tried it before they'd left as though he'd not trusted him to actually know how to lock a door. But the danger lurking in front of him demanded his immediate attention. He'd worry later about how the intruder entered. He stared at the young man with the thick brown hair and even thicker glasses. There was something vaguely familiar about the man, but he couldn't place him.

"You don't remember me, do you old man?"

"You're not one of my students." The Mystic cocked his head to the side. "I would have remembered."

"That's right; you never thought I was good enough to be one of your prized pets. But it didn't matter old man." Norman laughed, the evil sound filling his own soul and the rooms of the home as well.

Norman could feel his anger pooling. This wasn't an act. The Mystic truly didn't remember him. He felt jilted. He'd thought to make the Mystic look at him in wonder, realizing the foolishness of not teaching him, of treating him in the same disdainful manner, like Sal and Cassie had done, and all the others.

Norman closed his eyes and screamed, loud, long and guttural; filled with every moment of agony he'd lived whether real or imagined.

He looked at the old man hiding from him underneath his iridescent bubble. No one could sustain such a structure for long, even someone as skilled and gifted as the Mystic. Norman was better, he'd always been better.

He pulled five crystal hearts from his pocket and held them as close to the bubble as the energy permitted him to get.

"One for each of you old man," he roared. "I'm patient. The moment you lose focus, the first microscopic tear in your shield and you're mine. You're going to die tonight old man."

The Mystic sat crossed legged on the floor underneath his own energy field and looked quizzically at the man ranting and raving, trying hard to place him. "What have I done to you? Cassie, are you the one after her? The other psychics who have been harmed, are you the one responsible? What it is you want? Perhaps we can help you." He took a long look at the man. His entire aura was enclosed by a thick dark cloud.

The Mystic shivered and it went all the way to his soul. He'd never before encountered anyone without even a spark of light from somewhere deep within. This man had been feeding on his hatred apparently for a long, long time. He'd wager the hate started years before the talk began of mating Cassie to one of the psychic.

"Are you a...?" He stopped. He'd been going to ask the man if he were a psychic, because he thought he was aware of all in the psychic community. But it was apparent the man who had him trapped in his own home was indeed a psychic. He decided to try again, not because he was afraid for his own safety but, because the man was right. He couldn't keep the field up all night and he thought of the others. They would definitely need him. Here he was imprisoned behind a wall of his own making.

It was too soon to lose the daughter he'd been searching lifetime after lifetime for, much too soon. He thought of Blaine the grandchild, the seed of his daughter. Blaine with so much potential, if he died tonight the light would be taken from Blaine's eyes. He would lose his desire to study. He knew him so well.

Blaine really was much too sensitive to have been born a psychic. He would blame himself if something happened. Poor Cassie, what would happen to her? He even thought of Sal. A man he loved like his own son. He was so proud of Sal. What would happen to Sal's soul if they didn't find a way to save him?

Five minutes had already passed. He'd never gone past thirty, not alone. Now he had to try, the lives of all those he loved depended on it.

"Why me old man? Why wasn't I ever good enough?"

"I don't know. I'm sorry if I offended you, but I took on all students that showed a willingness to learn and a hunger. If I didn't accept you it was nothing personal."

"It sure in the hell was personal to me. You were the one person I came to for help, you and only you, but you were always so busy with your precious Salvatore and your precious Cassie. You shooed me away as if I were no more than a flea bitten dog."

"I'm sorry."

"Not yet, but you will be soon."

Norman turned from the Mystic. He didn't like the look of pity that had suddenly come into the man's eyes. He no longer needed his pity. That's all he'd ever had time to give him, him and Cassie. Well to hell with their pity, it was never what he wanted. He wanted their love, their acceptance. It was too late for all of that now. He no longer cared, the hell with both of them.

He did his best to push away the image of the little boy standing on the Mystic's steps, begging to be let into the group. The Mystic had smiled and given him a bag of cookies and sent him on his way. They'd gone through that same routine day after day for an entire year. Now to hear after all of that, the man didn't remember him.

Each time he'd given up and walked away Sal and Cassie would be walking up the steps laughing. Sal would punch him in the arms, push him down, or just say boo.

Once he'd pushed him down into the grass, and was attempting to make him eat it. Cassie had pulled Sal away dusting Norman off in the process and holding her hand out to him. And the look in her eyes, the pity. God how he hated that look from her. He would rather have Salvatore punch him until he was no more than a bloody pulp than endure that look from her. That was what finally made him give up trying to learn from the Mystic. Cassie's look of pity each day, never just a warm smile, maybe a piece of candy held between her delicate fingers, but pity, always pity, as if she knew he could never be what they were.

The last time he went, he was bold and shouted to her that he loved her. Sal had chased him and Cassie had chased Sal, pulling him away before he could do any real damage.

"I love you, Cassie," Norman had announced again.

"But you don't even know me." Her eyes held the oddest look, then instantly it was gone and she was back to keeping Sal from beating the crap out of him.

"I don't think you should come back," she'd said.

And he didn't.

Now the old man's eyes had the same pity they'd held for an entire year. Never once, not once in the year that Norman went there did the old man ever open up his home to him and invite him in, allow him to see the magic that the other kids found inside. For surely there had to be magic for a beautiful girl like Cassie to fall in love with a bully like Salvatore.

He thought of the others, all the ones the Mystic taught. They all laughed at him and threw rocks. The last few weeks had brought twenty years back with a whoosh.

Norman looked down at the crystal hearts, picking one and slipping the other four back into his pockets.

He turned back toward the Mystic watching the man's eyes watching him. He stared at the crystal until it took on a life of it's on. The ornament pulsated slowly at first picking up speed as the rhythm changed. Norman smiled; aligning the crystal with the beat from the old man's heart. He closed his eyes in awe loving the feel of the power of life and death being there in the palm of his hands. He was in charge. He opened his eyes and stared at the crystal willing it to once again begin a slow steady beat mimicking the functions of the real thing.

Norman smiled, "I have one for Sal, one for Cassie," he laughed gleefully counting off the names with his finger as a child might. "Then I had to include one for Blaine MaDia, and now one for the woman who's involved herself."

He saw the look of alarm instantly, the very second it leapt into the old man's eyes. She was more important than he thought.

"Who is she old man?"

The Mystic refused to answer, concentrating instead on reinforcing his barrier. The longer he held it the farther away Blaine, Cassie and his daughter would be. He could do it. He could continue holding the shield. He smiled suddenly. He didn't know the man that was holding him hostage, but if the man knew anything at all about him, it should be the fact that he wasn't a quitter. He would find someway to defeat the maniac. No, he still didn't remember the man, but he knew his instincts must have been right. The man had gone mad.

The Mystic felt bad enough that Sal had allowed some entity to use his body. But for this poor fool sitting in front of him, to have given him the gift of knowledge, in the hands of a loon it could have fatal results.

It was obvious someone had trained him. It was hard to tell if the man in front of him was a psychic who'd delved too deeply into the black arts. Or a masterful practitioner of the black arts with a little psychic powers. Either way, if he couldn't keep the barrier up they would all be in trouble. He pitied the world if Cassie was forced to give birth by such a monster.

It was over forty minutes, his energy was waning, but still he remained determined to hold on. A second before it happened, he saw it, felt the ping go through him, and knew he couldn't keep it up for very long. He had to find a way to alert them. He thought of Cassie, his poor dear Cassie. God how he hated to do it. He knew the pain her feeling his death would cause her, but it was the only way to let them know. She was an empath. Feeling his death might destroy her, but if he didn't alert them, her not knowing could very well destroy them all.

With all his remaining energy he concentrated as hard as he could on Cassie. He felt the barrier giving way, before the structure crumbled entirely, he felt the tight convulsing of his chest. His heart was on fire and unwanted tears sprang forth. He looked into the eyes of the madman, trying to imprint his picture to pass on to Cassie, hoping it would help.

He called with all his might to the cosmos to allow Cassie to hear him. He felt his jaw go slack as the pain became unbearable. He tasted the trickle of blood that ran from the corner of him mouth, then blessedly nothing, darkness and an end to his pain.

Chapter Twenty-Six

Norman bent over the body of the Mystic. It hadn't felt as good as he'd thought. He was going to put his finger underneath the old man's nose but something stopped him. He looked at the small pool of blood. It wasn't necessary. The old man was gone and now Norman would never get his answers, why he was thought to not be good enough. He shivered and pulled his bulky sweater around his body more to ward off the sudden chill than to disguise himself.

***

Michelle entered the room abruptly. With a startled gasp she rushed toward the disheveled body of the Mystic and screamed.

A moment of uncertainty claimed her soul and made her doubt. She didn't know whether to start CPR or call for help. She called for help first then began CPR her thoughts going in all directions. She wanted Blaine with her, and for the first time in months she again wished for Chance's help. He'd managed to save Larry. Maybe just maybe he could do the same with the Teacher.

She continued breathing air into the old man, no response. Maybe this was the price they would all have to pay for breaking the laws of nature. She thought of Larry, Blaine, Chance and her children. She loved them all. Then she looked down at the face of the Mystic, her father for many lifetimes. And her tears began to interfere with her poor efforts at best. Off in the distance she heard the wail of sirens and somewhere inside of her a comforting feel that Blaine was nearby. Perhaps with the three of them they would be able to help the Mystic. Her thoughts raced back to

Cassandra and she hoped that the young woman was alright. She'd not waited around to see. She'd had no choice, but to go to her father.

Her arms felt about to cave from the strain. Michelle summoned all the energy she could muster when Blaine flew through the door followed by Cassandra. She closed her eyes going back to her own body and in moments reentering the room just seconds ahead of the paramedics.

Blaine was pounding on the old man's chest. Tears filled his eyes. Michelle's glance slid to Cassandra. The young woman was still looking dazed though not the same shade of gray she'd worn earlier. Michelle slumped into a chair and stared, overcome by her sense of grief, her sense of loss. *No*, she screamed silently. It's much too soon, I haven't had a chance to get to know my father. She glanced toward Blaine and her thoughts flew to Chance. She didn't want to lose their son, not now. Not ever. *Chance*, she cried to herself. *Help us please.*

***

Blaine held the Mystic's wrist, a pervasive sense of loss filling him. This past year of his life had been filled with finding and losing. If he believed in curses he'd surely believe the deck was stacked against him.

Without warning a faint tingling began in his left wrist. It turned rapidly into a burn, enough so that his eyes were averted from looking at the face of his mentor to the spot on his arm. The stones of his bracelet were glowing, pulsating almost as if they had a life of their own. It was then he remembered.

"Michelle," he shouted, "Mother, Mother, come here." He clasped the Mystic's limp hand in his own and held on tight ignoring the paramedic's orders to move aside. When Michelle reached him he grabbed her hand.

"Grab his other hand."

"What?"

"Do it, do it," Blaine ordered. There was no time to talk, he sensed immediately the moment the change began. He scanned the Mystic's body and detected a faint hum of life.

Blaine glanced at Michelle. For the first time he was able to smile through the tears. As he'd expected the diamond that set in the center of Michelle's necklace was glowing with an unearthly light. He looked closely at the other stones, they too were glowing.

"We've got a pulse," came the excited voice of one of the men working on the Teacher. "Come on let's hurry up, this guy just might make it."

"Blaine."

Blaine had almost forgotten Cassandra. He observed her now, the worry coming back to rest on his shoulders. "Are you going to be okay?" he touched her gently, closing his eyes against the thought of losing her.

"You really scared me." Blaine whispered.

"I'm sorry, that hasn't happened to me in fifteen years. I used to have good control. It must be—"

"Someone you care about," Blaine interrupted. "You don't have to explain."

"And you don't have to make excuses for me." Cassandra squared her shoulders. "You were right, the herbs I've been taking to stop the visions, the feelings of others pains they've weakened me somehow. It's just that when the Mystic was dying it was too much for me. I love him so much, I couldn't take it."

"I know," he answered pulling her into his arms. "I feel the same."

"What happened?" she asked. "How did you and your mother? What did the two of you do?" She touched her hand to his bracelet. "It was glowing. Is this some kind of amulet?"

"Later," he cautioned. "I'll tell you everything later."

Blaine pulled Cassandra along behind him watching as they piled the Mystic into the ambulance, his grandfather, he still couldn't get over that fact. He helped Michelle into the back of the ambulance both of them overcoming the men's objections with mild mental commands. For once Blaine didn't feel guilty about entering someone's thoughts. It wasn't something he did on a whim but it was important his mother be with her father. She'd only just found him. Too many lifetimes had gone by with them not reconnecting, they needed this time.

Once they were in the car heading after the ambulance the weight of loss increased rather than decreased. He gazed in Cassandra's direction. "Is there anything I can do to help you if it happens again?"

Cassandra's eyebrow shot upwards. She knew he was thinking about the fact that they were heading toward a hospital, lots of pain, and lots of sadness.

"No, Blaine. Thanks, it's not like a disease that I can take a pill for. It's a gift."

He smiled in her direction. "Are you happy to have it now?"

"Well, considering that someone is killing psychics to get to me and we're chasing an ambulance down the street, no. But considering that I may not have ever known what was happening with the Teacher, that we may not have gotten there in time to save him, then I have to reconsider."

"Is that your only reason for reconsidering?" Blaine asked.

"Of course not. If it were not for my gift I would more than likely have never met you. So yes, I'm glad that I have it."

"Hallelujah." Blaine laughed out loud. "Then this night wasn't a total waste." He held tightly to her trembling fingers. His obvious ploy at levity known and accepted. For now they had no choice. They couldn't very well run and hide. They had to be with Michelle and the Mystic.

Cassandra held out her hand, in it contained the remnants of the red crystal heart. "Do you know what that is?"

"I'm afraid I do. I've heard of the practice being used in black magick, but I've never witnessed it. Do you think someone did this deliberately?"

"It certainly appears that way."

"Sal?"

"I don't think so. I didn't feel him there."

"But would you feel him still if he's possessed?"

"I believe so."

"You sure this isn't just more wishful thinking?"

"No."

"If it isn't Salvatore, we'd better find out fast who it was. Whoever it is seems to know a hell of a lot more about all of us than we do him." Blaine paused, the coldness increasing. If the Mystic couldn't protect himself against this man where did it leave the rest of them?

He let his thoughts fall as the doors of the hospital loomed in front of him. A second after he parked, the passenger door opened and Cassandra shot out of the car and sprinted toward the doors. Blaine followed thinking about the ride. She'd been especially quiet. God if only he hadn't promised, he'd scan her mind, just to see if she was doubting his ability to take care of her, to help her.

The strong smell of antiseptics put things in proper proportions. The Mystic was lying stricken somewhere and he'd promised to take care of the people he loved. No wonder Cassandra doubted.

"How did you know?"

Michelle was looking at him with eyes as big as saucers. "I don't know," he answered her. "I felt the warmth and remembered."

"Remembered what?"

Blaine turned to include Cassandra in the conversation.   "The Mystic made these for me. I gave one to my mother and father and kept one for myself."

"But how did it help him?"

"I'm getting to that."   He held up his hand, he'd not yet told Cassandra the full story. He glanced toward his mother and at her nod of approval he continued.

"Just recently the Mystic told me that he'd put little pieces of his soul's pattern on each of the pieces."

"Why?"

"Because he thought my mother might be his daughter. He's been looking for her for several lifetimes. He hoped that perhaps in the next incarnation, she would find him."

Blaine stopped and looked at both Michelle and Cassandra before running his hands wildly through his hair. "I think somehow our being here with the amulets and his own soul pattern that it somehow filled his soul and gave him the strength to hang on."

"Do you think it's going to be enough?" Cassandra stared from one somber face to the other.

"It's not complete." Blaine whispered. "It was made as a trinity. Michelle and I are only two parts of the trinity, there's another part."

"Your father." Cassandra's voice was soft. Blaine had told her of Chance and Michelle finding each other. She knew Michelle was married. Hell, she'd just had dinner with Michelle's husband, Larry a few short hours before. Her eyes caught Michelle.

"No, I won't call him."

"The Mystic may die." Tears stung Blaine's eyes as he looked at his mother.

"I still won't call him. Blaine, think what you're asking me to do. I'm not just thinking of my own life now or Larry. Though God knows I should. I don't want to put my marriage through anymore stress."

"I thought you said this wasn't about you." Blaine stopped Michelle, his feeling of helplessness making his voice harder than he intended. "It sure sounds like it."

"You didn't let me finish. Chance would be hurt also. How many times do you think he can continue to say goodbye? I won't call him."

"Even if it means your father may die?"

"You can get the amulet from Chance, we can just have that."

"I'm sorry to butt in," Cassandra's voice dropped to almost a whisper. "I don't think that's it. I think it has to do with the connection of the people involved. I think the three of you have to be together with the amulets to return him to good health."

Michelle stared back at Blaine and Cassandra. "He's lived many lifetimes, he understands that death is not an ending. He will be reborn again and again same as always."

"I'm sick and tired of hearing all of you talk so calmly about accepting death." Blaine screamed, the pain of his mother's words cutting him. He didn't want to hear anymore. "I don't care that he'll be reborn. For God sake, I've barely had time to get used to the fact that he's my grandfather. I don't want to lose any member of my family."

"I'm sorry, Blaine. I can't give you the okay to do this as much as I might want to. I can't. You have to understand."

Blaine glared at his mother. "The Mystic said together the three of us could defeat Sal, maybe he knew even then that Sal was possessed. I don't know. I just know he said that together our powers would be more."

"No. I will not call Chance."

"Listen to me, Mother," Blaine walked directly in front of Michelle. "This isn't over, there's a maniac out there on the loose killing people and we're all on his hit list. I'll do whatever it takes to keep you safe. Do you understand?"

"You call him and you'll ruin my life."

At that they both looked toward the voice calling Michelle's name.

Blaine looked in Larry's direction then glared once again at his mother.

"He's my husband. I called him," she muttered between clenched teeth and got up to go to Larry.

Blaine heard her explaining that the Mystic had an apparent heart attack. She left out of course that he was her father of several lifetimes. Blaine noted she also failed to tell her husband how they'd literally pulled the old man's spirit back into his body and that if they wanted to keep it there, they needed Chance. No, he noted bitterly she didn't bother to divulge any of that information.

He'd barely noticed the tugging on his arms. Now he looked down into the chocolate brown mist of Cassandra's eyes and he wanted to cry. He didn't feel up to the challenge. He wanted his father's help. He wanted anyone's help who could possible help him save the two women he loved. Neither of them seemed to understand how important it was to him. His mother was accepting of her death and Cassandra was more than ready to marry Sal and end all of this. Well, he wasn't ready to accept either of their decisions. He was going to fight and he intended to win by any means necessary.

"You can't ask her to risk her marriage." Cassandra whispered to him softly.

Cassandra's eyes were glassy with unshed tears. Blaine wanted so badly to kiss away the hurt he saw there. "I'm trying to save her life, all of our lives."

"At the expense of others? Plus what if it doesn't work? What if having the three of you together doesn't save the Mystic, what if it doesn't save us? You've given this manic and whoever is inhabiting Sal's body another victim. You could destroy the lives of Michelle's children and their children. Do you want that on your hands, Blaine?"

"I'm not going to allow her to die."

"It's not your choice to make. She volunteered to help out of her love for you. She knew the risks, you can't go against what she wants and she doesn't want you calling Chance."

Blaine looked toward Michelle crying softly in Larry's arms.

"I'm not going to let her die."

***

Damn. He'd never made a mistake like that. Norman was angry. He should have run a sword through the old man's heart, there would have been no way anyone would have been able to revive him.

Norman hit the wall with his fist. The old man was dead. He had to be. Cassie and Blaine were merely going through the motions.

A sound tore from his throat that frightened Norman for a moment. He'd had no intentions of screaming, it just came out and with it the anguish and pain of his childhood. They'd had their chance, all of them. For years he'd sat on the sidelines trying to be friends with them, not being accepted. Hell, he'd had as much right to the Mystic's teaching as they did. He was also a twenty-first generation psychic. That little fact had gone ignored by the entire community. He was sure when they counted the twelve they didn't include him. He wondered who they'd substituted to take his place or if they simply over looked his family's standing. Why not forget him? His family had.

Norman glared at the phone. Enough of this. "Look bitch," he barked into the phone, "the old man is dead you can't fool me with your tricks. And guess who's next? Where is your precious Salvatore by the way? Why isn't he with you now? Are you wondering how I know where you are and who you're with?

"I'm a fucking psychic, you stupid bitch! You pretend not to know me, but I'm telling you, soon you will know who I am. And you will scream out my name before I kill you. I'm not interested anymore in the prophecy, just in killing you."

With that Norman slammed the phone down, banging it hard for good measure. How he hated them, hated them all, but Cassie he hated the most because once he'd worshipped her, loved her with everything that was in him and she'd never known, never acknowledged his love. He was never good enough for her. He hoped she liked what he had planned for her, because she would acknowledge him now, of that he was sure.

The only thing marring his satisfaction was having to leave the message on a machine. He wanted to hear Cassie's voice, feel the fear creep in on her. He wanted to link with her, hold her pounding heart in his fist, feel her fear.

And kiss away her tears.

No, Norman stop that, stop that nonsense. To hell away with her tears. Her death, that's what he wanted, and he had no plans on comforting her.

***

Cassie rubbed her hands gently up and down Blaine's arms wishing again she had not brought him into her life. If only she'd done as she'd intended, kept two seats for herself, don't get involved with psychics, now here he was. It didn't matter what nonsense the Mystic spouted about Blaine's reincarnated parents having powers, it may well be true, but they needed those powers now, not hundreds of years in the past. Now, Blaine was here and he was not strong enough to battle Salvatore let along the psycho who was after them.

A feeling of sorrow filled her, sorrow that she almost couldn't bear. She was worried about Sal. They hadn't seen him in hours. What if they were too late to help him? She glanced at Michelle in her husband Larry's arms, watched her trying to explain to him why she wanted to stay with an old man she barely knew. The Mystic, Cassie had almost forgotten the harm she'd caused him. She'd always thought of him as invincible. He must have depleted his energies helping all of them train. No one should have been able to get to him so quickly. She wished she could see the man's face who'd hurt the Mystic, but she couldn't. She'd tried; all she could make out was the back of his head and thick brown hair. It could have been anyone, but thank God it wasn't Sal, she would know his dark black curls anywhere.

"Blaine, lets go, Michelle will call if there's any changes."

"I can't leave my mother."

"Your constant glaring at her is not helping."

"Blaine, for God sake, what can you do?" Her voice was harsher than she intended, she stopped as she saw Michelle turn to look at her. "I think he needs to rest for a few hours." Cassandra attempted to explain.

She watched as Michelle scanned Blaine's face, she saw the woman struggling with a decision and hoped despite her misgivings she'd side with her.

"Cassandra's right, Blaine, you go home I'll stay with your friend."

Cassie's hunch was proved. Michelle hadn't told her husband that the Mystic was her long lost father of several lifetimes in the past. *Good move*, she thought, then looked at the quizzical look on Larry's face. He had to be wondering why his wife was so worried about an old man she barely knew.

"I'm staying." Blaine declared.

Blaine glared at Cassandra before holding his mother's glance. The moment lasted so long that Cassie knew they were communicating psychically. She saw the precise second when Blaine became convinced to leave, the slight slump in his shoulders, and the defeated look in his eyes. How Cassie wanted to wipe that look away.

She said a hurried goodbye to both Larry and Michelle and held fast to Blaine as they left. He'd not spoken to either his mother or Larry, just turned from them and walked away.

She waited patiently on the elevator, not saying a word, the walk to the car the same, for two miles driving, where, she didn't know. She was quiet until she could take it no longer.

"Blaine, I know you're hurting, let me help you, let's talk. Where are we going?"

"We're going back to the Mystic's home. We're going to figure out what happened to him, together we're going to reconstruct what happened."

"Are you asking me...?"

"I'm asking you to use your powers. It's a gift, Cassandra, use it."

She was staring at him, his voice angry not loving in the least. She wondered if he blamed her, if he regretted having fallen in love with her. Closing her eyes absorbing the pain, a decision was made. She didn't want that. It no longer mattered how she'd fought against it, she loved him and she didn't want it to end before it begin.

"Blaine, are you angry with me?"

"Yes."

For a nanosecond there was only silence between them before he reached his hand down and found her fingers. "You're not the only one, don't worry, my mother is at the top of my list, the bastard that did this, Salvatore and who ever started this stupid legend. That's the reason for all of this."

"You're wrong, Blaine, it's not the prophecy, it's whoever is killing because of it. It feels so personal." She watched as Blaine squinted at her.

"It does, doesn't it? Is there anyone you can think of that would hate the Mystic?"

She laughed, "hate the Mystic, are you kidding, everyone loves him. He's taught forever."

"Not everyone loves him."

Blaine spoke softly making her wish she hadn't laughed. She'd meant nothing by it. Blaine was right, not everyone loved him or he would not be hovering between life and death at the moment, the doctors unable to find a cause. They had said as much when they'd told them, 'the Teacher was in God's hands now.'

Blaine opened the door to the Mystic's home and put out a hand to stop Cassandra from entering. He closed his eyes and walked forward again, mining for energy. He felt it, strong, powerful, evil and male, definitely male.

Simultaneously the temples of his head began to pound and his head filled with a whirring. His body swayed as he fought to remain centered in his body, dread overcame him and he linked with his mother.

"Are you okay?"

"Yes," she answered him. He opened his eyes and looked directly at Cassandra. "You can come in now."

She came slowly into the room. "Lock the door," Blaine called to her, ignoring her frown, this was the second time he'd requested the Mystic's home be locked.

"Cassandra, the man who was in here tonight, the one who attacked the Teacher, he was on the plane."

"How do you know?"

"He entered my mind at the same time that you did. I felt his evil. I feel the same evil now."

"It's not Sal."

For a moment he looked at her, heard the fear in her voice and a pang of sorrow pierced him. Would she ever feel for him what she felt for Salvatore?

"No, it wasn't Sal," he answered. "That doesn't make things any better for us. We still have to find him. I almost wish it was Sal," he sighed. "At least we would know what the person looks like."

At the same instant it seemed Blaine and Cassandra became aware of the pinging sound telling of a message on the Mystic's answering machine.

Blaine reached it first and pushed the button. The venom that came through the lines practically cracked with hatred. Blaine played the message over and over watching as Cassandra's face blanched.

"Who is he?"

"I don't know."

"You must, he knows you, and he hates you. He wants you to remember him."

"How can I? I never knew anyone that sick."

"Maybe he wasn't sick when you knew him."

"Blaine, I'm not going to start going through everyone I know and make them into suspects."

"We're trying to find a killer."

"There has to be another way. What you're doing is trying to create fear in me. I'm not going to look at everyone in my life and wonder if they're trying to kill me."

"If we don't find them before he finds you your life may be shorter than you think."

"If you want to name everyone who has the power to do this how about you?" Cassandra countered angrily. "You've been angry with the Mystic."

"I was with you."

"You can bi-locate, I know you can and so can your mother, one of you could have done it."

Blaine stood looking at her. She was trying to make him angry that much was obvious. She wasn't going to be any help for whatever reason. He meant it, he was going to protect her and he was going to protect his mother.

His eyes narrowed, he closed his eyes and his mind to her. He couldn't let her see, but he now knew how he would protect her. God help him. She would hate him, but he would protect her.

I don't want to fight with you," he said walking up to her letting his eyes roam her body freely, letting her see the lust that now came quickly.

"How can you want to make love in the midst of all that's happening?" Cassandra asked.

"Because I think it's just the rest we need, to fill ourselves. Besides if this nut is successful it will be my last chance to hold you."

"Blaine."

"I'm teasing," he whispered into her mouth tasting her breathe, holding back his own sorrow for what he must do. She must not know his plans or sense his pain.

"Blaine, are you all right?"

"Yes, I'm just thinking how much I want to protect you and Michelle, and how much I wish things could have been different for us." He pulled away to look into her eyes. "I do love you. I want you to know that, and believe it no matter what happens. I've never felt for anyone what I feel for you. I believe you're my soul mate that we're meant to be together."

"Blaine."

"Don't say anything. Just remember what I just said. I love you."

He held her to him feeling the shape of her body in his arms. He lowered his mouth to take in the hard pebble, the nipple practically jumped into his open mouth.

He kissed her, lavishing everything that he was and ever would be on making her know how much he loved her. *This will be the last time I get to make love to her*. The thought came out of the blue and he couldn't make it go away.

"Blaine, it won't be the last time. I promise."

Her arms wound around him and her tears scorched his cheeks, she'd read his thoughts. He had to be more careful, that was going to be damned hard. He had to be open. It had to be like last time, their souls had to mate or they would be doomed.

He gave up thinking as he trailed kisses down the plane of her belly, each kiss adding to the ignited fire in his body.

He felt the warmth of her hand as she slipped it into the waistband of his jeans. He shivered raising a little to give her easier access. With the snap undone he groaned aloud as she cupped him.

"Cassandra, I want all of you. Trust me, let yourself go completely."

Her legs slid open. Blaine touched his hand to velvet moss nestled in the vee of her legs. He felt her tremble. His eyes closed of their own accord and he saw the faint outline of energy that surrounded her body. Her aura was opening up to him.

How he wished he could just revel in the feel and taste of her, no hidden agenda, no motives, he sucked in a sigh. It was more important to save her life than preserve her love.

Blaine kissed his way down Cassandra's body, imprinting the taste and feel on his brain, this might have to last him throughout eternity. He kissed his way down until he was but a scant fraction of an inch away, he breathed in her womanly essence, the musty smell arousing his senses and his manhood. He felt his own flesh hardening as he dipped his tongue into her, tasting the droplets of moisture. He held her bucking hips closer, wanting never to let her go, he opened his eyes. Hers were closed as she writhed beneath him in ecstasy.

Sensing a change in her body it alerted him that he'd best stop his caressing of her. She was too vulnerable, her orgasm too close to the surface. It was too soon. How he wanted to continue, to make her come and start all over again, but he couldn't. He had one shot to get this right. He pulled away from her just as she moaned and reached her hands out to him, she was shivering in unfulfilled need, her eyes open to meet his.

"Blaine, why did you stop?" She asked.

"Because I want to see your soul, it's not there."

"But we can't let go like that again. I told you we're too unprotected in that state."

"I need to see all of you." He kissed her inner thigh his fingers dipping back into her moist well, her muscles quickly surrounding him, clamping his fingers imprisoning them in the yielding flesh.

"Trust me," he moaned, "meet me." He moved upwards, again licking every inch of her skin, touching her in ways he'd never done, every nerve alive in him knowing what it would take to send her over the edge.

He had to make her lose control; shed the barrier she was holding onto. "I love you, Cassandra, all of you." That did it. He saw the aura shimmer around her glowing with an ever brightening intensity. There it was again, the vivid whiteness.

"I trust you, Blaine."

Her words were soft, sweet, wrapping him in a cocoon of desire that he never wanted to leave, but he had to, for her sake he had to. There was no other way. She cupped him again in her hand rubbing her fingertips across the head of his penis driving him wild with wanting. Blaine entered her, finding her more than ready. He concentrated and sent his aura to meet hers, to join as they had before, soul to soul. He plunged in deeper and deeper until he heard her scream out his name. "Blaine, oh God, Blaine."

Now, he thought. He saw the shadowy forms of their souls grow brighter and brighter. It was as though he was viewing a television screen, until finally there was no turning back. He saw their two souls clinging together intermingling as the soft white light grew in radiance until it became so bright that he could barely look on them. All the colors of the rainbow shimmered and fell on them covering their bodies with their combined auras and the love of the entire universe it seemed to him. He plunged into Cassandra one last time.

"Forgive me," he shouted as he broke the connection and entered her mind. Her orgasm was so strong that he felt the tremors of it around and through him. His body shook also, because he couldn't complete the journey with her.

He saw rapid pictures flashing through her memories. He listened to the sounds, to the voice of the man who'd left her the vile message and he poured everything he had into concentrating on picking up his image. Please, God, he prayed. This has to work; this can't all be for nothing. I can't lose her and still be unable to protect her.

He saw a man, a mass of thick brown hair. Blaine went through the vision and came out on the other side until he was staring at the man face to the face. The ten inch thick coke bottle glasses, everything was imbedded there and he in turn burned the face into Cassandra's consciousness and held it there until he felt a shudder go through her spirit.

"Norman," he heard her say. "Norman Yates." Blaine pushed a little harder wanting her to be sure. "It's Norman," she screamed. "Now get the fuck out of my mind."

With that he released her and eased his way back into his own body. She was still pressed beneath him, he kissed her shoulder. "I'm sorry," he moaned.

Not a sound. Not one blessed sound then the torrent of pain. He held himself up and looked into her eyes. The eyes that had held love for him, trust, now were blank.

"Cassandra, I'm sorry. We had to know."

Still she cried. "I did what I had to do to protect you. We can fight him now that we know who he is."

Her eyes turned colder, her flesh appeared to harden. It felt as if a statue was lying beneath him. She pushed him away from her. What had he expected?

"How could you do that, Blaine? How could you plan and use me like that?"

"I had to."

"No you didn't have to. You made a choice. You used me."

"To save your life."

"You promised me you would never do that, never enter my mind without my permission, but this…this was so much worse. You deliberately made me defenseless, took away all my control in order to betray me."

"In order to save your life."

"Call it what you will. You could have asked, could have made me aware of your plans. Maybe I would have willingly agreed. Now you'll never know."

Cassandra walked slowly to the bathroom. She locked the door behind her wishing she were dead. How stupid of her to trust a psychic, he was just like the others only he was much worse. Even the entity that imprisoned Sal's spirit had stopped short of raping her. That was the correct word. Blaine, had raped her body, her soul and her spirit, and he'd done it deliberately.

She ran the water for the shower wanting to wash away every memory of him. She ached all over, the pain she was feeling was unbearable, she screamed beneath the water. Never in all her years had Cassandra felt pain like this. It was emanating from inside herself and she knew what it was. It was the death of her soul.

Chapter Twenty-Seven

"Chance, I need your help. Michelle and I..., we both need you."

Blaine ran his hand across his forehead. "Please get here soon it's a matter of life and death. You have a key to my house, meet me there. I'll come as soon as I can, but it may take awhile. I have to return to Michael Reese Hospital. Michelle's there."

A slight pause and Blaine rubbed his head again. "I'll tell you all about it when you get here." He knew his unwillingness to answer was giving Chance the impression that Michelle was ill. He didn't care, not now. They needed his help and if the only way he could get it was to lie to his soul father, then, so be it.

He hung up the phone, feeling weary. As he turned, he saw Cassandra staring at him, not glaring, just watching him. He should have known.

"We need more help."

"Why not?" she muttered woodenly. "You've betrayed me, why not your mother, and father?"

"I'm trying to protect her. I'm trying to protect all of us, keep us all alive."

"Is the price worth it, Blaine? You betray the people you say you love and they don't thank you for it. They hate you. Is that worth the price?"

Her words stung like a slap. "I did it because I love you."

She smiled at him, her face and eyes so cold that if she stretched her lips just a little more he feared her entire face would crack and fall to the floor. "I did what I had to do. I wasn't willing to lose either of you."

"You've lost me, Blaine. Even a baby psychic would know that."

Blaine stared at her. That was all he could do, his hands hung limply at his side. She hated him. *Was it worth it*, he wondered. He wouldn't know until this nightmare was over and she was safe. Then and only then would he be free to count up the cost. "You still need my help."

"I don't need anything from you, baby psychic." Cassandra taunted. She was being deliberately nasty and she didn't give a damn. "I'll work with you because you brought your mother into this and if it were not for me she wouldn't be involved. But make no mistake, when this nightmare is over I never want to see you again. And unless I miss my guess what you've just done might cost you your mother, you arrogant son of a bitch!"

"I had no choice," Blaine repeated as he watched something happen to Cassandra. In a flash she'd rushed across the room and was pounding him with her fists.

"I hate you, Blaine." she screamed, "for making me believe I could trust someone. I hate you. You didn't have to go to these lengths. I hate you."

He took her blows until she collapsed and fell against him, then he lifted her hands and kissed the closed fist, "I'm sorry," he said again as she shoved her body away from him.

He watched her go, watched as she went into a trance. And when she came out of it he watched her fingers pushing buttons on the phone and his heart broke. It hurt like hell, but it was true, he had lost her. He heard her talking to Salvatore.

"It's Norman Yates. No, Sal. Not Bates, you know how he hated that. I have no idea why he hates me so, but apparently he hates us all. Listen, he called me. Pretended to be you. He was good. I believed it was you, thought you were in danger and left the Mystic to come and help you. He attacked the Mystic. He's in pretty bad shape. He's over at Michael Reese. Meet me there, we need to put an end to this."

Blaine heard a slight hesitation, then her eyes found him and she glared. If she were a dragon she would have been breathing fire. He was thankful that unlike the little girl in Fire starter, Cassandra didn't possess that particular gift or he would have been toast. He attempted to smile at her knowing without a doubt it was too soon. Her next words confirmed it.

"Maybe we can talk to Norman, if we can't reason with him, then yes, you can announce to the entire community that I'll marry you."

She couldn't mean it. She was only angry, trying to get back at him, but one look into the depths of her brown eyes and he knew she'd meant every word. He opened his mouth to protest, but could only come up with, "You called Salvatore."

"And you called Chance."

He couldn't miss the ice in her voice, still he attempted to close the distant, pretend noting irreparable had happened. "We need Chance, he's part of the trinity, the Mystic...," he stopped because the look in Cassandra's eyes was freezing him.

"And I need Sal."

With that she walked from the room and out the door, out of his life.

                    ***

With a sigh of disappointment Blaine followed Cassandra into the hospital. From the Mystic's home now to his bedside, not a word passed between them. He would get through it, he would. He was more than used to women walking away from him. *But not one that you loved, one who's soul you touched.*

He hated the habit he had of talking to himself. If only he didn't have to analyze everything over and over, maybe that would make it easier. He glanced across the room at his mother wondering how long it would be before she too left him.

Michelle stood walking toward them her eyes glancing at Cassandra before coming to rest on Blaine. "You two didn't have to return so quickly, there hasn't been any change." She tilted her head slightly. "What's wrong?" she whispered and Blaine knew she was attempting to keep their conversation private.

Cassandra pivoted her head around spearing them both with a look. "Tell her the news, Blaine. We know who it is that's after me. Maybe now we can stop him."

"That's wonderful. Isn't it?" Michelle looked between Blaine and Cassandra for confirmation. "Isn't this what we wanted?"

"There's a little more." Cassandra smiled sarcastically in Blaine's direction. "Blaine, don't you want to tell your mother all of it?"

Focus, focus, he commanded his body. He looked into his mother's eyes. He had no choice but to tell her. "Where's Larry?"

"He went to get coffee," Michelle answered. "What's going on? Why is there so much tension between the two of you?"

"I called Chance." There he'd said it. He clenched his jaw and waited.

"You did what?"

"I called Chance."

"Tell me you're kidding, Blaine. I asked you not to do that."

"I had no choice."

"What do you mean you had no choice?"

She was angry, but he didn't see the same cold dismissal that was in Cassandra's eyes. She was merely angry, that he could handle.

"I never wanted to involve you in this, now that I have, I have to make the decisions for all of us. The two of you are thinking with your hearts, someone has to be reasonable." He glared at both women. Maybe if he became angry at them he could ignore the hurt and pain in both their eyes.

"What are you talking about? I'm here because I remember who I've always been." Michelle fumed. "If we can't handle this together what do you expect Chance to do? He's one man, Blaine. Did you stop to think that you're now putting his life in danger?" She turned away from him and he linked instantly with her telepathically. "Don't turn away from me," he pleaded.

"Have you thought about what Chance's coming back is going to do to Larry?" Michelle asked him.

Blaine lifted his brows trying to signal to his mother that Larry was back and standing behind her. She didn't heed his warning.

"I can't work with Chance, don't you understand that. Maybe this is all some romantic notion on your part to see the two of us together, reunited. It's asking too much of all of us. I'm married, Blaine. Larry's not going to like this."

"Not like what?"

Blaine, Michelle and Cassandra all looked at Larry. He was the true innocent in the room. He had no belief in anything he couldn't explain.

"What's going on?" Larry asked of no one in particular. Blaine started to answer but was stopped by his mother's glaring eyes. He watched in silence as she led her husband away wondering how she was possibly going to explain to him that she was involved in a psychic war.

Shit. Was it worth it? He asked himself. He looked toward Cassandra's stiff form then at his mother. He saw the trembling in her shoulders. All he knew at this point was that they were still alive. Surely that would have to outweigh even his mother's wish for an untroubled marriage?

For twenty minutes Blaine gazed out of the window, he tuned into the spirits he'd been ignoring for the past weeks. They knew what he'd gotten himself into and were appalled. Even the spirits were against him.

He felt a light touch on his shoulder. How he wished it was Cassandra's touch. Of course that was asking too much, he knew she meant what she'd said, she was done with him.

"Blaine.

Blaine turned to Larry, facing the man's determined look was easier than looking at the women.

"You'd better pray that my wife isn't hurt. When this is over, you're no longer welcome in our home or in our lives. I don't want you to call or see my wife again."

Blaine closed his eyes against the pain. He'd known it was coming. There had always been the thinnest lines there between friendliness and hostility between him and Larry. And he'd crossed it by inviting the one man Larry hated more than him. Chance, his soul father, the man his mother had found more than a year ago and had an affair with, Chance, the man she left Larry for. Sure he understood how Larry felt.

Is the price worth it now? His subconscious whispered to him. He glanced toward Michelle, she was talking to Cassandra. He wanted to remind her of her promise never to leave him, that she'd said she wouldn't put him out of her life. He thought of Chance, his father, who'd been forced to live the rest of his life without his soul mate. Well Larry had ordered him out of Michelle's life. Now they would both have to live without her.

Larry was glaring at him and he had no answer for him, he could only stand before him muttering, "I called him to help save Michelle. I wasn't trying to hurt her."

"I don't want you seeing her anymore. I don't care what your reasons were. You're not wanted or needed in our lives."

"Larry, don't."

Michelle had come alongside them and had her right hand around Larry's shoulder. "Don't say that." She was looking at Blaine while she talked to Larry.

"Blaine is my son. I'm not going to desert him."

"I'm your husband," Larry screamed angrily, "I don't want him in my home."

"Then he won't come to your home, our home. But no matter what he's done, I won't stop seeing him."

"Are you sure it's Blaine you want to keep seeing or were you hoping for something like this, that some time just by being with Blaine you'd see Chance?"

Was it worth it Blaine? The voice again. He still didn't have an answer. "Stop it. This is all my fault, I admit it." Blaine said. "Larry, I'm sorry. I've tried not to intrude in your lives. I've never mentioned Chance to Michelle, not once since she chose to live out her life with you. And I wouldn't have called him if I didn't think we needed him. But the Mystic said the three of us are the key."

"The Mystic?" Larry looked toward the still figure on the bed. "Okay, so now he's a Mystic. What does he have to do with any of this?" Larry asked exasperated with the entire explanation.

One look at him and Blaine could tell without the benefit of reading him. "It's too much to explain now, Larry. But if you want, when this is over I'll tell you everything."

The least he could do was help Michelle explain to her husband the tangled web of their lives. He'd be lucky if Larry didn't think they were all a bunch of loonies when he finished with his tale.

The glare in Larry's eyes would have melted a glacier. Blaine wished he would aim the piercing glare in Cassandra's direction, perhaps he'd melt her a wee bit. He wanted to smile, but common sense kept him from it.

He looked instead at Michelle. "I'll understand. You warned me. I didn't listen."

She turned from Larry to him, all her attention focused on him. "I meant it, there is no way I want you out of my life."

"I've been nothing but trouble to you since the day you met me."

"That's a lie."

Michelle smiled while Blaine watched her movements, surprised that her smile was genuine. She smiled until the muscles of her face would stretch no farther; still the smile appeared to get larger until her face glowed with happiness.

"If it wasn't for you, my God, Blaine, I would still be wandering around in darkness, not knowing who I am, who I was, feeling guilty for

242

DYANNE DAVIS

being a horrible mother, believing I didn't love my children, denying a big part of myself. Don't you understand, Blaine? I lived this entire lifetime worrying about you. Do you think I'm going to give you up?"

Blaine glanced toward Larry, ignoring the look in Michelle's eyes, the touch of her hand on his forehead brushing away the hair that had fallen there. He didn't deserve her love, not now.

He glanced back toward his mother seeing that her vision followed his own, to Larry standing near by sulking, a scowl on his face.

Michelle lifted her shoulder toward Larry. "He loves me, he'll have to get over it, he has no choice. I'm not letting you go again for anyone."

She touched her hand again to his forehead, reminding him that she'd done the same thing when he was lying in his apartment near death. He kissed her hand grateful for her love.

"Don't misunderstand, Blaine, I'm still angry at you, but that has nothing to do with my loving you. I love you. You're a part of me, my soul and my heart, you'll be that forever."

Blaine stepped away from her, he could not hold in his pain any longer. "Michelle, don't." He knew what she intended to do, could tell from the look in her eyes. It was too much to go through standing there defenseless with Cassandra and Larry glaring at them.

"No, Michelle," he whispered low, knowing as he knew her that she would ignore his pleas. She held him to her refusing to let go and like it was from the first he felt her energy going through him. He closed his eyes and gave into the whir of emotions, the memories.

There they were again, the three of them, Michelle, his mother, Chance his father, and him an infant. He watched through the eyes of the infant, saw his mother covered in blood, felt her pain and agony on her impending death and he allowed the tears to flow freely down his cheeks, still Michelle would not let him go. Not until...

At last he knew what she wanted. He concentrated and felt her never ending love for the infant, for him. He saw her pass her hand across his body imbuing him with her gifts, her energy and her powers and finally she imbued him with her never ending love.

He saw Chance kneel besides her and she placed his hand over the baby, begging him to take care of their son. With her last breath she expressed her love for her son, for her husband.

In that instant it hit Blaine exactly what he'd lost and what he'd found. He'd lost a mother in the last life, but was fortunate enough to find her in this one. The enormity of the situation struck him filling him with unbearable grief at witnessing her death yet again. Michelle held him to her and allowed him to mourn her passing, mourn an entire lifetime without her, but always he'd had her love. He didn't want to let go of her.

"Love never dies, Blaine."

She was repeating the same words that he'd once spoken to her, but this time he didn't think she meant the two of them. He pulled away and she inclined her head toward Cassandra.

Cassandra was staring at them, the instant she became aware that they knew she looked away, but not before Blaine saw tears in her eyes. He'd hurt her, and now she probably thought he did it all just to protect his mother. She was wrong.

"Thanks," he whispered to Michelle.

"For what?" she answered, "for finally getting a chance to love the son I lost? You've given me an incredible gift. To know without a shadow of a doubt that I lived before is one thing, to find those I loved and lost in another lifetime,...to find my son."

She shook her head, Blaine could tell she was overcome, she glanced toward Larry.

"I'll never give you up, never." She gave him one final kiss before turning her attention to her husband.

Whatever she said must have worked because Larry was holding onto her so tightly Blaine wanted to tell him to loosen his grip.

He wanted to go to Cassandra, but her eyes remained downcast. She wasn't looking at any of them. She appeared to be elsewhere, her stance not inviting him nearer.

"So what do we have here, a funeral?"

He should have known, just when he thought things couldn't get any worse, there was Salvatore. The obnoxious bastard had the audacity to joke about the Mystic's condition. Blaine watched him as he went toward the old man's bed.

He gazed on the Mystic body curiously, not the slightest hint of remorse touched his features. Blaine didn't trust Salvatore. Possessed or not, he didn't trust him.

His moves were too measured Blaine noted as he sauntered around the bed, his gaze landing on all of them. He walked toward Michelle and stopped. Cassandra made a small sound and immediately Salvatore turned in her direction his attention completely focused on Cassandra.

Blaine stood off to the side looking closely at the interplay between Sal and Cassandra. They weren't speaking but he could tell they were linked. There was a smirk on Sal's face when he viewed the still form of the Mystic.

Michelle had moved away from the bed, her gaze focused on Sal. For another moment Blaine watched her until it dawned on him that Michelle was positioning her body between Sal and himself.

She's trying to protect me. The knowing rammed into his head and heart. Blaine fought his emotions. He needed to be clear to focus.

Feelings of love mixed with anger toward his mother overwhelmed him. Until a few days ago she refused to admit she had any abilities, now she thought she knew enough to protect him, a professional for over ten years. The whole thing was incredibly ironic.

"So we meet again," Salvatore smiled at Michelle before turning his gaze in Blaine's direction. "Who is the baby psychic to you?"

He was trying to make her angry. Blaine took a step toward her. He would die first before he allowed Salvatore to touch her.

Michelle and Salvatore both turned in the same instant, both observing his actions. If anyone was placing his mother's life in danger it was him he realized suddenly knowing that it wasn't Michelle Salvatore was baiting, but him. He'd fallen right into his trap. Again.

A cool breeze rushed over the back of Blaine's neck and he felt a slight caress on his brow. Michelle was looking at him strangely. A split second later her voice filled his head. "Let me handle this."

Blaine remained motionless, his gaze fixed on his mother. "Don't you trust me to protect you?" he asked telepathically. She didn't answer.

"Why are you concerned with my relationship with Blaine, does it bother you?" Michelle asked Salvatore.

Blaine had his answer. Michelle had chosen to answer Salvatore, leaving him standing there like a small boy being protected by his mother from the town bully. He felt a flush of embarrassment cover his body and wished that he were somewhere else. For the briefest of instants, he toyed with the idea of bi-locating, anywhere to get away from Cassandra's hatred and his mother's smothering love.

Damn it, he'd had enough. He walked toward Salvatore to stand directly in front of Michelle. His left hand went out and he pushed his mother even further behind him. Enough of this nonsense. He would protect her with his dying breath if need be. But she would not fight his battles for him.

He remembered the feel of the electrical current flooding his body as in the last life, his mother had passed her gift on to him. He knew now that he could handle Salvatore. Sure the man was more trained, but if the Mystic was correct Blaine did possess the power to defeat Salvatore.

"Are you challenging me, MaDia?" Salvatore smiled wickedly at him.

"Are you so weak and afraid that you aim your glares at women?" Blaine answered in return.

"Touché."

Unexpectedly Salvatore laughed, causing Blaine to plant his feet more firmly. He already knew what was coming and decided to take the offensive position. His hand reached out and he forced a smile onto his face. "No hard feelings," he purred.

Salvatore took his outstretched hand obviously taken aback, but his recovery was swift. For in the span of a breath Blaine felt the coldness from the man's soul emanating through to his fingertips.

"The first line of defense, Blaine is your aura. Strengthen it." He heard the Mystic's voice so clearly that he almost glanced in his direction; instead he concentrated on strengthening his own aura, brightening the field until he was bathed in an iridescent purple light that radiated a foot in circumference.

Immediately warmth returned to the tips of his fingers and Salvatore released his grip.

"So I see the baby has been weaned."

"Look again Salvatore. the baby has matured and is a full grown man. More interesting than dealing with a woman, don't you think?"

He saw his mother bristle at his comment, but ignored it. She'd embarrassed the hell out of him. She deserved to be annoyed. He dared a glance to where Cassandra stood, her face expressionless, her eyes dull and lifeless. She wasn't reacting to anything or anyone.

Salvatore's eyes followed his glance. He smiled at Blaine before moving off to Cassandra. He'd found a better means of pushing Blaine's buttons.

Blaine watched helpless as Salvatore's hand went first to Cassandra's shoulder lingering a moment too long, as if he had a right, then the casual way he allowed his fingers to slip down touching her breasts. Blaine wanted to rush over and strangle him.

He glared instead at Cassandra who was looking into Salvatore's eyes staring transfixed, not objecting to his blatant sexual touches.

Blaine could understand her continued anger at him, but to allow Salvatore liberties only hours after making love with him, he was furious.

Cassandra's eyelids closed slowly and she leaned forward toward Salvatore. What the hell was going on? Two steps, two steps was all it would take to position himself between Cassandra and Salvatore.

"Do you really think you've grown up all that quickly, baby psychic?" Salvatore asked.

"We'll just have to see won't we?" Blaine answered. "Like I said you seem to enjoy your power over women." He gazed at Cassandra's face, passive in its acceptance. "Whatever you did to her, undo it. Now!" he demanded.

Blaine's shout was the first visible sign that Cassandra still existed on the same plane. She jerked her head toward him, a confused look in her eyes.

Blaine's raised voice had served to rouse more than Cassandra. Three nurses ran into the room, took a look at the assembled group and frowned.

"There's too many of you in here," the large plump nurse stated speaking to no one in particular. "Are all of you family?"

"Not all of us," Salvatore said answering for the group. "That woman over there," he said pointing at Michelle, "is a private nurse that the family hired."

Blaine watched the cool smile on Salvatore face, heard the audible gasps of delight as the women got a better look at him, causing Salvatore to grin in pride.

"I really do hate him," Blaine mumbled low, not wanting to admit that even a tiny part was do in fact to the effect that Sal had not only on the three nurses eyeing him as though he was a juicy steak that they couldn't wait to sink their teeth into, nor did he want to admit that in spite of her complaints there was something between the woman he loved and the man he detested.

They all stood there in awe watching Salvatore work his magic on the women. For a moment the women were so still that Blaine knew it was more than male charm he'd used. Salvatore had hypnotized the women, put the three of them under right there, and he'd done it so cleverly he'd almost missed it. Damn, that was how he'd done it. He should have known.

He glanced backwards at Cassandra, for the first time he was really looking at her half dazed expression. So that was it. That was his secret.

Blaine smiled in spite of the situation. He'd gone past annoyed. He was now royally pissed. How dare Salvatore break every code of ethic there was. To put the nurses under in order for them to be allowed to remain in the Mystic's room was one thing. To do it to Cassandra was going too far. With a disgusted snort Blaine turned his attention back to the little scene being played out in front of him.

"Ladies, you have nothing to worry about, we may get a little noisy, but you won't come in the room. Right ladies?" Salvatore purred at the women then laughed.

"Right." They repeated in triplicate and giggled like bumbling fools.

Blaine knew he was being harsh. His anger was not at the women, they couldn't help themselves, coupled with Sal's hypnotic suggestion, his charm had won them over. Both would have worked, but Sal had taken advantage of the women's gaga state over him, probably another show of his powers. They all watched the nurses leave the room still giggling.

"Like I said, Salvatore, you do enjoy your power over women. I wonder if it would work if you didn't hypnotize them?"

"Well," Salvatore replied coming closer. "I don't think I used anything when Cassie said she'd marry me."

Touché, Blaine thought, but didn't say it. That had been strictly Cassandra's anger. Blaine couldn't blame that on Salvatore.

***

Norman was tired of pacing the room waiting for the television stations to tell him the news of the Mystic's death. He'd tried to enter Cassie's thoughts, but the little bitch had slammed the damn door on him, viciously. Perhaps she knew who he was now, maybe his message made her remember him.

Well, enough waiting around, he'd only dared to leave the room once to go for food. Room service would have been easier, but he didn't want anyone coming in his room. The do not disturb sign, hung on his door permanently. He even took care of changing the sheets himself. Probably was the only way they'd actually get changed anyway.

Pacing around the room was getting him nowhere. He'd lost track of Salvatore, and was tiring of the game, he stopped and looked at his reflection in the mirror.

"Where's your precious Salvatore, Cassie, did he desert you? He probably knows that it's me and that I'm coming and he's going to get every square inch of his ass kicked. He thumped himself on the chest three times, each thump harder than the one that preceded it. "Yeah, yeah," he screamed to the top of his lungs.

It was time to end this game, he would go to the hospital and finish off the old man the way he should have done in the first place. Then he would take his time killing Blaine MaDia. That one he would enjoy. As for Cassie, now she would never know the pleasure of having his flesh buried deep within her body. No, he no longer wanted the whore. She'd soiled herself again with that fucking no talent psychic. She would just have to die without the pleasure of knowing what it would be like to lie beneath a real man. After that he would find Salvatore and he would make him pay for every moment of torment he'd dished out during his childhood.

Then like the phantom he'd been for the last ten years he'd once again disappear. Norman grabbed for his sweater laughing at his own joke. He really was probably the only spirit that Blaine MaDia could prove he'd talked to. He was a ghost, had been one for a decade, he would return to being one as soon as he'd made everything right.

Norman opened the door then thought better of it. He closed it quietly walking toward the phone. One last thing he thought as he dialed the hospital and waited to be put through to the Mystic's room. The moment the phone was answered he took a deep breath intending to say what he had to say calmly, but calm failed him.

"I'm coming bitch," he yelled into the phone.

"Who is this?" a voice other than Cassie's answered throwing him off for only a moment.

"Don't get cute with me; put that bitch on the phone."

"There are no bitches here," the voice answered him.

""You'll die also, for being flippant with me. Now put Cassie on the phone."

"No."

"No?" Norman growled. "Tell them all Norman's coming, and as for you, you stupid cow, I'm going to kill you first."

With that he banged the phone repeatedly on the desk top until it fell apart, then he banged it one last time for good measure and took off to complete his mission.

***

Michelle turned from the phone. "Well, it looks as if we don't have to search out this Norman character any longer, he's coming here."

She lifted a hand to stop the barrage of questions, her eyes honing in on Larry. "Hon, why don't you go home and wait for me, I should be along soon."

Blaine couldn't believe his ears. He wanted to pretend that he wasn't watching Larry, but he was not an actor. Besides, all eyes were on Michelle and Larry.

"If you think I'm going to leave you here with these people you're as crazy as they are. You stay, I stay." Larry's voice thundered as he glared at all of them.

"I'll look out for him," Blaine offered.

"No thanks," Larry countered.

"Beside, Blaine, who's going to look out for the baby psychic," Salvatore laughed. "Why don't you all go home and leave Bates, to us. Cassie and I will take care of him."

"Norman hates that name, Sal. Don't call him Bates, Norman always hated his name, always got teased because of it. His name's Yates."

It was the first time Cassandra had spoken more than three words since they'd left the Mystic's home. Blaine eyed her sharply, something was wrong with her, she was showing more concern about hurting the feelings of a crazed killer than she was in the fact that he'd threatened her, and was now on his way to kill her.

He had to snap her out of it. "Cassandra, why don't you go with Larry into the lobby? Here you can take my cell phone." He attempted to hand it to her. "Page me when you see Norman."

"I'm not leaving my wife," Larry barked, "forget it."

"You're not sending me off either," Cassandra added her opinion, her eyes cutting him into. "This is my fight. I think Sal is right, the rest of you can leave, and we'll handle Norman. You have no stake in this fight."

Blaine's glance flew across the room landing on the Mystic. "We have a stake. We're not leaving."

"Then might I suggest until we take care of Norman that we work together," Salvatore grinned showing perfect white teeth. "Your time will come baby psychic. When this is over you can take me on, psychic to psychic, no tricks." He grinned again.

Blaine wanted nothing more than to wipe that smug look off Sal's face. He was just the sort of person that gave psychics a bad name.

For a full minute Salvatore stood grinning then he put his fingers together giving them a flick as though he was swatting an insect. Blaine knew that was just the image the man had intended to send.

Sal turned to look once again at the body of the Mystic. "Did anyone attempt to heal him?" He asked.

Blaine noticed that Salvatore's voice carried disdain as well as his usual condescension while his glance flicked back and forth between Blaine and Michelle.

"Yes," Michelle answered him at last.

"Doesn't look as though it worked." Sal stared directly into Michelle's eyes.

Blaine smiled to himself, his mother was something else. He was so proud of her. She didn't even flinch under Sal's scrutiny.

He saw something flicker in Sal's eyes and for a moment it looked as if he took pleasure in Michelle's defiance. But the moment was over before he was sure. Salvatore's words letting then know what he thought of them and their abilities made Blaine forget the flicker.

"I guess I'll give it a try." Salvatore yawned. "I'm sure I have a lot more experience with healing, after all I deal with the living while you, MaDia deal with the dead." He cracked each knuckle, twisted his head sideways and stretched.

Mere theatrics Blaine realized, but still Salvatore Sharif annoyed the hell out of him. Now he was taunting them with his deliberate cat like moves.

Still, if Salvatore could help the old man, Blaine would take his contempt. He kept watching as Sal approached the old man's body. He glanced at each of them, nothing sparking his interest until his eyes found Cassie.

"Cassie, lets do this together, like the old days, just the two of us."

Blaine looked from one to the other of them, Sal smiling beguilingly and Cassandra's look of resignation. She moved like a robot toward Sal and held her hand out for his.

"I'm sorry," Blaine heard her apologizing to Sal, "I should have attempted to heal him. I don't know where my head was."

"Don't worry about it, sometimes when you're with amateurs you tend to get sloppy."

Blaine gritted his teeth. The remark was only more bait, this he wouldn't take. He remained where he was watching as Salvatore and Cassandra joined hands and moved them along the Mystic body. He saw the healing white light glow, go from their hands and descend to less than a millimeter of an inch from the old man's body before bouncing away and returning to them.

They tried repeatedly. Blaine was praying that it would work. Whatever it took he was willing to do. "Maybe we can help you," Blaine said to Sal. The more of us that try, it will give the attempt more energy. It can't hurt." Blaine finished.

Salvatore looked at him, and Blaine felt himself growing cold and threw up a mental block. This look was different than all of the others that Salvatore had cast his way. For the first time his look was one of pure hatred. Still Salvatore opened the circle and allowed Blaine and Michelle to enter. The four of them worked together sending the healing energy from their bodies. Again the energy came down, but nothing happened, no change in the old man.

"Maybe I can help." Said a familiar voice from the doorway.

Blaine felt the tremor go through Michelle as she dropped his hands, her eyes going first to Larry then resting on Chance.

"Sorry to bother you, Chance, but thanks for coming. We could really use your help here." Michelle admitted looking quickly at Blaine then back at Chance.

Her look told Blaine what he needed to know. His mother wanted Chance there. She had known he would call and she had known Chance would come. Blaine looked at both of his soul parents for the first time understanding how very hard it had been for Michelle to ask Chance to leave, and how very hard it had been for him to do so. Their love for each other was apparent. Blaine dared a glance in Larry's direction and saw the pain on the man's face. *Was it worth it*, he heard the voice in his head calling out to him again and shook his head to dislodge it and his own thoughts.

Thanks, Chance." Michelle repeated herself.

"No problem," he answered her. "When Blaine called I thought something had happened to you. Who is this and what are you trying to do?"

"This is a friend of Blaine's. He's a Mystic we're trying to heal him."

Blaine rubbed his bracelet hoping Chance would know what he meant. If they could get through this without destroying his mother's marriage, then all of this would be worth it.

"So let's try again," Chance answered Blaine as he walked toward the bed his eyes on Michelle only.

"I think we just need the three of us, we're the one's who can make it happen." Blaine said softly not wanting to look at any of the others not wanting to see the pain he'd caused by his actions.

"Then by all means go for it baby psychic." Salvatore dropped his hands and moved away taking Cassandra with him.

Blaine bit back any retort. Shit, he wished he knew what to do. It was getting a little tiring playing the role of the fool in front of Salvatore.

"The three of you Blaine, you're part of a trinity."

"You talk as though we're the godhead of something."

"Don't be ridiculous, I'm talking about the simple power of three, the three of you are a trinity unto itself. Scoff if you will, but the time will come when my words will be proven to you"

"How am I going to know what to do if it ever happens?"

I guess you'll just have to figure it out, I don't know the answer to that one."

Blaine's conversation with the Mystic came back to him. He could feel everyone's eyes on him. Michelle was smiling softly, her eyes lifted in maternal pride, while Chance waited for instructions. They'd both thought he would know what to do. Why shouldn't they? It was his idea.

He held his hands outstretched one to each of his soul parents and together they stood over the Mystic.

Nothing happened.

Blaine heard the snickers of Salvatore grow louder until it turned into a full fledged laugh. He looked nervously toward his mother and father, then at the too still body of the Mystic. He felt a squeeze of reassurance from their hands to his.

Out of the blue it came to him. It all made sense now. The trinity, a triangle. Immediately he dropped his parents' hands, pointing out positions for them to stand. Michelle stood at the bottom of the bed while Chance stood at the left side and Blaine stood on the right. The Mystic himself was the head, the pinnacle of it all. Blaine thrust his right hand into the air, his left outstretched across the teacher's body. Without one word, Michelle and Chance followed suit.

Their outstretched hands joined forming a triangle, while each of them divided the Mystic's body into thirds and worked on that section.

A bright light filled the interior of the room surrounding the Mystic's body with healing light. Blaine felt the energy going from him and flowing downwards. He dared a glance and he saw that their amulets were also glowing eerily. Damn it, it was going to work.

Michelle's face was beaming. He held her gaze, warning her with his look not to break the connection. He knew the Mystic would be healed. He knew until the slight prickle of awareness began creeping up his neck.

He was losing focus, the energy from his hand waning in intensity. He turned his head, a great silence filling the room and the outside hall. A sense of evil lurked about and was coming closer.

With that thought a man entered the room, rumpled, dark brown hair, something familiar about him. A second too late Blaine realized where he knew the man from. It was the man in Cassandra's memories, only without the coke bottle glasses.

For a moment everything stilled before all hell broke loose. The man, Norman pointed a finger at Cassandra and sent her flying through the air landing hard on the opposite side of the room.

Blaine took a step toward the intruder, his blood boiling, healing the Mystic forgotten for the moment. He had to save Cassandra.

Unseen hands slammed into his chest knocking the wind out of him and Blaine went sailing as well.

"Your first line of defense is your aura Blaine, use it." Again the Mystic's words rang out to him.

This man wasn't just a psychic. Blaine knew that the instant the stabbing pain struck him in the chest. Damn it they should have guessed, he was a master of the darkest of dark magick as well.

He watched dazed as the man turned his attention toward Michelle. "No," Blaine screamed out loud and erected an energy barricade encasing them inside and keeping Norman out.

Never in his life had he ever done anything like that. Hell, he never knew anyone could, until he saw the Mystic do it. He had no way of knowing how long it would work. He only knew he'd promised to keep his mother and Cassandra safe.

"Cassandra," he'd almost forgotten. He ran to where she lay against the door of the bathroom, Sal at her side, her look, stunned disbelief.

"Remove the bubble, baby psychic."

"No."

"I'm not cowering from Norman Bates."

"Yates," Cassandra muttered weakly.

"Are you stupid? Have you ever seen a psychic levitate someone across a fucking room? No. Hell no. The man's a practitioner of the dark arts, and unless you know something that I don't, I suggest you help reinforce the barrier, not get rid of it."

"Oh I know quite a bit more than you do, now remove the barrier, or I will finish our game now and remove it myself."

"Sal, no," Cassandra touched Salvatore's sleeve while Blaine looked questioningly at him.

"Salvatore doesn't live here anymore!" Sal laughed before standing and squaring off with Blaine. "Now are you going to remove it or do I remove you?"

Blaine looked around the room. Larry was quiet, his arms around Michelle, he was scared shitless and it showed. Blaine didn't blame him. He had every right to be afraid. As for Chance he stood next to them only inches away. From the look in his eyes Blaine knew he was ready to take the next bolt aimed at Michelle.

"MaDia," Salvatore screamed, breaking him from his trance. "It's not Norman Bates you have to worry about. Do you think I would let anyone have the pleasure of getting rid of you, but myself? There are twelve psychics, when I get rid of Norman, I will be the only one to fulfill the prophecy."

Blaine eyed him intensely, and then smiled. "Go for it," he said to Sal. Just as the barricade disintegrated, Blaine spoke again.

"The prophecy said thirteen male psychics."

He saw that Sal and Norman had both heard him and had gotten his meaning, but they were too busy with each other to worry about him.

As Norman's hand dipped in his pocket, he heard Salvatore laugh again and pull out several red crystal hearts,

"Are you looking for these, Norman?"

Blaine watched as Norman blanched visibly. It was obvious that he hadn't known Sal had the trinkets.

Blaine checked Cassandra for injuries as he gently helped her from the floor. He moved toward Michelle and Chance while beckoning for Larry to move behind them. *Was it worth it Blaine?* Now the voice was taunting him.

"Norman."

It was Cassandra. Blaine placed his arm protectively out in front of her. He didn't want her near the man, not to talk to him, nothing.

"Norman, why?" Cassandra repeated.

"Why do you think, Cassie?"

"I don't know. We never had any problems when we were children, we were friends."

"Friends?" Norman's voice thundered through the small room. "We were never friends. You, all of you wouldn't let me be your friend. You didn't think I was good enough. As for the teacher he wouldn't teach me because he didn't think I was capable of learning. I was as entitled to the fulfilling of the prophecy as any of you. I'm also a twenty-first generation psychic. Did any of you ever treat me that way? No."

"Norman, I was never mean to you."

Norman cocked his head as if in thought. "Did you love me as I loved you? Did you ever leave Salvatore once to walk away with me?"

"Norman, I'm sorry."

Cassandra took a step to walk toward Norman and Blaine's hand clamped down on her arm. "No, Cassandra." He held her gaze for a moment. "I can't let you endanger yourself. Don't do it."

"This isn't your fight, Blaine. I can take care of myself."

"If he kills me, you take care of yourself. Until then I'm taking care of you."

"You have no right."

"And we have no time."

"That's one thing you're right about, MaDia, you have no time, it's over." Norman lifted his hand to send Blaine flying but this time Blaine was ready. He thrust his hand out and met the bolt of energy that came from Norman, sending it back causing Norman to lose his balance.

From the corner of his eye Blaine saw Sal drop one crystal heart after the other, the trinkets breaking, shattering on the tile floor.

"Did you think I would have yours in with the others?" Norman turned to Sal so quickly his fury mounting, forgetting Blaine for the moment as he focused his anger on Salvatore.

His hand went into his sweater pocket this time bringing out a deep red heart twice the size of the others and so dense that you could not see through it. He smiled at Sal.

"Goodbye, Salvatore."

Norman squeezed the heart in his hand, opening his palm as Sal bent over, to do it all over again.

"I'm going to do this slowly and I'm going to enjoy it." Norman laughed.

Without thinking of the consequence Blaine ran head long into Norman knocking him off balance, wrestling him to the ground taking Sal's heart from him.

"You're going to die, MaDia."

"Not today, Norman, and not by you." Blaine touched his hand to Norman's heart beating beneath his shirt. "You're evil, but it's not my place to kill you."

He held on to him closing his eyes pouring all his energies into cleansing Norman's aura with purple healing light. I bind your powers, Norman, as surely as I cleanse your spirit."

With those words warmth radiated through Blaine's entire body. The diamond in his bracelet twinkled. He wasn't alone. He had the power of the triad, his mother and father positioned at his side. The purple light became blinding in its intensity and still Blaine held on to Norman until his aura was white with streaks of gold. Even then he held on.

When he finally let go Norman dropped to the floor limp and sobbing. *"Was it worth it Blaine?"* Even now the voice taunted him and he still didn't have an answer. Larry was in shock, not believing the things he'd seen with his own eyes, the Mystic remained unmoving on his bed, Cassandra out of her zombie state, but not fully herself and Sal, Sal who he would still have to defeat. "Was it worth it?" Blaine said back to the voice. "You tell me."

"So tell me baby psychic, what makes you a part of this prophecy? You're not a twenty-first generation psychic."

"You know, Salvatore, all this time you've all had the readings wrong, the prophecy say that after twenty-one generations a psychic would be born who would mate with a female psychic of equal powers and together they would produce a baby of unknown powers."

He pointed toward the Mystic. "He's my grandfather." Then his eyes lifted toward Michelle and Chance. They are my parents."

"How?"

"From my last incarnation. I remember them well."

"Okay, assuming that all of that is true and you're the thirteen male with the power, show me what you've got."

"Gladly."

Blaine smiled, this time not unsure, knowing exactly what it was he was going to do. He had told the Mystic he wasn't willing to kill, that remained true. But he was willing to save a life.

"I don't know who you are," Blaine spoke softly. "But you don't belong in that body and we want it back."

The man blinked. In that instant Blaine closed his eyes and linked with Salvatore. He held out his hand hoping Michelle and Chance would know what he needed.

They did.

Together the three of them saw Salvatore, the real Salvatore bound and they released him giving him the needed energy to push forward to reclaim that which he'd lost.

With a tremendous jolt Salvatore pushed the three of them out of his mind. They stood looking at Sal, knowing this time they were finally meeting the real Salvatore.

There was still that same cockiness but something in the eyes told them he was a different man. The two men stared at each other a moment longer before Sal's hand shot out in thanks and Blaine accepted it.

"Sal, it is you."

Cassandra's face came alive as she rushed forward to hug Salvatore to her. Blaine moved away. *"Was it worth it?"* Still the voice came.

"I'm sorry, Blaine, but we're not done."

Blaine glanced into the eyes of his mother. Tears were streaming down her cheeks. "You're right. We're not done." He held her to him for a moment while he viewed Cassandra in Salvatore's arms. "Come on lets get to work."

They resumed their positions around the teacher's bed sending their energy into the old man until they all felt the weakening of their own spirit, then they pulled back to wait.

"Was it worth it Blaine? He looked at Cassandra, the woman he loved, in another man's arms. He listened while he looked at the hungry, lost look in the eyes of his father, heard his mother tell him that he needed to find someone to love, that she didn't want him to be alone. He looked at the still body of the Mystic and he still couldn't answer the question.

Again Blaine was alone as he'd always been. In a room filled with people, he was alone. He glanced at each of them in turn his heart breaking, and for just a moment he wondered why he'd followed his mother's advice and clung to life. She'd been wrong. He still didn't have anyone.

"Is everyone all right?"

The voice was a bit weak but it was the Mystic, alive and well. Blaine stood in the back while the others rushed forward.

"How did you do it?" the Mystic asked.

"The baby psychic did it." Salvatore smiled at the old man then at Blaine.

"And, Salvatore, it is you this time isn't it?"

"Yes, teacher, the baby psychic did that also."

"How did it happen? You're much too powerful for anyone to take over your body. What happened?"

"I was doing a favor for a friend that died. We met in India. He asked me to help him make a couple of things right and I did. I thought it was kind of cool."

Salvatore blushed under his perpetually deep tan Blaine noted. That was one difference in him and the entity that had inhabited Salvatore's body. That entity would never have cared that he'd been so reckless. In spite of Cassandra's love for the man Blaine would much rather have him there than the evil that had occupied his body.

"So how did he gain control?" The Mystic asked struggling to sit up.

"He had help, some potions someone gave me and of course he had me, a more than willing victim."

"That was dangerous, Salvatore. I didn't know if we could get you back." The teacher scolded Sal.

"Blaine, the old man called out his voice sounding stronger. "Come here."

"So you've learned?"

"Perhaps," Blaine answered.

"And was it worth it?"

"Was it worth it?"

He should have known. Blaine stared dumfounded. "It was you. But how... you were...you were..."

"I was right there with you. Now, was it worth it?"

"But why, why did you put us through this?"

"Partly to teach you a lesson. You were getting too cocky. Partly to force you to use the powers that were given to you in the last life."

"What if I didn't, how could you have been so sure?"

"I knew what powers your mother possessed. I knew she passed those powers on to you. No brag, just fact."

"That was quite a risk you took."

"No risk, we're here aren't we?"

Blaine pointed toward Norman. "What about Norman, was he part of my training? Was any of this real?"

"Believe me, Blaine, it was very real."

"And the cancer? Was that real?"

"Yes, it was, but so was the healing. Thank you for that."

"But how...when?"

"When you revived me at my home it occurred to me that my condition would be a wonderful opportunity to teach you a major lesson. I guess I should apologize for putting the others through their paces in order for you to learn what you needed to know. But they'll understand and forgive me. Besides, I'm old."

"What about the other psychics, the one's—?"

"I've already healed the others. I didn't know Norman was using the heart of the soul. We only lost one psychic." He glanced at Norman. "Make that two."

"What are we going to do with Norman? We can't let him go. He killed a man and attempted to kill you."

"Yes, but we have no proof. Don't worry, Norman will have to pay for his crimes, it's called karma. But for now I'll do what I should have done twenty years ago. I'll give him the love I should have given him then."

"He no longer has any psychic powers, I bound them."

"You can't permanently bind a psychic's powers. Unless you were practicing the dark arts. Which you aren't and never will."

"Norman doesn't know that." Blaine whispered. "But until we find a way to rid him of the evil that was the best I could do."

"I think you did something even better for Norman. You took away his hatred and cleansed his heart and spirit."

The old man chuckled. "You haven't answered my question. You've violated your own code of ethics in the past week. You've violated the code of professional psychics. You've betrayed the woman you love and you've betrayed your mother. Now I ask you again, was it worth it?"

They were all waiting for him to answer, all wanting to hear what he would say. Blaine knew he should say no, say he was sorry for the way he'd handled things, he closed his eyes and again felt alone.

He felt the pain of the people he loved; his eyes opened to look at Larry. Larry's face was filled with confusion and pain. His mother was holding Larry as though he were her life line, not daring to look at Chance, afraid that her love for him would show through and she would not be able to let him leave her again. Blaine saw all of this.

He looked at his father and read his thoughts. Chance was wondering how on earth he was going to leave Michelle again when all he wanted to do was wrest her from Larry's arms, from Larry's life. He was filled with pain and Blaine shivered. His calling his father to help had caused his father's pain. He glanced again at his mother just as she looked toward him. Blaine saw her pain and blinked back the tears. Then he turned in order to view Cassandra more clearly.

I've lost her, he thought, as he watched Salvatore's arm tighten protectively around her. She'd said she was marrying Sal. Blaine winced at the hurt in her eyes. He'd never meant to hurt her, he loved her. He'd only wanted to protect her, save them all.

Pain sliced through him with the speed of a sword. All the people he loved were hurting and all in part because of him. He blinked back the tears. But they were alive. And the Teacher had said, he'd taken away Norman's hatred and cleansed his heart and spirit.

"Yes, it was worth it." He answered at last. "As I'm sure your using a really horrible event to teach me a lesson was worth it to you."

"You're learning, Blaine, the Mystic clasped his shoulders and gave him a hug before getting up and hurrying to meet Chance.

Blaine took a long look at all in the room then turned his back to them, to the pain etched on their faces. He'd lived his life alone he'd continue to do so.

"You don't have to."

He felt her touch light as a feather. He didn't move. Her arms came around him as her head pressed against his spine.

"You don't have to be alone ever again, Blaine."

"What did you do, read my mind?"

"Yes," Cassandra muttered as she slipped from behind him to come into his arms. "Yes. I love you, Blaine MaDia."

His arms closed around her. "I thought you hated me."

"Your heart was in the right place. I know that now. You saved Sal thinking I loved him, that I was going to marry him. You did that for me because you knew how much I love Sal."

"Then why?"

"Because I love Salvatore, baby psychic. But, I'm in love with you."

Like magic the heaviness lifted from Blaine's heart. He barely heard the Mystic scolding Salvatore for his foolishness or Michelle doing her best to explain everything over again to Larry. He barely heard anything over the beating of his own heart.

"I love you, Cassandra Boozer, with all my heart and soul." His lips claimed hers, his tongue probed her mouth to taste of her essence. His arms tightened around her. If he had anything to say about it he would never let her go. Thank you, God, Blaine whispered inside his head. Thank you for the gift."

THE END

About the Author:

 Dyanne Davis is a Multi-Published, Award Winning author of 16 novels. She has written dozens of articles for on-line magazines. She was one of the authors for the Premier Edition of, New Love Stories, magazines. Dyanne lives in a Chicago suburb with her husband of 43 years, William Sr.

She has been a presenter of numerous workshops. She hosts a local cable television show in her hometown, "*The Art of Writing*," to give writing tips to aspiring writers. Interviewing some of her favorite authors, LA. Banks, Robin Schone, Donna Hill, Melody Thomas, Ann Marcela, Cathie Linz, Jade Lee, Jenna Petersen and many more has been the highlight of doing the show. You can catch some of the clips on Youtube.

Dyanne also writes a vampire series under the name of F. D. Davis.

You can contact her by email:
        davisdyanne@aol.com
        adamomegavampire@aol.com
Visit her on the web:
        www.dyannedavis.com
        www.adamomega.com

www.ingramcontent.com/pod-product-compliance
Lightning Source LLC
Chambersburg PA
CBHW030125180626
46812CB00002B/559